The Last Mayor's Son

The Last Mayor's Son

Book 1 of the Nivaka Chronicles

Leslie Heath

Cover Design: matthillbookdesign.com

Editors: Maria D'Marco and Florence Weinberg

Copy Editor: Anita York

Printed in the United States of America
Copyright © 2016 Leslie E Heath
All rights reserved.
ISBN: 0692899168
ISBN-13: 978-0-692-89916-8

Dedication

This book is dedicated to my husband and daughter, Jamie and Amanda. They supported me as I chased my dreams, even when they didn't seem to make sense. Special thanks also goes to Kristy, for giving me the courage to begin.

Acknowledgements

It truly takes a village to raise a story from a solitary idea to a full-fledged novel. I couldn't have done it without the advice and support of Maria D'Marco, Alun Seymour, Connie Powell, and Lynn Fellows. Many others have helped through the process, but these four guided me as I developed this story into what it is today.

1.

The Letter

Eddrick huddled in the shadows near the edge of the arena and considered the recent changes he had seen. He remembered the old adage that change is the only constant in life. Maybe that wasn't entirely correct. Changes continued well beyond the grave. Now, he looked at life happening before him—the crowd of people cheering as two young swordsmen faced off in a tournament. One of them had once been his son, Aibek.

Aibek and his competitor, Intza, faced each other in one of three dusty circles marked out with fist-sized black stones. If either stepped outside the circle, the match would end, and the competitor remaining inside the ring would be declared the winner. They had each won six matches during the hot, humid day, and now traded blows in the final battle of the tournament. Only one could be the champion of the annual Xona Military Academy East versus West tournament, which pitted teams from the two branches of the Academy against each other.

In Eddrick's opinion, Aibek was a superbly skilled fighter, light on his feet with a lightning-quick strike. His adversary was larger and stronger, but Aibek had beaten him in an early round last year. This time, they faced each other late in the day, after hours of fighting in the blazing sun had drained both of much of their strength. Breathless, he watched as his son dodged an aggressive swing, then countered with a swift stab towards his enemy's chest. His blow glanced off Intza's shield with a loud clang of metal. Aibek ducked away from yet another heavy attack. He wiped the sweat from his eyes with the glove on his shield hand and watched for an opening in his adversary's defense.

The brightly painted fighting dragon on Aibek's shield announced him as a member of the West Xona team. His opponent's shield bore the likeness of the three moons of Azalin, the banner of the East team. The two emblems combined to form the insignia of the Army of Xona, which would employ all graduates from both branches as officers. Eddrick glanced away as the blindingly bright afternoon sun glared off his son's polished chain mail. He kept to the back of the crowd and moved to the other side of the arena for a better view.

Meanwhile, the two opponents danced in a slow circle, maintaining their weapons at the ready.

Eddrick shouted encouragement to his only son. Though he knew no one could hear him, he yelled with all the volume he could muster. He wished again he had been able to raise his son and silently cursed the cruel fate that had prevented it.

Glancing around at the wilted appearance of the other spectators, Eddrick was grateful he couldn't feel the heat. The shadow from the ancient brick building, the West Xona Military Academy, had long since moved away from the dusty circle where the oldest students battled for the championship.

If this matchup had come earlier in the day, Eddrick thought, Aibek would have easily beaten this slower, clumsier opponent. But, Aibek's armored chest heaved with exertion, Eddrick could see he'd had enough. The score was tied four to four. According to the rules of the tournament, one more precise, forceful blow to the torso would end the match—and the championship. With his son only one point from winning, Eddrick swore he could feel his heart pounding with excitement, though he knew that was impossible.

Aibek shrugged his shoulders (perhaps to keep his arms loose?) and raised his shield to defend his chest as the brutish opponent hacked at him once again. Both could taste victory. When his adversary's sword swung down once more, Aibek leapt slightly right. The sudden movement threw Intza off balance. Before his adversary could regain his equilibrium, Aibek used the last of his energy in a perfectly placed swing of the sword. The weapon clanged against Intza's chest-plate like a bell, signaling the end of the match. The rivals both fell to the floor, dripping sweat and struggling for breath. Their teammates rushed to their sides, tore off their helmets and the sweat-soaked padding beneath, and helped them to their feet.

Breathless from the close battle, Eddrick watched as his son accepted his award, and lingered until the young man disappeared into the crowd with his friends. Bursting with pride, he rushed home to tell his wife of Aibek's victory.

~*~

Aibek looked up at the cloudless sky as he left the arena with his team, laughing and celebrating the day's win. He remembered the cool, rainy weather he had hated the year before and wished they could have had such luck again today. The hot sun had baked him inside his armor and sapped his strength. His legs shook as he worked to keep up with his friends.

Still, everyone on the team had won at least one match

during the tournament. As the team captain, he considered the day a resounding success. He congratulated one of the youngest members of the team on an early victory, then looked up and saw his uncle Noral step toward him out of the crowd.

"Good job on the win today!" His guardian clapped him on the shoulder. He held on a moment longer than was necessary, and Aibek paused, glancing at him over his shoulder.

"Um…thank you." Aibek's steps faltered. He stopped, looked into his uncle's face, and then dropped his gaze to the pebbled path. He stood frozen in place and waited for his uncle's verdict.

"You know; you could have beaten him without the theatrics."

Aibek furrowed his brow but didn't raise his eyes. "I don't know what you mean," he mumbled.

"Oh, come on," Noral said with a laugh. "You know exactly what I mean. You didn't have to let him get four points on you! If that had been a real battle, you'd be dead, not wearing a trinket."

Aibek's blood turned to ice in his veins. He closed his eyes against the old, familiar feeling. He took several deep breaths to ward off the sense of failure and ran his hands through his sweat-soaked hair. "I put too much into the match before him. I used up all my energy."

Noral dropped his hands to his sides, and they resumed their progress toward the Academy where his nephew's friends were waiting. "Look, you know you can do better just as well as I do."

"I know. I'm sorry," Aibek answered quietly. "I'll be stronger next time."

"Exactly right; learn from your mistakes and get better… fight smarter." His uncle smiled. "Now, I have to get back to the shop. We'll talk more later." He strode away across the brown grass of the yard without waiting for a response.

Aibek stared after his uncle for a long moment, wondering if he would ever be able to live up to the expectations of his only father figure. A breeze ruffled his still-wet hair and brought him back to the moment. He kicked at the path in front of him, scattering pebbles in every direction, and made his way up the stairs at the front of the imposing brick building. His teammates had gathered between the enormous, red marble pillars that marked the entrance. He welcomed the joyous celebration of his friends. As always, he painted a broad smile on his face and joined their conversation as if nothing had happened.

~*~

Eddrick rushed along the streets to the entrance to his home and glided silently through the door, where he searched out his wife, Kiri. He found her sitting in her favorite chair, working a ball of brightly colored yarn. Several years ago, she had discovered she could still make hats and scarves. Since then, she spent much of her time knitting child-sized accessories that she deposited on the stoop of the orphanage in Xona in the dark of night.

Eddrick strode into the small room that was an exact replica of the sitting room they had shared in life. The golden curtains hung by the window had never faded, even in the twenty years they had remained there.

"I couldn't have raised him any better myself!" Eddrick grinned, his eyes nearly squinting closed from pure joy. "He's going to be a perfect mayor."

The lovely redhead rolled her eyes and continued knitting. "Of course he will, that was the whole reason we sent him to your brother and his wife. We knew they would do an excellent job. Now, what's got you so excited this time?"

A small smile brightened her face when she finally looked up from her knitting.

Eddrick roared. "Aibek did it again! He won the tournament at the academy for the third year in a row. And every day after class—even after his own tournament today—he's been helping some of the younger officers learn to fight. You just wait and see—"

"I know, I know, he'll be perfect," Kiri interrupted with an indulgent smile. "You've said it every day since he graduated from the university and moved up to the Academy."

Her smile faded to a worried frown. "I just hope nothing bad happens because we interfered with Tavan." Her voice dropped to a whisper as she stared into the empty fireplace.

"Shush!" Eddrick glanced at the windows to make sure no one was near. "We shouldn't talk about it. Besides, it's not like we actually killed anyone. We just made things a bit easier for the boys."

"I know, but I still feel guilty." She heaved a great sigh and shook her head. "You've always been the one with the crazy schemes. I always get caught whenever I try to break a rule."

Eddrick sat next to his wife and stroked her fiery red hair. "It'll be fine, you'll see. We didn't tell anyone what to do." He placed his hands on her shoulders and gazed earnestly into her eyes, "By the trees! We didn't even give them the idea. They came up with the plan and carried it out on their own—we just made it a tiny bit easier. Now, no more worrying. Aibek's coming home!"

~*~

"You know I'll beat you again next week." Aibek taunted his friend over his shoulder as they left the training grounds behind the Academy.

"Of course, you will!" Faruz choked out his words between breaths. "You're a foot taller than me and everyone else, but I'll beat you yet. It's only a matter of time."

They strolled toward Aibek's home, down the cobbled streets, past a row of low mud brick and stone buildings, common in this prairie city. The scrubby grass that would normally brighten the town with its brilliant blue flowers had turned brown and dry in the unseasonable heat wave. Aibek wished again for rain. It had been almost a month since they'd seen a single drop. At least the short, skinny trees that the last General had planted along the grounds of the school still had green leaves, though they hadn't flowered that spring.

They walked the familiar roads lined with low grey houses, laughing and talking about the day's tournament and the practice session for the underclassmen that had followed.

Aibek grinned when Faruz ignored the door to his own home and followed Aibek into his house. They entered without pausing to remove their shoes. Faruz made a beeline for the end of the couch near the window, as he did every day. He claimed it was so he could see his father when he passed by on his way home, but Aibek suspected he wanted the most comfortable spot. Aibek stood and stared at his friend for a moment, wondering how Faruz had gotten so lucky. His family was close, but not smothering, and his parents treated him like a capable adult. Aibek swallowed against the old envy and dropped his bag on the table by the door.

"Wipe your feet," Aunt Ira scolded, strolling into the room from the kitchen. "I don't want you tracking dirt through the whole house." She wiped her hands on her apron. "How was the tournament? I want to hear all about it. But first, put your things away. You can't just drop them on the table like that." She smiled fondly at the auburn-haired young man and his friend.

"Hi, Aunt Ira. I won!" Aibek grinned at his aunt.

The always-smiling, short, stocky woman moved closer to her nephew, tucking her chocolate-brown hair back as she walked. Behind her, the housekeeper entered the room carrying a heavily laden, wooden serving tray.

Aibek held up the palm-sized medal for his aunt to see and grabbed a glass of water from the tray the housekeeper had placed on the low table before the couch. Ira took the prize from him and examined it at length. She handed it back and crossed the room to her favorite worn leather chair.

Aibek gulped the cold liquid. "You know I wouldn't have left my things here." He started down the short hall with his satchel thrown over his arm.

The house was small, with only two bedrooms on the ground floor, the main room, a moderately-sized, open kitchen that held an enormous coal-fired stove, a large prep table, a deep basin for washing, and a cozy dining nook. Up a narrow stair by the kitchen was a small servants' quarters the housekeeper shared with their only maid.

It was a large home by Xona standards, but Uncle Noral often complained how cramped it was. He also insisted on wooden furniture, though it was quite expensive. In a region with no trees, wood was a luxury reserved for the very wealthy. Most homes in the city had iron or steel-framed furniture since the iron mines were less than an hour's walk to the north. The men and women who mined the ore worked long, hard hours. Still, Aibek had heard they earned a fair wage and were able to pay for food and shelter in the city or surrounding villages.

He had shared a room with his father's servant Serik since the day they arrived on his uncle's doorstep nearly twenty years ago, though he had spent several years living away from home while attending university and beginning his training at the Academy. Narrow bunk beds occupied the far wall of the room. Aibek slept on the top bunk since his roommate was too old to climb the ladder every night.

On the opposite wall stood a simple, dark wood wardrobe. He placed his books, sword, vest and hat in it and closed the door. A full-length mirror leaned against the wall next to the cabinet. He glanced at his reflection and wiped a smudge of dirt off his broad nose and swept his still-damp hair behind his shoulders before he turned and ambled back through the narrow doorway.

He returned to the main room, where Faruz had made himself comfortable on the large brown couch that took up the middle of the room. He grabbed a chunk of heavy, spiced cake from the tray by the sofa and settled in to relax next to his friend. Faruz was demolishing what looked like a muffin.

Just as Aibek reclined on the couch, Serik trudged into the room with a worried expression on his weathered features. "We need to have a talk." The old man spoke quietly as he slowly came farther into the room.

"All right. What's the matter? Has something happened?" Aibek examined his oldest friend. Had he gotten smaller since the morning? Serik's white hair had mostly fallen out over the past several years, leaving only a few wild tufts in various places on his head. His hands now held a wadded parchment, grasped tightly and crinkling under the gnarled fingers.

Serik limped to one of the two large blue armchairs opposite the couch. "I've received a letter from my old friend, the religious leader in Nivaka, the village where you were born."

The color drained from Aibek's face. He twisted his hands together in his lap as he fought the urge to jump to his feet. He'd never expected to hear from that village. For years, he'd had no idea whether the place had been destroyed or overrun in the invasion that had caused them to flee. Either way, he'd believed the townsfolk had no need of the last mayor's son.

"Why? What does it say? Why did they wait so long?" He glanced at his aunt, who sat still and pale in her favorite chair by the fireplace. He hesitated, gulped, and asked, "Does it say anything about my parents?"

"It does. Here, why don't you read it for yourself?" Serik handed the crumpled parchment to his young ward. The furniture was close enough that neither had to stand to reach across the gap.

The world could have imploded around him, and Aibek wouldn't have noticed. Nothing existed except the paper in his trembling hands. Deep down, he had always maintained the dream of meeting his parents someday, and his heart leapt into his throat at the hope that this letter would fulfill that fantasy. However, the grim expression on Serik's weathered features made Aibek doubt the note held good news.

He smoothed the wrinkles in an attempt to gain some composure before he read the neat script on the page.

My Dear Serik,

I hope this letter finds you well. I'm sorry so many years have passed without contact, but I couldn't find a way to reach you without exposing your location to our enemy. The night you fled, our village was invaded by Helak's *warriors. We were completely unprepared for the attack, and their victory was swift.*

Unfortunately, Eddrick and Kiri were killed in the battle. I'm sorry I don't have better news—I know you were close to them.

I'm writing today because things here have changed. The villagers have overthrown Helak's *governor Tavan and his guards, and now the townsfolk are trying to return to their previous way of life. No one here believes that Helak will allow us to live in peace without attempting to regain control of our village. We need Eddrick's son to return and help us defend the village from the inevitable attack. I trust you have trained him well.*

I am looking forward to welcoming you and Aibek home again.

Please respond in all due haste.

Anxiously waiting,

Valasa

Aibek read the letter twice before he slowly lowered it to his lap. His eyes blurred with unshed tears, but he swallowed hard against them. He had long suspected his parents must be dead. Otherwise, they surely would have tried to learn what became of their only child. They'd never answered any of the letters he'd sent through the years.

Now the villagers wanted him to return and lead them through what could be a brutal massacre. The invaders had beaten the villagers easily the first time, or so the letter claimed, but they seemed sure he could lead them to a better life. He was nowhere near confident of that outcome.

"How can I lead a village I haven't seen since I was

a baby? Villagers I've never met are relying on me—a total stranger—to save them somehow?" Aibek scowled as he tried to reason through the villagers' expectations. As he spoke, Faruz took the letter from his hand and scanned it.

"I 'm so sorry about your parents. Really, though, this is what you've trained for your entire life. You finally get to lead a whole army, and… and fight with something other than dull practice swords, Faruz babbled.

A long silence followed as Aibek struggled to come to terms with the news of his parents' death. His aunt and uncle had raised him carefully, and his aunt had always treated him as her own child, but they had always made sure he knew who his parents were. He'd always treasured the hope of meeting them someday and having a father who would cheer him on at every step.

Aibek took a deep breath to clear his thoughts and sat up a little straighter. His family had made sure he was able to defend himself and his friends if he were ever called back to Nivaka. Still, he didn't know how to lead a village. He'd always thought he would start out as a lower officer and gain responsibility as he learned from those above him. Now he was expected to assume the leadership of an entire village of strangers?

Serik sat quietly, with a blank expression. Aibek glanced at him and wondered what he was thinking. After all, this must be a shock for him, too.

Finally, Ira broke the silence. Tears streamed down her face, and she lowered the letter to her knees. "I always knew I would have to send you back someday. You were the answer to our prayers…"

While she was speaking, Noral quietly entered the room. He glanced from face to face, worry darkening his features. Aibek looked up at the interruption, then dropped his gaze before his uncle could meet his eyes.

Noral eyed his wife's tears. "What's happened?" He strode to her side and wiped her face gently with his handkerchief.

Serik spoke first. "We've had a letter from Nivaka. The time has come for us to return to the village." He hesitated. "As we suspected, Eddrick and Kiri were killed in the invasion."

Noral's head fell to his chest. His face flushed red, and Aibek stared at the muscles working in his neck.

"I've already penned a response to this note," the old man continued. "We'll gather our supplies and be off within the week."

Noral shook his head and looked toward his nephew. "Nivaka's a beautiful place; I only wish I could go with you. I haven't laid eyes on the forest since I was about your age."

Aibek sighed; it was time to return to the forest. He just wished he had parents waiting to welcome him home.

2.

Assignment

"They're coming! He's alive! And now they're coming back!" Valasa shouted as he ran into the main room of his home. "I was never completely sure they made it to Xona, but they did. And now they've sent word they're returning. Isn't this wonderful news?" He shoved the newly arrived letter into his startled wife's hands.

Ayja's face set in a grim mask. "What are you going on about? Who's coming? You know Helak's men will return before too long. Now's not the time for visits." She paused for a moment to read the brief note he handed her.

When she finished, smiled at her husband. "They made it, then… Now the child will return to help us. Although he's fully grown by now, isn't he?" She stared out the window at the low clouds. "It doesn't say when we should expect them." She stood and made her way to the chair by the far window, her favorite spot to sit and think.

Valasa watched his wife's movements. What could she be thinking? She didn't look as excited as he'd thought she would. His enthusiasm seemed exaggerated compared with her quiet thoughtfulness. He stared at the brilliant halo of her pure white hair illuminated in the late afternoon sun.

It had been the same color since they were children, and,

together with her delicate features, it gave her an ageless beauty.

"Wherever will they stay?" she asked after a long pause. "Eddrick's old house is a mess after Tavan and his guards lived there for so long. It'll take a great deal of work to make it livable."

Valasa weighed his wife's reactions. "I've been thinking about some of the particulars. They can stay in our empty rooms for a while." When she said nothing, he continued, "Also, I think Ahren would be the perfect person to show him around once they arrive. She knows every nook and cranny of this town and all of the gossip." He chuckled.

Ayja's head whipped around and she met his eyes with a startled glance. "Do you think that's wise? Why couldn't Dalan or Alija or any of the other young men show him around? How do you suppose the young men in the city behave around young ladies?" She scowled and he took a breath, determined to set her mind at ease.

"The lad was raised by Eddrick's brother. I have no doubt he'll be perfectly respectful." Valasa wouldn't admit his real purpose to his wife—that he wanted their new leader to see their son in action, training for war, rather than playing tour guide.

She scowled at him again, then glanced at the darkening sky outside the window. "I'm not so sure, but we have some time to work out the details. For now, I need to see to our dinner."

When she finished speaking, Ayja rose from her seat and strode toward the kitchen at the back of their home. Her husband stood as well, but hovered near the fireplace, unsure what to do with himself. He finally wandered to his workroom, which occupied most of the west side of the house. He was confident he would find something to do in there. As the religious leader of the village, he was responsible for the health and wellbeing of the entire population, from the smallest plant to the highest ranking villagers. He had several unread letters on his desk that had arrived with the one from Xona. Valasa was confident that reading and preparing replies to those letters would keep him occupied until it was time to eat.

~*~

A few hours later, Valasa sat at the head of the small dining table with his wife to his left and their son, Dalan, and daughter, Ahren, on the right. They often preferred to eat in the small dining nook near the kitchen rather than the formal dining hall. It was a cozy space painted in shades of green. Small shelves adorned the walls, each crowded with diminutive wood carvings. Ahren had a promising talent at sculptures, but her father wished she'd practice more. Valasa thought she could make a good living selling the tiny, exquisitely detailed animal statuettes in the market. He hoped they'd be able to market them again in the very near future.

His offspring were devouring a meal of roast foul and squash. Valasa had seen a considerable increase in Dalan and Ahren's appetites recently, and today was no exception. They dispatched the large meal in record time. He thought the change was likely due to the hours they spent every day learning to use the swords and spears they had found in the governor's armory.

When they'd finished their meal, Valasa stared thoughtfully at his seventeen-year-old daughter. She was tiny; the top of her head barely reached his chest, though she had blossomed into a lovely young woman. Her long white hair—just like her mother's—was bound tightly in a braid that brushed the ribbon tied around her waist. He wasn't sure how she would react to his announcement, but he was ecstatic that his child would have the honor of welcoming their leader home. He was a little uneasy about Ayja's reactions, too. His wife hadn't exactly consented to the plan.

After a moment, Ahren's crystal-blue eyes met his. "What? Do I have food on my face?" She wiped her napkin over her chin.

"No, not at all. But I do have wonderful news. Come with me to my study and we'll discuss it." Valasa stood and led the way out of the small dining nook.

~*~

Ahren trudged behind her father into his workroom. *How long is this going to take?*

She was anxious to join her new friends at the Pavilion. She'd met Tamyr and Ahni soon after the governor's assassination and had immediately liked them. Her other friends had been much less welcoming.

They must be worried about spies, Ahren thought.

That was the only reason she could think of that would explain her friends' suspicion. She shrugged off the thoughts and closed the door behind her.

As she waited for whatever grand news had prompted this rare occasion, she looked around at her surroundings. She had seldom been allowed in this room; her father only used it when he wanted to work undisturbed. Any other time, he preferred to use the small desk in the den. He'd always said he liked to be near his family. Her father was an important man. He was the Gadonu, or religious leader and healer of their town, and she'd learned at a young age that he was not to be bothered when he was working.

The workroom was wide, extending over the entire side of the house. However, it was only a few steps to the far wall from the door they had passed through. She turned her head from side to side, craning her neck as she tried to see the entire space.

Dark golden wood covered the walls, unlike the light red shadow-wood used in the rest of the building and most of the village. Four windows let in the evening light, spaced evenly along the west wall, each covered with a simple dark blue piece of heavy fabric she assumed was meant to pass for a curtain.

There were nearly a dozen ornately carved desks and worktables scattered down the wall, some under windows, others haphazardly placed between them. Papers, vials, jars, and bottles littered each weathered surface. Shelves covered the entire east wall, displaying all manner of books, bottles, drawings, paintings, and carvings. There were only two breaks in the shelving, which allowed for the heavy wooden doors that led to the main parts of the house. She leaned closer to get a better look at a tall, narrow bottle that gleamed red in the lamplight. "Don't touch that one," Valasa warned just as she reached toward it.

The sudden exclamation startled Ahren, who dropped her hand and walked to the desk near the center of the room, where her father lowered himself into the chair. Strands of silver streaked his long chestnut hair, catching the light from the lamp on the table. His beard had slowly turned gray over the past few years, and the solid silver presented a stark contrast to his mostly dark hair.

"I only wanted to read the label," she murmured, anxious to let him know she wasn't trying to meddle in his work or mess with his things. On her rare visits to this room, it had always felt alive somehow, and she never quite felt comfortable within its walls.

"It's best not to touch. Now, let's come to the point. I received the most wonderful news this afternoon." He grinned broadly and gestured for his daughter to sit in the chair across from him. "How much do you know of what Nivaka was like before Tavan's invasion?" Without pausing for an answer, he continued, "Were you aware that Eddrick and Kiri, the mayor and his wife, had a son only a few weeks before the invasion?"

"I've heard this was a peaceful, happy village, and that the mayor and his wife were very generous and loved by the people." She seated herself in the chair he indicated. "And I do remember hearing they had a baby who was killed with them in the invasion… but… that's all ancient history." She shook her head and opened her mouth to say more, but her father cut her off.

"I received a letter today from an old friend. It turns out he escaped with Eddrick's infant son. They fled to the city of Xona, where the mayor's brother and his wife took them in." He paused and his crystal blue eyes met his daughter's. "I learned today they're on their way home." He smiled widely. "Aibek, the baby, is now twenty. He's been raised as a leader and warrior and is coming back to help us keep our freedom."

He stood and walked around the desk to face his daughter before continuing.

"I want you to show our new mayor around the village." He grabbed her hand and held it between both of his. "And teach him the important points of our history here. He'll help us defeat Helak's troops when they return." Valasa grinned.

Ahren frowned as she tried to process her father's announcement. Someone from Xona was going to lead them? She'd heard they didn't even have trees that far north. What would this person know of life in the forest? How would he handle their unique living situation? Her mind spun with questions. Ahren had expected one of the young men who helped overthrow the governor to step into the mayor's role. Why should this northern stranger take that right away from those who'd fought for it?

Fury descended over her like a curtain. She struggled with her breath and stared mutely at her father. Long moments passed before she overcame the shock and voiced a reply.

"I… I don't understand. A stranger? Why not Dalan? Or Alijah? They're the ones who got rid of Tavan and his guards." She paused and considered what her father had said. "And why should I have to show him around?" She jumped up and ripped her hand from her father's. "There are so many men who've grown up here, who know our history and traditions and would be excellent mayors."

"Aibek is no stranger." Valasa's reply was cool. "He was born here. It is true we have an abundance of strong, intelligent young men in Nivaka, but none of them have been raised and trained to lead as Aibek has." He placed a hand on his daughter's shoulder and peered into her eyes. "This assignment is an incredible opportunity, and I fully expect you to treat it as such."

He spoke in the authoritative tone she'd heard so often as a child. There was no point in arguing.

She dropped her gaze to the floor and sighed. "If it means that much to you, I'll welcome this stranger and show him the important places in the village, but I hope you don't expect me to fall at his feet and call him 'my lord.'" She pulled out of her father's grip and turned to look at the brilliant reds and oranges of the sunset visible through the small window. The images blurred, and she wiped a hand over her eyes.

She'd always hated her tendency to cry when she got angry. She took another deep breath and tried to gain control of her reactions.

"I don't understand why we can't elect a mayor from the citizens who've lived here all their lives. There must be at least a dozen people who would be perfect." At that moment, another problem altogether occurred to Ahren. "Where will he be staying? He certainly can't live in the mayor's house on the square. It's a huge mess after Tavan and his guards remodeled it. It's hideous… and none of the other homes on the square have been repaired in years…" She trailed off as she remembered exploring the dilapidated buildings with her friends when they were children.

"I've decided our guests will stay here, in a couple of our spare bedrooms, until the mayoral home is repaired and ready." When he saw she was about to object again, he continued, "Aibek will be traveling with an old friend of mine, the same man who escaped with him to the city and has served as his advisor there. I'm sure I'll recognize Serik, so I'll know they are who they say they are." His voice hardened. "Really, it's nothing to cry about. I know you'll like him if you just give him a chance."

Ahren fumed as she listened to her father's response. She wiped at the traitorous tears streaming down her face again. He couldn't seriously mean to invite total strangers into their home, could he? But he was adamant. She struggled to find an angle to argue, but he had covered all her objections already.

After a long, tense pause, Ahren finally answered, "Fine. I'll help you welcome this stranger to our village—and our home—but please don't expect me to be happy about it. I'm not convinced that any one of the young men, or even any of the old men, wouldn't be a better mayor than some stranger from the city."

"All I'm asking is that you help us welcome him, and

give him a chance. Try to be kind." Valasa gestured to the door and followed his daughter out of his workroom and into the house.

Ahren ran out the front door to meet her friends at the Pavilion, angrier than she had been in years. She could hardly wait to tell the others what was happening, and, she hoped, find some sympathy and support. She met the group of women at their regular spot under the farthest corner of the Pavilion. When she stepped out of the deep shadows cast by the massive branches overhead, Zifa stopped pacing mid-step and stared at Ahren's flushed, tear-stained face.

"What's happened?" Zifa pulled a handkerchief from the pocket of her breeches and dabbed at Ahren's wet cheeks.

"My father…" She trailed off with a sob and turned her back to her friends. She leaned on the heavy rail lining the boardwalk and stared into the darkening forest. She needed to get control of herself. After a moment, she turned and stared into the concerned faces of her four closest friends. They'd all moved closer.

Ahni placed a gentle hand on Ahren's hunched shoulder. "Is he ill?"

Ahren sighed and dropped onto the delicately carved bench behind her. "No, he's quite well. He's written to Eddrick's son, who apparently escaped with a servant the night of the invasion." She paused and took a deep breath. "This… this person is coming back to be our new mayor, and my father wants me to head the welcoming committee."

"What? But what about our own men?" Tamyr exclaimed. "We have plenty of men who could take on that role."

"I know, that's what I said, too, but my father is sure

this city boy is the perfect leader." Ahni's spritely face lit with a mischievous smile. "What if we find a way to chase him back to the city where he belongs? Then our own men could take the lead."

"Aren't we getting ahead of ourselves?" Zifa asked with a frown. She sat next to Ahren on the bench and stretched an arm around her shoulders. "Your father is the wisest person I know. Why don't we give Eddrick's son a chance—see who he really is—before we start plotting against him?"

"That sounds like a good plan," Zyana agreed with a gentle smile. "You know I'd love to see Wayra as the mayor, or Alija or any of the others, but maybe there's a good reason your father thinks this young man is the best choice."

Ahren sighed. She'd hoped for more support from her friends. She looked up and met Ahni's eyes over Zifa's dark hair.

"We'll talk later," Ahni mouthed in silence, gesturing to include Tamyr in her plan.

Ahren gave a tiny nod and pushed herself to her feet. "All right, we'll wait and see. Now, we should get some practice in before it gets too late. Zifa, weren't you going to show us how you jump through the trees?"

They trained for a while, but Ahren had a hard time concentrating.

What could Ahni be planning? How can we chase this visitor back to the city, where he belongs?

She tried to leap to the next branch as all her friends had done but missed. She landed hard on the stack of cushions below, grateful for Zifa's foresight. That fall would've hurt if she'd landed on the hard wooden boardwalk. Maybe she should pay more attention to the night's practice. There was plenty of time to devise a plan before Eddrick's son arrived.

3.

Traveling

"This will be great! They're leaving today. Maybe soon I'll be able to talk to my son." Eddrick beamed, considering the possibilities.

Kiri set her knitting aside and furrowed her brow. "Now, wait just a minute. You know the living can't see you."

He waved her protest aside. "I do it all the time. I figured out that I can talk to certain people, but only if they're paying attention. Most people don't realize I'm there."

Kiri worried her lower lip with her teeth. "Who have you been talking to? I hope you're not trying to change things down there again. I feel bad enough about interfering the one time."

"Valasa's aware enough that we can communicate sometimes. I only answer the questions he asks, so I'm not breaking any rules," Eddrick said. His smile stretched wider.

"And exactly what questions does he ask?"

"We've only talked a few times, and mostly he's talked about what's going on in Nivaka and how his family's doing. I don't think he realizes I've been able to see them all this time." He wandered closer and sank down onto the chair beside her. "He did ask me about Aibek, and I told him how to contact Serik."

"Please be careful," Kiri pleaded. "I'm not sure exactly what all the rules are, but I don't think we're supposed to talk to them."

"What would be the point of being able to see our friends if we weren't allowed to talk to them? I'm only chatting with a religious leader, and nothing bad's happened so far. I'm sure it'll be fine," he answered defensively

"Just be careful. I don't want you getting us into trouble again." She squeezed into the chair with him and settled in to watch the rain fall over the forest.

~*~

Aibek tossed the last of his belongings into the leather bag his aunt had bought for the journey and took a final look at his room. The newly-bare walls echoed his melancholy mood, the dull brown curtains his aunt had put up yesterday flapping in the morning breeze. He'd sold or given away all of his books and belongings. He had tucked everything he had left into the leather pack on the neatly made bunk. He didn't know if he would ever return, either to this house or to the city where he had lived his entire life. Emotion squeezed his chest, robbing him of breath. He inhaled, relishing the scent of his aunt's favorite potpourri, and ran his hands through his thick auburn hair. He needed to be strong for Ira and Noral. His aunt had been tearful all week, and Aibek had worried about her.

He grabbed his pack and trudged out of his room for the last time. When he stepped into the hall, he almost collided with his uncle.

"There you are! I was hoping you wouldn't take too long. I have something for you." Noral closed the door to the master bedroom and gestured for his nephew to follow him down the hall and out the front door.

They walked the short distance to the blacksmith shop, and around to the small study in the back. Scraps of paper littered every surface in the cramped space, even the wooden chair that stood in front of the desk. Old bare-wood furniture filled the space, worn and dented from years of use. The dingy, gray walls were bare as well, except for one small iron frame that held a miniature painting of a much younger Ira.

Memories flooded Aibek, and he stood frozen in the center of the room. He had played here as a boy when he wanted to be near his uncle before he was old enough to be allowed in the workshop.

He remembered play-fighting in the small office with Faruz, using sticks for swords, jumping on and under the furniture, and causing such a ruckus his uncle sent them into the yard to play. Aibek smiled at the memories. He and Faruz had grown up together. Beginning this new chapter of his life alone would be strange. Of course, Serik was coming, but the old man only spoke when it was necessary.

"Ah, here it is." Noral's brusque voice startled the younger man out of his reverie.

His uncle had just come through the door that led to the workshop, holding a long, narrow sword, sheathed in a dark leather scabbard with a matching belt that would tie around the waist of the wearer.

"I've been holding onto this for some time; I was planning to give it to you when you graduated the academy. This sword belonged to my father and has been handed down through our family for many years." Noral spoke softly, unsheathing the weapon and holding it out across his open palms for his nephew. "I've kept it oiled for strength and reinforced the handle."

Aibek took the sword from his mentor and turned it over in his hands. His eyes widened as he felt the weight of the weapon in his grasp. It was finely wrought steel, with intricately carved vines and branches intertwining to form the elaborate guard and basket hilt. The blade was light but strong and sharp. It gleamed in the early morning light and he had no doubt it would be his most prized possession from that day on.

"Thank you," Aibek answered before he sheathed the weapon and tied it around his waist. "It's the most beautiful sword I've ever seen."

Noral caught him in a strong hug, holding tightly for just a moment. He released his nephew, and they walked back to the house together, knowing daylight was burning and the travelers would need to begin their journey soon.

"I know I've been hard on you," Noral said as he walked, "but I knew you'd have to return to the forest one day. You won't be fighting for trophies and medals now, but for your very life."

Aibek nodded, but couldn't think of anything to say to that. They finished the short trip home in silence.

When they reached the house, Aibek bent down and wrapped his arms around Ira. She looked so small and frail all of a sudden. He kissed her cheek and accepted her kiss in return. She hugged him in a viselike grip around his waist for a long time, and he wondered if she was going to let him go. Finally, he stepped back and kissed her soft, powdered cheek one more time.

"Thank you so much for everything. I'll write as soon as we get there and let you know I'm well. Maybe I'll even be able to come visit someday." Aibek grinned weakly at the only parents he had ever known, hugged his uncle once more and gestured to Serik.

This wasn't going to get any easier, and any delay now would only make it tougher on everyone. Aibek swallowed hard against the emotions that threatened to choke him and strode away next to his oldest friend. He was disappointed that Faruz hadn't come to say good-bye, but there was no time to stop. They'd already delayed well past sunrise—the time they had planned to be on the road.

Around them on the street, the city bustled in its usual way. Women hurried on various errands, some with small children in tow, others in groups chattered as they walked toward the shopping district. The stone side-walks teemed with people, and the dusty, cobbled streets overflowed with oxen pulling carts filled with various wares for the market. Serik led the way to the South Road, which would take them to one of three gates where individuals could enter and exit the city walls.

Aibek had never taken that particular road; he had only ever left the city through the West Gate to swim in the river with his friends. He would miss them all. His heart was heavy as he trudged toward the guards at the city gates, and he wondered again if he would ever return.

The throngs of travelers and merchants slowed to a crawl as they approached the city's exit. The stone wall sparkled in the morning sun, but Aibek barely noticed. He kept his eyes on the enormous iron gates that stood open, allowing travelers to exit on the left while arriving ones stopped on the right for inspection.

I hope this doesn't take long.

They had planned to be beyond the gates before the second moon, Ilodus, dropped below the eastern horizon. Their exit had been so delayed that now Thrimanca, the third and slowest moon, was about to set. It was nearly mid-morning.

While they waited with the crowd for their turn to exit, a commotion behind them caught the travelers' attention. Someone was pushing toward them through the throngs of people, and those being shoved aside shouted their anger. Aibek would have continued his progress toward the gates, but he paused for a moment. It sounded as if someone was yelling his name.

He turned again to scan the crowd and spotted Faruz, carrying a leather knapsack and making his way toward the gate. He wore his father's broadsword on his back and his smaller Academy sword at his side. When he finally caught up, he grinned breathlessly at Aibek.

"You didn't really think you were going on this adventure without me, did you?" He paused a moment and braced his hands on his knees as he panted for breath. "I didn't know you were setting off so early in the morning. I couldn't believe it when I got to your house, and you'd already gone. I didn't even have time for one of Ira's famous muffins!"

Aibek raised both hands. "What are you doing here? You can't seriously mean to travel all the way to Nivaka with me. What about your family? School? The Army? Do your parents know you're here? How will you ever get home?" He fired off questions without pausing for a response.

Finally, Faruz threw his hands up, too. "Of course they know. They didn't even try to talk me out of coming. But, really… I can't let you travel off into the sunset—or sunrise as the case may be—without at least one friend to help you along. I'm coming with you. And if you won't let me walk with you and Serik, then I'll follow behind."

Faruz matched Serik's pace as they passed the guards at the city gates and walked out into the open pasture area surrounding the city walls.

Aibek grinned faintly at Faruz. "All right, you can come along. But you'll have to carry your own weight on the journey. We've only brought the bare necessities with us, and we plan to hunt and fish for food along the way."

"Well then, you'll be even happier that I decided to tag along. I brought some fresh cookies that Mother baked for us this morning, some venison jerky Father picked up at the market, and some fishing supplies for the rest of the journey, and of course my own necessities."

Faruz grinned at his companions, but Serik frowned and fidgeted. He looked to Aibek. "Have you considered what may happen when we arrive at Nivaka with an extra person, sir? Where will he stay once we arrive? What will he do while you're preparing to take on the mayoralty?"

Faruz answered quickly. "That's easy. I'll share a room with Aibek like we have hundreds of times… and if they won't let me in, then I'll sleep under the stars. Plus, I'll be the perfect advisor for his Lordship, or whatever he'll be called, because I have no emotional connection to the place."

Just as Serik opened his mouth to object again, Aibek interrupted. "You said your mother baked cookies this morning? Are they still warm?"

~*~

They walked in silence for most of the day, through the plains and farms that surrounded and supplied the city. The excitement of the journey soon wore thin, as they walked forever without making any apparent progress. There were no trees or hills to break up the scenery, and late into the afternoon, Aibek could still see the shadow of Xona's wall on the distant horizon. The only difference he could see in the landscape was a gradual change in the grass from brown to green. When the sky began to darken in the evening, they found a soft, dense patch of grass and set up camp. They caught three fish in the nearby stream and built a small cooking fire. As they settled in for dinner, Serik asked if they wanted to hear some of the village's history. Both young men agreed they should know as much as possible about their destination.

Serik began, his voice soft, "Many generations ago, the people of the village were embroiled in a bitter dispute over who had the right to occupy the Tsari Forest."

Serik's companions leaned in closer to hear as he relayed what he knew of the origins of Nivaka.

"The villagers had been living there for about a decade when a nomadic group of natives tried to force them to leave. After several bloody battles, the leaders of both groups came together and agreed to a truce: the Nivakans would build their village in the treetops, and the natives would live on the ground, in a village they named Kasanto."

As they laid out their bedrolls on the soft grass and pre-pared to sleep, Aibek wondered what this treetop village looked like. He imagined quaint little treehouses con-nected to each other by rope bridges.

How can they cook? Surely they can't make fires in the tree-homes. Perhaps they have a fire pit on the ground. What about those enemies Serik had mentioned? Are they still around to trouble the tree-dwelling villagers?

Before he could ruminate further, the exhaustion of the day caught up with him, and he fell into a fitful sleep.

~*~

In the days that followed, they fell into a comfortable routine as they traveled the dusty, well-packed road south. They walked in silence most of the day, then hunted small game or caught fish for dinner, and Serik talked over the fire as they ate. He related the histories of some of the more prominent families in Nivaka and gave them a partial account of what he knew about the night they had escaped to Xona. Whenever they were near a water source, they washed themselves and their clothes with the soap Ira had tucked into Aibek's pack. He was glad she'd thought of something so practical; they would have arrived smelling like farm animals if she hadn't.

The first few days passed quickly, excitement spurring them on. The thrill didn't last long, however, before the monotony of the treeless landscape began to wear on Aibek. Each day, his eyes searched the unchanging horizon for a house, a scrubby bush or some small landmark he could use to mark the passage of time and distance. His legs ached from the endless hours of walking, and each evening he yearned for the sight of the Zobe River ahead of them.

After several days of traveling the wretched, never-ending plain, Aibek finally spotted trees ahead as they topped a small rise.

"Yes! The river. We're almost there," Aibek shouted, dashing toward the wood.

"Wait," Serik called. "It might be best to sleep here tonight."

Aibek didn't hear him. Though the afternoon light was waning, he rushed into the dim forest and instantly understood his error. His friends followed him into the murky, muddy bog. Relief flooded Aibek when Serik fashioned a torch from branches to light their way through the darkness. The old man walked just ahead of his two companions, holding the torch off to the side to avoid blinding the younger men. The stagnant air reeked of rotting vegetation and foul water. Aibek gagged repeatedly and wrapped his handkerchief around his face to keep the stench from his nose.

They trudged through the swamp for two days without stopping, since there was no place to set up camp or even to sit and rest. They took turns carrying the torch and leading the way through the bog. Tall trees with drooping branches surrounded them and blocked out almost all sunlight.

The eerie atmosphere made Aibek uncomfortable. His skin prickled with the feeling of eyes boring into his back. With every step, he expected to be accosted or attacked by whatever lurked in the dimness. Serik kept his eyes on the partially submerged path before him and pressed onward, his face a mask of grim determination. Only a slight tremor in his hand gave away his unease.

Aibek kept his hand on his sword and repeatedly startled at the sound of something massive moving through the water and mud nearby, though he never caught even a glimpse of the source.

"Hey!" Aibek shouted in alarm when something wrapped itself around his leg above his boot.

He splashed ahead a few steps, but the animal was gone before he could see what sort of foul creature it could be. Faruz stayed close to the others, alert but apparently unconcerned. He never once drew his sword but hummed quietly to himself as if this were a predictable stroll down the road near his home. Aibek didn't understand how his companion could be so relaxed in such a place, and the cheerful humming grated on his nerves.

After hours of gritting his teeth against the happy tunes, he exclaimed through clenched teeth, "Would you please stop singing?"

Faruz startled and dropped the bit of jerky he had just removed from his pack. It sank into the murky water beside him and vanished.

"What was that for?" He pulled another strip of the

tough jerky from his pack. "A little music helps keep my mind off this place." He gestured around him with the dried meat.

Aibek shook his head and held his tongue. He didn't want to fight with his friend. Faruz chewed noisily and resumed humming, though he kept his voice a bit quieter than before.

The road was barely discernible, and they trusted it merely because it was the only place not wholly covered with water. They trudged for hours through the ankle-deep mud, repeatedly bitten by mosquitoes and swarms of other flying, biting insects before they finally made it to the rise that marked the end of the swamp.

There, they stopped to enjoy a short break in the gathering twilight. Splashes of colorful clouds painted the sky in a brilliant palette of pinks and oranges as the scarlet sun descended toward the horizon.

Aibek sighed in relief but perked up his ears. A growing noise behind him caught his attention, and he frowned. A flurry of squeaks and clicks carried on the breeze. He turned to ask Faruz if he heard it but froze without a sound.

Before he could say a word, a colony of enormous bat-like creatures with brilliant blue eyes besieged the travelers. They came out of nowhere and caught Aibek by surprise. The flying rodents flew close to the travelers and brushed the men's hair and clothing as the animals ate their fill of the insects that swarmed around the three men's warmth.

Aibek fought the urge to scream as he shook his head and batted at the huge flying creatures. He had never seen anything like these bats. They were at least three times the size of the ones he had seen in the city, with scalloped, leathery wings beating against the evening air and brushing within a hairbreadth of his shirt and hair. They were close enough that he could hear the incessant clicking sounds as they located the tiny insects they hunted.

Panicked, Aibek swatted and shook and ran alongside his friends until they rid themselves of both the bats and the insects, then struggled to push their tired legs over a couple of higher inclines before they stopped and set up camp.

When the sun rose, Aibek groaned and burrowed into his bedroll. He wasn't ready to face another day of travel. Thankfully, neither were the others. They spent a full day resting from the ordeal of the swamp. They spread out their clothes to dry in the glorious morning sun while they slept on the soft cushion of grass.

They napped until late afternoon when Aibek's hungry stomach drove him to find food. He managed to snare a pair of rabbits while Faruz and Serik scrounged for wood. They scraped together enough for a tiny fire, just large enough to roast the meat. To Aibek, the gamey, unseasoned rabbit tasted like a king's feast after days of living on Faruz's jerky.

The friends rose at dawn to continue their journey. Finally, just before sunset four nights later, they saw the buildings that marked the border of Kainga, a small city nestled against the banks of the Zobe River. They agreed to spend the night in the river town, and they would complete the journey to Nivaka the next day.

Aibek walked a little faster as they entered the town, his head held high. Giddy excitement bubbled up in his chest, and he grinned at the expectation of a home cooked meal and the luxury of soft feather beds. Serik arranged for a room while his younger companions stood close behind. Aibek kept his eyes on the floor in front of his feet. Standing in the close hallway, he couldn't avoid the knowledge that they were dirty and smelled awful. His own odor assaulted his nose, and he tried to stay as far as possible from the other patrons. It had been several days since they'd last seen a stream, and a few days more since they'd had a full bath.

"Do you have a bathtub we could use?" Serik asked, echoing Aibek's thoughts.

"Yes, that'll be an extra two pieces of silver," the young innkeeper answered, smiling.

Serik glanced at Aibek and Faruz, who nodded their approval.

The tall young woman who showed them to their room was talkative and friendly. She showed no signs of noticing their unbathed state as she gave them information on where they could obtain any supplies they might need before they continued on their journey. While they climbed the steep wooden staircase toward their room on the second floor, she told them about the boat that ferried travelers across the river.

"If you want to catch the boat, you'll need to leave here by sunrise, though it's only a few blocks away. If you miss the first one, it'll be back in a couple of hours." She grinned and pointed toward the window. Aibek stared at the tall mast jutting into the sky outside the inn.

"It runs back and forth all day," the woman continued. "Of course, if you don't want to ride the ferry, you can take the South Road to Imah and cross at the bridge there."

"Oh? How far is it?" Serik asked.

"It's about two hours south, not much if you're looking to save some coin." The woman pulled out a key and opened the door to her right.

"Thank you for your help," Serik said quietly, stepping

into the room.

"The maids will be up shortly with your bath." She vanished down the hall in a swish of skirts, and Aibek dropped into the soft chair.

The single room had two fluffy beds piled with pillows and covered with plain yellow quilts that looked heavy. A smallish, faded red couch sat against the wall next to the single window, and a large, comfortable-looking, dark brown leather chair sat near the sofa. It looked like heaven to Aibek after nineteen days of hard travel. They each took a turn in the modest claw-foot tub that the maids set up behind the screen on the right side of the room.

Once all the men were washed and dressed, they headed down to the tavern for the evening meal. It was a large, noisy room with tightly packed wooden tables and chairs. Aibek couldn't believe how much wood they had used to decorate the building. Surely, they must be near the forest by now. Otherwise, how would the innkeepers have afforded such a luxury?

Revelers surrounded nearly every table, but Serik found one in the corner farthest from the loudest patrons. The simple country fare of rabbit stew with roasted vegetables and fresh bread tasted delicious to Aibek after the unspiced rabbit, fowl, and fish he'd eaten for nearly three weeks. There was butter for the rolls and vegetables, and the stew was well-seasoned and aromatic.

While they ate, Aibek enjoyed the energy and enthusiasm of their fellow travelers, many of whom had sampled the ale and were happily drunk. The conversations and laughter echoed through the room; the bare wood flooring and furniture did nothing to dull the sound. After the quiet solitude of their journey, the ruckus was deafening.

Aibek laughed along when a young man took a seat at the spinet and played a hilarious song about falling in the muddy waters of the swamp. He was still chuckling when the song came to a sudden stop.

"Sing something different!" someone shouted. "No one wants to think about that awful swamp, especially since they finished the new road and we ain't gotta go near it anymore."

Faruz and Aibek both stared wide-eyed and slack-jawed at the man who had interrupted.

What new road?

Serik leaned over and whispered something to the tavern maid, who laughed cheerfully and answered in a thick accent, "Yep, they just finished it last year. It's a bit longer now, but worth it to stay out of that miserable mud." She paused, then shuddered. "I'll happily walk an extra day to avoid going through that again."

Stunned, Aibek could only gape at the woman. He struggled to hide his reactions from Serik; the old man was already upset by the news and didn't need to feel worse. Oblivious to the reactions of the patrons at the table, the thickset woman straightened and cleared the dishes. She moved quickly and had the table cleared and wiped down in less than a minute.

"Excuse me," Aibek caught her attention before she could move away.

She turned to him and tapped her foot impatiently.

Not quite able to meet her eyes, he said, "I know you have work to do, and I won't keep you long, but do you know why they would have made the road go through the swamp in the first place? I mean, if they could avoid it."

The woman cocked an eyebrow at the young patron, then smiled. "Well, it wasn't always a swamp. I've heard stories that it was once a lovely valley that has slowly sunk and filled with water over the past few generations." She laughed and wiped at a spot on the table. "Now, I don't know that for certain, it's all just stories now. Like you said, no one would want to build a road through that bog."

Full from their meal and deflated by this revelation, the weary travelers trudged to their room for a good night's sleep.

4.

Arrival

Serik closed the door behind him. "I had no idea." Head down, he trudged toward the bed by the window where he would spend the night.

Aibek shook his head. "There's no way you could have known. We'll just keep the new road in mind if we ever travel this way again." He sighed and sank onto the bed, kicking off his boots. Aibek thought back to the discussion they'd had at that crossroads, and how he and Faruz had wanted to turn right onto the wider, smoother road. Of course, Serik had kept them on the path he knew would lead them to Nivaka. Aibek hoped Serik wasn't reliving that same moment, though the dejected look on the servant's lined face indicated he was.

"I didn't mind the swamp so much," Faruz blurted, startling Aibek back to the present. "At least it was a change from the boredom of the plains and… well, we've some great stories to tell, though I don't know who'll believe we were attacked by giant bats." He laughed at the memory and climbed into the soft bed.

Aibek raised his eyebrows and tried to see his friend's perspective. He gave up after a few moments and extinguished the only lamp before he crawled under the covers. He and Faruz shared the larger bed near the door, so Serik could sleep comfortably in the other bed.

~*~

Faruz stared at the ceiling in the darkened room and wondered if he'd be allowed into the village when they arrived tomorrow. He thought about the old man's warnings when they began their journey.

What if they turn me away?

He hoped he wouldn't have to make the return trip alone. He didn't know the way around the swamp, but he didn't think he could face that awful bog alone.

Surely, they'll let me into the village, right? Well, if not, I guess I could make his way back to this little town and find someone to travel with.

He lay awake for a short time pondering before sheer exhaustion overtook him and he fell into a deep sleep.

~*~

Aibek stared at the sliver of light sneaking through the curtains until it vanished with the fading moonlight. He wasn't ready to lead his own division, let alone a whole village.

How can anyone expect me to take over as the mayor of a town I've never even seen?

He flopped to his other side and tried to find a cool spot on the pillow but found himself looking at the back of Faruz's head.

How is Faruz snoring so loudly; isn't he nervous at all?

Aibek flipped onto his back and stared into the blackness above the bed.

What if I can't find a way to beat this army? Surely, they have some kind of plan in mind already.

He tossed for most of the night, falling into a fitful slumber a few hours before dawn.

~*~

Eddrick grinned. "I'm so glad we decided to go ahead with our plan. And now Aibek's on his way home."

"It looks like they'll arrive tomorrow, barring any trouble crossing the river." Kiri smiled as she sat on the comfortable sofa. "They've made good time."

"I wonder…" he trailed off as an older man walked through the door.

"Well, Agommi, I didn't expect to see you again so soon," Kiri said. "I hope all is well?"

"Not exactly." The visitor shook his hat as if to remove the rain and stomped his immaculate boots on the doormat. "We need to talk about the rules… You can't interfere with the living."

Eddrick spoke slowly. "I'm not sure what you mean. I've only chatted with one person, and even then I just answered direct questions."

The old man shook his head, advanced farther into the chamber and pointed at Eddrick. "You know very well that's not what I'm talking about. You planted weapons and ideas for those young men who assassinated Tavan, and have changed the course of their lives, perhaps forever."

"Well, we had to do something!" Kiri jumped from her seat on the couch. "That's our son. We couldn't let him walk into an ambush! What would you have us do?"

Agommi gestured to Eddrick. "You know I understand; it was awful to stand by and do nothing when my own son was killed. But the ancient laws exist for a reason. We have to let them live their own lives! You have changed the course of time. None of the ancestors knows what will happen now." As he spoke, he walked to where Eddrick sat. "They sent me here to inform you of your punishment. You are to be confined to this room until Thrimanca is full again—"

Kiri interrupted, "But that's more than a month! Now? It's such a critical time. Aibek's due to arrive in Nivaka tomorrow. Please let me see my son come home!" She sank onto the couch.

At the same time, her husband leaned forward in his chair. "That can't be right! I know I'm not the only one that's helped his family. There are hundreds of stories throughout history."

But the old man just shook his head. "Most of those stories aren't true, and the few true ones centered on advice that was given. None have blatantly interfered as you did. Your sentence stands according to the ancestors." He placed a hand on his son's shoulder, but the younger man shook it off.

Eddrick stood and crossed the room to sit with his wife. "Is there really no other way? We won't interfere again. We just want to see the day our son returns home."

Agommi bowed his head and stared at the floor. "I'm sorry. The ancients have decided. It could have been much worse. Forty-two days is nothing but a blink of an eye in the vastness of eternity."

As soon as he finished speaking, the visitor vanished from the room, leaving the couple distraught, trying to cope with their sentence.

Eddrick ran out after him, only to reappear before the door an instant later. Again, he struggled to leave, and again he was instantly transported back into the room with his wife. His shoulders slumped as defeat washed over him. He trudged across the room and sank onto the couch.

~*~

Aibek woke to Serik's voice and a firm hand on his shoulder in the predawn light. He groaned and struggled to hold onto the blissful slumber. He felt like he'd just fallen asleep. He rolled to the side away from the lamplight, but the old man was persistent. Finally, Aibek sat up and focused his bleary eyes on his friends.

Faruz sat on the edge of the bed rubbing a hand over sleep-reddened eyes. The realization that today was the day they'd arrive in Nivaka rolled over Aibek like a fog. He sat surrounded by blankets for a moment longer, then dressed quickly and headed down to the pub with his friends for a morning meal before they embarked on the final leg of their journey. They had decided they would cross the river here, by ferry. It would take too long to walk to the bridge.

Anxiety twisted Aibek's stomach, and he fidgeted in line while they waited to buy tickets for the ferry. He and Faruz occupied themselves by making up stories about their fellow passengers. It was a pastime they had enjoyed together since they were small boys waiting for Faruz's mother and Aibek's aunt to finish shopping in the city. They'd continued the habit whenever they were bored in a crowd, even after they were old enough to avoid trips to market with the women. Aibek found the childhood routine comforting amid the strange sights and smells of the river town.

Faruz gestured at a broad-shouldered young man they had seen earlier with a cart full of fabrics and dry goods. "You think he might be a farmer? I bet he traded vegetables and eggs for the goods in his cart."

Aibek glanced in the direction his friend pointed. "Maybe… and maybe he has a wife who'll be thrilled with the treasures he's bringing home."

He looked to the other side of the broad waiting area and waved toward a lovely copper-haired lady with red-rimmed eyes. "I'd bet she's on her way to an arranged marriage, and the man with her is her father. He's coming along to make sure she follows through."

Faruz nodded. "Could she be so sad because she's been forced to leave a favored suitor behind?"

Serik distracted Aibek from this line of thought with a small, worn bit of parchment. A faded number 54 took up the center of the parchment.

Oh, I wonder how many there are, Aibek thought as Faruz accepted a similar bit of parchment. He glanced over, noting that Faruz's ticket had a 55 on it.

They followed the line around the small wooden building that housed the ticket window and got their first unobstructed view of the ferry. Aibek froze mid-step, transfixed by the sight of the massive vessel. It was a flat-bottomed ferry like the ones he had seen in Xona, except larger than any he'd seen before. Two tall masts jutted into the sky, disappearing into the early morning mist that hovered over the river.

Aibek handed his ticket to the uniformed man at the riverfront and climbed the stairs that led onto the ferry. They wobbled under his feet. He clutched the post and mounted as fast as he could and hopped over the small gap between the step and the open rail to board the craft. He moved away from the stairs and stood for a moment, inspecting the flat, open space. It was already filling up. Ropes larger than Aibek's forearm surrounded the areas directly under and around the thick wooden masts. He stared at the lines for a long moment and listened to the soft flapping of the sails against the masts.

Shouts rang through the deck as passengers yelled their goodbyes down to the people assembled on the pier, and Aibek focused again on the inhabitants of the top deck. Farmers returning from the market clustered together at the far right, laughing and talking amongst themselves, various travelers milled about in groups. To his left, Aibek spotted the finely dressed family he'd seen climbing out of a carriage on the dock. The horses, wagon, and some farmers' livestock were all loaded onto the lower level of the large wooden ferry boat, and people on foot all milled about on the upper deck. As he watched, several individuals shoved their way through the growing crowd to the rail, waving to friends and family gathered on the pier below. Aibek, Serik, and Faruz were far more interested in the view on the other side of the river, so they made their way to the far side of the deck.

Faruz nudged his friend as they stood against the balustrade. They strained for several minutes, trying to see the forest beyond the mist-shrouded waterway.

Faruz slapped an impatient hand on the railing. "I can't see anything, can you?"

"Nothing but water and fog. It's so much wider than I expected. I'm glad we didn't walk all the way south to the bridge. I wonder if the river's narrower there, or if the bridge is this long…" Aibek trailed off, staring out at the endless water. He shuddered at the thought of stepping onto a bridge when he couldn't see the end, then wondered how deep the river was. The dark gray waves churned the surface and revealed nothing below.

Serik stayed close but kept his eyes on the workings of the sails as the brawny deckhands readied the ferry for its first departure of the day. Aibek gasped when the boat shoved off, the massive sails unfurling to catch the slight breeze. The vessel lurched under the sudden pull. Its swift jerk nearly knocked the young travelers off their feet before it evened out. The rocking movement of the boat made Aibek uneasy at first, but he adjusted quickly and enjoyed the sun on his face and the sound of the water lapping against the sides of the boat. Birds screeched and soared overhead and occasionally dove after a fish in the churning wake of the ferry.

The tangy, earthy scent of the water reminded Aibek of

the river near Xona where he'd swam as a boy, and he thought wistfully of his home. He missed Ira intensely and wondered if Noral missed him at all.

What kind of foolhardy thought is that?

He laughed a little at himself and turned his attention to the far horizon. From his vantage point on the front rail, he expected he would be able to see the far bank the moment it came into view.

"You know, we still have half a day's walk once we reach the other side," Serik reminded the excited younger men. "The village is deep in the forest, and it'll be harder traveling than the open road we've enjoyed these last several days."

Aibek didn't hear Serik's warning. Instead, his stomach dropped, and his heart leapt in renewed anticipation when he spotted a narrow pier jutting into the river.

The bank was in sight. Aibek sighed in disappointment when he saw that the forest didn't extend all the way to the river. They'd have to cross another mile or two of grassy hills before they reached the cool shade of the trees they could see beyond the small village on the riverbank. The younger travelers stayed at the rail until the ferry was ready to dock, then clamored to be among the first off the huge vessel, all but dragging Serik in their wake.

It was midmorning when they disembarked from the ferry, and unusually warm for that early in the summer. Aibek scratched at his shirt where it clung to his chest. He was hot and sweaty after standing in the sun on the deck of the ferry for so long; even the steady breeze hadn't made the muggy heat of the morning any more bearable.

Still, it was good to be walking again; he wasn't used to standing in one place for so long. It was a little less than half an hour later when they reached the edge of the wood. Along the way, they passed several cross-roads that led east or west to other villages, and after the last one, the road they traveled had narrowed noticeably. There, it became little more than a trail. Grass and weeds covered the dusty path.

"This used to be a busy market road," Serik remarked. He shook his head at the sad condition of the road now. "I wonder if they've stopped buying and selling in the river towns."

Aibek didn't know what to say to that but thought it must be significant. He considered the implications as they walked between the scattered trees and into the forest. Why would the market road be abandoned? That question led to another. What kinds of things would the tree-dwelling villagers have to sell at market? He didn't have long to wonder before the trees grew closer together and they stepped into the gloom of the forest.

At the edges of the trail, the trees and brush grew close and thick, obscuring most of the sunlight. Aibek stood blinking just inside the forest's border and waited for his eyes to adjust to the sudden dimness.

"We'll move slower from here," Serik said. "We need to watch where we set our feet. Beware of snakes on the path."

Aibek cringed and leaned over to peek under the nearest bush and stifled a relieved sigh. Nothing but brown leaves and a few beetles. He hadn't even considered the dangers that might lurk within the woods. He wondered what Faruz thought of the warning, but couldn't read any reaction on his face. Faruz was staring at a small branch that lay across the trail, perhaps wondering if it was a snake.

Aibek didn't spend much time thinking about his friend.

He was so nervous about returning to the village of his birth that he worried he might lose his breakfast. He took a deep breath to steady his nerves and thought he rather liked the earthy scent of the forest. He glanced around at the trees and brush and thought he saw something dart behind a bush. He squinted into the dim forest, but whatever it was had been too fast. He could see nothing but the leaves swaying gently in the warm breeze.

He kept looking around; the unnatural hush among the trees set his nerves on edge. He couldn't hear anything but the wind blowing through the leaves and an occasional squirrel that chattered beside the path. No birds or insects or other creatures made a single sound. What sort of animals lived here? He'd heard stories of enormous cats that could eat a man. And bears. Were there bears in these woods?

He placed a hand on the hilt of his sword, ready to defend the trio if any large animal attacked. Why was it so quiet? The silence felt wrong. Gooseflesh spread over his arms and the small hairs on the back of his neck stood on end. Shouldn't there at least be birds singing? Surely there were birds nested in these trees. He looked to his friends, but they continued into the forest, unruffled by the eerie quiet.

None of the travelers spoke as they carefully picked their way along the narrow trail. After a few minutes of walking, Aibek heard the first sounds of small animals moving in the brush, then birds singing overhead. He relaxed somewhat now that the silence was broken by what he assumed were normal sounds. A short time later, a new noise made his mouth water—the soft tinkling of water flowing somewhere nearby. The sound gradually grew louder as they walked, and soon Aibek saw a narrow stream with a rocky bed just to their left.

He picked up the pace and hurried toward the welcoming brook.

When he reached its banks, Aibek dropped his pack on the mossy ground and stooped to drink from the cold, clear water. Beside him, Serik and Faruz did the same. Though the trees shaded them from the midday sun, the heat and humidity were oppressive, and Aibek smiled as he splashed the icy water over his sticky face.

Aibek knelt on the stony bank and dunked his head under the swiftly flowing water. He gasped as he sat up, his hair dripping the cold water down his back and soaking his white linen shirt. He sat for a moment and stared up into the dense foliage above him. How could a village exist among those branches? What would the people have to eat? He looked down at the water again and watched school of colorful fish swim downstream. How would they cook food in the trees? He hoped he wouldn't be expected to eat everything raw from then on. He shook the water from his hair and bent to use his hands to drink from the cold stream again.

"It's not much farther from here," Serik said.

Aibek smiled to hide his apprehension. He rose to his feet and gathered his pack. He barely noticed Faruz's anxious expression as he waved his friend on by. They carefully picked their way over the crumbling bridge one at a time, with Serik leading the way. Faruz went next, and Aibek followed close behind.

As they walked, Aibek kept his eyes on the densely packed branches above, trying to spot some sign of the civilization that somehow existed up there. He thought about his earlier imaginings of rope bridges and small treehouses. Was that what his new home looked like? Would he be able to see it among the huge branches and thick leaves? He'd need to learn to navigate above the ground before he could consider taking over as the mayor.

A new stab of apprehension struck him. What if he humiliated himself trying to learn? At least the thick moss on the ground would cushion his landing if he fell. His thoughts kept his eyes trained on the foliage above the trail for long minutes. He looked down just in time to avoid colliding with a tree. He stopped short and looked around; his friends had continued around a bend in the path. Maybe he should pay closer attention to where he set his feet.

After that, he made sure to lower his eyes to the path at least once every three or four steps. Aibek certainly didn't want to arrive at his new home bloodied and bruised from a mishap on the trail. Still, his thoughts remained distracted. He'd grown up in an area with few trees, and he'd never seen anything like the tall, thick trunks packed close together in this forest. The dense foliage overhead obscured every trace of sunlight, leaving the path shrouded in shadow and darkness.

Finally, Aibek peered into the leaves above the path and thought he could make out a wooden railing between patches of leaves. It was high in the trees; a large house could easily fit underneath the hidden structure. It looked like some sort of walkway—a sidewalk made of wood suspended in the trees. As he stared and continued walking, more of the wooden structure came into view between the branches and leaves. He slowed his steps and nudged Faruz, mutely pointing up at the mostly-hidden structure.

At the same moment, Serik stopped in the middle of the path and looked up. "This is the north entrance to the village. It hasn't changed, even a little, in all this time. I wonder if anyone saw us coming."

Just before the old man finished speaking, someone leaned over the wooden rail along the edge of the boardwalk.

A great bear of a man shouted down at them, "Ho there! Serik! I thought you'd changed your mind and weren't coming after all. And who have you brought with you? Come on up so we can have a look."

With a great deal of creaking wood and falling dust, a broad wooden staircase descended slowly out of the boardwalk. It was wide enough that Aibek thought he could lie on one step without his head or feet hanging over the side. The whole device was made of a pale red wood that was unlike anything he'd seen before—but that wasn't much of a distinction anymore. Nearly every single thing he'd seen since they entered the river town had felt new and bizarre.

"Impressive, isn't it?" Serik gestured to the descending staircase. "Aibek, your great-great-grandfather designed the mechanism for the stairs. Before that, I'm told they had ladders to climb."

Aibek nodded mutely. It was impressive, all right. And there wasn't a rope ladder in sight. He grinned and watched in amazement as the stairs reached the ground and nestled perfectly into stone brackets planted in the path. His fatigue forgotten, Aibek ran up the dusty steps to the village nestled in the trees above the trail.

He stopped at the top of the stairs and craned his neck in all directions, trying to see everything at once. It looked nothing like he had imagined. He was a little ashamed of the images he had previously in his mind's eye of this incredible place. He had expected simple cabins propped against tree trunks; what he saw instead was glorious, breathtaking beauty. Where he stood, the boardwalk was wide enough for six men to walk abreast and bordered by an intricately detailed wooden railing. The carvings of tree branches, vines, and leaves were almost identical to the smaller carvings on the handle of the sword his uncle had given him.

Ahead, the walk widened farther as it extended deeper into the town—surely this was indeed a town. No mere village could be this… this…? His thoughts trailed off as he searched for a word to describe the splendor around him.

The buildings and homes were larger than he had expected, most of them at least two or three stories tall and much larger than the simple mud-brick dwellings in Xona. He suddenly understood why Noral had always complained about being cramped in their small house.

Then there was the decoration!

The houses he could see were as minutely ornamented as the wooden railing around the walk. Some had stone walls tiled in elaborate murals that depicted images of the forest or lakes or the sky. Others were carved wood in even more complex patterns and designs. The whole village looked magical as the golden light of the after-noon sun filtered through the leaves above them. Aibek glanced at Faruz and saw an expression of wondering surprise on his face. His mouth hung slightly open as he gazed at the beautiful buildings. Aibek snapped his mouth closed and grinned. He couldn't have been more wrong in his imaginings.

"Valasa, you haven't changed at all!" Serik greeted the giant who had come to welcome them.

The man threw his head back and guffawed. "Nonsense, I'm nearly twice the man I used to be." He patted his round belly and laughed again. "It's so good to finally have you home."

Aibek looked at the stranger and wondered if everyone

in the village was as big as that individual. He hoped not. The man was intimidatingly large. He was at least six feet tall, with a shining mass of graying auburn hair. His blue eyes shone with tears as he regarded the visitors. His face was broad and set above a thickly muscled neck. The man was built like a wall, and just as solid. Without warning, he caught Aibek in a crushing hug, squeezing all the air from his lungs.

"You look exactly like your father, boy. I'm so glad to see you looking well, and just as fine as if you'd been raised among us." His voice sounded strangled, and he gulped audibly as he set Aibek back on his feet.

Glancing up, Aibek paused. A young woman strolled toward them, keeping her eyes on the large man as she approached. She glanced curiously at the newcomers, then back at Valasa.

"Oh, this is my daughter, Ahren." He gestured to the young lady with a broad smile. "She'll show you around town and introduce you to all the village leaders tomorrow. I don't think there'll be time today," he added with a formal air.

The girl's features strongly resembled her father's, but the similarities ended there. Her hair was a brilliant white and flowed to her waist in shining waves. Aibek tried to remember if he had ever seen such pure white hair on someone so young, but couldn't think of a single instance.

When she raised her head, her crystal blue eyes met Aibek's. They were the same unnerving shade as Valasa's but contained none of the warmth he had seen in the older man's eyes. In fact, he was startled by the simmering rage he detected in their depths. Aibek wondered what he had done to provoke such anger in someone he was only just meeting and hoped he hadn't made some inexcusable mistake. He realized his hands were damp with sweat as he tried to figure out how to make amends for whatever he had done wrong.

On another level, he realized he had feared exactly that reaction. Would the rest of the villagers react the same way? He considered turning around and going home to Xona, but instead stood his ground and tried to make small talk. He'd never been in such a position before, but Ira had always taught him that politeness could smooth any situation. He wiped his shaking hands on his pants and inhaled through his teeth.

"Pleased to meet you," he said, trying to keep the tremor out of his voice. "I understand our families have been close friends for several generations. I hope we can continue that tradition."

"Pleased as well, I'm sure." Ahren's voice dripped ice, and Aibek wondered again what he'd done to offend her so quickly.

Finally, Faruz found his voice. "Ahren, a lovely name for a very lovely lady. I'm terribly pleased to have made your acquaintance." He bowed over her hand. He either hadn't noticed the tension in her meeting with Aibek, or he chose to ignore it.

She frowned. "Umm…pleased to meet you…sir? I'm afraid I didn't catch your name."

"I'm Faruz. Aibek and I have been friends since we were knee-high." He hitched a thumb at Aibek, "and I couldn't let him run off for such a fantastic adventure without me." He grinned at Ahren, and Aibek thought she almost smiled back at him before she turned away.

"And we're very glad you came along, Faruz," Valasa boomed. "Come along, and we'll get you all settled in your rooms so you can get washed up for dinner."

His powerful voice startled Aibek, and he jerked his

head back toward their host. The man called Valasa smiled and gestured for him and his friends to follow. They trailed after him as he led the travelers down the main thoroughfare to his home. He stopped several times to introduce the group to passersby, and Aibek realized the whole procession generated a great deal of interest among the villagers.

All of the older citizens gave a warm welcome to Serik and his companions, and most of the younger ones were intrigued by the entire entourage. Only a few showed any hesitation in welcoming the newcomers.

Aibek tried hard to remember everyone's name but feared it was impossible. He would no doubt have to ask them all again when they next met.

How long will it take before I feel at home here? Not long, I hope.

Right then, he felt like a creature on display in the traveling zoo that sometimes visited Xona. All through the village, people stopped and stared as they passed. Several of the villagers they met commented that he looked like his father, which he found odd but gratifying. No one had ever mentioned any resemblance before, even though his father's brother had raised him.

As they walked through the village, Aibek realized they stood out among the crowd and didn't look as if they belonged there. For one thing, the difference in clothing was evident to all and delineated the group as outsiders more clearly than anything else could.

The travelers wore loose linen shirts with brown leather breeches tucked into knee-high, black leather boots that were practical for walking long distances. None of the villagers wore anything made of leather or linen; they all wore clothing made of some fabric Aibek had never seen before, soft and flowing, which shimmered slightly in the sun-dappled lighting of the tree-top community. The men wore loose pants of various colors that came all the way to their ankles with closely tailored shirts in a complementary color. They wore odd-looking slippers on their feet that could have been the same unusual fabric. Aibek wondered if they had heavier shoes, or even boots, for those times when they left the smooth wood of the boardwalks and ventured into the forest below. Some of the women wore pants similar to the men's, while others wore long flowing dresses made of the same material, accented with lace and ribbons.

~*~

Faruz realized as he walked that he'd listened to Serik's stories of the village without believing they could be true. He trailed behind their guide as they moved along the boardwalks, his eyes wide, staring at everything around him. This was the kind of place where fairytales happened. Twice, he walked into Aibek's back when the entourage stopped, smacking his nose against his best friend's sweaty neck. He couldn't help it. He'd looked at Serik's or Aibek's back for the past twenty days—he was sick of that view. Plus, he'd never seen anything like this village. He'd never even heard stories of places like this. It was hard to believe it was real, though it was there in front of his face. He smiled, happy he'd come along. There was no way he would have wanted to miss this.

"Here we are." Valasa gestured as they stopped in front of the largest home they'd seen. The building was enormous by Xona standards, though only a little larger than the houses surrounding it in the trees. A simple design in shades of green stone decorated the front of the building, shining like diamonds in the golden light of the sun. There were very few branches above them,

so the house was fully illuminated by the bright afternoon sun. Faruz blinked furiously in the sudden bril-
liance and struggled to make out the details on the
exterior of the home.

Before he could determine anything more than the pale
green color and a vague geometric pattern, Valasa led
them through the door and into the main rooms of the
house. He continued up two levels of stairs and to a
group of rooms clustered together on the third floor just
above the staircase.

"You should all be comfortable enough here." Valasa
showed them into their respective rooms. "You'll have
to give us a little time to prepare a room for you, Faruz
since we weren't expecting you."

He started to turn to Serik, then whipped his head back
to Faruz. "But don't let that bother you a bit; we have
plenty of room and are extremely pleased to have you."
He walked a couple of steps farther down the hall and
added, "We'll eat in about two hours, so you all have
some time to rest and wash up from your travels. Serik,
your room is across the hall here, and it's all set up for
a nice soaking bath for you."

Faruz blushed and ducked his head. "You don't need to
go to all the trouble of preparing another room." He
rubbed a hand over the back of his neck. "I can easily
share with Aibek, really. We've been sharing space
since we were infants." Embarrassment heated his face.
He hadn't been invited and didn't want to make more
work for anyone.

"I wouldn't hear of it. Your room will be ready in an
hour or less, I'd wager since my wife has already
started preparing it. I sent Ahren ahead earlier to tell the
others we were on our way. Don't worry about a thing,
you're very welcome here, and we'll see to your com-

fort while you stay with us."

Valasa didn't seem to possess a normal speaking voice. His volume was overwhelming in the small space of the hallway, even with the bedroom doors open.

~*~

Aibek waited while Faruz thanked their host several times and ushered him into the room that Valasa had said was his. As he closed the door and looked around the room, awe muted him once again. The chamber was large and beautifully decorated without being fussy or ostentatious. The four-poster bed was hung with simple but heavy burgundy drapes tied back at the corners. It was at least twice the size of the bed he'd shared with Faruz at the inn only the night before. A mountain of pillows beckoned, and a thick golden quilt folded neatly atop the fluffy mattress promised warmth.

To the right of the bedroom was a small sitting room furnished with cozy-looking chairs and two matching tables carved to look identical to the railing of the boardwalk. It had a separate door that led into the hallway.

A soft mossy carpet covered the floor. It felt like heaven under his bare feet. Aibek and Faruz had both removed their boots at the door—it felt disrespectful to trample such a lovely room in booted feet. Aibek sank into the well-cushioned chair by the empty fireplace. The rich brown chair was covered in what looked like the same fabric the villagers wore. It was incredibly soft and felt luxurious under his hand.

"What is this fabric I keep seeing everywhere?" Aibek wondered aloud.

"Who cares about the fabric? We're to live like kings here! I've never been in such a beautiful room before. This entire place is like heaven! And you were going to leave me behind. Why didn't you tell me Nivaka was this lovely?"

"I haven't been here since I was a baby, and I didn't expect it to be like this, either. Come sit and we can relax for a bit before we figure out how to blend in at dinner," Aibek mumbled, already drifting to sleep in the chair.

"Don't tell me you're tired?" Faruz shouted. "How could you possibly sleep right now? First, we have to find some clothes. You're right, we need to blend in if we want to get to know everyone. Then, we both need to wash up and come up with a game plan for dinner. This whole place is totally unbelievable."

Faruz babbled on, uninterrupted, while Aibek tried to stay awake in the chair.

Aibek thought he used too many superlatives but tried to tune out his overly enthusiastic companion. The hard traveling of the day combined with the sleepless night was too much for him.

Faruz chattered on and on about everything they had seen, finally catching Aibek's attention when he exclaimed, "...and all the houses have fireplaces! I even smelled bread and sweets baking when we walked through town. I never expected there to be fires burning in the trees! I figured we'd be living on cold fruit and maybe bugs or birds or frogs from here on in, but the food smelled incredible. I can't wait to see what they serve for dinner."

The smoke coming from several chimneys in town had caught Aibek's attention, too. Even that bedroom had its own fireplace. Were these people not worried that the entire village could catch fire and burn to the ground? After all, all of it was made of wood.

5.

Welcome

After a brief moment, a servant boy came and led Faruz to his room. Aibek thought he would have a little time for a quick nap; however, the instant his friend left the room, a group of ladies entered carrying buckets of steaming water. They filled the tub in the small dressing room attached to the bedroom and arranged towels, a washcloth, and a bar of soap near the tub. As they were leaving the room, one maid pointed to a thick red pull rope tied to a ring in the corner and told him to ring when he finished so they could remove the water.

The soaking bath felt heavenly and eased his aching muscles. Hiking the hills, climbing over downed trees and stepping over large roots had left him sore, even in his excellent physical condition. He cocked his head and wondered how Serik was doing after their travels. The old man would surely be feeling it more acutely than he. Aibek soaked until the water cooled, scrubbed himself from head to toe, and stepped out of the tub. For a moment, he felt guilty about the water dripping onto the thick green rug beneath his feet. He shrugged off the feeling and wrapped himself securely in the fluffy towel.

What am I supposed to put on now?

He had brought only two other sets of clothes, and they were nearly identical to what they wore when they arrived. He hadn't thought of this when he was packing in Xona. He wished he had at least brought along one of his school uniforms; they were more formal and stylish than his plain traveling clothes.

His eyes scanned the room and arrested on a narrow door at the far end of the small room. Holding his towel around his waist, he crossed the smooth wooden floor to investigate. He hesitated when he reached the door.

Would he be trespassing if he looked inside? It felt odd to be a guest in a stranger's home; he'd only stayed with family and friends before this journey, and had never needed to look for clothing in their homes. He stood before the door and stared at the wavy patterns in the smooth golden wood as he tried to determine the best course of action. Twice, he nearly left the dressing room for his knapsack. Both times, he remembered how he had felt during the afternoon's march through the town in his old clothes.

After a long while, Aibek shrugged. Noral had always told him to be bold and decisive.

What's the worst that can happen? Maybe it's a broom closet, but maybe it's storage for some of Valasa's old clothes.

They'd be too big, but better than anything Aibek had with him. He tried the knob. It turned easily in his hand. When he pulled it open, the hinges protested with a soft squeak. It smelled like fresh flowers, not musty as he'd expected. Inside was a well-stocked wardrobe. He stood there for a long while, looking through the clothing and debating with himself whether he had the right to try something on.

Why am I so indecisive?

Noral had often scolded him for his hesitancy. He ran a hand through his hair and realized it was dry. How long had he been standing here? The door behind him whispered open, and he turned to see Serik silhouetted in the bright light from the bedroom.

"Well, go on then," Serik shook his head. "You need to get dressed – unless you plan to go to dinner in your towel, sir. And I'm quite certain they have something special planned for this evening, so dress accordingly." Serik was dressed as the villagers had been, in flowing garments of that same shimmery fabric.

The wardrobe contained clothing in every color and size, ranging from some tiny enough to fit a small child to others that would be too large even for their enormous host.

Aibek rubbed the soft fabric between his fingers. "What are these made of? And what do you mean they have something planned? I have no idea what's considered appropriate."

A hint of his anxiety leaked through in his questions, and his oldest friend smiled.

"This? It's called zontrec." Serik ran his hand over a shirt he had just pulled out of the wardrobe. "It's made from the leaves of the shadow trees, the big whitish trees that support and surround Nivaka. When the leaves fall or are blown down in a storm, they are gathered, washed, spun, and made into fabric for clothing and household goods."

"With all the trees around, it must be a huge job to collect the leaves in the autumn. What if someone needs some new clothes and there are none on the ground? Do they pick some leaves?" Aibek continued to peer into the narrow closet.

Serik squeezed in next to him and hunted through the tightly packed clothing. "No, we never do anything to hurt the trees. We wait for the leaves to fall." He spoke around the pile of shirts in his arms. The stack of garments swayed as he moved his head to talk.

"We keep a stock of leaves and fabric in storehouses near the outer edge of town. It's the same with gathering wood: when a tree dies or gets struck by lightning, the wood is harvested and stored for repairs to the village boardwalks or buildings, and we plant a new tree in the same place." He draped another shirt over his arm and continued. "The sap coats the wood and hardens as it cures. It's what makes the wood fireproof."

Serik handed him a shirt and pants in the same style he had seen earlier that day. "Here, these look like they should fit."

The shirt was a pale turquoise color, and the breeches were a much darker blue. Both of them fit Aibek perfectly, and he thought he had never worn anything nearly so comfortable. He tied the coordinating belt snugly around his waist to keep the pants in place, then looked around again.

Now, what about shoes?

None of the slippers in the small closet even came close to the right size. They were all far too small, and Aibek debated whether it was better to go to dinner barefoot or in his boots.

"Have you ever seen anything this soft?" Faruz came strolling through the open door, holding a pair of cream-colored slippers. "I finally found a pair of shoes that fit me, but my closet is full of these huge ones. They look closer to your size than mine." He tossed the slippers toward his friend.

"These are perfect. I guess I don't have to go barefoot to dinner after all," Aibek grinned in relief as he pulled the second slipper into place. "Should I ring for someone to clear the tub away? We could all wait in the sitting room instead of this little room. It might be a bit less cramped."

Faruz chuckled, and they filed into the much larger room. Serik pulled the rope in the corner before he followed the others out.

~*~

"How am I supposed to dance and act happy that Tavan's dead?" The pretty young woman asked her friend. She tied the sash around her waist and smoothed her skirt over her hips.

Tamyr looked up, shook her head, and returned to the work of fastening the buttons of her own gown. Tonight would be hard for her friend, and nothing she said could make it any easier.

The pretty young woman continued. "We were supposed to be married this summer, before my condition was obvious. Our child would have taken his place as governor someday."

She brushed her long hair into a simple style, then sank onto the chair near her bed. "What'll become of me, Tamyr? My father..." she trailed off, hiccupped, and started again. "He'll be furious when he finds out I'm with child. He never knew about my relationship with Tavan. We were planning to announce our engagement the week he died." She wiped a tear from her cheek and sniffled softly.

Tamyr walked over and perched on the arm of her friend's chair. She put an arm around the girl's slender shoulders and brushed the tears from her cheek. "We'll figure something out. You're strong. You'll get through this. Maybe, once we get rid of the interloper and his friend, your son can still lead the village."

The young woman sniffed and nodded. Squaring her shoulders, she stood and regarded her reflection once more. "It's time to go. You'll be there before the meal is over, right?"

Tamyr nodded and kissed her on the cheek. "I'll be there."

The woman picked up the note she had written earlier in the day and tucked it into her skirt pocket. She swept out the door in a flurry of skirts. Fighting tears for her friend's pain, Tamyr stared after her for a moment. When she'd regained control of her emotions, she grabbed the brush and finished getting ready for the festivities.

~*~

Serik peeked out the tall window. "It's just about time to go to dinner. Are we ready?"

Faruz preened in front of the narrow looking glass on the wall before he turned to his friend. "I'm starving. Let's go!"

Aibek sighed. "All right, I guess I'm about as ready as I'll ever be. I suspect we're about to be presented to the entire village." He made a face and hoped to conceal some of his apprehension. Most of the villagers he'd met today had been exceedingly nice. Still, the few who were less welcoming concerned him.

Serik led the way down the stairs since he knew where he was going, and they all filed into the comfortable den at the front of the house. Valasa's family had assembled there and reclined in vibrant orange and yellow chairs that stood out against the pale cream walls. They stood as the newcomers entered the room.

"Well, you all found something to wear, I see." Valasa's booming voice greeted them as the large man opened the front door and gestured for the group to precede him out into the gathering twilight. "That's wonderful, wonderful. All right, then, let's go to dinner."

The boardwalks were empty and strangely silent as

Valasa led the way toward an enormous pavilion at the center of town. Aibek took a series of deep breaths as they walked, trying to calm his out-of-control nerves. Fortunately, their destination wasn't far away, so the walk was brief. Once they arrived, Aibek saw why the boardwalks were abandoned—everyone was already there. As they entered the Pavilion, he was struck again by the breathtaking beauty of this place.

The Pavilion was a large open area covered by a broad wooden roof. The sides were open to the outdoors, with half-walls extending down from the pyramidal rooftop. The pale red wood gleamed in the lamplight. Aibek recognized it as shadow wood after Serik's explanation. The pillars supporting the roof were carved in the same style as the railings, and covered in intricate vines, leaves, and branches. Lanterns hung suspended on strings between posts, casting a warm glow over the whole scene. Hundreds of tables crammed under the enormous pyramidal roof, each surrounded by villagers waiting for their arrival. At the front of the Pavilion, on an elevated dais, was a large table, set for a meal.

Aibek realized with a start that this was their table. His stomach sank into the soles of his slippers; he forced himself to take another deep breath to calm the pounding of his heart. How was he supposed to eat with his stomach doing flips?

Valasa led the way to the front of the Pavilion and gestured for everyone to sit, then seated himself, leaving one empty place on the right end of the table. The chairs lined one side of the table, so the group would eat facing the throng of villagers just below them. Wide-eyed, Aibek smiled and took a seat between Valasa and Serik. Faruz sat to the left of the trusted servant, and Ahren slunk into the seat next to Faruz. On her other side was a fair-haired young man whom Aibek didn't remember meeting. The young man smiled warmly and leaned forward across the table, surveying the packed Pavilion. Valasa's wife sat on his right, completing their party.

Out of the corner of his eye, Aibek saw Valasa raise a hand slightly, and activity fluttered from the gloom on the far side of the Pavilion. A veritable army of tiny people, each barely as tall as his boots, and sporting large wings on their backs, came fluttering into the crowd carrying dishes heaped with food. Aibek couldn't believe what he was seeing. The tiny people wore brightly colored clothing similar to the villagers', and their hair was every color of the rainbow. Their wings were the same color and texture as a dragonfly's wings but were shaped more like a butterfly's.

Awestruck, Aibek turned to Serik and whispered as quietly as he could, "Are those truly fairies? I didn't know they actually existed."

Valasa must have overheard the exclamation because he leaned over. "Yes, they're fairies." He chuckled. "They serve the religious leader, or Gadonu, of each treetop village. Sometimes, they help out with large gatherings and special occasions. Most of the time, they carry messages between villages so we can stay in touch with our neighbors. In return, we provide them with food, shelter, and protection."

He gestured to a wooden cup in front of his plate, and a blue-haired fairy rushed over with a pitcher. She filled Ayja's cup, then Valasa's, and continued down the table until everyone had a drink. At the same moment, the rest of the fairies began heaping steaming servings of fish, red meat, vegetables, and fruits onto their plates. Aibek sipped cautiously at first, unsure what the beverage could be. It had a smooth, fruity flavor – sweeter than the lemonade he'd enjoyed during the summers in Xona.

"Easy," Valasa warned with a broad smile as he gulped from the carved cup. "You'll want to drink that slowly." Aibek set the cup on the table and savored the spicy citrus flavor of the fish and vegetables. The food was cooked to perfection and steaming hot, and Aibek's stomach snarled. Breakfast had been a long time before, and they'd hiked through lunchtime. His anxiety diminished as he struggled to remember his manners. He almost wished he could eat with the abandon of the children he saw at the front table. One child with chocolate brown curls, who looked just past the toddler age, used both hands to stuff the food into her chubby face. For a while, all conversation was at an end as everyone enjoyed the colorful and delicious meal set before them. A dessert course followed, and all the villagers and travelers ate their fills.

When everyone at the table on the dais had finished eating, Valasa stood and addressed the assembled villagers in his deep, resonant voice. "Today is a day of great celebration for Nivaka. Aibek, the only son of Eddrick and Kiri, has returned to us!"

He gestured for Aibek to stand and greet the villagers. Aibek flushed, but rose and waved to the people, determined to project a confidence he did not feel. A murmur went through the crowd, but Aibek couldn't make out any words.

Once the guest of honor was standing, Valasa continued, "He has been raised these past years by his father's brother in the city of Xona, and has trained in how to fight and lead. He has brought with him a friend, Faruz, who has also trained in the arts of war, and who will be an invaluable asset to our community." He waved for

Faruz to stand. Faruz beamed a wide smile and stood, waving to the crowd.

Valasa waited for the villagers to quiet again, then said, "In the days ahead, there is a great deal of work to be done as we prepare to face our enemy once again. But tonight, we came together to say 'Welcome home' to Aibek, Faruz, and our trusted friend, Serik."

When Valasa fell silent, the villagers erupted in a deafening cheer. Aibek smiled a little wider at the friendly reception and gave another short wave before he sank back into his seat. Within seconds, a quartet of musicians appeared from somewhere nearby and began playing a rousing tune. A group of villagers stood and cleared tables from the center of the Pavilion. Within moments, there was a significant empty space which filled again with groups of dancing citizens.

As the revelry increased in joyful movement, Valasa smiled and asked Aibek, "I'm sure this has been an overwhelming day for you. What questions do you have?"

Aibek glanced out at the crowd, then answered, "I'd love to hear more about the village." He looked back at his host and continued, "It's bigger than I expected. How many people live here? And what's happened here in the time we've been gone? During the journey, Serik told me a bit of Nivaka's history, but I'm sure there's much more to tell."

Valasa smiled, then sobered. His face grew serious as he considered his answer. Finally, he spoke. "I don't have an exact count anymore, but we have somewhere around eight hundred citizens now." He glanced down at the table, then looked back at Aibek, "The night you fled to Xona, the council was isolated and overthrown by Helak's army. All of the council members and their immediate families were killed, including your parents." His eyes met Aibek's. "You're the only one who survived that night. Other than the council, very few were killed. A dozen or so were seriously injured fighting, and a couple more were executed when they refused to surrender," he paused and looked down at his plate.

"How many were lost?" Aibek asked hesitantly.

"All totaled, we lost twenty-eight citizens." Valasa shook his head slowly and gazed out at the laughing, dancing throng. "We were all gathered here, in this pavilion, and the invaders announced that they worked for Helak and were here under his strict orders. Tavan, their leader, told us he had been appointed as our new governor under the rule of their overlord." All traces of his easy smile had vanished, and he twirled his fork in his fingers as he continued. "He was very strict, and life was drastically different from what we had always known. His rule was mostly fair—he didn't take sides in disputes, and he only punished people who were caught breaking his rules. And there were a lot of rules. He was harsh and merciless with any who opposed him."

He stopped and stared down at his plate, and Aibek wondered what he was thinking. Could he be reliving painful memories? Aibek's stomach turned as he considered the types of punishment the dictator could have used against the villagers.

Before he could ask, Valasa looked up and met his eyes. "Finally, about two months ago after a particularly brutal display, a small group of our young men decided they'd had enough. They swept through the village in the middle of the night, killing the governor and all of his guards and enforcers." He paused for a moment and looked around at the festivities.

Aibek wondered how the young men had handled the

experience of taking lives. He'd known trained officers who had struggled with guilt when forced to kill. How much harder would it be without the training and support of the army?

"Two days later, I sent the letter to Xona." Valasa laughed a little. "I half expected that the messenger would return with the letter still sealed. I didn't know for sure if you'd made it there, or if you'd gone to another family member somewhere else. I never knew for sure if you were alive, but I didn't dare attempt to find you sooner. I knew if I sent out messengers to search for you, Tavan would have sent men to follow them, so I just waited and hoped for the day you might come home."

Aibek hoped the man wouldn't be disappointed. He didn't know how to lead a town, and he was certainly no hero. He opened his mouth to speak, but Valasa didn't notice.

"I cannot describe my joy when I received Serik's note," Valasa continued. "Since that day, we've been busy preparing to receive you in grand, traditional Nivaka style. It's the first major celebration we've enjoyed since Tavan was overthrown." He watched the dancing for a moment. "Indeed, it's the first gathering of this style we've had since the invasion. Under the governor's rule, even our weddings were required to be small affairs that took place during daylight hours, and dancing was forbidden." His smile faded a bit, and he added, "The villagers are still afraid of what will happen when Helak finds out his governors were overthrown, but I've been told you trained to be an army officer. Is that right?"

Aibek nodded. "Yes, I was set to graduate next year."

"Then you can train our men to fight and defend themselves and our village." Valasa's smile was radiant.

"I'll do my best." It was the only response Aibek could

think of at that moment. It must have been sufficient for Valasa, who turned and murmured something to his wife.

Aibek felt slightly ill from the weight of the other man's expectations and overwhelmed by the amount of information he had been given. He took another sip of his drink and stared into the nearly empty cup. He felt a little dizzy. His stomach churned as he wondered again if he would be able to lead these people. He let his mind go blank as he watched the villagers dancing and celebrating in the golden light of the Pavilion.

6.

New Friends

Within an hour after sunset, the villagers began to disperse to their homes. Before they left, all the families came to the front table to introduce themselves, welcome Aibek and Faruz, and exchange a few words with Serik. Aibek tried to smile graciously as he struggled to remember everyone's names. After a few families had passed by, he gave up. It was impossible to learn so many people's names so quickly. He'd just enjoy meeting them all for now, then get to know them better over the days and weeks ahead.

At some point in the procession, a neatly folded note appeared next to Aibek's cup. A blob of red sealing wax pressed with an unadorned circular seal held it closed on one side. He didn't open it; there were still people in the receiving line waiting to meet him. He tucked the note into his pants pocket for later. His curiosity about its contents left him distracted through the rest of the introductions.

When the last of the villagers had left the Pavilion, Valasa stood and led their party back to his home.

As they walked, he paused and pointed. "There is the house that traditionally belonged to the mayor. It's where your parents and grandparents lived."

"Really?" Aibek said. He'd known his parents had their own home, of course, but he hadn't realized it belonged to the mayoralty. Honestly, he hadn't thought much about where he would live.

I just want to get through the first few days. Then we'll think about longer-term arrangements.

Valasa shook his head. "Yes, but it still needs a lot of work. Tavan and his guards lived there and left it a complete mess; they even built a shrine to Helak!" He hurriedly added, "But don't worry, you're all more than welcome to stay with us until it's ready."

Aibek breathed a small sigh. "Thank you so much for your hospitality." He didn't think he was ready to face the specter of his parents' home, especially now that he knew Tavan had converted it for his own use.

They finished the short walk in silence. The note pressed against his leg through Aibek's pocket; he couldn't think of anything it could possibly say. When they entered Valasa's home, he thanked his hosts again and bid them goodnight before rushing up the stairs to his room. He almost forgot to bid goodnight to Faruz and Serik, so he uttered a quiet "Sleep well," in their direction before he closed the bedroom door behind him.

~*~

Aibek strode to the small desk near the window and lit the lamp. The note had felt like a weight in his pocket all evening, and he couldn't wait any longer to read it. He adjusted the lamp to give enough light for reading, then settled into the chair and unfolded the note.

Not all are pleased the governor is dead. More blood will be shed in the coming days. You would do well to go home to the city. This is not your fight.

The note was unsigned. He scanned it, then reread it, stunned by its message. Aibek worked to remember who he had been speaking with when the missive had appeared. He racked his memory for any useful tidbit, but couldn't think of anything. The faces had all blurred together in his mind. He would show the note to his friends in the morning and see if they had any insight.

His mind was numb, dazed, and slow as he prepared for bed. So much had happened that day. It felt strange that just that morning he had awakened in the inn. The exhaustion of a poor night's sleep the night before and the events of the day descended over him like a curtain. He fell into the mountain of pillows on the bed and quickly fell asleep.

~*~

Faruz made his way to Aibek's room as the sun was rising. Just behind him, Serik entered carrying a tray of fruit, muffins, and some mugs filled with a hot, steaming liquid. The rich aroma made Aibek's stomach growl.

"Something smells fantastic!" He turned and smiled when Faruz ducked through the door. "Good morning." Aibek gazed in concern at Serik as the servant limped across the room. "Are you feeling all right?"

Serik grunted as he set the tray down on the table in the sitting area. "I'm just a little sore from yesterday's hike. But don't worry, I'll be fine with a little rest. I plan to spend today sitting and visiting with my old friends." He smiled, even as he winced and lowered himself into a soft chair. "I learned this morning that most of your parents' servants have been working here—in this house—for the past ten years or so."

Serik grinned, and Aibek didn't think he'd ever seen the old man smile as much as he had since they arrived yesterday.

They each took a muffin, some fruit, and a mug and relaxed in the chairs surrounding the fireplace. They sat quietly for a few minutes and listened to the morning song of the birds outside the window, the sound now and then punctuated by other animal noises the younger men couldn't identify. While they ate and listened to the sounds of a forest morning, they conversed in short bursts, alternating with long minutes of quiet reflection.

"This is a great way to start the morning," Aibek said after a break in the conversation. "We should do this every day."

Faruz nodded. "Great idea!"

"I used to start the days with your parents this way.," Serik said, smiling. "You're right; it is a lovely way to spend the morning."

Aibek grinned and took a swig from his mug. The hot drink was delicious, bolder than tea with a hint of sweetness. Serik told the younger men it was a drink called famanc, made from steeping the seeds of the shadow tree.

During a lull, Aibek blurted out, "Someone gave me an odd note last night." He pulled out the note and handed it to Serik. "What do you make of it?"

Faruz read the missive over Serik's shoulder, then let out a low whistle. Serik shook his head.

After a moment, Aibek blurted, "I thought everyone was happy to be free. Who would be unhappy about Tavan's death?"

After a long moment, Serik answered, "We'll show the note to Valasa and see what he thinks." He met Aibek's eyes. "I wouldn't mention this to anyone else, at least for now."

Aibek and Faruz nodded, and the conversation died. Aibek stared out the window at the growing light while he sipped the last of his famanc, then refilled the mug.

Faruz stared at Serik for a long moment. "So… what do you think will happen today?"

"I'm not sure." The servant set down his mug and looked out the window at the hazy blue light. He sighed. "It doesn't seem like many of the old customs have survived."

Aibek grabbed a muffin from the tray. "What would be the custom?" He spoke around a huge bite of cake, then gulped down a swallow of famanc and repeated his question so his friends could understand. "This muffin is unbelievable!" He took another bite, savoring the sweet berry flavor.

"I know," Faruz groaned. He grabbed the last one from the tray and looked back to Serik. "Well? Do you think we'll get to meet more of the people?"

"Traditionally, visitors would attend the market, meet the artisans, and tour the village with their hosts, but I didn't see any booths for the market, and no one mentioned it at dinner. Come to think of it, the market road was in pretty bad shape..."

Aibek smiled. "A tour sounds perfect. I'd love to see more of this place."

Faruz repeated himself. "Do you think we'll get to meet some of the villagers? The food last night was great, but it was awful to be stuck at that table while everyone else had fun."

Aibek nodded. He hadn't considered before now how hard last night must have been for his friend. Faruz deeply loved people and was never happy unless he was in the thick of a crowd. He never really cared if they included him in their activities, he simply preferred to be surrounded by people with the energy they brought with them.

Faruz startled his companion out of his reverie. "There was a big group of people our age at the center of the dance floor last night. Maybe we could get to know some of them."

"That would be great." Aibek smiled and drained the last of his drink. "But I'd prefer a tour first. I can hardly wait to explore all the corners of the village. I can't believe how big it looks."

"I thought the same thing. I hate to admit it, but I expected a bunch of treehouses clustered together," Faruz said, blushing.

The friends all laughed, and Serik suggested they venture downstairs. The sun had risen while they talked, and he thought it was late enough now that the family should be up and ready for the day.

~*~

Faruz descended the stairs behind his friends, trying to be quiet in case they were wrong about the time and the family wasn't awake yet. They weren't sure what the daily patterns of the village were anymore. Serik had told them over breakfast that Nivaka had always had a fairly late start to the day, and the villagers enjoyed socializing late into the night. However, Valasa had told them that for the past twenty years, no one had been allowed out of their homes after darkness fell. As they came into the sitting room below, Faruz saw that the entire family was assembled and waiting for them.

Valasa greeted them and stood as they entered the room. "Well, well, you're finally up and about, are you? We usually start the day before the sun rises, to make the most of the daylight. I can't tell you how wonderful it was to be out so late last night, celebrating by lamplight in the Pavilion like we used to do." The enormous man smiled warmly.

As he spoke, he began gathering a cloak and cane, preparing to leave for the day. Faruz's face flushed in embarrassment. Why had they spent so long talking in

Aibek's room while his hosts were apparently up and waiting below? He'd hate for them to think he was the sort of person to sleep late into the day. He opened his mouth to explain that they had been awake for a while, then closed it again when someone spoke.

"I'm Ayja, the lady of the house." A soft voice issued from the rocking chair by the fireplace. "I'm truly sorry we weren't introduced properly yesterday, but it was such a hectic day for all of us. We're very happy you've come." She rose and crossed the room while she spoke.

Faruz could see where Ahren's diminutive size came from. Ayja had come to stand next to him as she introduced herself, and the top of her head barely reached his chest. Aibek was even taller and towered over her when she moved closer to him. Her hair was a bright silvery white and was tied on top her head in an intricate design of braids and curls. She wore a simple flowing dress in pale purple, made of the same fabric he'd enjoyed wearing for the first time the night before.

It was so much more comfortable than linen. Faruz didn't think he'd ever wear his traveling clothes again, at least not if he had this zontrec as an option.

"I don't think you met our son, Dalan, either," she continued, drawing Faruz back to the present. "He's been very busy recently with his training." She gestured to her son, then picked up a pair of gloves from the table beside the door.

Dalan stood near the fireplace and addressed the visitors quietly, always keeping his eyes on the floor in front of his feet. "I heard you were both being educated to be officers in the army. Is that true?" He continued without pausing for an answer. "My friends and I would be very pleased if you could practice with us a bit if you're not too busy."

Faruz guessed the young man was close to his own age, though it appeared he had also inherited his mother's stature.

Valasa answered before the visitors could form a response. "You know, your sister is planning to show our guests around the village today and introduce them to some of the important leaders in town." He smiled and added, "I'm sure they'll have plenty of time to help you improve your fighting skills another day."

Faruz sauntered over to the young man and said, "If you don't mind giving me a quick tour first, I'd love to help you out… but only if you and your friends will spar with me a bit, too." He grinned at Dalan and gathered his sword.

He had known immediately that he didn't want to spend the day with the girl glaring daggers at him and Aibek, so he jumped at the chance to do something enjoyable instead. At the moment, he didn't care what customs he might be violating by turning down the official tour. He glanced in the direction of the group gathered at the door to make sure he hadn't offended anyone, but no one was upset at all, at least to his own mind. They still looked friendly and smiling, except for one.

"I guess that should be all right. I daresay you'll enjoy sparring more than discussing the history of the council, anyway." Ayja's words removed any last doubts he may have had, and he rushed out behind his new companion before anyone could voice an opposing view. He carefully avoided meeting Aibek's eyes as he left.

As planned, the two young men went for a brief tour of the major points of the village, lingering near the enormous cisterns at the north end of town.

Faruz was fascinated by the enormous structures. "You said these collect rainwater?"

Dalan nodded.

"Amazing. Then how do they get the water into the houses?"

Dalan pointed to a heavy iron pump at the bottom of the cistern. "Each day, the servants or residents of each house come and get their water. They can come back once or twice throughout the day if they need more. There are more cisterns throughout the village, but these are the largest. Each house has an assigned cistern."

"Is that iron?" Faruz asked, knelt for a closer look. "Where can they keep a forge in the woods? I know Serik said the town is fireproof, but a forge? Really?"

Dalan laughed. "Yes, we have a forge in the village, not far from here. There are a couple of blacksmiths who keep the iron parts of the cisterns and stairs in good repair."

Faruz was impressed. He had several more questions but decided to keep quiet. He'd made an awful lot of wrong assumptions about this town. He also thought it rather odd that the citizens insisted on calling this place a village. He thought it much too large to be a proper village. It was at least a town, and possibly a small city.

They lingered a bit longer, then hurried to meet with three others at one of the open areas, or parks, in town. This particular park had never attracted very many children, Dalan explained, because there were no games or other attractions for them. The absence of small children was, in fact, its biggest draw for the young men who assembled there now. Each had some type of sword, and two of them also brought small daggers to use for practice. Faruz hoped they had brought something without a real blade, so he could demonstrate techniques without harming his new companions.

As they drew near the group, Dalan shouted to his

friends, "Hi, everyone, I want you to meet Faruz. He's staying with my family for a while and wants to practice with us."

The newcomer was enthusiastically welcomed, and was extremely grateful Dalan hadn't announced him as an army officer-in-training. He was uncharacteristically nervous and sincerely wanted to be liked by these young men. He had worried that Ahren's friends might share her anger at the visitors, but the smiles on the men's faces reassured him. He beamed as the locals stepped forward to meet him.

"This is Wayra." Dalan gestured to a tall, lanky young man with very short, dark hair. Then, he turned to a shorter, muscular man with shaggy black hair and a thick beard, "and over there is Kai."

"I'm Alija." The last member of the group stepped forward to introduce himself. He was about the same height as Faruz, but with blonde hair and a slender build.

"I'm very glad to meet you," Alija continued. "You arrived with Eddrick's son yesterday, didn't you? Can you tell us something about him? Some people are afraid he'll be as bad as Tavan before we got rid of him." He came to stand close beside the newest member of the group, fidgeting with a string hanging from his shirt. He looked expectantly at Faruz.

Faruz let out a little laugh and shook his head. "Well, I don't quite know what to say to that, except that Aibek has no plans to come here and assume any kind of control over your town or its residents. He only wants to help the people protect their new freedom and learn more about the place where he was born."

He was more than a little uncomfortable with the direction this conversation was heading, and quickly added, "But I have no doubt he will be loved by all within a

very short period of time since he is a very good sort of person." He flashed a brief smile, raised his eyebrows and continued, "Did you say you got rid of the governor? How did you manage it? It must have been difficult, or he wouldn't have ruled for so many years."
Now they all scrambled closer, talking over each other to tell their tale.
"We waited until the middle of the night," someone shouted near his ear.
"We planned together and got all the leaders at the same time."
"I sliced the villain's throat with my new sword!"
Faruz couldn't distinguish who was saying what, since they were all shouting at once, so he stood still and quiet for a breath, laughed, and asked them to choose one person to tell the story. They all glanced around at each other, then all turned and looked to their ringleader. Dalan relayed the story as the rest listened eagerly.
"We've all been friends for as long as any of us can remember, and we've always helped each other in everything we do. The four of us have been in trouble together more than a few times, but that day was different. A group of the governor's monitors caught us sparring with our fathers' swords in a small clearing below the east end of the village, and hauled the lot of us in front of Tavan for judgment."
Faruz cringed and realized this might not be the story he had expected to hear.
"We were offered the 'opportunity' to join the invaders' army," Dalan continued, "and told if we declined we would severely regret it since the only swordsmen were members of their army. Of course none of us were interested in joining them, so the governor sent us away while he decided on our punishment. We were held in

a smalls rooms for about an hour, then brought out one by one and threatened again, separately, so we wouldn't have our friends for support."

A sudden knot of anxiety twisted in Faruz's stomach as he listened intently. He thought he knew where this story was going but hoped he was wrong.

"When none of us would join them, he decided that the best punishment would be to make the others watch while one took the beating for the group." He paused for a moment and looked around at his friends, his gaze lingering on Kai.

"It was the most awful thing he could have done to us. We were shackled and couldn't do anything as our best friend was beaten in front of us. When it was over and we were free at home, we decided together that enough was enough." He stopped and took a deep, shaky breath before he continued. "We discovered that the guards were rather careless with their weapons. We found several swords and daggers they'd left out on benches near the watches. We collected them and prepared our plan." As he spoke, he kept his eyes on the toes of his shoes. He only rarely looked up at his friends or their guest.

"It took about two weeks before we were ready, and Kai was healed enough to fight. On the chosen night, in the darkness of a moonless sky, we split up and killed Tavan and all his top guards and advisors as they slept. Kai had the honor of dispatching the governor since he had endured the beating." He stopped again and took a few more deep breaths.

Several long minutes passed, and Faruz wondered if he would continue. Wayra started to say something, but Dalan held up his hand, and his friend remained quiet.

"Finally," he continued, "once the leaders were dead, we spread out and disposed of the guards on watch, then waited and killed each new guard as he came to take over their posts. By the time the sun rose, we were free again. It took about half the day for the news really to make sense to the rest of the town, but I can't even describe how happy we all were."

Faruz hadn't been there, but could almost feel the joy the villagers must have experienced. If the torture these men had endured was any indication of the governor's brutality, the citizens here had every right to celebrate his death and fear his replacement. Faruz's mind strayed to the note Aibek had shown him that morning. Clearly, at least one person was unhappy with the new freedom.

"That day, we carried all the invaders' bodies down to the lake and had a huge pyre to destroy their carcasses, but we held no ceremonies for their spirits. Soon after that, my father sent the letter to Xona to summon your friend, and now here we all are." Dalan raised his head and looked squarely at Faruz as he finished his tale.

"The village is still finding its way without the rules of the governor or the leadership of a mayor. No one's quite sure what will happen next, but we all want to be prepared for when more warriors come." While he spoke, Dalan stood as straight and tall as he could, and gestured to his sword and his friends. "Now that we're free, we come here nearly every day to train and practice with our weapons. This is where we sorely need help. None of us have had any real training because there's been no one to teach us."

Faruz grinned at the group, "Well then, let's get started. You clearly have the bravery and planning ability to be amazing warriors. I can help with technique. I trust you have some sticks or dull blades to use for practice?"

The friends hadn't considered practicing with anything other than their real blades, so they spent a little time locating strong, straight sticks they could use. Once they had appropriate practice weapons, Faruz had two of them show him what they had been doing, and he wasn't surprised to see a classic error.

He called them together and asked, "Do you see any problems you feel you need to address? Where do you think we should begin?"

They all looked around at each other, but no one answered.

Faruz broke the silence. "The first thing I see is that you're each aiming for your opponent's weapon. When you're battling an enemy, they'll aim for your body or your head. You'll need to use your weapons to block their attacks and disable your enemy. You'll aim at their bodies, their legs, their heads – anything you can hit."

Dalan nodded. "That makes sense. Should we practice?"

They spent the rest of the day learning to parry, thrust, and block. Sometimes they paired off for a practice bout, and other times their teacher would match up with one member of the group to demonstrate a new technique while the others watched. While they learned, they talked and laughed together, and Faruz was thrilled to be accepted and welcomed. He beamed his joy through the entire experience and thought the only thing that would make this day better was if Aibek were there. He couldn't wait to tell his best friend about all of this. Twice, he almost brought up the note to the locals, but Serik's words from the morning stopped him both times. He'd wait to see first what Valasa thought, then perhaps ask more of the citizens.

Halfway through the day, someone produced leftover fish and vegetables from last night's feast, and they gobbled the cold fare before continuing their practice. The sky had turned orange with the beginnings of the sunset when they finally parted and went to their respective homes for the night, fatigued and hungry from a day of extreme physical exertion.

7.

Tour

Ahren strode swiftly away from the house, keeping her chin up and never looking back to see if Aibek was with her. He trudged behind, dragging his fingers through his hair. He walked considerably slower than she did, and she stopped at the end of the walk and waited for him to catch up. He still had no clue what he had done or said to make her so angry, but he'd decided to set it to rights during the day.

As they strode down the various boardwalks, Ahren pointed out landmarks and important citizens' homes but didn't speak at all beyond what was required. Aibek stared wordlessly at the detailed carvings throughout the village and the height of the trees. Over and over, he found his footsteps faltering as he gaped at a new carving or architectural wonder. At these times, Ahren stood with her hands on her hips while she waited for him to catch up. He was pleased to note that all of the homes they saw were pretty and picturesque, though most weren't nearly as large as those in the center of town. He could hardly believe the size of the cisterns near the edge of the village that captured and stored rainwater for the citizens' use. These, alone among the structures in the village, were built on firm ground. Not even shadow trees could support that many tons of water. He assumed their heavy metal construction made them safe against enemy attack.

A question came to his mind and he blurted it out. "And…erm…waste products? What does the village do with them?"

Ahren tapped her foot, eyebrows raised as if this were a foolish question. "Recycle. We recycle everything. As a tree-top village, we have no choice." She abruptly turned and walked on. He'd have to find out how some other day.

When they moved back toward the main parts of town, Ahren explained that the innermost part of Nivaka, where they were staying, was known as the Square—even though it was more of a hexagon—and all the homes there belonged to important members of the community. Most were empty and in need of repairs since they had been vacant for two decades. Those were the homes reserved for the council members and their families.

The other houses were built out from the Square, nearly perfectly aligned in concentric rings around the center of town. Boardwalks connected the circles like spokes of a wheel, jutting out from the Square at regular intervals. He noticed several large openings in the boardwalk at unexpected places, though they had ropes around them to keep anyone from falling through. Hopefully, Ahren would warm up at some point, and he'd be able to ask her about the openings.

At the very center of the village stood the Pavilion, which they had seen last night, and several open areas were scattered haphazardly throughout the town. Ahren coldly explained that these were parks, where children played, and young men and women practiced their fighting skills.

The tour was interrupted several times by individuals

who wanted to meet the visitor. At these times, the change in his guide was unbelievable to Aibek. She was smiling, gracious and witty with these citizens. He frowned, mouth agape, and wondered again what he had done to offend her. As much as he tried, he couldn't think of anything he might have done wrong. He considered whether she might have had something to do with the odd note he'd received, but dismissed the idea. She clearly didn't like him, but she seemed happy enough with the town's freedom.

After a couple of hours of walking through the village, they stopped at a park for lunch. Ayja and Valasa joined them and provided a meal of warm vegetables and smoked fish. They ate quietly, then Ahren's parents said something about finishing their morning's work and walked away toward the center of town.

Ahren immediately rose and strode off down a boardwalk they hadn't yet explored. Aibek followed behind, wishing she would at least pretend to be pleased he was there. Instead, she barked out the names of homeowners and identifying landmarks as they rushed through the town.

They rounded a corner to head back toward the east end of the village after she had shown him the south entrance when he stopped and asked for a break. It was a lovely spot with a bench and dense branches overhead to block the hot mid-day sun. Here, they could discuss whatever was bothering her without attracting too much attention from nearby villagers, but they weren't so alone that their absence would cause gossip. He sat on the bench, which gave her the advantage of height when she chose to remain standing.

"I think we might have started off on the wrong foot—you're clearly unhappy with me. What have I done? Or said?" He waited a moment to see if she would respond. When she said nothing, he continued, "I hoped we could at least be civil, since you're one of the few people I've met so far, and I'm staying at your house for now. Even if we'll never be friends, I'd love to move beyond this… hostility." He looked hopefully up at her as he spoke, but she kept her eyes on the trees.

After a long pause, she suddenly met his eyes with an angry glare and asked, "What would ever make you think you can just show up one day and take over?"

He gaped at the force of her anger, but couldn't think of a reasonable reply before she continued.

"You ran away before when things got hard. Now, you come back and try to assume the title of mayor, just because of who your father was! And you came back only after our people got rid of the governor on their own!"

He frowned and tried to say something in his defense, but she got louder and kept going.

"There are dozens of people who have lived here all their lives and know what we've endured who would be perfect leaders for this village. They don't get that chance because you decided to come back here and pretend you're better than all of us." By this time, tears were streaming down her face, and she swiped viciously at them.

Once she had finished, Aibek sat very still for a long moment. He stared absently at a bright purple flower beside the bench, while he determined how to best answer her charges.

"You know; I didn't come here to 'take over' anything. I was asked to come and help Nivaka defeat its enemy, and that's why I came." He paused to give her a chance to respond. After a moment, he continued, "I don't know how to be a mayor; I've trained all my life to be an army officer." He paused briefly as something else she had said struck him forcefully.

"Did you just accuse me of 'running away' because things got difficult? I was a baby, carried out of the village in a knapsack. How is that my fault?" Aibek tried to maintain his calm demeanor, though he was seething inside.

Ahren sneered. "You cannot seriously mean to tell me you didn't come here expecting to take over the mayor's role! You have certainly enjoyed the privilege thus far! And, yes, I am aware you were an infant when you left, but why did you never return?" When he opened his mouth to answer, she cut him off again. "I'll tell you why! You were a coward who stayed where it was safe until the danger had passed, then came to claim your birthright. It's not hard to figure out." She was shouting now, uncaring of who might see or overhear their heated exchange.

"A coward?" He began, his voice growing softer as the discussion progressed. "I was a child, a little boy who wrote dozens of letters and tried again and again to learn something of my parents. I didn't know if this village still existed, or if the invaders Serik talked about had wiped it out completely. Then, one day after twenty years of silence, we received word that the village was intact, but my mother and father were dead." He paused to choose his words and took a moment to regain control of his emotions. "I'll find my way back from here. You don't need to stay and usher me around town." He stood and walked quickly away from the bench, not sure where he was going or how to get there.

~*~

Ahren sank down onto the bench he had vacated and

wept out the rest of her anger. As his nearly whispered words echoed in her ears, she began to think she may have been too harsh. To be sure, he still had no business trying to become the mayor, but perhaps she had mis-judged his motives and shortcomings. She wouldn't let him see those second thoughts, though.

She sat on the bench until the light began to fade. Slowly, she walked back to the large house on the Square.

Has he made it back already? What if he told everyone about what happened?

She flushed and hoped he had kept it to himself. He'd been pretty upset when he walked away. She didn't know how she'd face him at supper.

~*~

After striding away from the tour and the failed attempt to patch things up with his guide, Aibek didn't know where to go to regain control of himself. He craved solitude to think through the events of the after-noon. He was in no condition to encounter either well-meaning or hostile villagers while still so angry after that exchange, so he quietly slipped out of town using the south entrance Ahren had shown him just a little while ago.

His heart pounded in his ears as he pulled the lever, grateful she had shown him how the mechanism worked. When he reached the bottom, Aibek locked the stairs down so he could re-enter the village when he was ready. He decided to explore the world below the village on his own for a while but would return in time for din-ner. He was glad he had chosen to delay that conversa-tion until after lunch, so he had plenty of time to calm himself before anyone would expect him back.

With the boardwalks and buildings above blocking most

of the sunlight, the forest floor was nearly dark as night. He wandered among the trees, reliving his encounter with Ahren and trying to decide how to handle that nightmarish situation. He kept a careful eye on his location, finding odd-looking trees and rocks to distinguish his path since he didn't want to get lost in the dark forest. He wandered and walked and explored for several hours, and found a stream that ran near the village. He thought it might be the same one they had crossed on their journey just a day before. Slowly, Aibek became aware of quiet sounds of movement around and behind him.

"Is someone there?" he loudly asked the shadows, but all he heard was silence.

The only sound was the leaves rustling in the breeze. It was the same eerie quiet he'd noticed the day before. No birds were singing, no animals moving about. Even his breathing sounded loud in the profound silence of the woods, and the crunching of dried twigs and leaves underfoot echoed through the still air. Gooseflesh erupted along his arms, and the little hairs on his neck stood up. He tried to convince himself he had imagined those soft sounds, or maybe they had been made by curious animals watching from the shadows. He breathed in the fresh, earthy air.

Stop it. You're being ridiculous. Nothing is following you in the forest, Aibek scolded himself silently. The admonition did nothing to ease his anxiety.

He regretted that he hadn't brought his sword with him. He hadn't thought he'd need it for the tour, and he hadn't been rational enough to consider whether he'd need it before he left the village. Honestly, he wouldn't have returned to the house at that point anyway; it would have been awkward to explain to the family why he was alone, and why he needed a sword.

The shadows around him Had grown deeper.

Could it be nearing sunset? Have I been gone that long? Aibek realized he was starting to get hungry, so maybe, but the dimness made it difficult to guess the time. Given the turbulence of his thoughts, it wasn't unlikely he had wandered through the entire afternoon.

Aibek turned back the way he'd come. He was almost certain the dimness of the forest was turning to the darkness of night. He hurried back to where he thought the village entrance had been, but the stairs weren't there. He searched the vicinity for the way back in, but couldn't find any mark that identified the spot. His mouth went dry with budding panic, but before he could shout to anyone above that he was lost outside the village, something struck him hard on the back of his knee. He lost his balance and dropped to all fours. He rose to his knees, brushed the pebbles and dirt from his hands, and looked around for the source of the blow.

The deepening shadows made it hard to see much, and Aibek took his time standing again while he searched for whatever had knocked him down. Just as he regained his feet, something struck him again, hard, in the middle of his back. This time, he remained on his feet and spun to face his assailant. He just caught a glimpse of a small person darting back behind a tree. In the darkness, Aibek wasn't sure he could trust his eyes. He thought he saw a person the height of a child but heavily muscled and carrying a knobby club.

8.

Nightfall

The sunset had painted the sky above Nivaka a deep red before Faruz and Dalan trudged through the front door. They had enjoyed a day of bonding over physical exertion, and Faruz looked forward to a bath and a hot meal. The rest of the family reclined in the den's plush chairs. Faruz searched the room for his best friend, looking forward to the opportunity to tell all he had learned about the villagers during the day.

When the door closed behind them, Valasa frowned. "Isn't Aibek with you? I thought he went looking for you after lunch today."

Faruz scanned the room again. "No, we haven't seen him since we left here this morning. Wasn't he supposed to spend the afternoon meeting the elders of the community?"

Alarmed, Ayja blurted, "Ahren, when was the last time you saw him? Where exactly was he, and which way was he going?"

Ahren answered hesitantly. "After we ate our midday meal… he said he was tired of being led around and he wanted to explore on his own for a while. I last saw him walking away from the south entrance; I showed him how the stairs work."

Faruz stood frozen just inside the front door, looking from person to person, trying to fathom where his friend could be. The concern written on the faces of his hosts made him more worried than he otherwise would have been. It wasn't unusual for Aibek to wander on his own when he wanted to explore a new place, but the family's reaction made him uneasy. Their eyes were wide, and their mouths were taut, and they were all a little paler than they should be.

Valasa frowned and looked at his wife in concern. "I was at the south entrance a short while ago, because I had work to do over there. The stairs were down. Do you think he could have gone to explore the forest?"

Faruz broke in. "I don't see why he would leave the village so soon. He's in love with this place—the people, buildings, even the railings on the boardwalk have caught his attention. There's no way he left on his own to go wandering in that jungle—without his sword no less." He had spotted Aibek's sword leaning against the hearth as he spoke.

"Well, he may have," Ayja replied calmly. "If the stairs are still down, then he shouldn't have any trouble getting back. We'll wait a bit and see if he makes it home before we get too worried."

Valasa flinched and turned a pale green as the color drained out of his face. "I pulled up the stairs," he whispered. "I thought the hunters had left them down by mistake. It never crossed my mind that someone could still be down there this close to sunset."

Horrified, Ahren exclaimed, "It's not hard to imagine that he would have gone down to the woods. We had a terrible argument, and he said he wanted to be alone."

Valasa grabbed Aibek's sword and gestured for Dalan and Faruz to follow him out the door. The younger men were still wearing their swords from their training session.

The three of them ran through the village toward the south entrance. As they ran, Faruz wondered what danger his friend was in. He hadn't understood most of what was said about darkness and the forest. He barely noticed the girl, Ahren, following them along the boardwalk.

They reached the south end of the village just as the last rays of the sunset dimmed. Nearly frantic, Valasa fumbled with the latches that secured the stairs. Finally, the last closure came loose in his hands, and he released the safety catch that prevented the stairs from dropping too quickly.

~*~

Aibek swung around in the gathering darkness, trying to locate the little person and figure out what was happening.

"Hey! Who are you, and why are you attacking me? What do you want?" Aibek shouted at the shadows where the person had disappeared.

His back smarted from the blow, and he scanned the ground for the stone that marked the way back into the village. When he looked up again, many more of the little people surrounded him in the dimness of the forest. They wore brown and green draping clothes and carried spears, clubs, and staffs. Some were very slim, with slightly pointed ears. Others, like the one he had seen a few minutes before, were heavily muscled and had thick beards that tumbled halfway down their chests. Still searching for the way back into the village, he tried to make conversation with the menacing group.

"Um… Hi. I'm new here. Can you tell me how to get back into the village? I seem to have lost my way."

They laughed and circled closer, brandishing their weapons and making clear their intent.

He scanned the ground again, this time searching for anything he could use as a weapon, and spotted a downed branch a few paces to his left. It looked perfect, heavy enough to have some strength, but not so large that it would be impossible to swing. It had a few twigs still attached at one end, but all the leaves had fallen off. He looked around at the threatening group, gauging his chances. They glared and slowly circled closer. He'd have to risk it. He took a deep breath and prepared to fight for his life. He leapt with all his strength toward the branch, snatched it off the ground, and swung to face his attackers.

Two of the muscled, bearded men charged toward Aibek, and he swung the branch toward their low knees in an attempt to knock them off balance.

One man jumped over the thick branch, but Aibek made contact with the second. His short legs flew into the air, and the man landed hard on his back. Aibek took a moment to pin the bristled end onto the ground under his foot, jerking upward. The end snapped off, leaving a sharp point.

Aibek jerked the branch up in time to deflect an axe swinging toward his flank. He whirled again and hit his attacker square in the chest. The small man stumbled backward, but remained on his feet. Aibek's eyes darted around him in all directions. They had him surrounded. There was no way he could hold off all of them without a real weapon.

The entrance has to be close, he thought, searching between the trees for some sign of the stairs.

The sound of footsteps echoed from above, and Aibek opened his mouth to shout for help.

He didn't have a chance to make a sound before something collided with the back of his head, knocking him to the ground and leaving him dizzy and breathless. He reached up and felt something warm and sticky matting his hair and running down his neck. He wondered dazedly if they'd hit him with an axe or a staff, and how the little people had gotten to him so fast. He thought he should get up in case they struck again, but when he moved, the whole forest spun around him.

As if from a distance, he heard Valasa's resonant voice. "Back off, all of you! He's with us. Oh, no. What have you done?" Aibek felt himself being rolled to his back, but his head was still spinning too much to make any sense of the situation. Nearby, someone laughed.

~*~

"We… did… nothing!" The elf gasped between bouts of laughter. "You did it yourself! You dropped your stairs on him. I've never seen anything so funny!" The elfin spokesman had a hard time getting the words out, bent over at the waist, laughing so much tears rolled down his face. His friends were all laughing just as hard.

"Are you all right?" Faruz ignored the laughter and tried to determine if Aibek was well enough to walk into the village.

He gently prodded for broken bones or bleeding wounds and was thankful to find none, other than a small cut on Aibek's scalp. There was a significant lump on the back of his head, and a tender bruise on the left side of his ribs, but nothing that looked unmendable. Faruz pressed his sleeve against the cut for a minute, and the bleeding slowed to a trickle, then stopped. He'd feel much better about the situation if his friend would answer him. Aibek had passed out while the elf was still talking.

Faruz struggled to carry Aibek's torso up the steep staircase while Dalan took his feet. He glanced up as they passed Ahren standing near the top of the stairs. What was she doing here? Instead of asking, he grunted and hoisted his unconscious friend onto a nearby bench. Alija had shown him how the seats could come off for easy repair. In this case, they removed it to use as a stretcher to carry Aibek home.

I hope he'll be all right, Faruz worried. He needs to heal fast so he can see how incredible the people here are.

Valasa led the way back to his home, and a silent Ahren trailed behind. Bits of Valasa's grumbling carried to Faruz as they walked.

"We need to find a way to remove that catch," Faruz heard him say, "It just isn't safe to let those stairs fall like that. Someone could be seriously hurt."

If he hadn't been so concerned about Aibek, Faruz probably would have laughed. As it was, he stifled a grin and hoisted the bench a little higher.

~*~

"I can't believe they've locked us in here," Eddrick lamented again. "I even promised not to have any contact with the living, if they would only let me watch him come home."

"I know this is hard, but would you have done anything different if you had known what the punishment would be?" Kiri asked calmly, without looking up from the scarf she was knitting.

"I would have suffered through much more to keep my son alive, and you know it." He replied gruffly, as he came and flopped down onto the sofa next to her. "I don't think anything could have made me sit back and watch him walk into an ambush. If we hadn't intervened, he'd have come looking for the village after graduation. He was already making plans." He wadded up the tangle of yarn she'd been working with and tossed it to her other side. "Tavan would have killed him on sight. We had to do something!"

"Well, then stop your grumbling and serve your sentence. You just need to find something to occupy your mind. We've already made it a week," Kiri reminded her husband. "Three more and we can see how he's settled in. I hope he's making friends with Valasa's boy."

"How am I supposed to 'occupy my mind'? I'm glad you have your knitting, but I make a mess when I try making things from yarn." He moaned, jumped up, and paced the room again. "You know I can't have a forge in here! It has to stay an exact replica of our rooms in Nivaka." He shook his head in frustration.

"There must be something you can do besides complaining. Don't you have any more ideas to plan out? You've been planning the next step in Aibek's life since the day he was born. Don't tell me you've run out of inspiration now."

"I don't complain! I'm just not a 'sit and watch' kind of person. I need to take charge. It's what I've always done." Eddrick pounded his fist into his palm to emphasize his words.

"I know, I know." She stood and crossed the room to join him by the window. "That's one of the things that made you such an excellent mayor. We'll think of something to keep you busy…"

~*~

All through the night, Faruz stayed by Aibek's side. Serik checked on them frequently and supplied broth for the patient and snacks for his dedicated friend. Faruz spent the time making sure the cloths on Aibek's head were fresh and cool. He rinsed them frequently in the washbasin he'd dragged into the bedroom.

In the early light of dawn, Aibek, at last, awakened. He suffered a stabbing headache but otherwise felt like himself. He asked for a bath first, hoping the heat would help soothe his aching back and head. Then he wanted to sit with his friends and learn what had happened yesterday. Most of his escapade in the forest was a bit of a blur.

As they sat around the fireplace, drinking famanc and eating warm muffins, someone knocked softly on the door, and Valasa entered the room.

"Ah, wonderful, you're awake. How does your head feel?" His face showed his concern as he looked at the freshly cleaned wound on Aibek's head. It was the first time Aibek had heard him speak softly.

"It hurts a bit, but I'm sure I'll be fine in no time."

"I'm so sorry about last night." Valasa murmured. "I guess it's a good thing shadow wood is so light. If it had been heavier, like oak or even pine, that would have been a very serious accident."

"What exactly did happen?" Aibek frowned, struggling to remember. "I know I was surrounded, and I couldn't find the stairs. The next thing I knew, I was waking up here with a splitting headache." Aibek gingerly probed the sore spot on the back of his head.

Faruz explained the events of the evening, but Aibek didn't understand how the stairs had fallen fast enough to knock him down. They had taken several minutes when he'd lowered them to explore the forest. He shook his head and asked a different question.

"But who were those people, and why were they attacking me? I didn't do anything to provoke them." The confusion was making Aibek's headache even worse.

"We've been enemies with the elves and dwarves for hundreds of years," Valasa said pressing his fingers near the wound on Aibek's head. "They're the reason Nivaka was built in the trees, rather than on the ground."

"Ouch!" Aibek exclaimed when the healer moved to press his sore ribs.

Valasa moved his hands away from the sore spot. "Our ancestors signed a treaty several generations ago. It allows us to come and go as we please during daylight hours, but as soon as the sun sets, we're trespassing if we're on the ground."

The healer reached into his shirt for a vial of ointment, which he rubbed gently onto the bruises on Aibek's torso as he spoke.

"They most likely followed and watched you as long as you were on the ground, then attacked as soon as the sun set. That's been their pattern for hundreds of years. We haven't had a lot of trouble in the past several years, since we've all had to be in our homes so early, anyway. I'd nearly forgotten about that old animosity, but clearly, they have not."

He cocked his head to the side and stared out the window for a long moment, then continued with a shrug. "I've heard that their village, Kasanto, isn't far from here, but I don't think I've ever seen it. They're experts at camouflage."

Later that afternoon, Aibek sat by the empty fireplace. A soft knock sounded on the door. He waited to see if one of his friends would enter, but the door didn't open. His head was still throbbing, so he moved slowly as he rose from the chair and went to see who was there. Before he could get to the door, he heard the knock a second time—just one soft tap on the outer door.

"Hold on; I'm coming." It was frustrating to have to move so slowly, but his head spun if he tried to walk any faster. He crossed the room at a snail's pace, then finally made it to the door. He inhaled sharply and wobbled a bit on his feet at the shock of seeing Ahren standing there. He closed his eyes against the dizziness and considered closing the door and going back to his chair, but instead, he opened it farther and invited her into his sitting room. He left the door open to alleviate any concerns about propriety.

She entered the room without a sound and walked to a chair, but stood beside it instead of sitting. She watched as he slowly crossed the room and lowered himself into his favorite seat, and still said nothing. When the awkward silence had stretched for several minutes, Aibek had to say something.

"Is there something I can do for you?"

"Umm… yes." She paused and chewed on her lower lip. "I, um, wanted to say I'm sorry." She dropped into the chair and brushed her hair back from her face before she continued. "I shouldn't have been so awful to you, and I shouldn't have said the things I did."

Aibek cocked his head, trying to figure out what had changed. "Did you mean them when you said them?"

"Well… yes… but that doesn't make it right." She picked at the skin around her fingernails. "I should have given you a chance to explain your absence first."

"I think I understand." Aibek's eyes narrowed suspiciously. "You feel guilty because I got hurt. If I hadn't left the village—hadn't gotten hurt—would you be here now?"

Some of the anger he had seen the day before flared again in her eyes. "I don't know," she snapped. "I just know that I feel awful about what happened."

He spoke calmly, though the ghost of the previous day's hurt and anger stirred in his chest. "I don't need your pity or your guilt. But if you truly want to talk about it, I'd be happy to put yesterday behind us."

"Look, I just wanted to apologize and make sure you

were okay, and I have, and you are. That's enough for me." She stood and stormed out of his room, though she stopped to close the door gently after her.

Aibek's pulse pounded in his ears as he tried to decipher her last statement. He wasn't sure what she'd said, but he understood she had no interest in smoothing things over. He sighed and decided to take a nap. His headache was getting worse as the day went on. He burrowed under the blankets, still fully dressed, and drifted off to a peaceful slumber.

~*~

Ahren rushed down the hall away from Aibek's room. *How could I have thought that would be a good idea? Who can I talk to that'll understand?*

All of her friends had bought Dalan's story that Aibek and Faruz were the greatest thing that could have happened to the village.

I know, I'll go talk to Tamyr. She doesn't think a city visitor should be the mayor, either. Maybe she'll have some idea how to stop this craziness. Really, how dare he talk to me like that! Like I was some... some... child who didn't understand how to make up for my mistakes! Really! Would it have killed him to accept my apology?

She fumed all the way to the washhouse at the edge of town where Tamyr worked. It was a large, three-story building perpetually in need of a coat of paint. The slate gray finish was flaking in places and completely gone in others, revealing aging wood beneath. The windows were so dingy Ahren doubted anyone could see through them, but the peaked roof had been replaced the previous summer, so it still looked new. The dried sap gave it a deep red color similar to the other buildings in town.

Ahren strode to the weathered front door and walked in without knocking. She passed through two large, open rooms where women stood folding piles of linen. She didn't stop until she stepped into the cavernous space she recognized as the rinsing room. She could usually find her friend there. Half a dozen flushed faces looked up when the door opened. It was uncomfortably warm in the room, even with all the windows propped open. Every woman in the room wore faded gray breeches and matching short-sleeved shirts. Each one wore something to cover her front. Some of the younger women wore towels tied over their shirts, while the more experienced, higher-ranking women wore heavy aprons. Ahren felt out of place in her bright green dress. She turned to search the room for Tamyr, trying not to compare herself to these women. They performed a valuable service.

An enormous tub filled with gray water filled the center of the room. The women stirred it constantly with long sticks. Ahren had been there once before, so she knew they were rinsing the soap out of the newly washed linens. The women all lived there, in the upstairs rooms and worked for the village elders who had homes on the Square. It was the women's jobs to make sure each house on the Square had clean linens at least twice a week, though that had become much easier since they didn't have to wash for Tavan's battalion anymore.

Ahren scanned the women and found the kindly face she was searching for.

"Ahren! Is everything all right?" Tamyr stepped away from the basin and dried her hands on the towel tied around her waist.

"Do you have time to talk?" Ahren asked.

"Of course. I'm due for a break."

Ahren's shoulders slumped a little in relief. She waited while her friend excused herself and followed Tamyr into the courtyard behind the wash house.

"What's happened?" Tamyr asked gently.

A tear rolled down Ahren's face and she swiped at it as she seated herself on one of the benches lining the courtyard. She hated that she cried when she was angry. She told Tamyr all that had happened the day before on the tour and that morning in Aibek's sitting room. When she'd finished, she leaned back against the bench, her anger exhausted.

Tamyr shook her head. "Why are you letting him get to you like this? You know we're going to get rid of them."

Ahren sniffed. "I know. It's just that my whole family thinks he's so great. I wanted to see that he could be decent, I guess." She leaned forward and stared over the rail at the moss-covered ground below. "So what do we do now?"

Tamyr's grinned. "I have a few ideas. Give me a little time to get them together."

9.

Messengers

The week passed without incident while Aibek remained indoors to allow his injuries to heal. He spent hours every day staring out the window at the bustling village, yearning to get out and meet everyone. However, he rested without complaint—partly because too much movement made his head hurt, but mainly because he didn't want to offend his hosts. They were solicitous and made sure he never needed anything for more than a moment. Even Ahren went out of her way to offer him anything she thought he might want at dinner. In fact, he was starting to feel a little suffocated. He didn't need another blanket, or a glass of water, a cookie, or another sip of famanc. He wanted to be outside, to hear the birds in the trees and breathe the fresh scents of the forest.

While he was recovering, several of the village leaders stopped by to introduce themselves and to inquire about his health. It was quickly apparent to Aibek that the people had dearly loved his parents, and the older villagers were eager to appoint him as a leader in their places. Their implicit trust flattered him, and he assured them he would do his best.

He used some of his free time to consider Ahren's accusations.

Do others in the village feel the same way? He wondered. I'll have to take things more slowly.

He didn't want to be seen as another appointed governor, taking control of a village he didn't care about. **Honestly, I'm not sure I want to be the mayor at all; I'd be perfectly content just to help them form an army and teach them to fight.

Finally, the morning came when he woke without the slightest trace of a headache.

When Serik and Faruz came for their daily chat and famanc, he explained his plan to get outside and meet the people.

"Finally!" Faruz shouted. "I've been dying to get back out there."

Serik nodded. "Just be sure you don't overdo it."

Valasa and Ayja tried to convince Aibek to spend one more day resting, but he insisted on joining the day's activities.

Faruz had told him about his day fencing and practicing with his new friends, and Aibek could hardly wait to join their group today. He was dressed and ready long before his friends joined him for breakfast, and had his sword strapped on before the sun had risen. He couldn't wait to get some exercise after so much time indoors.

Aibek fidgeted as they approached the Pavilion. Anxious to be accepted, he tried to plan every word he would say. Once they arrived, he noticed that the locals pressed close together and maintained their distance. They murmured amongst themselves until Faruz stepped forward to make the introductions.

"Everyone, this is Aibek." He gestured behind him to his friend. "And this is Kai, Alija, and Wayra." He pointed to each one in turn.

All at once, the friends rushed forward to meet the newcomer for themselves.

Aibek gave a short laugh and flashed a shy smile. "I'm

so glad to meet you all."

Wayra frowned. "Well, why haven't you come before now? We expected to meet you last week."

"You mean Dalan didn't tell you?" Aibek laughed. "There was a bit of a... um... accident... the day after I arrived."

Alija cocked his head to the side and looked at the stranger with a confused expression. "No, no one said anything about an accident. What happened?"

"Well, you see..." Aibek began, then quickly relayed the tale of his wanderings on the ground, without mentioning his argument with Ahren. Faruz filled in the gaps, and before they'd finished, the whole group was laughing so hard they could barely breathe.

"Wait, so you're saying you ended up with a staircase falling on your head? That was the grand rescue? That's hilarious!" Alija could barely speak for laughing. Once he had regained his composure, he clapped a hand on Aibek's shoulder and welcomed him to Nivaka, then led him to the park where they liked to train.

Aibek smiled and inhaled deeply as they walked to the park. The whole village smelled of an intoxicating blend of summer flowers, wood smoke, and spicy foods cooking. They spent the morning fencing and working on stances before they headed to the north end of the village for a picnic lunch with some of Valasa's friends.

When they arrived, the crowd startled Aibek. At least a hundred people had gathered in the small park and milled about in clusters and groups.

Ayja greeted Aibek and Faruz with a wide smile. "I think our small picnic got a little out of hand. I hope you don't mind. Everyone wants a chance to get to know you."

Faruz laughed and said, "That's fine with me! I want to

meet all of them, too."

Dalan led Aibek and Faruz through the park, introducing them to each person. The group of sparring partners stayed together through the luncheon. Several young ladies gathered to meet the man who would likely be the new mayor, and Aibek tried to be gracious and friendly despite the nervous knot in his stomach.

While Aibek struggled to conceal his anxiety, Faruz basked in the attention. Before long, a group of giggling girls surrounded him. Faruz entertained them for a while with jokes and tall tales from his days at the academy. Eventually, he extricated himself and heaped another serving of fruit and pheasant on his plate. When he finished eating, he walked around the picnic area, smiling and laughing with a lovely dark-haired woman before returning to his friends and the dessert table.

Aibek kept an eye on his friend while he chatted with Ayja and her friends. He'd always wished he could be as relaxed in a crowd as Faruz.

Despite his nervousness, he enjoyed mixing and mingling with the villagers. This had been Aibek's aim since he'd arrived. He beamed at the realization that Ahren's small group seemed to be a distinct minority in thinking him unworthy, and everyone else seemed glad to meet him. A few young women were hesitant, but none were unfriendly or angry as Ahren had been. Overall, Aibek considered it a satisfactory afternoon, and he exited the picnic area happy and more relaxed than he'd been since he'd left Xona. It would be good to help these people, but beyond that, he'd love to be one of them. Maybe it wouldn't be so terrible to be the mayor.

As they were leaving the meeting area, a tall, muscular man with a shiny bald head and a scraggly beard ran to them and introduced himself in a breathless, rushed voice.

"Excuse me, sirs." He nodded respectfully to Aibek, then turned to Dalan. "My name is Amiran. I am guarding the west entrance today, so we don't get taken by surprise again. Anyway, two men came this afternoon. They say Helak sent them. We've taken them to the Meeting Hall and told them we were going to find the governor. What should we do now?"

His jerky motions, shaking hands, and disjointed speech said more clearly than words how panicked the man was, and Aibek tried to calm him.

"We knew someone would come eventually. At least it's only two men. Why don't you take us to them? We'll see if we can get some information from these visitors." He looked around at his companions, hoping they wouldn't mind being included in this assignment. He needn't have worried. Every member of the group immediately voiced his assent.

Aibek trailed behind the others and tried to pay attention to his surroundings as they rushed through the village. He realized as they ran that he needed to spend some time just wandering around to learn his way through the town. It was a surprising distance from the park on the edge of the village to the Square. He'd been so focused on his nervousness that morning that he hadn't paid much attention to where they went.

When they finally stopped, he panted, "Hold on, I need to catch my breath." He braced his hands on his knees and focused on his breathing.

The others leaned against trees or assumed the same bent-over posture and worked to slow their breathing. After a short while, Dalan straightened and moved to the front of the small group.

"I'll do most of the talking if that's all right with you."

His eyes searched Aibek's. "I know more about the governor and the answers they're looking for. You all pitch in if I miss anything." He glanced around at his friends, seeking agreement. When he had received the go-ahead from everyone present, he opened the door and led them inside.

Deep shadows painted the room in strange shapes. The only lighted lamp was next to the door, illuminating only a small area of the cavernous space. Rows of chairs lined up around the room, forming a semi-circle around a large table at the back of the space. Two fierce-looking men sat at the table, heads bent close in quiet conversation. They looked up from their discussion and frowned at the young men walking down the center aisle toward them.

"Who are you, and what do you want here?" Dalan started questioning before he had even made it halfway to the table.

"I come long way to see Tavan," the dark, wild-haired man on the left spat angrily, "not the local children."

"I asked who you are. It would be wise of you to answer the questions since we're all armed, and you are not," Dalan retorted as he drew himself up to his full height.

"Where Tavan? And why we have to give up our weapons? Helak's still in charge," the short, dark man declared as he and his companion both rose to their feet on the far side of the table.

The other man, though taller than the speaker, otherwise looked similar. They both had the same wild, untamed hair and beard, but the other stranger's black, pointed teeth made him appear much more dangerous and frightening. They glared at the villagers while they waited for a response. Dalan stared back, and Aibek watched to see how the younger man would handle this difficult situation.

Alija finally spoke, ending the stare-down. "Tavan is dead. So are all his guards, advisers, and assistants. You will be too if you don't answer our questions." His blonde hair caught what little light the lamp put out, ringing his face in white fire.

Dalan moved closer to the men at the table. "What do you want here? Why have you come?"

The short visitor's hands twitched at his sides, and Aibek inched closer. After a long moment, the man on the right spoke again. Aibek had to listen carefully to decipher their distinctive dialect.

"I thought that might be. I Siddet, and this Namay. Helak send us. We need know why Tavan stop sendin' reg'lar messages. Who kill him?" The short man stood ramrod straight with his head tilted back. His eyes narrowed to slits, and his mouth twisted into a sneer.

Every movement was deliberate and careful, and Aibek wondered if he was about to turn on them. He looked around at his companions and nodded. Each one had a hand on his sword.

Aibek advanced to stand at arms' length from the messengers. "We'll ask the questions. Why would anyone want control of this tiny, remote village? What could your leader possibly gain from it? We're not strategically located, and there's no nearby river or highway to the city or the sea."

Even with all his military training, or maybe because of it, he couldn't make any sense of the overlord's drive to control the forest. His stomach twisted into a heavy knot. The tense standoff would likely end soon, so didn't take his eyes off the intruders. He stood with his feet braced for attack, his hand on his sword and looked the man called Siddet straight in the eye as he spoke.

Before he finished, Namay spat at him. "We not goin' tell you a ting. Helak don' care 'bout this nuttin' lil village. He squash you all, even the lil teeny people hidin' under yer town."

Without taking his eyes off Aibek, Siddet raised a hand to silence his companion. "Why I tell you a ting? If you was goin' kill us, you'd have done it by now." He barked a short, humorless laugh. "Whatsamatta, din't your papa teach you howta use dat sword?"

Aibek refused to be distracted but repeated, "Why does he want this village?"

As fast as lightning, Siddet leapt over the table and lunged for Aibek, grappling for his sword and kicking at his feet in an attempt to get an advantage over the much larger man.

"Hey!" Aibek shouted and shoved at the desperate man. As the messenger stumbled backward a step, Aibek unsheathed his sword, only dimly aware of his friends rushing forward at his sides.

His adversary regained his footing, spun, and ran toward the back of the room with Aibek close on his heels. He jerked open the door to the right of the table and disappeared into the darkness.

~*~

Before Faruz could register what was happening, Namay thrust a pointy elbow into his ribs and sprinted for the main door. Alija and Wayra gave chase, and Faruz took after them as soon as realization struck. His ribs smarting with every breath, he caught up with the other men several paces from the door. Alija held out his sword, pointed directly at the messenger's throat. Faruz watched as they moved step by slow step toward the outermost row of chairs. He stood back, breathless, until the enemy stumbled, then lurched to his right—and ran smack into Faruz's chest.

"Oomph!" Faruz grunted, then grabbed the messenger by his hair and dragged him to the nearest chair. Wayra and Alija closed the circle, each with a blade aimed at their adversary.

~*~

Aibek kicked the door open and stopped just inside to gain his bearings. Dalan came hurtling through the door behind him and nearly smacked into his back in the darkness. His eyes adjusted enough that he could make out a storage room, with neatly arranged chairs and tables near the front of the space where Aibek stood. There was a row of tiny windows near the ceiling, but they were so dirty only a few slivers of light penetrated into the room. The cavernous size of the chamber surprised Aibek. The building hadn't looked large enough from the outside to house this. His footsteps echoed in the dimness as he advanced farther into the space.

He scanned the room for the man called Siddet and spotted him standing near a row of tables shoved against the wall. Between them, broken chairs and tables stacked on top of each other littered the floor. When Aibek started toward him, the cornered enemy ran farther into the room, throwing more chairs on the floor and overturning tables as he went. Aibek gestured to Dalan to circle to the right and indicated he would go left. In the center of the room stood a ceiling-high, impassable mass of mangled wood that looked as if it might once have been an enormous sculpture

Aibek picked his way through the room, careful not to trip in the cluttered space. He took a deep breath to calm his pounding heart and fought the urge to spit when dust filled his mouth and nose. His breathing echoed in the large space as he closed in on his adversary, and he could hear Dalan kicking broken pieces of wood out of his way as he moved around the other side of the room. The shouts from the Meeting Hall had fallen silent, so Aibek hoped his new friends had subdued the other messenger.

He glanced over to check on Dalan's progress, and in that instant a chair leg flew toward his head from the other side of the room. The splintered wood stung like a bee as it grazed his cheek and he winced, wiping away blood with his sleeve.

~*~

Faruz shouted, "Why does Helak want control of our village?" He struggled to keep his sword steady as his hand trembled from the adrenaline coursing through his body.

"I not tellin' you anyt'ing," Namay spat through clenched teeth.

Alija pressed the tip of his sword to the enemy's chest and said, "You called this a nothing little village. Why would he care what we do?" He pressed forward until a bead of scarlet welled onto the tip of his sword.

The fierce-looking man pressed back against the wooden chair, dropped his head, and stared at the floor between Alija's feet.

"He plannin' ta cut the shadow wood ta build da strongest city eva. He's already drawn up da plans."

Faruz winced at the grinding noise when the warrior shoved an impossibly long black fingernail between his teeth. He continued the grinding for a long moment, then dropped his hands to his lap and looked into Alija's face.

"You unda-stand how spes-ial these trees are? Dat wood is strong, light, and canna' burn—the perfect buildin' mater'al, and easy 'nough to move about."

At the moment he finished speaking, he kicked Alija's

hand, sending the sword skidding across the floor. He leapt for the loose weapon, crashing into Wayra and sending the unsuspecting villager sprawling.

~*~

"Is that the best you can do?" Aibek taunted as he jumped over a table and sped toward his adversary.

This time, a chair flew through the air, landing with a crash beside him.

Siddet grumbled as he overturned another table, "You don' even know da waste dis is! Dis wood worth more dan gold, but it sit here like pile of dirt."

Aibek ducked away from a flying painting and crept closer to his adversary. He tried to keep track of Dalan in the dimness of the room and thought he saw his companion moving toward him from behind the sculpture-thing. Aibek's head throbbed again, but he ignored it and focused on Siddet. They were only a few paces apart now.

He tried to take a deep breath but choked on the dust filling the air. He bent his knees, poised to jump over the last obstacle, but before he could leap, the shorter man lunged over the broken table and tumbled into him. It was all Aibek could do to hold onto his sword as he fell. They landed in a heap on the floor, throwing up another cloud of dust, and Aibek rose to his knees as he pummeled at the man's face and neck with his free hand. Siddet lunged for the sword, but Aibek was quicker. He swung the weapon and slashed at the messenger's thigh. The dark man grunted and rolled to the side, struggled to his feet, and grabbed a splintered table leg, wielding it like a spear in front of his chest. Aibek leapt to his feet and kicked the makeshift weapon, sending it flying across the room.

At that moment, Dalan jumped over a broken chair

beside Siddet. He landed with a grunt and dispatched the messenger with a swift slash to his throat. The man stumbled and fell, making an awful gurgling, gagging noise before silence descended in the room. Breathing heavily, the friends moved back toward the door, blood dripping from their blades.

~*~

Faruz's heart pounded against his ribs as he jumped to catch Namay, who raced toward the exit. Namay clumsily swung Wayra's sword. The blade was too long for the man's smaller size. Faruz easily blocked the blow, lunged forward with his own weapon, and sliced into the inner part of his enemy's upper arm. Crimson blood spurted from the wound and Namay dropped his sword. He stumbled backward, impaling himself on Alija's ready blade. With a shocked expression, Alija yanked his weapon free of the messenger and watched, eyes wide with horror, as the fierce man coughed a fountain of blood and fell, silent, to the floor.

~*~

The woman tugged hard on the front of Tamyr's apron, all but dragging her down the boardwalk toward the center of town. "We have to hurry."

"What's going on?" Tamyr broke the younger woman's grasp. "Where are we going?"

"Someone came looking for Tavan! Maybe they can take me with them when they report back to their leader. I'm sure Helak will be overjoyed to learn that Tavan fathered a child!"

Tamyr stopped in the middle of the boardwalk and stared at her pretty young friend. "You plan to tell complete strangers about your predicament?" She began to shout. "You haven't even told your father!" She shook her head and grabbed her friend by the shoulders. "What will your family think when you disappear with these men? Will they come after you? Get themselves killed in some misguided attempt to save you?"

Tamyr had been worried about her friend lately. The pretty young woman had been distraught since Tavan died, especially since a few days later she'd discovered she was carrying his child. Her family was important in the village and wouldn't likely accept the baby.

"I have to try!" The woman sobbed and yanked free of Tamyr's grasp. "I thought you understood. My family won't accept this child. They hated Tavan. They're happy he's dead. I had hoped they could get to know him—that they'd come to love him as much as I did—but there's no chance for that now." She began running down the deserted boardwalk once again. "Maybe Helak's people can help me raise the child."

Tamyr raced after her friend, following close behind until they reached the edge of the Pavilion. They stopped under the edge of the large structure, unable to move forward through the wall of villagers. The woman paused, wiping her face on her sleeve and looking around. Tamyr followed as she crept around the border of the crowd toward the front of the Pavilion.

"Eddrick's son just ran right in." Tamyr heard one man tell the person standing beside him. "He'll take care of us now."

Tamyr's friend gasped and spun back the way they'd come, nearly colliding with Tamyr. The washwoman wrapped her arms around her friend's small form and walked her back toward the rear of the crowd. They could wait there until someone emerged from the Meeting Hall.

10.

Council

Aibek stepped out of the dusty room and inhaled, letting the fresh, clean air of the main meeting space clean the dust from his nose and throat. He scanned the room and saw the other messenger lying on the floor near the back of the hall. He wasn't moving. Faruz and the rest of their group stood nearby. Their heads were close together, but they all looked up as he and Dalan moved toward them. Breathless and shaking from the fight, Aibek sank into a chair near his friends. "Is everyone all right?"

Faruz nodded. "We're all fine. What happened in there?"

Dalan filled them in on the events in the storage room. "We didn't get any information out of him."

Alija gestured to the dead man. "Well, his friend told us everything we wanted to know, but Valasa's going to want to hear about this, too."

They filed out of the hall and found Valasa and the village elders waiting with a crowd in the Pavilion. The assembled villagers fell silent when the friends stepped under the roof. Dalan announced that the enemies were dead, drawing cheers from the villagers and a concerned look from the religious leader.

Alija strolled to the rail and retched violently over the side. He stood for a while, white knuckles holding fast to the railing as he peered at the vegetation below. Aibek followed and placed a hand on the man's shoulder. Taking a life was hard on a person, even when you knew they'd kill you if you didn't.

"You all right?" Aibek asked softly.

Alija nodded and wiped the back of his hand over his mouth. Aibek worked to contain his own emotions as Alija's tear-filled eyes met his.

"Let's get back to the others." Aibek gently guided his new friend toward Valasa's retreating form.

The Gadonu walked back toward the Meeting Hall. "Well, let's see to cleaning up the mess and disposing of their remains, then we'll talk about what they wanted. Did you get any answers from them?"

Wayra nodded and filled him in on what Namay had told them.

Aibek added, "That makes sense. The other one said something about the wood being more valuable than gold."

Valasa opened the door and waited for the younger men to enter before following them. "I think it's time to elect a council and begin to make some hard decisions. Helak won't stop sending messengers. When these two don't return, he'll likely think the worst and send an army. I don't believe his only goal is to build a city."

They spent the rest of the afternoon quietly cleaning up the mess from the fight but had their families spread the word that a village meeting would be held in the Meeting Hall just after sunrise the next morning.

~*~

Ahren greeted the weary men with a tray of cookies when they finally made it back home. Valasa declined politely and retreated to his workroom, and Dalan and Faruz walked by as if she hadn't spoken, but Aibek gratefully accepted the offer. He was starving. He downed three cookies before he noticed the worried expression on Ahren's face. She was ignoring him, entirely focused on her brother's tear-stained countenance.

"Is everything all right?" she asked, placing a gentle hand on her brother's shoulder.

Dalan nodded and took a cookie from the tray. He didn't say more, so Aibek answered for him.

"No one here is used to battle. It's hard to get past the guilt that comes when you take a life, even when you know it's your life or his. Just give him a little time." Ahren sighed and nodded, then moved to hand her brother a carved wooden cup filled with water. Aibek watched her closely. He hadn't seen her so quiet and supportive. Tear stains streaked her face. Her eyes were red, too.

Why has she been crying? Shouldn't she be relieved and happy, like everyone else?

Aibek shrugged away his questions and trudged up the stairs to his room. He really wanted to be alone for a while. Faruz followed him up the stairs but continued down the hall to his own room.

I guess he needs some quiet time, too.

~*~

"We've been locked in here for forty-two days," Eddrick moaned. "I've watched as Koviom turned full twice and Ilodus went from full to new and nearly back again; finally, finally, all three will be full tonight. Is anyone coming to let us out? What if they've forgotten us? We could be stuck in here for eons before the ancestors free us."

"Thrimanca won't be full until tonight, but I wouldn't get too worried just yet. I'm sure someone'll be here soon." Kiri sat calmly on the couch and stared into space while her husband paced the room.

She hoped Agommi would return this morning and free them; she desperately wanted to know what was happening in Nivaka, and how the villagers liked her son. She had stayed near Aibek through his entire life and had enjoyed watching him grow into the strong young man he had become.

The time locked in their suite had been excruciating. Kiri glanced around at the pile of scarves and blankets she had knitted. She'd never gone so long without checking on her boy. Eddrick hadn't fared any better and had worn a track in the golden wood floor with his pacing. She sometimes envied her husband's boldness in appearing to the living. She didn't think anything could be better than talking to her son, but she'd always feared the consequences would be unbearable. These long weeks had proved her right.

Finally, after several hours, a loud clack echoed outside, and she stood beside her husband in front of the sofa. A few moments later, the only door to the large room opened, and Agommi entered.

"I hope these weeks haven't been too awful for you. The ancestors have discussed your situation at great length and have decided there's nothing more to be done. You are free, but be careful—they're watching you closely."

"Thank you, Agommi," Kiri wept as she caught him in a strong hug. "Being trapped here was beyond terrible."

"You can say that again," her husband chimed in. "I've never been so miserable. Thank you for freeing us, Father. I've learned my lesson."

"I hope so," the old man replied as he released Kiri and hugged his son. "Believe me, I know this is hard, but you cannot interfere any more in the world of the living. We still don't know what consequences your meddling will have on the future."

As soon as he'd finished speaking, Agommi left the room and closed the door behind him. Eddrick stared at his wife for a moment, then headed for the door.

"I'm going to check in with Valasa," he blurted out just before he ripped the door open. He was gone before Kiri could react.

With her heart in her throat, she followed her husband out the door. She wouldn't follow him to Valasa's house. She decided to wander around Nivaka and listen to what people were saying about her son.

~*~

Dinner that evening was an unusually quiet affair. Aibek scooted his food around his plate, distracted by worries over what a village meeting entailed, and how he and Faruz would fit into the plans. He pondered the topic of a mayor.

Will they bring up the mayor's empty house? What if they nominate me for the role? What if they don't?

He couldn't decide which would be worse.

Based on what Faruz had said earlier in the day, he thought his friend was probably worried that the villagers wouldn't allow him to join the meeting. In a way, his concerns were valid. He had no justifiable reason to be included; he wasn't family to anyone in the village. Still, Aibek hoped Faruz would be able to join the meeting, even if he wasn't allowed to vote.

After dinner, Aibek went straight to his room. He didn't have the energy to smile and socialize with the family. He flopped into his favorite chair by the fireplace and stared out the window, basking in the silence of the room. He wasn't alone for long before Faruz slipped through the door.

"Are you all right?" Faruz's face reflected his concern.

"I'm fine, but I'm a little worried about our new friends. They didn't handle that so well, did they?"

"I think they're trying to figure out how to cope." Faruz crossed the room and sank into the chair next to Aibek's. "You and I knew to expect these reactions, but they've never had anyone to teach them. I can't help but wonder how they managed after they killed Tavan and his guards. They seem to have recovered quite well."

Aibek nodded and stayed quiet. He didn't want to mention his worries about the meeting. Faruz had never understood why he got so anxious about things like that. Still, he wondered if he would have to decide whether to accept the position as mayor or worse if the people would decide they didn't want him to fill that role. He stared silently into the empty fireplace for a long while.

Eventually, Faruz yawned and stood. "I'm going to get some sleep. You should try to rest, too." He didn't wait for Aibek to respond before he strode out the door and down the hall.

Aibek woke earlier than usual the next morning, and Serik entered soon after, carrying a tray of muffins, fruit, and famanc as he did each day. Faruz strolled in behind the servant, settling into the soft chair to the right of the fireplace and staring out the window at the early morning light.

Serik greeted Aibek cheerfully. "Good morning, my lord. This'll be an important day for you. The talk in the kitchen is a new council will be elected today, and you'll be installed as mayor. This is the day you've been preparing for your entire life!" Serik smiled broadly at the younger man as he handed him a plate.

Panic welled in Aibek's stomach. He snapped at his friend. "I really wish you'd stop calling me that. I'm not your lord. I've never paid you a penny. You're my friend, not my servant."

It had bothered him for years, but Aibek had always held his tongue to keep from hurting the old man's feelings. That day, his nerves were on edge, and he wanted his friend's support without the artificial rank imposed by an antique tradition.

Serik shook his head. "I believe you are mistaken, sir. Your parents paid me handsomely the night we fled Nivaka. Your mother handed me a purse containing more coin than I could spend in a lifetime. That money paid for your education and purchased our supplies to travel here. I consider myself paid for the rest of my life, and have more than enough to retire on eventually. For now, it's enough to see you take your rightful place among the people of Nivaka."

The old man grabbed Aibek in a fragile hug, clung for a breath, and turned to the wardrobe, laying out clothes for the day ahead.

Chagrined, Aibek quietly dressed. He'd had no idea his parents had paid their servant so well since he had never known enough to ask anything about it. He could've missed any number of details over the years. He silently vowed to be more careful in his treatment of his friends. The rest of the morning passed in relative silence, including the walk to the meeting hall. Aibek found himself too absorbed in his thoughts and worries to make polite conversation, and he thought Faruz was a bit preoccupied, too. Villagers filing quietly and quickly toward the meeting filled the boardwalk, an occasional greeting and response punctuating the otherwise silent procession.

The walk took only a few minutes, and soon they entered the same heavy, engraved doors they had used the day before. Now that all the lamps gave off light,

Aibek could see the room in its entirety. It was strikingly simple in comparison to the rest of the village. There were no carvings or embellishments here, only plain green walls and unadorned wooden benches and tables. The sole artwork in the room was a single painting of a shadow tree covered in large blue blossoms that hung above the long desk at the front of the room. The picture was nearly as wide as the table; its branches spread to a broad canopy covering the entire council space.

The villagers filled the room, each headed to designated seats that correlated to the part of the village where they lived. The citizens in the rear of the room wore noticeably worn and faded clothing, and Aibek realized he hadn't had much interaction with anyone from the edges of town.

What do they do to contribute?

Serik had explained that everyone in the village had a purpose, a role they filled in the daily running of the town. The elders and administrators lived near the center of the village, and the majority of the homes in the middle area homed wood carvers, millers, and seamstresses. The craftsmen had long been the backbone of the community, Aibek had learned. Even during Tavan's reign, they had continued to hone their crafts and had sold their wares to Helak's men.

Valasa had arrived before the rest of the family and stood at the back of the room holding a hushed conversation with a group of elderly men. Other small groups clustered around the room, each carrying on quiet discussions. Ayja led her family to their designated seats and pointed Aibek, Faruz, and Serik to a row of chairs just in front of her own.

Within a few minutes, everyone in the room had settled into their seats, and Aibek realized with a start that they were the only ones in the front row. Only the rail stood between his chair and the table that was the focus of the room. He felt conspicuous and on display, and every villager stared at his small group as they waited for the meeting to start.

After what felt an eternity, but was only about ten minutes, Valasa came and stood in front of the table. "Today is the day we have both anticipated and dreaded for many years," he began.

Aibek jumped a little at the sudden booming speech.

"We are once again free," Valasa continued, "and need the leadership of an elected council. Our enemy has not forgotten us. Before long, more warriors will descend upon our village, and we must be prepared to defend ourselves, or meet the same fate as before."

A chorus of gasps went up from the crowd. Aibek wondered what they had expected to hear, that those words came as such a surprise.

"In order to get through our business today, we will vote on all measures before taking a brief recess to allow the ballots to be counted." Valasa continued speaking as if the villagers hadn't reacted. "Once the votes have been counted, the meeting will resume to announce the results. Beneath each of your seats is a stack of papers and a pencil. You will use these to cast your votes."

His booming voice projected to every corner of the room, and as soon as he quieted each citizen shifted and gathered the supplies from beneath their benches. Quiet murmurs and shuffling papers filled the room for several minutes.

Aibek leaned over to Serik and whispered, "Can everyone here read and write, then?" Only the wealthy in Xona were literate, so the announcement of written votes struck him as decidedly odd.

"Yes," Serik whispered back. "Your father's grandfather—the one that designed the stairs—felt it was important for the people to be able to read and write so they could draw up contracts and take orders from clients in the market town."

"Oh. I guess that makes sense." Aibek nodded and settled back into his chair, waiting for the voting to begin.

He glanced over at Faruz, who clutched his paper in his lap and grinned.

The first part of the meeting passed quickly, with a dozen individuals nominated for council seats, and votes cast. As the last order of business, Valasa asked the villagers to vote on whether to install Aibek as mayor, as would be expected by their customs. He gave them the option to be led solely by the authority of the council, with no mayor as head of the village. He recognized that some had voiced concern that a mayor who wasn't raised in Nivaka could not effectively lead them.

Aibek smiled a little at this since he didn't want to be voted in solely because there was no other choice. He still wasn't sure he was capable of leading anyone, let alone this incredible town. He debated on whether he would accept the position if they voted him in, or respectfully decline. Strangely, the overwhelming anxiety he had suffered through the past weeks had vanished. He felt calm and collected and ready for whatever might happen.

The fairies carried baskets among the rows and aisles, collecting the ballots for each vote in a different bucket. They wore sober brown and green outfits that were appropriate for the occasion, rather than the bright colors they'd sported at the banquet.

After a long morning, the meeting broke for lunch and for counting the ballots. There was little conversation outside the meeting hall, and each family group went home for a quick luncheon before the meeting resumed. Aibek ate his meal without tasting the food. Some of his anxiety had returned during the assembly, and his stomach twisted when he thought about the results of the vote. He hated that he'd spent so much time confined indoors after his injury and hoped he'd made a positive impression on the villagers in the brief time he'd socialized. However, he still wasn't sure he could be the mayor they needed. The noon hour passed in a blur of anxiety and concern.

Finally, it was time to return to the meeting hall. The villagers arrived early and took their seats, everyone eager to hear the results of the voting. Once again, Valasa stood at the front of the room, calling the meeting to order and beginning to announce results.

"It is the will of the people that Aibek, son of Eddrick and Kiri, be installed as the new mayor of Nivaka."

His words landed with the force of a boulder on the one they most concerned. He felt as if someone had dumped ice water into his veins. He was both elated that the villagers trusted him enough to vote him in as mayor and terrified that he would lead them wrong. While he wrestled with his reactions, he forced himself to pay attention as Valasa read the rest of the results.

"The new council will be made up of the following members: Alija, Kai, Dalan, Wayra, and Zifa," Valasa continued. "Many of you voted for me, even though I was not nominated. While I am honored by your confidence in me, I am not able to take an elected position. My role as Gadonu requires that I remain an impartial advisor to the council, but I am grateful for your votes. Now, will our newly elected council please come forward?"

Valasa nodded to Aibek when he hesitated.

The council lined up in front of the table. Valasa gestured for Aibek to stand on his right, and the others lined up shoulder to shoulder beside the mayor. The sole person on the stage that he hadn't met was Zifa, though he recognized her as the same young woman Faruz had entertained at the picnic.

Was that only yesterday? It felt like a month, at least.

She was tall for a woman and slim. Her capped-sleeve dress revealed slender, muscular arms, and he wondered what she did that made her so strong. Her eyes were a striking turquoise color that stood out against her long black hair.

Valasa turned to Aibek first and swore him in as the new mayor of the village of Nivaka. He repeated the vows solemnly and felt the weight of the oath settle upon his shoulders. Valasa patted his shoulder and turned to the next person in line, swearing in each council member, one at a time.

Once all the newly elected leaders had said their vows, Valasa presented the council to the villagers and adjourned the meeting. The new leaders remained at the front of the room, and all their constituents came forward to shake their hands and congratulate each of them. Several villagers told the new mayor how much they had loved his parents, and how they hoped he would follow in his father's footsteps. A few even mentioned a family resemblance. Aibek smiled at the comparison and welcomed the thought that he looked like a man who was so well-loved by the citizens he had once led. He hoped he could live up to the legacy.

When everyone had said their congratulations, the villagers moved to the Pavilion, where they celebrated the newly elected council. The first election in more than twenty years had energized the people, and the joy of freedom demanded an outlet. Someone produced a musical instrument, and some villagers began dancing to the music. This time, Aibek and Faruz joined in the revelry and danced until darkness fell, even though they didn't know the songs or the steps. They would have stayed longer, but no one lit the lamps, and each family had planned to serve their dinner at home. Laughing, Aibek strolled with the family to Valasa's house and enjoyed a celebratory dinner with the family.

While they ate, they discussed the new council. No one was surprised that all the men who had worked together to free the village were elected to lead them. Even Zifa's election wasn't a shock to the family, who knew her as a leader among her peers and a strong climber. Ayja explained that Zifa had been friends with Ahren for many years, and had helped keep their impetuous daughter out of trouble with the governor more than once.

Ahren herself remained relatively quiet, only responding when she was asked a direct question, as she had since the night Aibek was injured. He wondered what she was thinking, as he often did. Had she changed her mind about him at all? At least she no longer glared at him constantly. Now, she avoided eye contact altogether. He couldn't decide if that was better or worse.

As they headed upstairs to bed for the night, Valasa caught Aibek in a brief hug. "Your parents are so incredibly proud of you," he whispered and walked away down the hall.

The new mayor, dumbfounded, wondered what his host meant. A heavy ache settled in his chest as he considered the Gadonu's words. His parents had been dead for twenty years. Surely Valasa meant his parents would have been proud? Aibek pressed his fingers to his temples for a moment and took a deep, calming breath.

What a crazy day, he thought.

He drifted slowly to his room and prepared for bed in a fog. What an overwhelming day! He replayed the entirety of it in his head before falling into welcome oblivion.

~*~

Aibek woke the next morning to the sound of birds singing. He sat up, realizing with a shock that he had overslept. The stress of the election must have worn him out. He swung his legs over the side of the bed and nearly jumped out of his skin when he came face to face with all of the members of the new council, as well as Faruz and Serik.

He glanced frantically from face to face, stopping when he got to the only female in the room. He needed a moment alone to tend to his morning business, but he wasn't sure how to ask the others politely to step out. Grateful that he had never slept in the nude, he jumped up and hurried to the small dressing room adjacent to his bedroom. As he dressed and prepared to face the assembled council, he silently grumbled to himself about the unconventional meeting in his bedchamber.

I have a sitting room, he thought, *why aren't they waiting in my sitting room?*

Through the closed door, he heard the unmistakable sound of laughter, Faruz's chortle was the loudest, but he could distinguish several individual voices.

They all think this is funny! Is this some kind of joke? Have I been had?

He wasn't sure, but he tried to find some humor in the situation.

He must have looked like a total mess with his rumpled

hair and wrinkled pajamas. He looked down and realized his pants were inside out. The more he thought about it, the funnier the whole thing was, and before he left the dressing room, he was laughing along with the others.

When he reentered his bedroom, Aibek found it empty. The whole group had withdrawn to the sitting room.

It was definitely a joke, then.

Still chuckling, he followed them and lowered himself into his favorite chair.

"So glad you decided to join us," Faruz greeted him with a laugh. "We were starting to wonder if you were going to get up at all."

Aibek laughed along and replied, "You got me. Whose idea was this?"

Wayra struggled to control a smile. "We didn't really come here to play tricks on you."

Dalan handed the new mayor a muffin and said, "We thought we'd get an early start and have a breakfast meeting. We didn't think you'd still be in bed."

"But since you were," Faruz interrupted, "It seemed like the perfect way to start your life as a mayor." He erupted again into fits of laughter and tears streamed down his scarlet cheeks.

Aibek smiled and poured himself a mug of famanc. Though he wouldn't have chosen it, he appreciated the unconventional start to the day. He smiled, enjoying the time gathered with the council for the first time without the anxiety that would have flared before a planned meeting. He sipped his drink and realized that he liked these folks, maybe even more than some of his friends in Xona.

~*~

The council agreed to meet every morning until they

had a plan in place. They gathered in the Meeting Hall. The first day, a few dozen villagers followed them in and seated themselves in the first rows of chairs. At first, the new council worked on getting to get to know each other and developing a structure for meetings, as well as discussing how to fortify the village against attack. They had to learn how to manage the business of the village, and they spent a great deal of time debating the particulars. Valasa's experience and advice were invaluable as they learned the requirements and traditions surrounding the council. The spectators sat silently watching throughout the discussion and debate.

At the beginning of the second meeting, Alija said, "We have all the time in the world to figure out how to run the town, but probably not much time to come up with a plan to defeat Helak. I think we should make that our priority."

The others agreed and looked to Aibek. He smiled self-consciously and pondered how to fortify the town. Even though the locals insisted on calling this place a village, he couldn't reconcile that word in his mind. It was too big to be a village.

"Could we have the blacksmiths put spikes along the rails? That would make it harder for enemy soldiers to climb over. They'll likely use grappling hooks to scale the sides."

Alija eagerly agreed. "That sounds like it would work. I'll talk to my uncle tonight and see if he thinks it's feasible. He's one of the blacksmiths."

Aibek tried to consider how the enemy would attack this unusually placed town. They wouldn't be able to use a trebuchet in the confines of the forest, so they'd have to find other ways to climb onto the boardwalk.

"What if they try to climb the trees?" he asked. "Could

we somehow put spikes on the bottom of the trees to stop climbers?"

Wayra shook his head. "How would we do that without damaging the trees? We can't harm the shadow trees, even to defend ourselves."

Aibek agreed at once. "We'll have to think how to do it safely. What about digging a trench around the perimeter of town?"

"Have you ever tried to dig a hole in the woods?" Zifa asked flatly. "It's nearly impossible. You can't dig even the depth of a hand without hitting tree roots."

"Oh. I guess that won't work then. Does anyone else have any suggestions?"

They all stared at him silently.

All right, I'll have to work on this on my own. Faruz might have some ideas, too.

They adjourned the meeting for lunch soon after that exchange. The council had formulated a lot of questions, but Aibek didn't think they had nearly enough answers. He wished the villagers who had come to watch the meeting would join the discussion. Surely some of them had some good ideas.

~*~

About a week after their first meeting, Aibek awoke to a dizzy nausea that sent him running for the washbasin in his dressing room. He retched until he was sure he'd lost everything he'd eaten the day before. His head felt like the carpenters had used it for practice pounding nails. He dragged himself back to his bedroom, longing for some fresh water to rinse the awful taste from his mouth. His skin burned. He pulled off his nightshirt and gasped at the blisters covering his entire body.

A moment later, Serik backed into the room carrying their breakfast tray. His eyes widened when he noticed

Aibek's shirtless appearance.

"What happened? What are those from?" He asked, pointing to the angry-looking blisters.

Aibek slowly shook his head. "I have no idea. I feel awful. Do you think Valasa's awake yet?"

"I'll get him," Serik answered. He plunked down the tray and swept out of the room.

Aibek crawled back into bed and tossed from side to side, trying to find a comfortable position. He gave up after a short while and moved to his sitting room. Dropping into a chair, he examined the sores on his arms and hands. They had spread even more since he'd been in bed. What were they? It didn't look like any disease he'd ever seen, and he didn't think he had a fever.

Eventually, Serik returned with Valasa in tow. The Gadonu gaped, knelt in front of Aibek, and examined the blisters and welts. He stood and scanned the room.

"Were you in the forest yesterday?"

Aibek shook his head. "No, I haven't been on the ground in nearly a week. Why?"

"This looks like a reaction to atpyrum, a poisonous plant. I haven't seen any in quite some time," Valasa said.

"Open your mouth," the healer demanded suddenly. Aibek frowned and glanced toward Serik, who nodded slightly. Aibek opened his mouth and tried not to breathe as his friend moved closer to his face. He knew his breath smelled terrible after his bout of illness earlier. Valasa turned Aibek's face toward the light and peered into his mouth. Aibek wondered what the man could be looking for.

"Do you feel anything besides the rash?" Valasa asked quietly. "Any dizziness or headache or cough?"

Aibek nodded. "I threw up earlier. Now I have a bit of

a headache, and I feel a little weak, but I don't have a cough or any dizziness." He still had a sick feeling in his stomach, but he wasn't sure if that was a reaction to the worried look on Valasa's face or an effect of the plant.

Before the healer could respond, a young servant girl burst through the door. "Mister Valasa, come quickly! Mister Faruz is very sick!" Her eyes widened as she took in Aibek's shirtless form on the chair. "Oh, no! Is it contagious?" She turned to Valasa.

"No, it isn't contagious. Let's go see Faruz. Serik, come with me. I think I'll need your help treating these two."

Aibek dozed in the chair while he waited for Valasa to return. While he hovered in that place between sleep and wakefulness, Valasa's words swirled in his head. How had he come into contact with a poisonous plant? He'd spent most of the past several days meeting with the new council, and he'd spent the evenings training in the park. None of his friends had been on the ground since before the town meeting.

The door flung open, and Aibek sat up with a start. Valasa strode into the room carrying a selection of bottles and vials, followed by Serik, who brought a tray loaded with a pitcher, bowl, and towels.

Valasa pressed a small vial into Aibek's hand. "Here, drink this."

Aibek poured the contents of the vial into his mouth and forced himself to swallow the bitter liquid. He gagged on the foul taste, and Serik rushed to hand him a cup of water.

Valasa wet a rag and patted the blisters on Aibek's arms. "I'm not sure how this happened, but all the council members are suffering from the same malady this morning. Where have you been going to train after your meetings?"

Aibek made a face. The tincture Valasa dabbed on his arms stung. He felt as if he'd stepped too close to Noral's forge and been burned. He brought his mind back to the question at hand. "The same park we've always used. The one over by the big cisterns."

"Hmm," Valasa mumbled something unintelligible and dabbed cold ointment on the blisters on Aibek's chest.

Serik stepped forward and handed a small bottle to Valasa. "Do you suppose this could have something to do with that note you received the night of the banquet, my lord?"

"What note?" Aibek asked, his head swimming from the burn of Valasa's treatment. Then he remembered. He'd tucked it into a drawer in his sitting room and forgotten it—and the warning it contained. So much had happened since that night.

He leaned over, opened the drawer on the small table near his chair and found what he was looking for. Aibek carefully unfolded the missive and handed it to Valasa.

"Yes, this does make more sense now. Someone must've poisoned you. But who? I don't know of anyone who was unhappy to learn of Tavan's death."

Aibek slowly shook his head, struggling to concentrate over the burning in his skin and the waves of nausea the vile tincture he'd drunk had caused. "If I were going to poison someone, I'd want to do more than just cause a rash, even if it is an awful one."

Serik gave a short, humorless laugh. "This poison will do much worse than give you a rash, my lord. If it gets into your airway or your blood, it can kill you."

"Oh," Aibek grunted as he clenched his teeth against another stinging application. The strong fumes of whatever ointment Valasa was rubbing over his blisters made Aibek's head swim. "How's Faruz?" He struggled to overcome the dizziness.

"He didn't get it nearly as bad as you," Valasa said gravely. "Once I have you cleaned up, I'll go see the others. We still need to figure out how someone could have gotten this all over you. It's the plant's oils that are poisonous. Most people only get a spot or two on their legs or arms when they touch the plant by accident."

Aibek's face twisted in confusion. "But it's all over me."

Valasa agreed, "Yes, it is. I think that does it. Where were you when you first felt the itch?"

Aibek stood and stretched as Valasa and Serik gathered up the used cloths and piled them onto the tray.

"I felt fine when I went to bed last night. I didn't notice anything until I woke up this morning." Aibek gestured to the bed, then looked to Valasa in horror. Now that the room the morning sun streaming through the windows lit the room, he could see oily streaks all over the sheets. Serik picked up Aibek's nightshirt from the floor and held it to the light. The oil covered the shirt, too.

~*~

It took two days of Valasa's careful treatments to restore Aibek to his usual perfect health. Once he felt better, he went to check on each of his friends. Thankfully, they were all doing quite well. Only Alija was still recovering. He'd received the largest dose of the poison and would need at least another day before he could leave his home.

During his visits with the council members, Aibek learned that each had been poisoned the same way—with dangerous oils in their bedsheets and clothes.

Aibek found Valasa in his workroom and hesitated at the door until the Gadonu waved him in. He'd never been in this room before, but now wasn't the time for gawking.

Aibek walked the short distance to the desk and seated himself across the table from his host. Valasa had papers strewn over the surface but looked up as Aibek spoke.

"Do you have any ideas? Who could have done this?"

"I don't have a name yet, but I'm nearly certain this came from the washhouse. All the homes near the square send their linens to the laundry on the same day." Valasa peered down at a sheet of paper on the table and sighed. "The real question is how the individual managed to poison only the council members, without any other members of the households getting sick."

"Who's responsible for putting the sheets back on the beds after washing?"

Valasa didn't answer immediately. He shuffled some of the papers into a stack and placed the note from the night of the banquet on top. Finally, he said, "That's the question I've been trying to answer. Normally, the maids make the beds and put away the clean clothes." He frowned and moved another paper to the top of the stack. "This time, the washwoman told the housekeeper she had scented your sheets to make you feel welcome and asked to make the beds of the council members personally. I'm not sure why she included Faruz, except that he's your friend and spends time with the council."

"So we have our culprit, then," Aibek's face showed his relief. "We just have to figure out who the woman is, and that shouldn't be too difficult."

"Well, it's not quite that simple." Valasa shuffled more papers onto his growing pile. "There are dozens of women involved in washing the linens, and we don't know for sure that the person who delivered them is the person who poisoned them. Still, we need to figure out who was behind this."

11.

Fishing

Tamyr watched quietly while her pretty friend paced in the courtyard behind the washhouse.

"This was the best you could come up with? Poison ivy in their sheets?" The woman screeched at her.

"It was atpyrum, not poison ivy. It's much more dangerous and should have been deadly in that dose. Besides, what did you want me to do? I'm a washwoman. My best chance to kill them is to poison their clothes. I'm not important enough to be able to get close enough to them to try anything else."

"Well, it's only a matter of time before they come here asking questions. Are you sure none of the others will talk?"

"They've all sworn to keep our secret." Tamyr wasn't sure of all the women, of course. She feared some would be quite open to spilling what they knew in exchange for a bribe.

She was starting to doubt the wisdom of helping her young friend. Even if they did succeed in killing off the leaders, the town would elect new ones. What did her friend hope to gain? Tamyr wished she'd thought of this before she'd agreed to this crazy scheme.

How can I back out now?

~*~

The next day, the council met again. They agreed

they should stick to their pattern of daily meetings until they had some firm answers. They'd kept the poisonings quiet, so only their closest friends and families knew what had happened. It would be better not to announce that they were at risk until they identified the culprit.

Between meetings, Aibek and Faruz spent a great deal of time mingling with the people of the village. When they weren't working to learn all they could about their new home and its people, the two friends spent their days practicing their fencing and fighting skills with Dalan and his friends. On a couple of notable occasions, they also helped Ahren, Zifa and some of their friends improve their technique. The days felt surreal to Aibek, who hadn't expected to enjoy forest life so much, even though he was much more careful after the poisoning.

One afternoon, while the others squared off in a practice match, Wayra and Dalan told Aibek about an upcoming wedding.

"We'll need a group of eight or ten people to go fishing for the wedding feast," Dalan said. "We'd love for you and Faruz to come along."

"We only get to eat fish for special occasions," Wayra explained. "It's just too hard to catch enough fish for everyone more often than that."

"Of course," Aibek said, grinning. "I'd love to go along. I know Faruz will, too. When should we go?"

"Tomorrow?" Wayra said.

"Perfect. We'll meet at the south entrance at daybreak," Dalan replied.

~*~

That night, it stormed for the first time since the travelers had arrived in Nivaka. The wind shook the trees, and the whole village trembled with each clap of thunder. Valasa and his family gathered in the den for a game, but Faruz and Aibek had never experienced such a violent storm.

Aibek tried to disguise his fear by laughing with the family, but after only a few minutes they gave up and retired early to his rooms. Faruz followed Aibek up the stairs and into his sitting room. They sat together and waited out the storm, for the first time, Aibek doubted the safety of his new home in the trees. Each rumble of thunder rattled the house, and the winds tried to knock the entire village to the ground below.

A couple of times when the lightning flashed, Aibek thought he saw the shape of a woman standing in the corner of his room. She disappeared with the flashes of light, and Faruz never looked in that direction, so he thought it best to keep it to himself. He wondered if he was starting to lose his mind. He'd never experienced anything like this before, and he wasn't sure how to explain it. He'd never really believed the stories Ira had told him about spirits, but that looked like a spirit to him. He was sure it had to be the strange light playing tricks on his overstressed mind. He gave his head a hard shake and tried to continue his conversation with Faruz, but couldn't remember what they had been talking about.

The torrential downpour lasted late into the night, and eventually, the two friends fell asleep on the chairs while the wind whipped the trees outside the window. Aibek woke in the stillness before dawn and wondered if the village had survived the storm.

Serik found them still in the chairs where they had waited out the storm and informed them that they would have to delay the fishing expedition. The storm had knocked several Shadow wood branches down, and the villagers needed to work together to harvest the wood and gather the fallen leaves. The citizens would work together to prepare the wood and leaves for storage, so they would age and cure into useable goods. Aibek and Faruz followed Serik out to the south entrance, where they learned that the huge building on the very south end of the village was a warehouse where workers prepared, cured, and stored shadow wood for future use. They helped carry the stored lumber out to the workers, who used it to repair homes that had been damaged by falling branches during the storm and to repair an area of the boardwalk that had been struck by lightning.

A little later, Aibek and Faruz worked with a group of men on the forest floor, cutting large tree branches down to manageable pieces, hoisting them up to the boardwalk, and carrying them to the storage building. Once there, the wood had to be cut into boards and hung from chains attached to the ceiling so it could cure properly. The workers told Aibek the wood needed to hang for at least six months before they could use it. That time allowed the sap to dry and harden, rendering the wood fireproof and giving it added strength. Meanwhile, women and children gathered the leaves from the forest floor in large baskets and took them to the storage building where they were laid out to dry on wide shelves lining the perimeter of the building. The work kept the entire village busy all day, and they finally finished all of the preparation, storage, and repairs about an hour before sunset. By that time, everyone was tired and dirty; they trudged home in groups while they chattered happily about all they had accomplished that day. The friends had rescheduled the fishing trip for the next day, and the same meeting place and time agreed upon.

The morning dawned cool and clear, and the group met as planned at the south entrance. Aibek had only expected the six men who usually stayed together, but Ahren, Zifa, and their friends Tamyr, Ahni, and Zyana, also joined them at the entrance, so eleven set out together for the lake.

The forest was lovely; the bright colors of the leaves signaled the progression of autumn. As they walked along the path, Aibek gaped at the clusters of shadow trees with their brilliant yellow foliage and many other trees with vibrant orange and red leaves. Even the brush bordering the path was changing colors. Aibek breathed deeply and luxuriated in the heady scent of the autumn flowers mingled with the fresh scent of the woods after the rain. Their trek through the woods was a colorful adventure. The group was cheerful and noisy as they progressed towards their goal, some of the women boasting of the delights they had brought along for lunch, and the men threatening to steal the baskets and eat all the food during the walk.

As they strolled along the path, Aibek glanced over, surprised to find himself beside Ahren again. The first few times that had happened, he had slowed down a bit to allow her to get ahead of him, and she had rejoined her friends. This time, she stayed next to him even when he changed his pace. She had barely spoken to him since their argument in his room, but she was making an effort to stay near him.

She finally spoke, her voice soft. "I voted for you for mayor." She leaned away from him and kept her head down, but her words were unmistakable.

"I thought you wanted someone else in that role. I haven't been here nearly as long as most of your friends." He kept his voice low, so those walking

nearby wouldn't overhear. She was visibly uncomfortable, and he didn't want to make things worse.
"I did, and I still think there are others who would be
better mayors." She glanced at his face, but he kept his
expression neutral. "But everyone says we need to
return to our customs and regain our identity as a community. Tavan stole so much from our people. If elect-
ing the last mayor's son can help give some of that
back, then I'm all for it."
She snapped a twig off a bush as they walked, then continued snapping it into smaller pieces. He kept quiet
and waited for her to proceed.
"And it's not like you're standing alone, ruling over the
village. The whole council is made up of locals, so
they'll keep us moving in the right direction." She
kicked a loose stone down the path as he took a
moment to choose his words.
"Thank you for your vote. It really means a lot, and
thank you for telling me. I know you didn't have to."
He tried to express his gratitude without sounding arro-
gant. For some reason, the girl's opinion mattered to
him. Maybe, if she was starting to come around, then
whoever else opposed the new council would change
their minds, too.
They walked on in silence for a few minutes, then she
blurted out, "I really am sorry about the way I acted
when you first got here. I've felt terrible about it for
weeks." She kicked another stone down the path. "It
was my fault you got hurt."
"That wasn't your fault at all," Aibek said with a smile.
"I should know better than to wander alone in an unfa-
miliar forest. Besides, there's no way you could have
known your father would drop a staircase on my head."
He grinned, and she laughed.

"You're right. No one could have predicted that."
They laughed together and continued on their way, but
before long she caught up with her friends and finished
the walk with them. He couldn't help but notice the dis-
approving look Tamyr gave Ahren when she rejoined
the group after talking to him.
After about an hour's walk through the woods, the
group entered a clearing which led them to the banks of
a small lake. The forest surrounded it, and a wide band
of short scrubby bushes and tall grass grew near the
water's edge. As they progressed toward the bank, the
group scared a cloud of colorful butterflies, which took
to the air by the hundreds, a stunning contrast against
the brilliant blue sky. The air was filled with the bright
yellow and red insects for an immeasurable moment
until they had all flown higher and landed in the trees
around the lake.
When they reached the water, the men set about the
business of catching fish while the women spread blankets and started gathering fall berries. The fish were
biting, and the men strung them on twine in the water
to keep them fresh. It was an idyllic morning of fishing
and gathering, talking and laughing.
Aibek learned that Wayra was to be the groom in the
upcoming wedding, and he was marrying Zyana, who
had also come along. She was great friends with Ahren,
so he thought it was surprising he hadn't met her before
today. She was a tall, slender, pretty young woman,
with rich brown hair, golden eyes, and a dusting of
freckles across her nose. She stayed near her betrothed
all day, even when the other women had gone off into
the woods following a line of berry bushes. Wayra
acted like a love-struck youth; he constantly smiled
when he talked about her and leaned close any time she

stood near him.

Aibek soon got bored with the village gossip, stood and stretched his arms over his head. He wasn't accustomed to sitting in one place for so long. He glanced around and decided to go for a walk on the path the women had taken. He wasn't sure he wanted to catch up with the girls, but he needed to move around. He slipped quietly into the woods and took a deep breath. There was something about this forest, something peaceful that made a man let down his guard and relax deep inside.

In the sun-dappled woods, it was hard to remember why he'd been so anxious. He still didn't know how to lead a village, but decided he would lean on the council and Valasa and they could figure it out together. As Ahren said, he wasn't alone. Still, he wished he had someone to ask for advice. He missed his Aunt Ira and wished she had been able to come along.

He wandered down the walk and let his mind go blank as he took in the bright colors of the autumn. After a while, he realized he had somehow managed to lose the trail he'd been following. Too relaxed to be alarmed, he simply continued in the direction he was heading until he found another, narrower trail.

He was strolling along, enjoying the slight breeze and looking around for signs that would lead him back to the lake when someone shoved him hard from behind. He stumbled forward a couple of steps and turned to see who was behind him. His mind jumped to another day and another attacker, and he hoped he wasn't about to meet more of the elves and dwarves. At least this time he could count on his own abilities; there were no village entrances within several miles so no one could drop stairs on his head.

He scanned the trail behind him for signs of an attacker and saw none. He looked closer at the bushes and trees, trying to discern anything unusual. It took several minutes of searching before he noticed what looked like leaves floating in the air in front of a tree.

"Aha! I see you now!" He shouted, then immediately felt foolish.

Who says things like that? This isn't one of Aunt Ira's bedtime stories.

To his surprise, a dozen or so elves emerged from the bushes around the trail and surrounded him. One elf stepped onto the path directly in front of Aibek.

He sneered. "You're on the wrong trail, tree-dweller,"

"I think I may have gotten lost," Aibek admitted as he combed the immediate area for anything he could use to defend himself, since—once again—he had no weapons with him. Seeing none, he wondered if he could talk his way out of this. "I'm still pretty new to the area, and I'm not sure how to get back to my friends at the lake. If you'll point me in the right direction, I'll be on my way." He tried to move past the closest little warrior person.

"Slow down." The elf held up his hands, and his friends moved to block the path. "What's the hurry?"

Suddenly, the mayor found himself face down on the dirt trail with a heavy weight on his back. It felt as if a pointy knee or elbow dug into his spine between his shoulder blades. Aibek struggled to get free, but he the little people outnumbered and outmaneuvered him. A minute later, he found his arms tied behind his back and realized something heavy held his feet to the ground.

An elfin face appeared before his own near the dirt. The little warrior spat out a warning, curling his lip. "Listen here, Mayor, you may be important to those simpletons in the trees, but you are less than nothing to us. We won't kill you now, but only because it would violate the treaty. You keep to your end of the forest, and stay away from Kasanto and our trails."

As soon as the little man had finished speaking, he and all of his companions disappeared into the forest. They left Aibek bound on the trail, wondering how to get back to the lake. It didn't take him long to pull a hand out of the bindings around his wrists and twist into a sitting position. He spat the gritty dirt from his mouth and wiped the dust off his face. Then he moved the stones weighting his legs, stood and looked around. The elves had drawn a series of arrows in the dirt indicating the direction he should travel, so he followed the marks and soon found himself back on the main path. Before long, he heard his friends' voices in the distance, so he stopped to compose himself. He was considerably shaken but decided not to tell anyone about his encounter. After all, it was his own fault for wandering off, and they hadn't harmed him. He stepped into the clearing and blinked for a moment in the bright sun, then walked over and rejoined the men on the bank where they were still fishing and laughing. He did his best to join the conversation and was relieved that no one mentioned his prolonged absence.

Soon, the sun shone down from overhead, signaling lunchtime, and the women emptied the picnic baskets onto the blankets. The group of friends continued laughing and joking as they ate, and they consumed the food in a flurry of activity. They repacked their jars and filled the baskets with the berries the women had gathered earlier in the day.

As the men returned to fishing, Kai shouted, "Hey! They're getting away! The twine must have broken!"

He pointed to a string of fish drifting deeper into the lake. He splashed in after them, trying hard to retrieve their catch. He stretched and reached for the line of fish, but couldn't quite reach it. He hesitated before going farther into the water.

"It's too bad you never grew any taller!" Alija taunted his friend, "Just go out a little farther, and you'll have it!"

Kai laughed, nodded, and waded just a few inches more into the lake. He grabbed for the string of fish and held it above his head in triumph, then yelled and peered into the water. He jumped away from whatever he saw there, only to land in deeper water. His friends watched in horror as his black head disappeared beneath the surface.

Everyone jumped up at once, shouting together for their friend. When he hadn't surfaced after a few seconds, Aibek jumped in after him. He waded to the spot where Kai had vanished and dove beneath the surface without a moment's hesitation.

~*~

All their friends remained clumped together on the banks of the lake, watching anxiously for the men to break the surface. Faruz ran into the shallow water, prepared to help either man or jump in after them if they didn't emerge soon. He held his breath to gauge when Aibek would run out of air and likely need help.

12.

Wedding

Faruz's lungs burned. Aibek would be running on less air than he had, so he exhaled and drew a deep breath, preparing to dive in after his friend. Aibek's auburn hair broke the surface of the water, followed quickly by Kai's lifeless form, draped in the string of fish that had been the source of trouble.

Dizzy with relief, Faruz helped his friend carry the unconscious man to the bank, rolled him to his stomach, and pounded on his back until water poured from his mouth. Everyone cheered when Kai finally gasped and coughed violently to clear the remaining water from his lungs. His friends gathered around and helped the choking young man to a sitting position, then stayed near him until his breathing returned to normal.

~*~

Aibek filled his lungs with a relieved breath as Kai reached for his hand, gripping it tightly as he mumbled, "You saved my life."

"That's what friends do—they help each other, right? Don't you know how to swim?" Sweet relief flooded Aibek at the sound his new friend talking. He'd worried that he might have been too late.

"Nobody in Nivaka can swim," Dalan explained. "Why would we? We live in the trees. That was amazing. Where did you learn to do that?"

"We used to swim with our friends in the river that borders Xona, so we learned when we were little boys," Faruz said. "It was a favorite pastime on hot summer days. We didn't have trees to shade us from the sun."

Aibek stared at Kai in concern, then turned and gazed out at the lake. "So… what exactly happened out there?" His brow furrowed as he turned back to his friend. "You looked down as if something was after you, then disappeared under the water."

Kai was silent for a long while, and Aibek wondered if he would answer. Finally, he said, "No, nothing attacked me. Something brushed against me—maybe a fish? It felt like a fish. It startled me, and I tried to get away from it, but I stepped off into deep water."

As soon as Kai had recovered sufficiently, the group gathered their belongings, packed the strings of fish into the baskets, and headed into the forest. The day was warm enough, but a cool breeze blew through the woods, and no one had brought dry clothes. The men who had gone into the water were chilled and shivering, so Ahren and her friends wrapped them in some of the blankets they had used for the picnic. The walk home took longer than the walk to the lake because Kai was exhausted from his ordeal and often needed to rest.

They made it back to the village just as the sun slipped below the horizon. Faruz and Dalan helped Kai to his house, and all of the others wasted no time going home for the evening. Aibek trudged back to Valasa's house, exhausted from the day's excitement.

The next morning, the village was abuzz with the arrangements for the wedding. Dalan and his sister were to take part in their friends' wedding, so they were occupied for the day. That left Aibek and Faruz with nothing to do. They agreed to wander on their own for the morning, then return to get ready for the wedding before the afternoon turned to evening.

As they strolled along the boardwalks, several people stopped to talk to the new mayor and his friend. Not infrequently, the villagers congratulated him for destroying the enemy's messengers and for saving Kai from drowning.

The attention made Aibek a little uncomfortable, and he worried that they would try to paint him as a hero. He knew a battle was coming, and he still wasn't sure how they could win it. He feared letting everyone down more than death and wanted to see them all survive and thrive when it was over. With each handshake, Aibek felt the villagers' expectations settle more weight upon his shoulders, and he slumped under the burden. He had to fight harder for each smile as worry etched his face.

How am I supposed to save these people from an enemy we know nothing about?

Aibek and Faruz spent the entire day walking around and talking with the villagers and had a light lunch with some old men who told them stories of hunting and market days before the invasion. Aibek enjoyed spending time getting to know the people who lived in this lovely place and was starting to feel he belonged there. He was quietly proud that they only got lost twice, and both times managed to find their way back without asking for help.

They returned to Valasa's house in time to get ready for the wedding. Aibek had no idea what to expect from the afternoon's celebration. Maybe it would be like the banquet on his first night here. This time, he intended to join the festivities.

The whole family had a light snack at the house, then headed to the park at the east end of town for the ceremony. The entire village was there, and all wore their best clothes for the event. The women wore flowing gowns in satin and silk with lace sleeves and lacy accents on the skirts. Aibek was a little shocked—that was the first time he had seen anyone wear something other than zontrec, though he'd noticed a few fur cloaks hanging in the wardrobe. The women pinned their hair up in a variety of unique and complicated styles, and he thought they each looked lovely. The men wore darkly pigmented shirts and pants, which looked similar to their usual attire. Aibek and Faruz both wore dark brown suits Valasa had given them.

The groom stood next to Valasa, beneath an arch made of colorful autumn leaves, awaiting the arrival of his bride. Aibek felt a stab of sympathy for his friend as he noticed Wayra fidgeting with his shirt cuffs, stepping forward and back again. His obvious nervousness only added to the general excitement of the day. The groom wore a yellow silk suit with a red flower pinned on its lapel.

Valasa was wearing the robes of his station, which the new mayor and his friend had never seen before. The outer robe was a deep forest green, each layer underneath a lighter shade than the one above it. There were at least seven layers, making the robe a veritable rainbow of green. The innermost layer was pure white, but Aibek only glimpsed an occasional sliver when the Gadonu moved. Pale pink washed the sky as the sun dropped near the horizon.

Soon after Aibek's arrival, the musicians began playing, and the bride entered the park. She wore a long, flowing gown of rose silk, embroidered at the hem and the long draping sleeves with white and yellow flowers connected by dark green vines and leaves. She shuffled toward the arch, holding the arm of a much older man whom Aibek assumed must be her father. Her rich brown hair was swept up to the crown of her head, where her curls interwove with little purple flowers. She smiled at her father, then turned tear-filled eyes to Wayra.

Aibek smiled at the sweetness of the picture they presented, then inhaled the flower-scented evening air. He hoped this was the first of many such celebrations for the people here.

The ceremony was short and solemn, but very sweet. Immediately after, the newlyweds led their guests to the Pavilion, where the celebration was to take place. The fairies had decorated it with magnificent garlands made of red and orange autumn leaves wrapped around each pillar and strings of lanterns casting a golden glow on the festivities. The lamps, strung along the boardwalks for two hundred yards in each direction, made the entire area look magical. The scent of flowers hung heavily on the humid evening air, mingling near the Pavilion with the scents of fish, vegetables, and cakes.

The area at the front of the Pavilion, where the long table had been on the night of their arrival, was set up as a huge buffet. On the front table, displayed in ornate, colorful arrangements, were several dishes of fish, the bountiful catch from the day before featured with obvious pride at the center of the room.

The workers had arranged more tables around the perimeter of the lower space, but they'd left a large area cleared for dancing in the center of the Pavilion.

Fairies fluttered about the tables, dressed vibrantly once again for the joyous occasion. Aibek wasn't sure he would ever get used to seeing them; he'd grown up thinking they existed only in the stories his aunt read him as a child. As they approached the celebration, Aibek basked in the noise of merriment drifting from the Pavilion. He smiled at the sounds of laughter and chairs scooting as people found seats for the festivities.

The bride and groom assumed their position in the center of the dance floor, and the musicians began a slow, lilting tune. They danced in circles, their tempo increasing every few steps as the music sped up. Before long, the couple was dancing furiously as the crowd clapped to the beat of the music and cheered for the newlyweds. By the time the song ended, the bride and groom were both breathless and laughing. They left the dance floor and headed to the buffet, where a line formed behind them. Other villagers filled the dance floor, choosing to eat later in the evening and avoid the long lines at the buffet.

Aibek and Faruz joined the dancing couples, each paired with ladies they had met over the past few weeks. Aibek struggled to remember the name of the girl he danced with but gave up when he realized in horror that he didn't know the steps to the dance. He stepped right when everyone else moved left, then stomped on his partner's foot. He tried to watch the other dancers through the corner of his eye, but they moved faster than he could. When everyone around him twisted into a turn, he bumped into the man dancing near them, then laughingly gave up even though they were only halfway through the song. His companion laughed with him for a moment, then went off into the crowd in search of a more competent dance partner.

Still laughing, he inhaled the aroma of the banquet mingling with the perfumes of all the dancers and reveled in the sounds of laughter and the clatter of dishes. Looking around, he realized his friend hadn't fared any better, so he made his way to where Faruz stood alone, next to a pillar by the edge of the dance floor.

"Well, that was fun," Aibek shouted over the noise once he had his friend's attention.

Faruz made a glum face. "I don't know if 'fun' is the right word for it. We may need lessons on these dances before we try again. That wasn't the impression I was hoping to make."

"Lessons don't sound like a bad idea, but it's a bit late for that tonight. Why don't we get some food?" Aibek tugged his disgruntled friend in the direction of the buffet. There were very few things that couldn't be made better with a good meal. However, before they made it to the tables, Zifa flagged them down. She had Ahren by the arm and dragged her along.

"That was a great try at a really tough dance. May I show you the steps?" The dark-haired beauty flashed a shy smile at Faruz, then leaned close to hear his response in the noisy Pavilion.

"That would be great, but maybe not out in the middle of the dance floor, where everyone can watch me fail." He smiled and raked his hands through his long blonde hair. "Is there anywhere else we can practice for a bit?"

"Sure, we can use the boardwalk over here. They lit lamps along the walk, and since everyone is in the Pavilion, we can have a bit of privacy while you learn." Zifa grabbed his hand and led him off into the night, leaving their two friends standing awkwardly in their wake.

Ahren made a quiet suggestion. "Well, do you want to go, too? I could teach you the steps at the same time, and that way there won't be rumors about the two of them tomorrow."

Aibek had to strain to hear her words over the din of the party.

"We can do that, but only if it's what you want to do. I don't want to be responsible for you missing the fun." When he looked up, her crystal-blue eyes met his, and she smiled.

"I wouldn't mind helping you a little. It's only dancing." They followed the path their friends had taken into the lamp-lit night on the boardwalk beyond the Pavilion.

Within a few yards, they approached the other couple, slowly practicing the steps to the dance near a bench. Ahren stopped several feet away and started walking Aibek through the steps. It took him several tries to catch on to the basics, and before the song ended, they were both laughing at his attempts. When the next song began, she showed him the dance that went to that music. The new one was a bit easier, and he caught on much more quickly.

Within a few minutes, he swung her easily through the turns of the dance and thought how lovely her eyes were in the lamplight.

Now that's a dangerous thought. This girl is my host's only daughter. I don't need to get any ridiculous ideas about her.

He needed a clear head to help steer the village through what was sure to be a rocky road ahead. Besides, he didn't even know where he stood with the lady at the moment. She'd been pleasant enough yesterday, but she hadn't been in a hurry to dance with him tonight—Zifa had basically forced her into it. As he steeled himself against any thought of attraction, she pressed closer in the dance, and he had to start all over again reminding himself why he shouldn't try for more.

When the song ended, Aibek called out to Faruz and Zifa and invited them to join him and his partner for a trip to the buffet. He needed to put some distance between himself and Ahren, and besides, he was getting hungry.

Aibek and Faruz were finishing their meal at a small table near the front of the Pavilion when screams pierced the night. Aibek jumped up, knocking the wooden chair to the floor in his haste. He tried to push toward the source of the screams but found himself facing a wall of retreating villagers. He squeezed between and around the terrified citizens until he finally broke through the crowd. It took a moment for his mind to process the shock of the scene in front of him. Alija lay on the wooden floor, a puddle of blood growing around him.

Aibek shouted, "What's happened?"

The blood flowed from Alija's left side. Aibek knelt beside his friend and gingerly turned him over to examine the source of the bleeding. Alija groaned in pain at the movement.

The back of his shirt was torn and plastered to the bloody gash beside his spine. The wound was deep enough that Aibek could see a glimmer of bone where the weapon had struck ribs.

Whoever did this clearly had no knowledge of the human body, Aibek mused as he examined the wound.

The cut was vertical and off-center, slicing through the thick muscle of the upper back. It didn't look as if the weapon had gone deep enough to hit any major organs, but that wouldn't matter if he didn't stop the bleeding.

Aibek ripped the ruined garment up the middle and folded an end to make a dressing, which he pressed into the wound to slow the bleeding. All the while, his mind raced.

Who could have done this? Surely someone must have seen something in this crowd.

They were only a few steps from the newly-empty dance

floor. The area would have been packed with people a few minutes before. Aibek looked up and met Faruz's worried glance.

"Start asking around. Someone saw who did this."

Faruz turned and scanned the faces of the onlookers.

Where's Valasa?

Aibek continued to hold pressure to the gash on his friend's back as warm, sticky blood squeezed between his fingers and ran down his hand. He pressed harder, and Alija grunted. Finally, the bleeding slowed to a trickle, then stopped. Soon after, Valasa came rushing into the Pavilion and knelt beside the wounded man. He scanned the scene and nodded to Aibek.

"Good work. It doesn't look like it's bleeding anymore." The healer turned his attention to Alija. "Do you think you can stand? We need to get you to my home so I can get a look at you and clean the wound."

Alija struggled into a sitting position, waving off Aibek's attempt to help. "I can walk."

He grabbed Aibek's outstretched hand and gingerly pulled himself to his feet. Aibek stayed close as Alija braced his hands on his knees, then slowly straightened. The wounded man took a few slow, painful-looking steps toward the boardwalk, then stopped to rest. Aibek didn't think he'd be able to make it all the way to the Gadonu's home, which also doubled as the town's hospital, but Alija stubbornly refused to let his friends carry him. Thankfully, he didn't have far to walk.

13.

Home

Eddrick spun his wife in a slow circle as they danced along with the revelers.

He whispered in her ear. "This is wonderful."

"Yes, it is." Kiri looked around. "But where's Aibek? I don't see him anywhere."

They stopped dancing, and both looked for their son among the dancers.

"It seems there's someone over there on the boardwalk. Maybe he needed some fresh air." She pointed to a small group in the lights outside The Pavilion, and they drifted closer to investigate.

Eddrick's lips widened into a huge grin when he saw his son dancing in a close embrace with Ahren. He wrapped an arm around his wife and spun her into the dance.

"Let's give them a little privacy, shall we?" he whispered in her ear.

"I didn't think she even liked him," Kiri replied, then laughed as he suddenly whirled her in the other direction.

He dipped her low to the ground and answered, "How could she not? He's really very likable. And they make such a lovely couple."

The song wound to a close and the joyful parents watched as their son and his friends left the boardwalk in favor of a meal. They decided they'd seen enough of the party they couldn't join and headed back to their quiet suite of rooms.

Eddrick spoke apropos of nothing as they walked toward their own space. "I'm running out of ideas how to get him to see me. I've tried every day since our punishment ended, and he doesn't even notice I'm there."

Kiri frowned at her husband. "What are you talking about? Who doesn't see you? I hope you're not interfering again."

"No, nothing like that. I want to talk to Aibek. He should know he's not alone."

For a moment, she gave him an intense stare. "Oh, it would be lovely to talk to him. I think he saw me the other night during the storm, but I'm not completely sure. He didn't say anything."

Eddrick nodded in understanding. "It was easy with Valasa. I just talked to him while he was meditating. Aibek doesn't meditate though, and I don't know what else to do."

"We'll just have to keep trying. He should know we're here for him."

~*~

Aibek waited impatiently in the family room while the healer treated Alija's wound in the Gadonu's workroom. Most of the council members, including Wayra and his new wife, were perched on the edges of the chairs in the room. Faruz and Dalan had stayed at the Pavilion to gather as much information as they could before all the villagers went home, and they hadn't yet returned.

The room was silent, except for the occasional rustling of fabric as someone shifted position. Valasa and Alija had been in the workroom for well over an hour, and Aibek was growing more apprehensive by the minute.

He stared at the door they'd gone through, willing it to open.

What's taking so long? Was I too late to stop the bleeding? Was the wound more serious than it looked?

He hadn't thought the blade had breached the ribs, but in that lighting, he could easily have been wrong.

Aibek jumped when the front door swung open behind him. He leaped to his feet and spun toward the sudden sound. He gaped at the sight of Faruz and Dalan leading a woman into the room, each holding one of her arms as she twisted and tried to get away.

The woman wore less finery than most of the villagers had that night; her simple yellow zontrec gown accented only with a pale green ribbon tied around her waist. It impossible to miss the bloodstains on the cuff of the right sleeve. The woman herself was slender and short, the top of her head just reached Faruz's shoulder. In spite of her small size, the woman had a hardness about her that Aibek recognized from his days in the city—this was a woman accustomed to manual labor. Her strength reminded him of the men and women who worked the rock quarries and coal mines outside of Xona. Her shoulder-length, dark hair tumbled about her face. It was hard to tell what color it was because of the sweat that dampened the heavy curls, sticking a few strands to her tear-stained cheeks.

"We caught her cleaning this not far from the Pavilion," Faruz said flatly, holding up a large carving knife. There were still dark spots—dried blood maybe?—near the tip of the blade.

Aibek considered the struggling woman. Possession of a carving knife at a banquet wasn't necessarily a crime, but cleaning it outside the Pavilion was enough to arouse suspicion.

And how did she get blood on the cuff of her sleeve?
The meats at the wedding feast had been prepared elsewhere and carried to the banquet by the fairies and cooks. He glanced back toward the door of the workroom.

After a long moment, Aibek asked, "Is there somewhere secure where we can hold her until we can gather more information?"

He didn't see any point in allowing her to speak right now. The rage in her chestnut brown eyes told him she'd deny any involvement, even if she'd wielded the knife herself—which he doubted. She had no blood on the front of her gown, which would have been hard to avoid if she had been the one who'd attacked his friend. The only bloodstains on her dress were on the very edge of the right sleeve.

He had too many questions, and he didn't really care to ask them at that moment. The answers didn't matter until he knew whether Alija would survive.

Dalan answered quietly, "Tavan converted the top floor of one of the houses on the Square into a dungeon. The keys are still in the guards' room there, but I'm not sure who would guard the girl." He looked uncomfortable and shifted a bit, adjusting his grip on her arm. "We released all of Tavan's prisoners the day we took our freedom back."

Everyone turned as Valasa swung the workroom door open and stepped into the den. He glanced around at the worried-looking friends, then eyed the woman who still fought against her captors.

"Alija will recover, as long as no fever sets in." Valasa never took his eyes from the prisoner. "The wound was deep, and took some work to clean and close, but I don't believe it did any lasting damage." He turned and met

Aibek's eyes. "You did well. It's a good thing you got the bleeding stopped. He'll heal much faster because of your efforts."

"What should we do with the woman?" Faruz gripped her arm with both hands. "Who can guard her until we can sort out the details in the morning?"

"Take her to Tavan's prison," Valasa answered gravely. "It's the only secure place in town. I'll have someone meet you there to take over." He slowly assessed the woman's appearance, his gaze lingering on the blood stains on her sleeve.

At least that's settled for the night, Aibek thought.

Exhaustion had hit him like a wall once he knew Alija would live, but he thought he'd wait for Faruz to get back. It wasn't likely this woman was the assailant unless she'd changed her gown. That meant the real attacker was still out there, and Faruz and Dalan could be in danger transporting the woman to her cell. He started to sit, thought better of it, and grabbed his sword. He clicked the door closed behind him and followed his friends into the night.

~*~

The next morning began much the same as all the days before, with the friends meeting in Aibek's room at sunrise. They'd slept late after the commotion of the day before, but Aibek was in no rush to leave his rooms. The trip to the jail had been uneventful, and they'd left the woman under the watch of Amiran, the man who had told them of the messengers' arrival only a week ago.

Aibek stared out the window at the growing light and allowed his mind to wander. He absently grabbed a cake from the tray Serik had brought and nibbled at a corner. *How's Alija doing this morning?*

He'd left his friend sleeping quietly in one of the small

bedrooms on the first floor. Before last night, he hadn't known those rooms were even there, but apparently, they served as a sort of infirmary. Valasa had explained that he liked to keep some patients close so he could monitor their treatment.

After a long while, when they'd eaten almost all the food, and the friends were finishing the last of the famanc, Faruz finally broke the silence. He rambled on about the dancing and the food, but mostly he talked about the people. Aibek only half listened to his friend, his mind trying to unravel the mystery of Alija's attack. Still, he gradually found himself listening more carefully to the conversation around him.

As Faruz talked about the wedding celebration and all that had happened before Alija's attack, Aibek realized that Faruz was falling hard for the dark-haired beauty, Zifa.

He tried to be tactful. "You know, now really isn't a good time for romance. We've got bigger problems to deal with."

"I know, I haven't known her long enough to see if we have anything in common at all. But I really like her, and she smells amazing." At his friend's hard look, Faruz continued, "I'll take it slow, I promise. We still have to figure out who's trying to kill us, then win the battle for the village before anything can happen with a girl."

"I hope so. We really don't need to make things more complicated than they already are."

Faruz gave him a crooked grin. "You know, you could take your own advice. You were getting pretty close to Ahren last night, too."

"I don't think there's anything to worry about on that front. Ahren's done her level best to hate me since I got here, and she wasn't in a hurry to dance with me last night."

Faruz laughed. "Oh, please! The way she was plastered against you during that dance made it pretty clear she likes you."

"I thought so, too, but then she avoided me for the rest of the night." Aibek sighed. "Really, it's best if she does keep her distance. I have enough other problems."

Faruz nodded and stuffed the last muffin into his mouth, and they headed downstairs to join the family. Aibek stopped to check on Alija before leaving for the day. He found his friend propped against a pile of fluffy pillows, eating a bowl of porridge. He still looked terribly pale. They chatted quietly for a few minutes, and Aibek went to meet Faruz and Serik in the den.

Today, Aibek planned to tour the traditional mayor's home. His stomach churned with fears of what he might see, and he repeatedly wiped his hands on the fabric of his pants. This was the place where his parents had lived their lives and where they'd died. He knew it wasn't ready to be lived in yet, but workers had removed Tavan's outdoor altar, and they had almost finished the interior work. The workers wanted his opinion on some details, so it was time to face his fears. Serik and Faruz planned to come along to see the house and to provide some moral support.

The three of them bid good morning to the family before they left the house, then together walked the short distance to the mayoral home. Their destination at the other end of the Square looked rather modest compared with the Gadonu's enormous house. It had two floors and many windows on the front of the building. The main entry doors were propped open to allow in the cool breeze while the repairmen worked. The exterior looked like a simple log home, except for the carvings along each log. The elaborate designs mirrored those on the boardwalk and the Pavilion, in what Aibek now recognized as typical Nivakan style. Dark green trim accented the windows and doors, giving the home a warm, welcoming appearance.

I should have grown up here.

Aibek stopped for a moment and inhaled a few deep breaths to steady himself before he took the step into his parents' home. The area immediately inside the front door was a large, open space. The floor was bare wood, and a large stone fireplace filled one wall. He recognized the foreman coming to meet them as soon as they stepped inside.

"All the furniture in here was ruined by that gov'nor, so we had to replace it all," he began. "We're getting ready to upholster the sofas and chairs, but need your opinion on colors and such." The worker went straight to the issues at hand in a no-nonsense manner that Aibek appreciated. He chose a few fabric samples from a selection on the hearth, then began a slow tour through the rest of the home.

Every room showed evidence of repairs underway, and the whole house smelled of paint and sawdust. The pounding of hammers made conversation difficult in some areas. Here and there, undamaged old paintings leaned against the walls, waiting to be rehung after the workers finished the repairs. They didn't talk much as they toured, except an occasional comment on this repair or that color.

Aibek relaxed almost immediately, relieved that it merely looked like a construction zone. Before he'd made it through the first two rooms, the sick feeling had left his stomach, and he wished he had eaten more at breakfast.

The foreman assured him everything would be done to his specifications. Aibek didn't think he could bear to claim his parents' bedchamber as his own, so he asked to have that space converted to a meditation room and told the foreman he would take the next largest chamber for his room.

He stood for several minutes in his parents' empty room after the others had left to explore the rest of the house. Even with the bare wood and sawdust, this room felt almost alive, somehow. Aibek thought he could sense his parents here. He shook his head against the ridiculous thought. He didn't believe in ghosts, and his parents had been dead for twenty years. He took a deep, calming breath and ran his hands through his hair, then strode down the hall to catch up with the others.

At the back of the house, Aibek and Faruz found a small outdoor courtyard, lined with benches and empty planters. In the center stood an empty fountain, its top broken off and sitting nearby. With a few repairs and some plants, this could be a special retreat. Serik showed him a hidden gate at the far end of the courtyard and explained that it led to a secret entrance to the village.

"This is how I got you out the night of the attack. I was afraid you'd cry and give us away, but you slept right through all the noise and we made it safely out of the village."

The old man then showed them how the secret stairwell was hidden by a bench, which had helped keep their escape a secret. They climbed down the stairs and found a splintered crib, infant chair, and dozens of tiny clothes and rattles still piled in a heap near the entrance. Serik told them the servants had thrown it all out so the invaders wouldn't know to look for a child. They stood in the forest and looked around quietly for several minutes before ascending to complete their tour.

By the time they had finished the tour of their future home, choosing curtains for this room or a paint color for that one, it was almost time for lunch. Faruz wanted to join the others for fighting practice that afternoon, but Aibek wasn't quite ready to leave. He sent Serik and Faruz to meet Dalan at the park and went back into his future home.

He assured the foreman that he was pleased with the repairs and told the man he simply wanted to hang around for a bit, then slowly wandered back toward his parents' room. There was just something about that space.

Aibek couldn't explain why he felt so drawn to that room, except that it was where his parents had spent their time. The latch clicked as he closed the door behind him and advanced into the space. Ira had always been loving and supportive, but he'd grown up longing for the opportunity to meet his parents. He'd always dreamed of having a father he could turn to for advice, and he'd often daydreamed about meeting his mother. Never knowing if they were alive or dead had weighed heavily on him throughout his childhood. He sat in the middle of the bare floor and stared at a whimsical painting leaning against the wall. The brilliant colors drew his eye, and he wondered how it had survived all those years without damage.

He rested there for a while, his mind drifting over all that had happened since he'd arrived in Nivaka nearly two months before. It was hard to believe how much his life had changed in such a short time. As his thoughts moved towards the uncertain future, he thought about how much he wished for his father's guidance.

He spoke aloud to the walls as he dropped his head into

his hands. "I wish you were here to help me."

A voice came from behind him. "I am here. I always have been."

Startled, Aibek jumped up and turned toward the voice. Gooseflesh erupted over his arms and neck. His eyes quickly scanned the barren space. It was empty. He thought at first he must be losing his mind, but Aibek was sure he had heard those words.

"Be calm, and you will see me," the voice resumed.

Aibek backed up until he touched the wall behind him, then sat facing into the empty room.

After a moment, the voice came again. "Close your eyes, and clear your mind."

Aibek did as he was told, and waited for whatever would happen next.

"You have never been alone. We've always been near you, even when you thought we didn't care. We would have given anything to raise you ourselves, but that wasn't meant to be."

Aibek took a deep breath and opened his eyes. Across the room stood a man who looked like an older version of himself.

"Father? Is that really you? How is this possible?"

Eddrick repeated, "We've always stayed near to watch over you."

Aibek shook his head. "I don't understand. Why haven't you talked to me before? I've never wanted anything more than this."

"I've tried so many times, but your mind wasn't open. You always said you didn't believe in spirits... I didn't know how to make you see me."

"I thought I saw someone in my room during the storm. Who was that?"

"That was your mother. She's never been far away,

either."

"This is incredible," Aibek grinned. "Can you help me lead the village? I don't know how to be a mayor."

"I can only answer direct questions, and I can't tell you what will happen. But I'll always be here to help you."

"Can you tell me who poisoned us? Or who stabbed Alija?"

Eddrick looked as if he might answer, then turned at the sound of footsteps in the hall.

They heard the foreman's question. "Aibek, sir, are you still in there?"

"Yes, I'm here," Aibek said through the closed door.

"I have to go for now," Eddrick whispered, "but know that I'm never far away."

Aibek was alone in the room when the foreman opened the door and strolled into the room. "Your friends are looking for you, sir. Can I tell them you're on your way?"

"Yes, I'm coming." The mayor followed the foreman to the front door, where Faruz and Serik stood waiting.

Faruz looked hard at his friend in concern. "Are you all right? You're awfully pale."

Serik stared at his friend with a concerned expression and silently placed a hand on the young man's shoulder. Aibek shrugged. "I'm fine; I just feel closer to them here."

Faruz slanted his head to one side, eyes narrowed. "I see... Are you ready for some lunch, or do you need more time?"

Aibek's stomach snarled aloud, and he realized for the first time he was starving. The friends laughed at the loud grumble, and they headed off to Valasa's house together.

As soon as the friends came through the door, Aibek

knew something was very wrong. The Gadonu and his wife stood in one corner of the den, leaning close together in earnest conversation. Nearby, Ahren and Dalan stared blankly out the window. No one even acknowledged Aibek or his friends as they came into the room.

Aibek braced himself for more bad news, then asked, "Has something happened? Alija?"

"Alija's doing well. He's resting now," Valasa began. "You know that part of my job is to maintain communications with the other villages in the Tsari, right?"

At Aibek's nod, he continued. "Today I received several messages from our neighboring villages." He took a deep breath and looked away, then said, "They've overheard Helak's guards and governors talking about a large battalion of soldiers preparing to come this way."

Aibek nodded again and chose his words carefully. "We knew this was coming. We'll have to work harder to build our forces and finish fortifying the village..."

He trailed off and stared into the empty fireplace, then turned back to the room.

"Have the villagers heard this? I would prefer to keep it quiet for now and inform the people all at once. And, I think we should call a council meeting immediately."

Aibek paced the floor while he thought out loud, "Can we send someone to bring them here? Is that acceptable? Or is there some chamber somewhere we can use for a private meeting?"

He was sure the entire council should know of this warning so they could have at least the outline of a plan in place before they told the villagers of the army's preparation.

Valasa looked thoughtful, then said, "I think... I could have the fairies notify the others, and there's an empty room upstairs that should be perfect for a small meeting."

In less than an hour, all the council members except Alija assembled in the small sitting room on the third floor of Valasa's home. It was a cozy room, with a few small tables and several comfortable chairs arranged around the room. One sofa dominated the wall under the large picture windows. It was an ideal place to sit and discuss their problems and plans at length, though Aibek thought it smelled a little musty. The servants hadn't had much time to air it out for their meeting.

Aibek didn't wait for Valasa to call the meeting to order. Instead, he blurted out the news they'd gotten that afternoon and added, "I know we expected this, but I thought we'd have more time."

The council members stared at him in stunned silence until Aibek started to feel a little uncomfortable.

Finally, Valasa spoke again. "Yes, I think we all thought we'd have more time to prepare." He turned to look at Aibek. "You're the only one in this room with any training for this type of thing. What should we do?"

Zifa broke in. "Now hold on! He may be the only one with an education, but we all have to work together on this. As he said before, many of the techniques he learned in school won't work here in the trees."

Kai peered up at Zifa from where he sat perched on the edge of a chair "Well, what ideas do you have then?"

Zifa shrugged but remained quiet as she settled farther back into her chair.

Dalan let out a loud sigh. "Look, we don't have to come up with all the ideas today, or even by ourselves. What if we put it out to the citizens at the meeting and see what they come up with?"

Aibek grinned for the first time. "That's a great idea. I'd

thought about that at our last meeting, except I didn't think to ask them. I just hoped they'd pitch in and help us generate some plans."

Valasa explained, "They'll never speak during a council meeting unless you ask. Before the invasion, the meetings were open for spectators, but they had to keep quiet. There are enough people still here that remember the old rules that I doubt any would try to interrupt a meeting."

Aibek nodded thoughtfully. "That makes sense. Do village meetings work the same way?"

"No," Valasa continued, "Those meetings are designed to allow citizens to voice their concerns and opinions, so they'll be more vocal there."

"Perfect. Then we'll have a village meeting today and ask for input from the citizens," Aibek said. He frowned and looked around at the other council members. "As long as we all agree, that is."

Valasa called for a vote, which was unanimous. Aibek wished he could ask Alija for his vote before they proceeded, but there wasn't time. They would hold a village meeting that afternoon. The council members spent the rest of the time trying to come up with an agenda for the village gathering and preparing for likely questions. Meanwhile, Valasa went down to spread the news and prepare the Meeting Hall for the assembly.

~*~

What the new mayor hadn't considered was the reaction of the townsfolk when they heard that a secret, emergency council meeting had been called. In a town of only eight hundred individuals, it wasn't long before everyone knew that the six community leaders had gathered in an upstairs room in Valasa's home, rather than in the designated place at the meeting hall. Within half an hour of their assembly, the villagers gathered outside the house, demanding to know what was happening and why they were meeting in secret.

Ayja did her best to keep the growing crowd calm, and once Valasa emerged, she dispatched several individuals to spread the news that they would hold a town meeting in two hours' time. That news appeased some in the group, and they wandered off to wait. But for every one who was satisfied, two others refused to leave without knowing what was happening in that room upstairs. While Valasa prepared for the meeting, his wife took it upon herself to feed the more willful Nivakans cookies and famanc to keep them calm and happy while they waited.

14.

Meeting

The small woman strode past the guard with hardly a glance. "I'm here to question the prisoner," she announced in an authoritative tone.

Amiran stood aside but didn't leave the room. He'd been alternating guard duty with one other man since the night before, with each guard taking two-hour watches. He was nearing the end of this turn and was beginning to look tired, at least to Tamyr's weary eyes. Tired or not, he kept his keen, unwavering gaze on the rumpled prisoner in the cell as her visitor approached.

Tamyr could have wept—again.

What's my pretty friend doing, coming to this dirty prison? Why has she come?

The woman turned to Amiran with a pointed question. "You don't think she's going to talk with a guard listening, do you?"

"Of course not, madam." Amiran nodded and ducked out the narrow door.

Tamyr assumed the guard would wait just outside the door, probably with an ear pressed against the wooden barrier, so she spoke as softly as she could. "What're you doing here?" A single tear ran down her cheek.

"I had to make sure you were all right."

The woman pressed her face between the bars and inspected her friend through narrowed eyes. Tamyr cringed under the silent examination. She must look terrible after a day spent in the cell without even a chance to wash her face.

"You look tired. Didn't you rest at all?"

Tamyr swiped a hand over her face, her fingers lingering over her eyes. She knew they must be red and swollen from a seemingly endless and miserable night.

Why did I ever agree to help this woman?

The headmistress of the washhouse had come by early in the morning and informed Tamyr she'd need to find a new place to live and work. They didn't want someone like her living with young, impressionable girls.

"I slept a little. I've had a lot to think about," she said after a pause.

The young woman knelt next to the bars, stretching a hand toward Tamyr. "I heard they put you out of the washhouse. What will you do?"

"I don't know yet. I'm hoping my father will believe I'm innocent and take me in, at least for a time." Tamyr moved away from the outstretched hand. She wrapped her arms around herself and turned away from her visitor. It was getting harder to think of the young woman as a friend. The girl had turned Tamyr's life upside down but had managed to remain free of suspicion so far.

Tears welled in Tamyr's soft brown eyes. "I have to find a way to clear my name somehow."

"How will you do that? You'll keep my secret, right?"

Tamyr jumped and spun toward her friend as the door flung open. Amiran and the other guard walked in together, nodding in deference to the young visitor.

"That's a long enough visit for now. The Gadonu wants her brought to his place for questioning," the new guard announced.

"I'll come back soon," the young woman promised

before she ran out the door.

Tamyr listened to her quick steps on the stairs and looked up at the guards. Her day was about to become much worse. She'd never actually met the religious leader, but she'd seen him across the room many times. He was nice enough most of the time, but she'd heard he could be harsh if he got angry. She took a deep breath, drew herself up to her full height, and followed the guards out the door.

~*~

Finally, it was time to leave for the town meeting. Aibek, pleased that the council members had agreed to ask the villagers for input and ideas, worried about their reaction to the news that Helak was forming an army. Widespread panic would be difficult to avoid, even though this wasn't unexpected news.

The council emerged together from the small room and trudged to the meeting hall without a word spoken among them.

When they arrived, they found the entire village already assembled, everyone in their predetermined seats and waiting expectantly for the arrival of their mayor and council. Aibek shrank under the weight of every gaze as the villagers watched the council members walk down the aisle toward their seats. He took a deep, calming breath as he lowered himself to his chair, deliberately keeping his eyes off the empty chair at the table. Alija should be at this meeting.

Once the council members had taken their places at the front of the room, Valasa called the meeting to order.

"Today, as part of my regular duties, I received communications from several neighboring villages, all with the same basic message. Helak is gathering a large battalion of warriors to regain control of Nivaka. We've called you here this evening so we can work together to devise a plan to defend our homes." As he spoke, the villagers began to shift in their seats and murmur to their neighbors. By the time he finished, his voice was barely audible over the dull roar of the villagers exclaiming over the announcement.

Aibek rapped his knuckles on the table to regain the attention of the assembled people. After a moment, they quieted with expectant looks at their mayor. Aibek nodded to Valasa to continue.

The Gadonu went on to explain that they had time to formulate a plan and train their own army, but they would need everyone's help. When he finished, he asked the assembled citizens if anyone had a suggestion on how best to defend their homes.

A hush fell over the room as the people looked at each other. After a long moment, a frail, elderly man in the middle of the room stood and raised his hand. His voice trembled but was clear and loud enough to be understood by the council members.

"I don't like this talk of fighting. It certainly didn't work the last time." He stopped and took a deep breath, then balled his weathered hands into fists and shouted, "Why don't we save ourselves the trouble and the bloodshed, and send Helak notice of our surrender? His rules were strict, but life was peaceful and predictable." When he finished, the old man sat down and lowered his head.

Wayra stood and addressed the old man and the assembly. "Thank you for your input, Eder. You lost a great deal in the last attack when your son and his wife were killed, and again in the revolt, when your nephews both died. Fighting means we could lose much more. Your idea has some merit. How many gathered here are in favor of a rapid and peaceful surrender?"

Nearly two dozen hands went up around the room as the council members gave the villagers time to consider and respond to the question.

When it appeared that no more hands would go up, Wayra asked, "And how many think we should defend our home in battle? We've had a few months of freedom. Who wants to remain free?"

Nearly every person in the room raised a hand, including some of those who had voted for surrender. Several stood and shouted their votes, and Aibek sighed in relief. There wouldn't be anything he could do but return to Xona if the citizens voted to give the village back to Helak.

Aibek gestured for those standing to sit and addressed the assembly, "We will fight, and we will win!"

He waited for the loud cheers to die down before he continued, "Every successful battle begins with a plan. We'll escort anyone who wishes to evacuate to the river town of Kainga. I have been there recently, and they have well-apportioned inns where our citizens will be welcomed."

At this, a few murmurs went through the crowd.

"Does anyone have any ideas for a plan to defend ourselves? Any strategies to help us defeat this enemy?"

Once again, the room was silent as the gathered villagers looked around, waiting for someone to speak.

Eventually, Serik stood. "I think we should ask our neighbors for help. There was a time when the people from all the villages would gather together regularly to mingle and celebrate. I don't see why they would hesitate to help us now. They could greatly increase our numbers and our chances of success."

Valasa responded quickly, "Thank you, Serik, that's an excellent idea. Let's have a vote. How many are in favor of asking our neighbors for help?"

Nearly every hand in the room went up, so the Gadonu continued, "Wonderful. I'll send messages to the other villages first thing in the morning."

This started the flow of ideas, and the meeting continued late into the evening. Many ideas came out, most of them immediately discarded for one reason or another. One individual even went so far as to propose moving the village, arguing that Helak's army couldn't defeat them if they couldn't find them. They rejected this idea as impractical; it would be impossible to move an entire village during daylight hours, let alone quickly enough to avoid this assault. Several villagers proposed useful ideas, however, and Aibek thought they would have enough to begin fortifying the village.

At last, the villagers, tired and hungry, called for an end to the meeting. The crowd dispersed in haste, and most rushed home to their dinners.

When the noise of chairs scraping and neighbors talking had quieted in the emptying hall, Wayra turned to Aibek, smiled and rose to his feet. "That went better than I expected."

Kai hopped to his feet and nodded. "I agree; I thought it would be a riot."

The others nodded as they stood and stretched. They walked together to the door.

Aibek yawned and made a suggestion. "We should meet again in the morning to finalize our plans, maybe at Valasa's house so Alija can join."

Dalan slapped him on the back. "That's a great idea. We'll meet in that upstairs sitting room an hour after sunrise if that's all right with everyone."

They all agreed and parted outside the building, each heading in the direction of home.

Before Aibek had made it very far from the meeting hall, a tiny old woman with bony hands and paper-thin skin pulled him to the side of the boardwalk. She held him with a surprisingly strong grip for one so small and frail. She spoke in hushed, quick phrases. "I didn't want to talk in there because most of them won't like my suggestion. There have been times during our history when Nivaka has partnered with the ground folk."

His eyebrows shot up as she grabbed his hands and peered into his eyes.

"You will be much more successful in defeating this army if you have the support of the elves and dwarves." She dropped his hands and sighed. "They will help you only if it serves them, and they cannot be trusted not to use any opportunity to attack our people." She pointed down the boardwalk in the direction his friends had gone. "Your servant knows how to bargain with them. Talk to him, and he will tell you how it is to be done." When she had finished her speech, the little old lady walked quickly away.

Aibek frowned and stared after her for a long moment as he considered her advice. He decided to do as she said and ask Serik what he thought of the idea, then walked as slowly as he could toward Valasa's house. This had been an eventful day, and he needed some time to digest everything that had happened. Had he really talked to his father's ghost? It felt like a dream, though he knew it wasn't. He wondered what his father would say about tonight's meeting and again worried that the village faced an unwinnable war.

Besides that, there was still someone in the village who was trying to kill the council members. Aibek was confident that the woman in the cell was not the person who had stabbed Alija. Valasa had planned to question the woman today. Aibek wondered absently if he'd gotten any information from her. He'd have to ask about it in the morning. Tonight, he needed to unravel the old woman's advice and find out what Serik knew about the ground folk.

15.

History

An unusual quiet reigned at the dinner table that evening, though Aibek was so distracted he barely noticed. He did take note of Ahren's empty chair.

She must be indisposed again, he thought.

She'd had several headaches that had kept her in her room for days.

When they'd finished the meal, they each retreated to their separate rooms, instead of gathering in the den as they normally did. Aibek checked on Alija and found him sleeping soundly, then trudged up the stairs on leaden legs. He wanted to ask Valasa what information he'd gotten from the prisoner, but he didn't have the energy. He'd have to make a point to talk to the Gadonu before the council meeting the next morning.

Serik followed Aibek to his room and began laying out clothing for the next day. Meanwhile, his friend sat in one of the large chairs by the fireplace, staring into the flames as if the answer to his problems could be found there.

The old man laid a hand on the mayor's shoulder, startling the younger man out of his reverie. "Is there anything I can do for you, sir? You've had a rough day."

"I don't know what I'm doing, Serik. How am I supposed to lead these people? Is there any way I can help them win? Maybe the old man was right, and it would be better to give in peacefully." He took a deep breath and knotted his fingers together. "The first battle this village fought would have been a massacre if that had been the invaders' intent. This time they'll be angry." He raked his hands through his long auburn hair and cradled his head in his hands, then whispered, "What if they aren't as merciful as the last time?"

His confidence had been growing steadily over the past several weeks as he began to understand the roles and traditions of this community. That day, Aibek had realized again that he didn't have the knowledge or experience to guide them. He'd been shocked when the first suggestion from the villagers had been surrender. He'd trained his entire life to become an army officer but had expected he would be taking orders from officers above him in the chain of command until he had learned enough to earn a higher rank and more responsibility. He wasn't ready to take on the leadership of such a large-scale battle plan, especially with so much at stake.

The two friends were quiet for a long while. Eventually, Serik sat down next to his friend, patted him on the knee, and asked, "Have I ever told you the story of the night of the invasion? I know you've heard bits of it all of your life, but do you know the whole story?" His voice was nearly as soft as Aibek's had been.

"I… don't think so. I only know you evacuated with me when you realized we wouldn't win, but that has nothing to do with now. I'm not leaving this time." He didn't want to waste any time thinking about that long ago battle. He was too consumed by his worries over how to lead the village to victory this time.

"It was the day of your naming ceremony," Serik began, his voice just above a whisper. "The day had been perfect. Everyone turned out to celebrate your birth." He looked up and met Aibek's eyes. "You were a long time coming. Anyway, the celebration was still in full swing at the Pavilion, but your parents brought you home to put you to bed just before sunset. I think they were hoping for some rest, too." He turned and stared into the fire. Aibek could tell that his friend's mind was transported back in time to that awful night.

~*~

The servant entered the room with a tray of snacks for Eddrick and Kiri, who were caring for their new baby and getting ready for bed. The fire, burning brightly, had warmed the room just enough. It cast a warm light across the chamber. Paintings of fairies and elves danced in the shadows cast by the flames.

"Thank you." Kiri took the tray and set it on the small table near the bed. She took a large muffin and turned back to Serik. "I don't know what we'd do without you." He had enjoyed helping care for the newest addition to the family and smiled at the compliment. He'd served the mayor's family since just after Eddrick learned to walk, and often spoke of staying until the babe was a father himself. Kiri would laugh and say that it was a little ambitious to plan that far ahead, since he was already quite old, though he didn't think she knew his exact age. Serik thought his white hair and stooped posture made him look older than he was. His hair had turned white while he was still a young lad, and he'd injured his back a few years later, but he was still quick on his feet and skilled with his hands. He bent to turn down the covers on the bed.

While he worked, Eddrick asked, "Serik, what do you make of these rumors of unrest I keep hearing from the West? Don't you have people in the mountains out there?"

"I do have family in the mountains, sir, but I haven't heard from them in several months." Serik shrugged and hummed softly to himself as he continued his work.

They had spoken of the skirmishes before, and he knew the mayor didn't expect any trouble in their secluded little corner of the world. He thought Eddrick probably felt it was his duty to know what was happening beyond the boundaries of the Tsari Forest. Azalin was a large land, with every type of landscape and climate, and many small disputes had come and gone between areas and factions over the years. This one would be no different.

The mayor took a few pieces of fruit from the tray and strolled toward the window of their chamber. The sun was finally setting, and he had always loved the view of the town in the twilight when people lit candles and lamps, and the village glowed with light and activity. It had been a glorious day. It had been only the mayor's second time back among the council since the birth of his son. A great feast, with mountains of food, flowing drink, joyful music and plenty of dancing had followed the meeting and naming ceremony.

Eddrick suddenly exclaimed, "What is going on out there?"

In the instant he reached the window, a loud, rhythmic pounding shook the floor. Each thunderous sound rattled the entire structure. Serik and Kiri ran to join the mayor at the window. Outside, chaos was breaking out. Townsfolk were using whatever weapons they could find, mostly ancient display swords, and were fighting against a large number of heavily armed strangers. As they watched, one of the swords broke in half, and the man wielding it went down on his knees before the intruder.

Just at that moment, the housekeeper came running into the chamber, shouting, "We're under attack! They're trying to break down the front door, and it won't hold much longer." She handed a leather bag to the new father and started passing him clothes to put in it.

"You have to get out of here!"

With panic in his eyes, Eddrick turned to the servant. "You have to take Aibek out of the village. Save him!" He handed the bag to Serik. "Take him to my brother and his wife in Xona. They won't turn you away."

"But… sir, shouldn't I stay and help defend Nivaka?"

It was difficult to hear over the noise of hundreds of booted feet marching on the boardwalk mingled with the sound of villagers shouting and fighting for their homes and lives. The rhythmic pounding had stopped briefly but started up again, this time louder than before.

"You can be more help by saving my son." Eddrick reached for his grandfather's broadsword where it was mounted on the wall. The panic had vanished from his face; in its place was a steely resolve.

An army of servants rushed into the room and silently carried out the cradle and infant clothes, and Serik realized the housekeeper had left the room. They removed every sign that an infant lived there.

Kiri tearfully kissed her baby's cheek, hugged him close for a brief moment then bundled him into several blankets. She then placed him in the knapsack so he wouldn't be visible and retrieved a large leather purse from the wardrobe and put it in the bag beside the baby. She handed the entire bundle to Serik.

"You have to save him. There's enough coin here to purchase the supplies you need once you're out of the forest. Do whatever you must, but keep him safe."

Serik nodded, then quietly slipped out the servants' entrance just as the main door exploded into a thousand pieces. The noise was deafening, and he knew he had to move quickly if they were going to escape from Nivaka. His ragged breathing sounded to him like trumpets in the unnatural silence of the service hall.

He moved swiftly to the private entrance in the mayor's courtyard to get out of the city and onto the perilous ground below. As he hurried quietly from the building, trying to keep to the shadows, he couldn't help but notice that the townsfolk were losing. Many had surrendered and were being led down the wooden boardwalks toward the village center where just a few hours before they had celebrated the birth and naming of their next mayor.

As the servant made his way down the ladder with the infant sleeping quietly in the bag on his back, he wondered how he could accomplish the task he had been given. He had no food, no supplies, and no milk for the baby. He only had a small fishing kit, a few blankets, and the purse Kiri had stashed in the knapsack. Serik thought of the desperation on the young mother's face when she'd handed him the bundle and knew he'd have to figure it out.

He took a deep breath, looked around in the dimness of the forest and racked his brain for a plan. There were several villages and towns between the northern border of the forest and the river city of Kainga. He could find someone who would sell him a goat to milk for the baby, or possibly a wet nurse who would be willing to make the journey with them to Xona.

He froze and realized there was still one major problem to be dealt with before he could worry about a plan to feed the child. The sun was setting, and he feared they would escape the clutches of the army only to land in a battle with their enemies on the ground. Panic again clutched at his throat when he heard a twig snap in the woods to his right. He waited for an eternal moment, expecting to see an enemy soldier or an army of elves and dwarves. When neither appeared, he decided the only chance was to try bargaining with the ground folk, so he walked straight toward their village. He didn't get very far in the darkening woods before the anticipated group of warrior elves appeared before him on the trail. He held up both hands and asked to speak to their leaders on an urgent matter. They nodded silently, turned, and led him through the forest to their village.

They took him through an underground tunnel to a cavernous room with a long table in the middle. At one end sat a small person with bright yellow-blond hair and slightly pointed ears. He was dressed in the browns and greens of the forest and wore a sword on his back.

"May I please speak, sir? I have distressing news for you," Serik whispered. When the king nodded, he continued, "Nivaka is under attack, and I have the task of attempting to save Mayor Eddrick's only child. I fear the villagers have no chance against this army."

Serik bowed his head and waited to hear his fate, fighting the urge to weep. His friends above were likely dead, but he had no time to grieve. He wouldn't make it out of the forest without the assistance of the king; the warriors would destroy him even if he were able to escape this room.

The elf king spoke slowly, apparently weighing the gravity of the situation.

"You know I have the utmost respect for Eddrick, mainly because he has done so much to prevent skirmishes between the elfin people and the villagers." He waited until Serik looked up before he continued. "If I help you, what guarantee do I have about the kind of man this child will grow to be?"

"I promise you that the child will be raised to be a leader equal to his father, and will return and bring peace back to our home. I plan to take him to Eddrick's brother, and I have no doubt he will be as fine a man as his father."

The leader stood and paced the long room, then replied, "An army has been cutting down Shadow trees at the edge of the forest, and has fought my people several times." He took a deep breath. "I'm afraid this is the same army that has attacked Nivaka tonight. I fear what will happen to the Tsari under the rule of such an enemy."

They agreed that the mayor's child was the forest's best hope for a long-term victory, and his elves helped them out of the forest. Serik made it unmolested to the edge of the forest with an escort of elfin warriors.

~*~

Serik had stood and begun pacing as he told the story, but returned to his chair and stared into the fire as he finished the tale.

"We stopped at a farm for the night, and the farmer's wife gave me milk to feed you. She said we could buy a goat to milk once we made it past the river. The next day we crossed into Kainga, gathered supplies, and set off for Xona."

Aibek thought the frail old man had shrunk even more during his tale. He now looked as if a slight breeze would blow him away into dust.

Serik continued, "I had never been to the city, but I had memorized your uncle and aunt's address from your father's correspondence. The journey was uneventful after that, and the rest you already know. Your family welcomed us gladly, and were happy to raise you as their own." The old man looked directly at the mayor. "So you see, there's a great deal of difference between that terrible night and the all-out battle you're expecting. Your parents weren't expecting trouble and were unprepared for the attack. This time, you have the advantage of preparation, and I have no doubt this battle will have a much different outcome."

After he had spoken, Serik fell silent. He had never told the entire story before this moment, and tears flowed freely down his leathery cheeks.

Neither man spoke for a long while until the old man stood and headed for the door. "I'll leave you to get some rest. Your uncle and I made sure you have the skills you need. Sleep well." The latch clicked softly, and the mayor sat alone in the quiet.

Aibek remained in his seat for a long while, considering everything that had happened during the day. It was impossible to believe that only one day had passed. Had he really talked to his father's spirit? How had he never heard the story of the night they escaped Nivaka before tonight? Why had he never asked? He sat and stared into the fire for what felt like hours, asking himself questions that had no answers.

Finally, exhaustion started to close his eyes, and he got up from his chair and burrowed into the blankets on the bed.

He slept fitfully, dreaming of ghosts, elves, dwarves, and invasions as his waking thoughts continued to plague him in his slumber. He woke well before the dawn and dressed, but stayed in his rooms until his friends joined him for their morning routine.

~*~

Eddrick burst through the door to their private space and grabbed his wife in a huge hug. He shouted beside her ear. "I talked to him! He saw me, and we talked!"

Kiri winced and hugged him back before she stepped

away. "Who saw you? What are you talking about?"

A huge grin spread across Eddrick's face. "Aibek! I talked to Aibek! It was incredible. He was just sitting in our bedroom, and he relaxed his mind enough to hear me." He struggled to keep his voice below a shout as the excitement threatened to consume him.

"Really? He heard you? That's wonderful! Do you think it was a one-time thing, or can I talk to him, too? When are you going to try again? I'm going with you." She asked all of her questions at once without giving him a chance to respond.

Her husband took a deep breath, held it for a few seconds, then exhaled slowly, slightly calmer. "He was in our room, just staring at the walls. I think he'll be more open to talking to us now. He even said he saw you in his room the night of the storm. He was so happy to see me that he nearly cried. I know I did after he'd left with his friends."

Kiri cradled her husband's face in her hands and smiled. "I can't believe I let you go without me."

"Next time, we'll go together."

They stood like that for a long time, laughing, hugging, and celebrating together.

~*~

You're awfully quiet this morning, sir. Is something wrong?"

"No, Serik, nothing's wrong, exactly." Aibek continued to stare out the window at the growing light. "I need to talk to Valasa this morning before the meeting. He was supposed to question the prisoner yesterday, and I never got a chance to ask him about it."

Faruz set down his mug of famanc. "What is there to ask? We caught her trying to clean a bloody knife less than an hour after Alija's attack. She's obviously guilty."

Aibek shook his head. "I'm not so sure. Wouldn't she have some blood on her dress if she'd stabbed someone? I only saw stains on her sleeve, which could be from holding the knife. Could she have been trying to dispose of the weapon to help the real attacker?"

Faruz frowned. "Hmm. I didn't look at her gown, but you could be right. Do you know if Alija saw anything?"

"No, he said he was walking toward the buffet for dessert when he felt the attack. He was at the edge of the crowd, but there were a lot of people around. Anyone could have done it. I think I'll go downstairs. Maybe Valasa's awake by now."

Serik broke in, but hesitantly. "Before you go, there's something else you should consider."

Aibek waited impatiently for his friend to complete the thought, but Serik just continued to sip his drink. "What else is there?"

"I'm not sure it's connected, but have you noticed how strangely Ahren has been behaving recently?"

Aibek laughed. "When isn't that girl acting weird? Besides, have you seen the way she looks at Alija? She hates me, but she all but worships him. I don't think she had anything to do with this." He stood and set his empty mug on the tray next to Serik, then left the room and went in search of the religious leader.

16.

Decisions

A light shone under the door of Valasa's private work-room. Aibek hovered uncertainly nearby.

Should I knock?

Valasa only went in that room when he wanted to work undisturbed. Aibek turned to leave but stopped when he heard an unexpected voice inside the room. Alija was there with Valasa. That made sense. The healer kept all his medical supplies in his workroom. Aibek knocked firmly on the heavy door.

After a moment, Valasa opened the door and smiled. He waved Aibek in, then closed the door behind him. Aibek glanced around, taking in the heavily laden shelves and stacks of papers piled on various tables. To his right, Alija laid face-down on one table, his wound exposed to the harsh light of several lamps. A neat line of sutures held the skin together.

"How does it look?" Alija glanced up and saw his friend staring.

Aibek answered honestly. "It looks good. There's no redness or signs of infection, so it should heal well. Valasa did an excellent job closing it."

Valasa added, "There's no drainage from the wound, either, and very little bleeding. As long as no fever sets in, you should be back to normal in a couple of weeks."

The healer moved back to Alija's side and smeared salve

over the exposed wound before he covered it with a clean dressing. He wound a cloth around Alija's chest to hold the bandage in place.

"That's good to hear," Alija ground out through clenched teeth as he worked himself into a sitting position.

Valasa helped the wounded man off the table. "Today will be the worst of the soreness. You'll need to take it easy and let yourself heal."

Once Alija was standing, Valasa turned his attention to Aibek, who was inspecting the titles of the books on the nearest shelf. "Now, what can I do for you this morning?"

Aibek glanced at Alija. "Were you able to question the prisoner yesterday, as you had planned? Did you learn anything useful?"

"The girl insists she's innocent, but she can't—or won't—explain how she came to possess the knife and why it was covered in blood."

Aibek barked out a humorless laugh. "That's not surprising. Of course, she won't confess. What do you think? Is she guilty? Or is she helping the one who is?"

Valasa remained quiet as he replaced his medical supplies neatly into the bag on the table, then removed the soiled bandages to a basket near the door. Finally, he looked up and met Aibek's gaze. "I think it may be too soon to say. She definitely knows more than she's saying. The girl took her time thinking through her answers yesterday."

Alija broke in. "Is it true she works for the washhouse? She may have been involved in poisoning our linens."

Aibek cocked his head and considered his friend. Where had he gotten that bit of information? It made sense that her first attempt would involve linens if she worked in the laundry.

Valasa lifted the basket of soiled rags in one hand and gestured for the younger men to precede him through the door. He waited patiently while Alija moved gingerly into the den, then said, "We need more information. I plan to ask her friends, family, and neighbors about her behavior lately. Maybe something has changed recently."

Aibek paused in the den and glanced through the large windows. The sun was already bright on the front of the house. He'd be late for the meeting. Oh, well. At least he'd have Alija with him. The two friends moved up the stairs toward the sitting room, frequently stopping for the wounded man to rest from the exertion.

~*~

Aibek strolled into the sitting room and looked around. Everyone was already there, including Valasa. The healer must have used the servants' stairs. Since they'd planned the morning's meeting, Ayja had arranged trays of muffins, cookies, and drinks arranged on a small buffet near the door.

The mayor began the day determined to observe his new friends and listen to their ideas and input, rather than trying to take charge and possibly miss something important. They knew this area and these people far better than he did and would be better able to gauge the villagers' responses to the final plan.

Valasa called the meeting to order and brought up the option of surrender. Exclamations of rejection rang through the small space. The council quickly agreed that giving up was not an option they were willing to consider, especially when they had other choices.

Valasa nodded. "We should begin by discussing the ideas presented at the town hall meeting. The villagers voted to ask our neighbors for help. As the council, you have the final say in these matters. What are your thoughts? How should we proceed?"

Aibek leaned forward in his seat, curious to hear his companions' thoughts. The idea intrigued him, but he didn't know enough about the politics of the forest to have a real opinion.

He watched as Kai nervously ran a hand over his goatee. The stocky man answered, "I don't think we'll have enough warriors without their help, and we can pledge our assistance to them if they decide to overthrow their governors later… but how would we get them here?" He looked around at his friends. "They'd need a good reason for all of their strongest men and women to leave the villages at the same time, and we can't let their governors know they're headed here—they know an army's coming."

The other members voiced their support of the plan to recruit neighboring fighters, but Valasa was noticeably silent. Aibek understood his hesitance and asked, "Is this possible? Where would we house all those people?" Slowly, thoughtfully, the large man answered. "Yes… I think it can be done. Once the rest of the homes on the square are repaired, there will be plenty of space for a large number of people." He stared out the window and said no more, though a slow smile spread across his face.

Satisfied, Aibek turned back to the council members, then jumped when the religious leader nearly shouted in apparent relief. "I can send messages to the other Gadonu by fairy, and they can extend the invitation to the villagers in such a way that the purpose is understood, but the governors aren't tipped off." He grinned. "The official invitation could be for a fall festival in

Imah, the little town by the river."

It would be great if he'd learn to use a normal volume indoors, Aibek thought as he settled back into his chair. However, it was nice to see the usually serious leader get caught up in the thrill of planning such an event.

Zifa leaned forward and flipped her long hair behind her shoulders. "How do we know when help should come? We don't know how long we have before this army shows up."

Kai answered quietly. "I think they should come as soon as the rooms are ready and repairs are completed. The sooner they're here, the more time we'll have to train together."

The Gadonu's excitement spread through the room, and the council members agreed that the invitations should go out immediately. They would call it a grand autumn reunion, and invite as many as could be spared from every village in the Tsari Forest. Most of the morning was spent working out details and writing invitations to the various villages. They had to employ some creativity to convey the message. They wanted strong, able-bodied individuals to come, but they couldn't say outright that they needed individuals who could fight.

When they'd finished that task, Alija asked if anyone had ideas for keeping the enemy out of the village. "Surely, there must be something we can do to make it harder for them to climb to the boardwalk, right?" He fastened his gaze on Aibek.

"Umm, there are a few things I learned about at the academy, plus the things we've discussed before." He stared past his friends at the floral curtains as his mind considered and rejected a hundred possibilities. "The blacksmiths are already working on spikes to line the rails," Aibek gained confidence as his ideas rushed out,

"And they've been experimenting with some heavy spiked balls that we could drop on enemy soldiers. They're trying to make them easy to move but heavy enough to be dangerous. Has anyone thought of a way to attach spikes to the trees?"

Dalan answered, "What if we used some of the sap we've collected as glue? Do you think that would be strong enough?"

All eyes turned to Valasa once again. "I think it might be. It would be worth a try."

Aibek's lips widened into a small smile. "Good. I'll ask the blacksmiths to work on spiked collars for the trees, too. What other ideas do we have?"

After a long discussion, the council broke for lunch, and everyone moved to the balcony attached to the sitting room to enjoy the sunlight and fresh air while they ate. As they enjoyed the sandwiches and cookies Ayja had provided, the friends talked of everything but the reasons for their meeting: about the autumn colors, the cool breeze, Wayra's new marriage, and the progress on the old council members' homes. Aibek avoided any mention of his parents. Mostly they joked and laughed and tried to take a break from the stress of their assignment, even if it would only last an hour or two. Alija joined in now and then, though Aibek thought he was beginning to tire.

Aibek leaned back on the bench and enjoyed watching the breeze blowing the leaves on the boardwalk below the balcony. As he watched, a few children chased the leaves and gathered them into a basket. Intrigued, he asked his friends, "Is there any part of the shadow tree that we don't use?"

Zifa answered first. "We use all of the trees. We gather the leaves when they fall. We make the autumn leaves into clothes, and the green ones that fall because of wind or storms are made into furniture or curtains."

When she paused to take a breath, Wayra jumped in with more details. "When a tree dies or branches fall, the bark is wound and carved into the decorations and designs that adorn the town, and of course the wood is used for building."

Alija interjected, "Even the roots are useful. When a tree dies, we make a small hole where the old one stood, and plant a sapling in the same place. That way, the supports for the village stay in the same place, and the roots of the old tree nourish the young one as it grows."

Dalan waited for an opening. "We make the excess sap that drips out while the wood cures into healing salves and tinctures. There is no waste."

The mayor nodded thoughtfully and smiled at his new friends. "I guess you've just explained the openings I saw in the boardwalk during the tour, the day after I arrived here. That's where an old tree died, and it's left open so the new sapling will get enough sun to come up through the gap." He stared off into the trees and wondered what else he still needed to learn.

Soon, it was time to reconvene their meeting, and the group headed back into the little room. As soon as everyone had returned, Valasa stood and addressed the council.

"We've made a great deal of progress this morning, but we have more to discuss." He looked at the mayor. "Aibek, if I'm not wrong, you were approached after last night's meeting by a villager with a less popular suggestion, weren't you?"

The mayor was a bit shocked since he had believed the others had all been inside while he was talking with the elderly citizen. He sat up a bit straighter and looked hard at the Gadonu through narrowed eyes. "Yes… someone did approach me last night. The old woman thought we should ask the dwarves and elves for help. She said they couldn't be trusted with much, but they might help by alerting us when the army enters the forest."

A collective gasp went up in the room as all the council members sat up and stared at the mayor. Before anyone could voice opposition to the idea, Aibek quickly related the portion of Serik's tale that pertained to the elves. He wanted the other council members to know that these individuals could be reasoned with and had helped at least one Nivakan before. He deliberately left out any mention of his encounters with the ground folk since his arrival.

"It would be helpful to have warning as soon as the army reaches the forest, and only they can provide that," Aibek added at the end of his tale.

While the others gaped in silent shock, Zifa jumped up and faced him, her gold eyes flashing, with both hands on her hips.

"What would ever make you think we can trust them? They try to kill us every chance they get! Why would this be any different? You've lived here for what, two months? And already you think you can change the way things have been for hundreds of years!"

Aibek watched cautiously—and somewhat curiously—as Dalan touched her on the shoulder and calmly gestured for her to sit back in her chair. The old woman had warned him that the idea wouldn't be well received. Dalan faced Zifa. "I don't know that I agree with you. I don't trust them either, but the night after Aibek arrived here, he was accidentally locked out of the village for a while at sunset."

He waited until he knew he had her attention. "When

our enemies attacked him, they waited for him to find a weapon and allowed him to arm himself. Their leader said they found no sport in fighting someone who couldn't defend himself."

Dalan looked at the mayor and took a deep breath. "They could have killed him long before we got there, had that been their aim. I've heard stories of times when they've helped our people throughout history."

Wayra shouted from his spot on the sofa next to Valasa. "This is foolishness! Zifa's right. We cannot possibly be so desperate that we are willing to ask one enemy for help defeating the other." He pointed at the Gadonu and frowned. "You can't believe they'd be willing to help us. Why should they?"

Aibek remained silent in his chair and listened closely to the council members. It made him uncomfortable to see the old friends shouting at each other. He soothed himself by thinking that they had surely disagreed before and had remained friends. He thought the idea of getting the ground folk's help had merit, but he was also the first to admit that he had a less than complete understanding of the complex relationship between the citizens on the ground and the villagers in the trees. He kept quiet about the story of his encounter with them the day of the fishing trip and was glad he had never shared that tale with anyone.

Again, Dalan answered softly, so the others had to strain to hear his words. "Remember what Helak's messenger told us? They want to cut down the shadow trees to build a city. The forest is home to the elves and dwarves, too, and I would wager they want to protect it. They just might help us if they understand the stakes."

Zifa stood again and paced back and forth in the small space. "You cannot mean to tell me you actually think this is a good idea! Who's to say they won't kill whoever goes to ask for their help? We can't trust one enemy just because we're threatened by another!"

There was silence in the room while each member of the group considered the arguments that had been presented. Finally, Kai spoke up. "I think this could work. We wouldn't be asking them to fight with us, and I see no harm in asking the elves and dwarves to alert us when Helak's army reaches the border of the forest. Some advance warning would be helpful."

Valasa's booming voice startled Aibek again as he broke the brief silence. "Let's take a break and gather our thoughts, and when we return, we'll have a vote."

The council members milled about for several minutes, eating and drinking from the trays that had been refreshed by a servant while they debated. Even Alija stood and moved gingerly toward the food. Aibek watched him as he wandered through the room. He thought Alija had gotten paler during the afternoon. He hoped this wasn't too much excitement for the wounded man. Valasa had advised him to rest today.

No one spoke or left the room; they simply stood, ate, and paced until it was time to return to their seats and cast their votes.

"All right, let's vote." The Gadonu reconvened the meeting without fanfare. "We will move around the room and give simply a 'yea' or 'nay' answer to the suggestion of asking the elves and dwarves to alert us when Helak's army enters the forest." He turned to the only other person on the sofa. "Wayra?"

The lanky newlywed shook his head vigorously as he shouted his answer. "Nay."

Valasa continued to the next chair, where the mayor sat, watching the proceedings with interest. "Aibek?"

"I don't think I should vote on this. I want to hear the will of the council."

The Gadonu nodded once and continued his circuit of the room. "Dalan?"

he gave his answer as calmly and quietly as his arguments earlier. "Yea."

Once again, Valasa's resonant voice urged an answer from the next member. "Zifa?"

"Nay," she responded flatly.

Alija spoke without waiting to be called upon, and with a firm, "yea," his vote was cast.

Valasa turned to the last member. "Yours is the deciding vote, Kai. What do you think?"

"Yea," the stocky man stared hard at a point on the floor as he continued, "I think we can use all the help we can get. If we can have a little notice that the enemy has arrived, it will give us an advantage."

Valasa addressed the group. "I think you've made the best possible decisions today. This solution of asking the elves and dwarves to warn us of our enemy's arrival is ideal since it doesn't ask them to do too much."

He looked around at the new council. "A small group of four or five people should address their leaders directly. I suggest you send Serik as one of this party since he has negotiated with them before." He turned and strode from the room, leaving the council members staring after him long after the door had closed.

Aibek stood and looked at the rest of the group. "I think those who voted in favor of this plan should be the ones to carry it out, except for Alija." He looked at the pale young man who had leaned back against the cushions of his chair. "You need a few more days of rest. I will accompany the group to Kasanto, and we'll ask Serik to come along as well. Does anyone object to this plan?" No one did, and he continued. "Then I suppose we're done for today." He swallowed against the knot of unease in his stomach. "Those of us going to Kasanto should meet here first thing in the morning, then the whole council will meet after lunch to discuss the outcome of the meeting with the ground leaders. Thank you all for your input today."

When the mayor finished speaking, the council members stood and began to file slowly from the room. They kept their eyes on the floor and walked silently down the hall. Aibek waited with Alija while the others left the room, then helped the wounded man to his feet and down the stairs.

17.

Kasanto

Once he'd helped Alija to bed, Aibek went in search of his oldest friend and advisor. He found the quiet old man enjoying the sunlight on a bench in Valasa's courtyard. Serik sat quite still and stared into the forest beyond the village. Aibek sank on the seat next to him and touched his frail shoulder to gain his attention before speaking.

"The council decided to ask the ground folk for help. We want you to come with us to their village since you have a history with their leaders. Will you come?"

They sat in silence for a while, and Aibek wondered if he would get an answer when Serik finally spoke.

"I thought you might ask—I heard the whisperings of the trees. I would be honored to join your group. You have done very well so far, learning the ways of this village and these people. You've taken your time and let the people know you care about them." The old man turned tearful eyes toward his charge. "I think your father would have been proud of the man you have become. I know I am."

When he had finished speaking, the old man stood and moved swiftly toward the house. Aibek was astonished—yet again—that someone so old could move so quickly.

Aibek sat and stared after Serik for a long while. The servant had never been talkative and had generally remained a silent fixture throughout the mayor's child-hood. He'd probably spoken more since they'd embarked on the journey back to Nivaka than in all the years leading up to their departure. He'd certainly never been emotional or demonstrative, and the unusual display of emotion clutched at Aibek's heart. At the same time, he wondered what the old man meant about the trees whispering, but dismissed it with a shrug.

Sometimes old folks say the strangest things.

He was deep in thought and enjoying the sunshine on the bench, so he jumped when Ahren suddenly asked, "May I sit with you?"

His head whipped around, but he calmly replied, "Sure. It's a nice day to be outside."

She lowered herself to the bench beside him. "I heard that the meeting was pretty rough this morning."

"Um… it got a little heated, but I don't think it was too bad." He considered asking about her connections to Tamyr. Ahren had spent a great deal of time with the woman before her capture.

Before he could ask, Ahren blurted out, "You know; you might have better luck if you listen to the others more."

Aibek's brow furrowed, and he glanced sideways at the lovely young woman. "What do you mean?"

"Look, I know you have your own ideas about what's best for the village, but it'll all go smoother if you listen to people who've lived here all their lives."

Incredulous, the mayor stood to face her. "What are you talking about?" He remained as calm as he could. "I've done nothing but listen to everyone else. I haven't tried to 'take over' anything, or whatever it is you're accusing me of this time."

Ahren looked up to meet his gaze. "Are you saying you didn't sit in there and talk everyone into doing something they didn't want to do? I know my friends, and they would never choose to go talk to our enemies."

"I didn't bring up going to Kasanto, I didn't participate in the debate, and I didn't vote on it. The decision was made solely by the council."

She jumped up and faced him with her eyes flashing. "It sounds to me like you're just looking for someone else to blame for your bad ideas."

Aibek shook his head and walked toward the edge of the boardwalk. He pressed his fingertips to his temples and tried to see things from her twisted perspective.

He turned back toward her and said, "I don't know what to say to you. I didn't vote or discuss it; the council made the decision without my input. Your father was the one who brought up asking the elves and dwarves for help."

Neither spoke for several minutes. Aibek wondered again if he could ask her about the prisoner, then dismissed the idea. She'd never give him any useful information—at least not while she was angry. Finally, Ahren heaved a great sigh and stormed into the house. Aibek sat on the bench and wondered what had just happened. *Did one of the council members talk to her and blame me for everything? Or did she hear that they were going to the ground village and decide it was my fault?*

His mind wandered again over all the events of the previous two days until a cold breeze blew across the courtyard. He looked up and was surprised to see the clouds painted a brilliant orange. Another day had ended, and he still wasn't any closer to figuring out who had stabbed Alija. Maybe after dinner, he'd go and question the prisoner. She probably wouldn't give him any real answers, but it was worth a try. Another cold breeze ruffled his hair, and he rose and turned toward the rear door of the house.

Shivering from yet another blast of cold wind, he made his way into the den, where he found Dalan admiring the sword Aibek's uncle Noral had given him back in Xona. He had removed it from its scabbard and rubbed a cloth down the gleaming blade and over the intricate basket hilt that was designed to protect the swordsman's hand.

Dalan turned to his new friend, who settled himself into one of the comfortable chairs near the fireplace. "Will you bring this to Kasanto? It's a beautiful sword."

"I hadn't thought about it until now, but wouldn't it be better to go unarmed? If we're hoping to reason with them, we shouldn't look like we want a fight. I think I'll leave it here."

Dalan re-sheathed the blade and set the sword aside. "That makes sense, I guess." He paused. "We'll go unarmed, then. I can't pretend that doesn't make me a little uneasy, but you're right—we shouldn't go looking like we're ready for a fight."

The two men talked on about the upcoming trip to the ground village until Faruz joined them. He'd spent the day with some of his new friends. Alija seated himself nearby and announced his intention to return to his home that evening after dinner.

Dalan looked concerned. "Don't you think you should spend another day or two here? It's barely been two days since your injury."

Alija smiled. "I'm sure. It isn't a very serious wound, and I'll be back to normal in no time. In fact, Valasa said it would be fine if I go with you to Kasanto tomorrow." He beamed as the others gaped at him.

Aibek shook his head. "That…might…not be such a great idea. You looked pretty worn out after sitting in on today's meeting."

"I don't know what you're talking about! I was fine. I only lay down after the meeting to keep Valasa happy. He told me to take it easy today."

I think he's actually enjoying my discomfort, Aibek thought. Is this a joke? Surely he can't mean to hike through the forest in the morning.

"Besides," Alija added, "We're just walking to their village, then walking home, right? I'll be able to keep up, as long as there's no fighting."

Dalan agreed, though his voice was hesitant, "Well, if you think you're ready, then I guess we can't stop you."

"We won't think less of you if you take the time to heal. You don't have to push yourself," Aibek blurted out. "We already know you're tough."

Alija laughed heartily for a long moment, and Aibek joined in, though his laugh came out awkward and forced. After another moment, Dalan and Faruz dissolved in laughter, too.

A moment later, Ayja appeared in the doorway and announced that supper was ready. The friends filed eagerly into the informal dining nook and took their seats around the table. They chatted cheerfully through the evening meal, then Aibek excused himself, grabbed a lantern from the table near the door, and slipped out into the night, while Dalan and Faruz accompanied Alija back to his house at the other end of the Square.

The moons Koviom and Ilodus were bright overhead, and Thrimanca hovered near the horizon. Together, they lit the boardwalk almost as effectively as the sun, and Aibek extinguished his lamp. He made his way across the Square to the house that served as the prison, shoved the heavy door open, and climbed the narrow stair on his right.

Lanterns lined the wall, casting a bright, cheerful glow

over the green-painted stairwell. Aibek climbed to the third floor and tapped on the door at the top of the stairs. The dark wooden door swung open with a slight creak, and the broad form of the guard appeared, silhouetted in the bright light from the room behind him.

He blocked the way. "Only one visitor at a time."

Aibek took a step backward, surprised. "Someone else is here? Who else is visiting the prisoner?"

"That's all right, we're finished," a soft, feminine voice came from inside the room, a breath before a small form rushed past Aibek and down the stairs. She had a dark cloak pulled close around her face, so Aibek couldn't tell who the visitor had been.

"Well, I guess you can come in, then," the guard said, pulling the door open farther.

"Do you keep a record of who's coming to see this woman?" Aibek asked as he stepped into the narrow room.

He glanced around at the bright yellow walls and high windows. An iron-barred cell covered the length of the far wall, and a woman huddled in the back corner. The fireplace beside the door blazed, heating the room to an uncomfortable warmth, and the odor of sweat and unwashed bodies permeated the space. Aibek suppressed a grimace. Couldn't they open a window or two? The windows lined the wall along the ceiling, but the tall guard should have been able to reach them.

"No, sir, no one ever suggested we should keep any records," the guard said awkwardly, his face flushed. "Do you want us to start?"

"Yes, that would be helpful." Aibek marched over to the bars. Someone had placed a chair near the cell for visitors, and Aibek dropped onto it, leaning forward to peer into the small enclosure.

"Has she been allowed to wash?" Aibek asked the guard, who hovered near his shoulder.

The burly man cocked his head to the side, frowning. "No, sir. No one's suggested that, either. I'm afraid I'm not doing a very good job. Tavan's guards always had this duty. I've never done it before this week."

"No, you're doing fine," Aibek reassured him. "She's safe and secure, and she can't get away. Those are the most important things. Could I have a moment to speak with her in private?"

"Of course, Mister Mayor," the guard stammered, then rushed out of the small room. The door closed with a creak and a click, and Aibek turned his attention to the woman in the cell.

"I'll have one of the women bring you soap and water in the morning."

"Don't bother being nice. I won't tell you anything," Tamyr spat.

Aibek nodded. He'd expected her anger. "Regardless, you deserve to have your basic needs met. I trust you're getting enough to eat? And plenty of water?"

She answered sullenly, "They're feeding me just fine."

She sat in the farthest corner from him, her back to the wall and her knees drawn up to her chest. Her skirts hung limply around her ankles, exposing her dirty bare feet to the light.

"I know you didn't do it," Aibek murmured.

She stiffened, and her eyes went wide before she dropped her forehead to her knees. She sat in silence for a long moment, and Aibek wondered if she would answer.

He waited a while longer and added, "You didn't stab Alija, but you know who did, don't you?"

She heaved a noisy sigh, then dissolved in loud tears.

Her sobbing discomforted Aibek, and he glanced around for something to offer her. He hadn't brought a handkerchief, and he didn't see anything else in the room that would be helpful. He frowned at the sobbing woman, trying to figure out if her tears were genuine or a ploy to get him to leave.

She continued for several minutes until his patience wore out. "All right, that's enough. You won't get out of here that way."

She sniffed and looked up sharply, her watery eyes finally meeting his. "We both know I'm not getting out of here at all," she wailed.

"That's not true." He barked a short laugh. "We certainly won't keep you in this tiny cell forever. We don't have the manpower to keep you guarded indefinitely."

She gave him a hard look and wiped her hands over her wet cheeks.

"Honestly, I know you didn't do it, so why don't you tell me who did, and we'll get you out of this miserable place and into a nice, hot bath."

"Do you really think I'd betray my friends for a bath?" She jumped up and stalked closer to where he sat. "Why should I talk to you? You think since they made you mayor that I'll just fall at your feet? You don't belong here, and your friends have no business pretending to rule this village."

The venom in her voice surprised Aibek a little. She'd switched from tears to anger with stunning speed. He frowned, recognizing a marked similarity between her attitude and Ahren's.

"If you think the council shouldn't rule, then who should? Who should protect this town and take care of the people?"

"Helak!" She spat. "Tavan was doing a fine job before

those fools interfered. But now he's dead and everything is ruined!" She slumped back against the wall and dissolved into tears again, though this time she kept them silent.

Aibek had nothing to say to that. It was the first time anyone had voiced that sentiment aloud in his earshot, though he'd gotten the same message in a note on the night of his welcome banquet. Surely she wasn't serious. From the stories he'd heard, Tavan had been a brutal governor and a strict taskmaster. Aibek stood and moved slowly toward the door, then turned back to the weeping woman.

"It really isn't that bad, if you'd just give us a chance." She didn't respond, and he opened the door, nodded to the guard, then moved swiftly down the stairs and back to Valasa's home. He'd have to find Valasa and see what could be done about providing clean clothes and soap for the prisoner. They couldn't keep her locked up without taking proper care of her, even if she had tried to kill off the council.

~*~

Alone in his room a short time later, Aibek tried to remember the events that had led up to his meeting with his father's spirit. What exactly had he been doing? He desperately wanted to get to know his parents, but he had no idea how to talk to them.

"Are you there?" He asked the empty room.

He stood against the wall and held his breath while he waited to hear something. He waited so long the room spun, so he exhaled in a great rush and chided himself for being foolish. He wasn't entirely sure he hadn't dreamed the encounter, so standing here talking to the walls probably wouldn't help. Maybe he could try again once he moved into the new house.

~*~

The next morning, Aibek, Dalan, and Serik waited for the others near the south entrance to the village. The brisk autumn morning made Aibek shiver as a cold wind blew through the trees. The sun shone overhead but did little to warm the air. A few puffy clouds dotted the brilliant blue sky, a lovely contrast to the vibrant yellow and orange leaves of the treetops. They didn't wait very long before Aibek spotted Alija and Kai walking toward them, each with a sword in hand. Alija moved much easier, and even had a spring in his step as he approached the waiting friends. Aibek realized at that moment that he hadn't told the others about their decision to go unarmed.

He welcomed the friends before anyone else could comment. "Good morning. I trust you slept well. Are we ready to head down?" He pulled the lever and released the catch to lower the staircase but stopped when Kai pointed to Dalan's unadorned waist.

"Where's your sword?"

Dalan fidgeted with his sleeve. "We thought it might be best to go unarmed, so it doesn't look like we're expecting a fight."

Kai looked around him and glanced from Aibek to Alija before he responded. "Hmm... I hadn't considered that. I wouldn't have thought to approach our enemies without a sword, but it does look rather aggressive, doesn't it?"

Alija quietly agreed, and both friends removed their swords and placed them under a bench near the entrance. As soon as that was done, the group descended the stairs and headed into the forest. They all whispered among themselves as they followed the same path they had taken to the lake when they went fishing.

The trees thinned enough there that brush could grow along the path. The colors of autumn were nearly at their peak, and everywhere he looked Aibek saw brilliant reds, yellows, and oranges in the shrubs and trees around them. Trees were rare in Xona, so he had never seen such a display and was impressed with the beauty surrounding them. Before they had gone very far, Aibek realized someone was following them. Twigs snapped in the brush beside the path, and an eerie quiet reigned in the forest: no birds chirped; no small animals chattered. Aibek glanced at Serik, who nodded in encouragement.

"We know you're there, and we mean you no harm," the mayor shouted. "We wish to speak to your leaders on an urgent matter."

The group of friends stood still on the path and waited for a response from the enemies hiding in the underbrush. They stood bunched together for a breathless moment until several fierce-looking elves exited the brush and stalked toward them from the north. They wore the colors of the woods, with bright leaves attached to their clothes and hats. One carried a bow and quiver of arrows on his back, and the others bore axes or staffs. Aibek wondered if he had made the wrong decision in leaving their swords behind. He'd left his friends exposed and vulnerable, and now they were surrounded by armed enemies.

The two groups faced each other for long, tense moments before one of the elves stepped forward. He stood about three feet tall, slender but with well-defined muscles on his bare arms. His bronze skin gleamed in the sunlight, and his leaf-adorned cap hid his hair.

"Our leaders will see you. We thank you for not bringing weapons since we could not have allowed you to bring them into our village. Please come with us."

He spun on his heel and walked to the right, through the brush and to another, narrower path nearby. They continued south, walking parallel to the walkway they had been using, moving in the direction of the lake. Aibek thought this looked like the trail he had been on when he got lost the day of the fishing trip, but he couldn't be sure. He searched for anything familiar as they moved through the woods.

Soon, Aibek heard the sound of the waves gently lapping the banks and knew they were near the lake, though he couldn't see it through the dense shrubbery. Then they turned abruptly west onto another hidden path and continued toward a wall of vegetation.

Their guides moved aside a curtain of vines, then led them through a gate hidden in the wall. Suddenly, they were in a quaint little town. Most of the houses were small, with thatched roofs and stone chimneys. Little benches sat in front of many of the homes, and the whole place looked welcoming and homey. Aibek felt like a giant, since he was as tall as most of the buildings, and he wondered where they would meet the leaders of this village. He remembered that Serik had described a room, so he hoped there would be a building large enough to hold them all. Everywhere he looked, elves and dwarves gaped at the group of strangers in their midst.

The party from the treetops waited in the center of town for a short while as the midday sun beat down from overhead. The walk had taken longer than Aibek expected. He tried to smile at the frightened-looking ground folk while he waited but gave up when the locals retreated further behind the trees and buildings. Finally, their guides returned and wordlessly gestured for the friends to follow.

They followed the elves through a smaller gate at the other end of the village, and toward a door that led into the ground beneath an enormous shadow tree. Aibek looked around at his friends, uncomfortable with the idea of going unarmed into a cave behind their enemy's village, but Serik looked unruffled and nodded slightly.

They descended a steep packed-dirt staircase into a narrow tunnel. Torches mounted every few feet along the wall lit small circles of the dirt-floored path, but Aibek thought he heard the distant echo of trickling water. Their chaperons moved swiftly through the dimness and Aibek had to be careful not to trip and fall on the uneven ground. The walls were only a few feet apart, and Aibek experienced the panicky feeling of claustrophobia for the first time. He could touch both sides of the dark tunnel without stretching out his arms, and he had to walk stooped to avoid hitting his head on the rocks above.

Their guides, oblivious to the visitors' discomfort, moved at ease through the passageway and soon led them into a large, brightly lit room. The walls and floor were smooth stone that sparkled like millions of diamonds in the lamplight. A small stream wound its way through one side of the space, fed by a narrow waterfall that trickled down the wall opposite the doorway where they stood.

The visitors stood blinking in the sudden brightness of the room. Once he had adjusted to the unexpected light, Aibek stared mutely at the long, white stone table in the center of the room. At one end sat an elf more plainly dressed than those they had met in the forest. Next to him was a dwarf dressed elaborately in fur-lined purple zontrec. Aibek swallowed against a knot of unease. He took a breath to introduce himself, but the regal dwarf spoke first.

"I am Idril, the queen of the Dwarves and ruler of Kasanto. Serik I have met before. Who are the rest of you?"

Aibek stepped forward and gave a brief introduction of each member of their party. They stood awkwardly in the doorway after their guides left them, unwilling to come further into the room without an invitation.

After a moment, the elf spoke. "We were told you have a matter to discuss with us. I am Turan, the king of the elves. Idril and I rule this village and the ground level of the Tsari Forest. What has brought you to seek our counsel?"

Aibek stepped farther into the room and addressed Turan. "I am sure you are aware that Nivaka has overthrown Helak's brutal government and has re-established a council."

He waited for some response from the smallfolk. When they remained silent, he continued, "I am Aibek, the son of Eddrick, and I have returned to help the village fight for a more permanent peace. Our enemy is sending an army to regain control of our home."

He couldn't help but notice the bored looks on his hosts' faces. Desperately, he went on, "His ultimate plan is to cut down the Shadow trees and make them into lumber to build a city in the desert. We are here today to ask for your assistance. We would like for you to alert our village when the army enters the forest, so we can be ready to fight. Will you help us?"

The king and queen whispered between themselves, leaving their visitors standing in the doorway while they discussed the request. Finally, Turan spoke again. "Please, come sit, and we will discuss this matter in detail. We were indeed aware that your village had disposed of the appointed governor and his guards, but what makes you think an army is coming, or that they would want to cut down the forest?"

This time Dalan answered, walking toward the table as he spoke, "My father is the Gadonu and has received messages from our neighboring villages. The guards stationed in those villages are saying that an army is preparing to enter the forest and re-establish control over Nivaka. As for the rest, Helak's messengers were bragging to us about how they plan to cut the trees to build a fire-proof city, and how easy it would be to transport because the wood is so light."

The visitors all took places at the end of the table farthest from the king and queen. As they were seating themselves at the table, Kai whispered to Alija, who was sitting next to him, "They aren't going to help us. I knew this would be a waste of time."

"What was that you said?" Idril frowned and stared hard at the two Nivakans. "If you believed you were wasting your time, why did you come in the first place?"

Kai apologized. "Forgive me, madam; I meant no disrespect. I had hoped to win your assistance this morning, but I'm afraid you won't help us."

She looked around at the others gathered at the table. "You would do well to remember that things are not always as they seem. Do the rest of you believe you are wasting your time? Are you ready to leave already?"

Dalan answered firmly. "We're not ready to leave yet, madam. We would greatly appreciate your assistance. Early warning of our enemy's approach would give us a substantial advantage. Please, can we count on your support?"

Turan stared hard at the young man. "You speak boldly for one who is begging your sworn enemy for help. Is this how you normally conduct your business?"

Aibek stood before the conversation could devolve any further. He nodded to their hosts in a show of deference. "Please forgive my companions. Emotions are running high, and we seek help from any available avenue. You helped save me once before, and we will be forever grateful if you will assist us once again. Will you please help us?"

As soon as he finished speaking, Aibek took his seat once again and waited for a response. The tension in the room was palpable as the king and queen stared at their visitors in silence.

"What exactly do you want us to do?" The elf king asked with a thoughtful air. "You surely do not expect me to send my people into your village."

Aibek answered respectfully, keeping his eyes on the table. "No sir, we would hang a lamp at the south end of town and one at the north end and would ask you to light these lamps when the army has entered the forest. Your network is vast, and you gather information about the entire Tsari quickly. This simple alert would give our warriors time to prepare to fight."

He wondered what their hosts could be thinking as they looked from face to face around the room.

It was Turan who finally spoke. "I do not think we can agree to anything today. Please come back and visit soon. We have much to discuss, but I believe we are finished for today." His gaze bored into Aibek's. "Please leave your friends at home the next time."

Having apparently lost interest in his visitors, the elf king turned and began talking to Idril about how colorful the leaves were this year.

The Nivakans stood and trudged to the door, and their escorts led them back through the village and to the main trail. No one spoke, but everyone appeared disappointed in the outcome of their visit. They walked quickly back to Nivaka. The sun was beginning its descent toward the horizon when they reached the southern entrance. Just before they re-entered the village, Aibek asked if anyone needed to meet with the rest of the council for discussion. No one did, and they went their separate ways once inside Nivaka. Aibek thought Alija had held up quite well during the day, but the wounded man looked tired and pale as he shuffled toward his home.

18.

Fairies

Aibek watched his new friends disperse within the borders of the village, then he retreated down the stairs they had ascended a few minutes earlier. The weight of the day's failure crushed him, making breathing difficult, and he sank onto the bottom step. He cradled his head in his hands and wondered what to do as the frustration of the past few days settled on him like a heavy cloak. He had let down his friends. He should have been able to convince the ground rulers to help them. If they were going to have a chance to win, they needed a warning that the army was near. Deep down, he knew that if they lost, no other villages in the Tsari would attempt to win their freedom.

Then there was the issue of the prisoner. Aibek was confident the girl wasn't the one who had attacked Alija, but she was protecting whoever had.

What am I missing? Have the other council members visited the woman? Have they gotten any more information than me? Who was the woman who visited the prisoner last night?

He stood and wandered down the path through the dimly lit wood, kicking at stones as he went. He relived the entirety of their visit to Kasanto in his mind and realized that things had only gone sour after Kai's whispered lament. He had offended the queen and ended the day's discussion. Aibek fought against the tide of anger that rose in him and tried to remember that Kai had only reluctantly agreed to ask their enemy for help.

Ultimately, the fate of the entire forest depended on the outcome of this one battle. If no one fought against Helak, the dictator would cut down the most cherished trees in the wood for his own plans.

He stayed in the dim solitude of the forest for what seemed an eternity, wishing for someone to guide him or tell him that things weren't as bad as he thought. He watched the leaves blowing in circles on the ground and listened to the rustle of branches overhead, then inhaled the earthy scent of the forest. It was a salve to his soul, so he repeated the exercise and let the calm of the Tsari seep into his being.

Finally, the deepening shadows forced the mayor to return to the warmth and safety of the village. There was still much to be done. Besides, the king had said they had more to discuss. Maybe there was hope, after all. Perhaps the king had simply been upset by his friends' behavior. He decided to find Serik and see what he thought of the visit.

Re-energized, Aibek bounded up the stairs and into the village. He secured the entrance and went in search of his oldest friend. He found Serik in Valasa's courtyard, on the same bench where Aibek had found him yesterday.

He cleared his throat and laid a hand on his dear friend's frail shoulder. "Well, that didn't go as well as I'd hoped."

"No, it didn't go well at all."

Aibek waited for more, then said, "What should we do now? They said there was more to discuss. Should we go back without the others?"

Serik finally opened his eyes and looked at his companion. "Yes, I think that is exactly what we should do. Your friends need to learn when to keep their thoughts to themselves."

Aibek nodded, and they agreed to return to Kasanto later in the week without the rest of the group.

They sat in comfortable silence and listened to the chirping of a brilliant red bird until it flew away, then went to check on the progress of the mayoral home on the square. They found the work progressing quickly and were pleased with what they saw. Aibek wanted to visit his parents' room once again but ultimately thought it best not to disturb the workers. Instead, they wandered through to the courtyard and discussed the events of the day until it was time to return for the evening meal. Aibek's stomach rumbled. The king and queen had offered them no food or drinks during their visit, and no one had thought to take any with them.

~*~

While their friends were visiting Kasanto, Faruz and Wayra agreed to accompany Ahren and Zifa on their errands in the village. They began the day gathering leaves with a large, noisy party of villagers. Ahren had told Faruz the workers would make the fallen leaves into zontrec, which the seamstresses would then turn into upholstery and curtains, as well as clothing for the villagers.

He was enjoying the energy of the group as they all laughed and joked with each other. Faruz basked in the joy of being included as one of the locals in such a fashion, and he wondered if he would ever want to leave and go back to the city. He thought he just might stay here forever.

As he worked alongside Ahren, he decided this was the

perfect time for a long-awaited discussion. He kept his hands busy gathering leaves while he searched for the right words.

"Why did you hate us so much when we got here, anyway? What did Aibek do that made you so angry?"

The white-haired girl flushed bright red, dropped her head and said, "I thought he was just another stranger coming to take over and control our lives."

Her voice was so low that he had to strain to hear her answer, then she began gathering leaves again with renewed energy. He wanted to ask if she knew anything about the attacks on the council, but before he could, she stood and rushed over to where Zifa was working on the other side of the clearing. The rest of the morning passed quickly as they all worked to gather and prepare the leaves for storage.

When they'd finished gathering and washing the leaves, Faruz and the others returned home for lunch. As they were eating a cold meal of autumn squash and leftover fowl, Valasa approached them with an assignment for the afternoon. A fairy had fallen ill and he needed them to take a vial of medicine to her. Faruz was intrigued; he'd never seen where the fairies lived and had never considered that they might get sick like anyone else. The Gadonu handed the tiny ampule to his daughter, and they promised to take it to the ill fairy as soon as they finished eating.

Faruz couldn't remember anyone mentioning the fairies' homes before, and he was sure he'd never seen any tiny houses. "Where do the fairies live, anyway? Are they near here?"

Zifa looked up at him and smiled. "They live in little cottages suspended from the branches in the very top of the trees. To get it to them, we'll use a hoist to raise someone up to them. Ahren will probably go up since she's the smallest and lightest of our group."

The others nodded in agreement, and the friends continued their meal in comfortable silence.

Faruz tried to picture this and failed. He shrugged and decided he'd see it for himself soon enough. He thought that dangling from a rope above the boardwalk could be fun, but also quite dangerous.

When they had finished eating, they shuffled out the door to complete the assigned task. The group headed to the north end of the village, talking and laughing as they went. After a few minutes trying to get Zifa's attention, Faruz touched her lightly on the arm and leaned in close to point out a pair of small monkeys playing in the branches of a tree at the edge of the boardwalk.

She turned in the direction he pointed and laughed, "Look how funny they are! I haven't stopped to watch them in ages."

She smiled and looked up, then realized that Ahren and Wayra hadn't stopped with them. She straightened quickly and hurried to catch up to her friends, though she was still smiling. He followed at a somewhat slower pace and wondered what she thought of him. She was so serious most of the time; her smile had been like a rare ray of sunshine lighting up her face. He hoped he could coax more smiles from her during the afternoon.

After a short walk towards the west end of town, Ahren turned and pointed to a platform about ten feet above the park where they stood.

"Here we are!" Zifa announced with another blinding smile.

Faruz stared until she turned away, then followed her gaze into the trees.

A ladder attached to a nearby tree led up to a narrow

platform. Without waiting to see if the others would follow, Ahren nimbly made her way to the top. The rest of the group scrambled up after her, and in a few minutes, everyone stood on the structure above the boardwalk.

"Now comes the hard part," Ahren said. "One of us has to climb the tree and attach our rope to the hook hanging from the hoist."

She pointed to a hook secured to the trunk of a tree another fifteen feet above them. Faruz tilted his head back to peer into the tops of the trees, then felt a little dizzy and focused his eyes on the wood at his feet.

"The fairies keep it up high, so children don't climb up and bother them. They like their privacy," she explained. Zifa volunteered, "I'll do it. I've done it several times before."

She started climbing the nearest branches before anyone could answer. Faruz realized this must be why the women here wore pants as often as they wore dresses—so they could climb the trees without getting tangled in yards of fabric.

He watched, enthralled, as Zifa swung gracefully to the hook, freed it from where it was anchored to the tree and attached it to their rope. She released the other end of the line, and it extended just past the top of Faruz's head. When she finished the task, she shimmied down the rope to the platform where the others waited.

Wayra clapped her on the back when she landed on the wooden floor. "Well done! I've seen you do that before, but it's always amazing to watch. Excellent job!"

Faruz echoed his praise, but she shook her head. "I never took an interest in learning to sing and dance and sew like all of the other girls. My mother all but gave up on me because I always preferred to be outside climbing trees. We live in this wonderful place where we're surrounded by branches and trees that are perfect for climbing. Why not enjoy them?" She grinned shyly and looked up through her lashes at him.

Faruz thought she sounded a little defensive and wondered at the reason. He thought she looked graceful and lovely swinging from the trees. Her strength, confidence, and coordination were impressive.

While they were talking, Ahren strapped herself into the harness, clipped it onto the end of the rope and held up the other end. "Who wants to pull me up?"

Wayra stepped up and took the rope from her hand. "Ready?"

Ahren replied with a grin. "I'm ready whenever you are."

Wayra immediately started pulling his end of the rope, hoisting her into the air as the others watched.

Faruz watched their progress for a while, then peered up into the trees. This time, he focused on individual branches and small details to ward off the dizziness. He'd never seen a fairy house before, and he wanted to see what they looked like. It took several moments of hard searching before he could make out the shapes of the tiny homes suspended among the treetops. They looked like elaborate birdhouses, except that they had doors instead of perches.

They were clustered close together on the branches and held apart from one another by wooden rods attached to the bases. One house had a tiny lantern lit outside the door, and it was this home that apparently held the ill fairy. As he watched, Ahren reached the house and tapped gently on the door with one finger. She waited until a little person opened the door and took the vial from her. He couldn't hear what was said, but the fairy appeared to thank her and closed the door gently as she went back inside. Ahren signaled for Wayra to lower her back down.

When he looked down again, Faruz noticed Zifa watching him intently.

"I forget sometimes that this is all new to you. Fairies are forest creatures, and you grew up in the city. Had you ever seen one before you came here?"

"No, I honestly thought they only existed in the bedtime stories my mother told me when I was young." He gave a little laugh. "I've seen a great deal here that's new to me. I don't know if I'll ever be able to go back to city life after this."

"Is that your plan?" She looked down at her feet.

"It was at first. I had no idea how wonderful this place is, or how quickly I would feel like I belong here." He was a little concerned by the sadness he saw on her face, so he tried to change the subject. "What about you? What are your plans?" He tried to hold her gaze as he asked.

"I don't know." She glanced at her friend descending through the trees and fidgeted with the ribbon at her waist. "Most girls dream of starting a family and taking over the duties of a retiring seamstress or cook." She gave a short, mirthless laugh. "I've always wanted something more than that. I want to fight along with the men to save our home. I refuse to be shuffled away somewhere 'safe' to wait and wonder what's happening. After that, I don't know."

Faruz frowned. "Is there some rule against women becoming warriors here? In Xona, there were several women in my class at the academy. They're accepted as outstanding officers and fight alongside the men to defend the city."

"I don't think there's a rule against it. For hundreds of

years, there haven't been any warriors here at all, but everyone thinks it's the men's job."

She kept her eyes on Ahren's descent, though he wished she would meet his eyes.

"I'm sure you aren't the only one who feels this way," he reassured her. "It's a good thing you're on the council, so you can be an example for others who want to protect their homes. Aibek said the other villages will likely send women, too, so you won't be alone."

Just as he finished speaking, Ahren reached the platform, and Zifa rushed over to her friend. She stayed near Ahren for the rest of the afternoon.

As they walked back to the square, Ahren told the group the fairy had said she wasn't sick. The tiny person had been injured by one of Helak's men in another village when she was returning with a message for Valasa. Zifa wondered aloud if they had lost any critical information – or any fairies – that way. They discussed this possibility briefly but finished the walk in silence. It had been an eventful day. Faruz was pleased to see that Aibek and Dalan were in the den when he entered the house. He had a great deal to discuss with his friend but thought it would have to wait until they could be alone after supper.

~*~

Zifa came in with Ahren and stayed through the meal. It had been a very long time since they'd had a sleepover, and she thought it was time to resume the habit. The two friends left the men in the main room as soon as they finished eating and went to Ahren's sitting room. They'd been best friends since they were toddlers, but they hadn't had much time to themselves lately. Zifa led the way in and plopped down on the fluffy sofa in the center of the room. Her friend followed more slowly, pausing to close the door behind her before lowering herself to the armchair near the couch. They chatted amiably for a while about everything that had been happening, including the marriage of their two close friends.

Zifa sighed. "I wonder if I'll ever get married."

"I'm sure you will. It won't be long before one of these buffoons realizes how gorgeous you are."

Zifa laughed. "You're right. Maybe one of the men coming from the other villages."

"Or maybe one that's already here," Ahren hinted. At her friend's confused look, she continued, "What about Faruz? I've seen the way he looks at you."

"He's funny, but I don't know if he's even going to stay here. Honestly, I don't think he knows what he's going to do yet. I'm not willing to leave Nivaka, so we'll just have to wait and see."

They both chuckled and talked some more about the local men, their strengths and foibles. After a while, Ahren remembered the trip some of the council members had taken today. "I wonder how the visit to Kasanto went."

"I don't know. No one said anything when we came in. I hope it went well. I feel really bad about the way things went in that meeting yesterday."

Ahren looked incredulous. "Why would you feel bad about it? It wasn't your fault Aibek tried to convince everyone to make nice with our enemies."

"What?" Zifa frowned. "That's not what happened. Your father told us a villager suggested we try to get the ground folk to help us, and we all voted. Aibek said he didn't know enough to participate and didn't debate or vote on it."

Ahren fell back against the cushions and heaved an

enormous sigh. "Oh. Why do I keep making myself look like a total fool where he's concerned?"

"What do you mean? What happened?" Zifa prodded gently.

"I heard a group was going, and I assumed it was his fault. I got angry that he was putting my friends in danger, and I said something to him about it. He probably thinks I'm a complete idiot."

Zifa tried to reassure her. "I doubt that. He probably thinks you're concerned about your friends." She paused as another thought occurred to her. "Speaking of friends, weren't you getting pretty close to that Tamyr girl, before she got caught? You didn't get involved in her scheming, did you?"

Ahren flushed and looked away. "Tamyr's innocent. She didn't stab Alija."

"What about the rest? Wayra said she all but confessed to poisoning the council members' bed linens. And what else is she planning? Tell me you haven't gotten involved with her plans." Zifa grabbed her friend's shoulders and shook her gently.

"No, I haven't been in on any of her plans," Ahren parroted.

Zifa examined her friend's face through narrowed eyes. They'd been friends for so long; she knew instinctively that Ahren was hiding something. "What's really going on, Ahren? You're not usually so quick to judge people."

Ahren sat quietly for a moment, avoiding Zifa's eyes. Eventually, she sighed. "I don't know what to do anymore. My two groups of friends have opposite goals."

"What do you mean?"

"You and the others are happy Tavan's gone. You want to get on with the business of freedom, and enjoy governing ourselves." She shook her head and looked out the window at the darkening sky. "But the others... Tamyr and Ahni and their friends aren't happy—not even a little. Tavan had promised to make their lives better. They would be important. Now that he's dead, they're lost. They hope that Helak will come back and keep all of Tavan's promises."

Zifa worked to conceal her gasp of surprise. How was Ahni involved in this? Her family were prominent community members—her uncle had been one of the last council members and had been executed by Tavan during the invasion. Her father and grandfather were considered elders in the town and were treated with respect and deference by all of Nivaka. Zifa wanted to ask more about the girl's involvement but was afraid to alienate her friend. Ahren wanted to do the right thing, Zifa was sure of that much. She just needed a nudge in the right direction.

Instead of pressing for more details, Zifa picked up a brush from the vanity and began to draw it through Ahren's long, silky hair. They sat in silence for a long while, as Zifa brushed and braided her friend's hair. Eventually, the conversation restarted, but the friends avoided any further mention of the council and Ahren's other group of friends.

19.

Preparations

Faruz watched the young women disappear down the hall, then turned and trailed after Aibek. He followed his friend into Aibek's sitting room and dropped into one of the chairs near the hearth, reveling in the warmth of the small fire. He had too much to say to wait for morning, and he wanted to hear what had happened in Kasanto. The two friends talked late into the night, with Aibek relaying the tale of the trip to see the elf king and the dwarf queen, and Faruz telling of his afternoon at the fairy houses.

Eventually, the conversation slowed, and Faruz shifted uncomfortably in the well-cushioned chair.

"How long do you think I can stay here with you?" he mumbled. "I don't know that I could ever go back to city life. How would I cope with the boredom?" He stood and paced in front of the dying fire.

Aibek started and stared at Faruz with a surprised expression. He recovered quickly. "You know I'd never throw you out—"

"I know you wouldn't," his friend interrupted, "but do you think I'll wear out my welcome? I wasn't really invited…"

"In the next week or two, we'll move to the traditional mayoral home, and you can live there with me for as long as you please. I have to admit; I'm a little shocked.

I thought this was all just a grand adventure for you before you went back to your life in the city."

Faruz nodded. "I planned it that way, but this place and these people are amazing. I just can't imagine leaving. I was thinking…" He trailed off, then tried again. "Well, I thought… maybe I could lead the Nivakan army. That way I could contribute something and not feel like I'm taking advantage of your hospitality."

"That's a great idea," Aibek exclaimed with a huge grin. "I'll present it to the council tomorrow and see what the others think. We plan to meet here before the town gathering in the afternoon. Let's get some sleep for now. I'm exhausted."

Aibek had been laying out his clothes for the next morning as he spoke and was ready for bed as soon as he'd finished.

~*~

The next morning began much the same as every other day since they had arrived in Nivaka, with the friends discussing their plans for the day over muffins, fruit, and famanc. A drizzling rain pattered against the window, and Faruz was thankful for the fire the servants had laid on the hearth.

While they ate, Aibek encouraged his friend to stay nearby during the morning council meeting and told him they would likely invite him into the session to speak on his behalf about the idea of his becoming the captain of the still-to-be-formed Nivakan army. Serik thought it was an excellent idea. He said it would give the warriors some much-needed leadership, and would also give Faruz a purpose in the village. They finished their breakfast in a rush when they realized the dimness of the rain had made it seem earlier than it was, then headed downstairs to join the family.

Within a short time, the rest of the council arrived, soggy from the rain, and discarded their thick leather boots at the door before they climbed to the small room upstairs for their meeting. Faruz waited in a cramped sitting room near their meeting space and stared at the rain outside the window while he waited anxiously to be called in. He knew it could be a long wait; they had to discuss yesterday's unsuccessful visit to Kasanto before Aibek would bring up the possibility of his assignment.

Meanwhile, the meeting got underway with a detailed report of yesterday's visit. Everyone who had gone contributed to the discussion and those who had stayed behind expressed regret they had missed the opportunity, at least until Kai told of his whispered admission that he thought they were wasting their time and the queen's response.

Zifa was outraged. She struggled to keep her seat when she shouted, "How dare she criticize you like that? Sure, you shouldn't have said that out loud, but she certainly shouldn't have pointed it out to everyone!"

Aibek, concerned that the meeting might be sidetracked by a discussion of shoulds and should nots, tried to regain the attention of his friends.

His voice was stern as he spoke, "Poor manners were displayed by both sides until our hosts called an end to the meeting. Serik and I will return to Kasanto tomorrow to try again to win their support, but for now, we need to make plans for this afternoon's town meeting."

This speech succeeded in decreasing the rising tensions in the room and the meeting continued in a calmer mood. They discussed in depth the plans that needed to be made and what needed to be accomplished before the arrival of their anticipated visitors from the other villages. At the end of this discussion, the mayor finally felt the time was right to bring up his friend.

"I have one more item for the council to consider before we break for our meal." He ignored the knot of anxiety in his stomach. "You all know Faruz, who came with me from Xona. It has been suggested that he would be an excellent candidate to organize and help train our warriors. What would you all think of naming him the captain of our army?"

Wayra spoke first. "I've been sparring with him for weeks. He's an excellent swordsman and an even better teacher. I can't think of anyone better to turn our fighters into an army."

Alija looked doubtful. "What are his qualifications? I know you were both studying to be military officers, but should we accept a student as our captain? Is he ready for such a big responsibility?"

The mayor declined to answer the question but said that the best person to answer it would be the person it most concerned. He suggested calling Faruz into the meeting from the other room, and the others agreed that he should be included in this conversation. They brought Faruz into the room and briefed him on the discussion.

Almost immediately, Zifa repeated the last question to Faruz. "We've all heard that you were a student at the military academy in Xona. As a student, are you ready to lead our warriors? What makes you more qualified to lead than locals like Alija, who participated in the attack that freed us?"

Faruz had expected this question and had prepared for it. "You're quite right; I was a student at the academy when I left the city, less than a year from my graduation date." He took a deep breath and shifted his weight to his other foot. "That said, I've led several teams in the mountains, where I taught villagers how to defend themselves from raiders who had been pillaging their homes. I have the schooling and the experience of how to turn individual fighters into a unified force."

He paused and looked around at the council members and took a deep breath.

"Besides all that, I've really come to love this village and the people here. I plan to stay long after the battle is over, and I want to do all I can to help."

Wayra nodded. "Well said, my friend. It has been wonderful to train with you."

Valasa, who had been silent up to now, asked if the council was ready for a vote, and when everyone indicated they had made a decision, asked Faruz to step out of the room.

He did as requested, and Alija stood to address the council before the voting could begin. "Since Zifa mentioned it, I want to be clear: I have no desire to lead our army. I had no problem helping my best friends get rid of the governors, but leading the whole fighting force is a very different thing. Please don't turn down an excellent candidate because of me."

The Gadonu asked if anyone else had anything to say, then began the voting process. It was unanimous; Faruz would be the new captain of the Nivakan army. He was brought back into the room and congratulated on his new position, then the group broke for lunch and planned to reconvene at the Meeting Hall. Aibek hoped the villagers would come out in the cold, drizzly weather.

He needn't have worried. Eager Villagers packed the Meeting Hall, filling every seat. The council members took their places at the front of the room, and Valasa called the meeting to order.

Kai gave the citizens a brief rundown of the events of

the previous two days, though he deliberately omitted any mention of Alija's stabbing and the prisoner, then announced that help would be coming from their neighboring villages. Finally, he added that they were attempting to bargain with their neighbors on the ground. When grumbles went through the crowd, he reminded them that they needed all the help they could get.

"We're not in a position to turn down assistance from anyone," he reminded the villagers. "We all want to keep our freedom, and that may mean swallowing our pride and asking for help where we can get it."

Aibek listened intently as the council members relayed the plans they had made to the villagers. Though they heard a few complaints and concerns, the overwhelming majority voiced their support of the council.

Once they'd explained all of their plans for the reunion celebration, Aibek stood at the center of the dais and shouted over the growing noise, "I know you've all been considering your roles in our freedom." When the citizens settled into silence to hear the mayor, he continued. "Immediately following this meeting, we will hold sign-ups for our fighting force, our own army. We need as many men and women as we can get to help us fight for our homes."

The villagers looked around at each other, exclaiming at the announcement that women would fight, but Aibek didn't pause to hear them.

"Those who wish to evacuate before the battle should meet with Serik at the left side of the building, while those who wish to enlist in our militia are meeting on the right side. The captain of the army will be Faruz, who comes to us with a great deal of experience from the Xona Military Academy. Thank you all for coming.

Please make your way to the tables to sign up to fight or to evacuate."

Even before he had finished speaking, the villagers stood and began moving toward the tables set up next to the large outer doors. The majority moved to the right, with only a few individuals showing an interest in evacuation.

They spent the rest of the day recording the names and talents of the individuals who would form the army and deciding how to organize them into a functional fighting force. No one willing to fight was turned away, and only the elderly, frail, and women with small children expressed any interest in evacuating. Aibek was thrilled to see such a show of support for the village, and hoped their enthusiasm would last through the difficult days ahead.

~*~

The next morning, Faruz watched as the villagers arrived in groups to the designated areas within the Pavilion. The council members waited at tables lining the far side of the space, ready to issue the new warriors weapons and assign each one to an area to begin training. Most of the women were sent to the dais to meet with Zifa, so she could teach them how to fight while maintaining their feminine modesty. Faruz had laughed at Wayra when he'd made that suggestion, but had ultimately agreed that some instruction could be helpful. Still, he suspected Zifa would merely tell the women to wear pants for training and battle.

They divided the men according to the talents and interests they had declared yesterday. They formed groups for archery, swordsmen, and other types of weapons, such as spears, axes, hatchets, and daggers. Immediately following the meeting, the citizens broke into smaller groups to begin training. Faruz moved between the groups of swordsmen, and the other council members led the archers and other groups.

~*~

While Faruz was building the beginning of an army, Aibek and Serik left the village at dawn to try again to win the support of the ground folk. They followed their guide to the same room as before, but their hosts had removed the large table. In its place were several comfortable-looking chairs that matched the colors of the autumn leaves outside. The two friends lingered in the doorway until Idril gestured for them to continue into the room. She sat in an elevated red leather chair.

"Please, have a seat. We will discuss your proposal."

Aibek tried to suppress the anxious fluttering in his gut as he left his place near the door and sank into one of the smaller chairs arranged near Idril. As they settled into their seats, Turan strode into the room and seated himself in an empty chair beside the Dwarf Queen. Today, they both dressed simply in shades of brown and green.

The Elf King abruptly broke the silence. "We have some questions about what it is you want from us."

"You mentioned something about lamps?" Idril asked at the same time.

Aibek wasn't sure which one he should answer, so he addressed them both, glancing between them as he spoke.

"We would like you to have your warriors light a lamp near the village to warn us when the army has entered the forest."

"And why is this important to you? So important you're willing to beg your enemies for help?" Idril asked coldly as she looked down her nose at the visitors.

"I am willing to beg if that's what is required. But I sincerely hope it won't come to that. The warning is important because it would give us an enormous advantage over our enemy and keep us from being caught unaware yet again." When he saw doubt creep into her expression, he decided he should change his tactic. "This army intends to cut down the shadow trees. All of them. Please help us stop them," he whispered.

The rulers of Kasanto exchanged a long look, then Turan said, "We have discussed this at length and decided we will light the lamps."

He stared into the waterfall for a breath, then looked hard at the mayor.

"If you fail, it will send a strong message to the other villages, and they may not try again. We want to rid the Tsari of these invaders as much as you do."

Aibek hadn't realized he had been holding his breath until he exhaled in a great rush. The sudden relief left him dizzy and shaking.

"Thank you… so much… for your help," he stammered.

"We hope you succeed," Idril replied, then stood and left the room in a swirl of fabric.

Aibek and Serik both stood and bowed to Turan before following their guide back out of the cave and to the main trail. Aibek helped his friend up the stairs to the village and walked with him a short way, then turned and went in search of a quiet place where he could be alone. He found himself back at the stairs they had just climbed and descended once again to the solitude of the forest, just as he had two days before. Had it only been two days? So much had happened in the time he'd been here, some days had felt like a week.

He counted out the days on his fingers. Only five days had passed since the wedding feast and Alija's stabbing. Could that be right? Yes, it was five. The very day after the wedding, Aibek had toured his parents' home and spoken to his father. That same day, they'd received the warning about the coming army and held the town meeting, then Serik had relayed the tale of the invasion. The day after that, the council had made more solid plans, and he'd argued with Ahren again. The day after that had been their first, disastrous visit to Kasanto and Faruz had seen where the fairies lived. Then yesterday, the council had voted Faruz in as army captain, then hosted another town meeting and encouraged the citizens to sign up for the army. And of course today he'd gone back to Kasanto to plead with their enemies for help. It was almost too much to comprehend.

He closed his eyes and emptied his mind, listening only to the sounds of the forest around him. The birds and squirrels chirped and chattered, and a soft breeze rustled the fallen leaves on the earthen path. Aibek took a deep breath, opened his eyes, and began walking again.

As he meandered through the silent wood, he considered Turan's warning. He hadn't given much thought to the idea that Nivaka was setting an example for the other villages, but of course, the elf king was right. If their enemy regained control, it would send a strong message to the others that a revolt was futile and would strengthen Helak's hold on the forest. What would Noral say about Aibek's success today? He felt elated, but at the same time breathless with fear. Even with the warning, it would be difficult for the villagers to fight off a trained army.

"Father? Are you there?" Aibek asked the wind as it whispered through the trees.

He tried to let his mind go blank while he waited impatiently for an answer. He stared up into the heights of the treetops and wondered if he had dreamed that miraculous visit. Here in the loneliness of the forest, it seemed impossible that his father could have spoken with him from beyond the grave. He felt a few fat raindrops pelting his back and shoulders through the branches and decided it was time to return to the village.

Once there, he hurried along the boardwalk through the falling rain and found the newly formed army practicing in small groups under the roof of the Pavilion. Aibek searched out the council members and gathered them together, then told them of the morning's success. Kai and Alija had been uncomfortable with the idea of the mayor visiting Kasanto without the other members and again voiced their distrust of their enemies on the ground. They had little privacy for discussion in the crowded space, so they agreed to delay the debate and carry on with their training for now.

Aibek spent the rest of the day helping Faruz train the groups of swordsmen, then collapsed, exhausted, into bed at the end of the day. He fell immediately into the welcome oblivion of a deep, dreamless sleep.

20.

Moving

In the week that followed, the army gathered each morning at the Pavilion for training and drills. Faruz and Aibek closely monitored the practice and Aibek was impressed with how quickly their fighters learned the new skills.

While the citizens were learning how to defend themselves and their homes, Valasa and the council spent time each morning exchanging messages with their neighboring villages and the ground folk. Aibek and Serik made two more trips to the underground room to discuss their tentative truce with the rulers of Kasanto and gained assurance that the elves and dwarves would not attack those who were traveling to Nivaka from the other villages.

In between his other responsibilities, Aibek visited the prisoner, Tamyr, three more times, but each time she sat silently staring at the floor of her cell. She refused to look at him or in any way acknowledge his existence. Aibek's frustration with the woman was growing. He was confident she hadn't stabbed Alija, which meant the attacker was still free. Would that person strike again? Whom would he or she target this time? Thankfully, the army-in-training was practicing with dull weapons, so Aibek could walk among the practicing villagers without fear of a sword in his back—at least for now.

Meanwhile, work on the homes along the Square continued, and the workers completed the repairs faster than Aibek had believed possible. Less than a week following the town meeting, the workers announced they'd finished the mayoral home, and Aibek, Faruz, and Serik moved their meager belongings, supplemented by the wardrobes provided by their hosts, to the newly renovated home.

Aibek's room was down the hall from the one which had been his parents', and the workers had transformed their chamber into a peaceful chapel and meditation room. Deep blue curtains hung from the windows, and cushioned benches lined the walls. The parental bed had been removed and replaced with a table and four chairs. The original paintings hung over the hearth and on the walls, and Aibek felt closer to his parents in this room than anywhere he had ever been before.

Faruz chose his room from the guest chambers. He picked the largest one on the same hall as Aibek's room. It was a generous space with dark green and gold décor that he felt suited his personality, though he lamented the fact that it had polished oak floors instead of the lush carpet he had enjoyed at Valasa's house. Serik reclaimed the room that had been his two decades before. Though the workers had repaired it, they'd made no significant changes to the style or design of the room. The trusted servant told Aibek it felt like home when they toured the space on moving day. The friends agreed to continue their routine of meeting in Aibek's sitting room to begin each day.

Late that night, after everyone had finished exploring and had settled into their new home, Aibek walked the short distance down the hall to his new meditation room. He sat quietly in the dim light of a single candle on the table. He stared into the flickering flame and tried to let his mind go blank.

"This is a bit creepy, don't you think?" Faruz asked from the doorway. "You should at least light a lamp."

Aibek jumped and turned to face his best friend. "You scared me half to death."

Faruz crossed to the table and dropped into a chair. "What are you doing in here? And why is it so dark?" He looked closer at his childhood friend. "Are you all right?"

Aibek answered with a short, self-deprecating laugh. "I'm fine. I just feel close to them in here. I thought I'd spend some time here every day. Valasa said I should start meditating." He bit his tongue to keep from blurting out that he wanted to visit with his parents' ghosts. Faruz would think he'd gone mad.

"Do you want to be alone? I thought you might need some company for your first night here." Faruz stood and lit a lamp on the mantle, then returned to his chair at the table.

Aibek stared at the painting on the mantle. The flickering light made it look like the fairies were dancing. "You can stay..." He jumped again when Faruz interrupted.

"You know... if you're hoping to talk to their spirits, sitting alone and silent in a dark room might not be the best way to go about it."

Aibek jerked around towards his friend. "What?"

"Look, I talk to my grandfather from time to time," Faruz explained, "and I know you've had a couple of spirits hanging around you for years. All you have to do is talk to them if that's what you're trying to do. They can't hear your thoughts though, so you have to talk out loud."

Aibek chuckled and looked up at his friend. "So you

don't think I'm crazy?"

"I know you're crazy," Faruz laughed. "You left your home on a moment's notice to come play at being a mayor in some little jungle village that's about to be attacked by an army from the desert."

Aibek smiled. "I'll admit that sounds a bit far-fetched."

Faruz's smile faded, and he added, "Wanting to talk to the parents you never got to meet isn't crazy at all. I'd call it completely normal. Do you think they'll show up if I'm here? I'd love to meet them, too."

Aibek rearranged the flowers in the vase on the table. "I don't know. I haven't had much success on my own."

"I don't have anything against meeting you," Eddrick said from the other side of the room. "You've been a great friend for my son."

Aibek gasped and stared at the spirits. He was sure they hadn't been there a moment ago.

Faruz grinned and nudged his friend. "See? I told you it was easy." He looked at the ghosts who were approaching the table. "Thank you, sir. What should I call you?"

"You can call me Eddrick, and this is my wife, Kiri,"

The woman didn't acknowledge the introduction at all—she was completely oblivious to everything but Aibek. She sat in the chair next to him and smiled.

"I've waited so long for this," she whispered.

Aibek gawked at the lovely redhead and realized he had her eyes. "I wish I'd known it was possible." He raked his hands through his hair.

Faruz frowned at his friend. "Hey, we're not going to get all weird and emotional now, are we?"

Aibek laughed and looked around again at his best friend and his parents, who had seated themselves in the remaining chairs at the table.

"Who's emotional? This is amazing."

The four of them talked and laughed late into the night, remembering funny things that had happened as the boys grew up. Aibek was surprised by how many details his parents knew and accepted that as proof they had been there throughout his life. When they finally separated for the night, he went to bed feeling more at peace than he ever had before.

~*~

Before the sunrise brightened the sky in the morning, and before the friends had even dressed for the day, the new housekeeper ushered a small cloaked figure into Aibek's sitting room. As he and Faruz watched in disbelief, Ahren shrugged out of her heavy cape and crossed the room to sit on the sofa across from Aibek. He regarded her with unveiled shock on his face, realized he was staring, and glanced away. Why on earth had she come? Something picked at the edge of his consciousness, but he couldn't put his finger on it. There was something about the way she'd looked as she huddled into the room that was eerily familiar, though he didn't think he'd ever seen her dressed for the cold before.

She shifted uncomfortably on the new furniture for several minutes as Aibek waited expectantly to hear the reason for her visit. As she opened her mouth to speak, Serik burst through the door carrying a tray with their breakfast. He set the tray on the table in the center of the room, then looked up and noticed the young woman.

"Oh! Hello, miss. I didn't expect you this morning. I'll get another mug and plate." Before she could object, he bustled out of the room.

Ahren stared after him and shifted in her seat again. As soon as the servant was through the door, Aibek jumped up and hurried to get her a mug of famanc and a muffin.

"I'm sorry," she choked out. "I didn't mean to interrupt your breakfast."

"You aren't interrupting anything." Aibek handed her the hot drink. "Please… have a muffin or some fruit. We always have more than we can eat." He deliberately ignored the fact that this was his first morning in his new home and therefore didn't know how much they would have.

"Thank you." Ahren chose a fruit-filled cake from the tray.

Before Aibek poured his drink, Serik returned with a smaller platter. He placed it carefully next to the first one, the edges of the trays just touching, and poured himself his morning beverage. They ate in silence until they'd finished off the food, then Aibek looked to their guest again.

She swirled the last drops of liquid in her cup, placed it on the table and arranged her heavy skirt around her on the sofa.

"I'm so sorry; I didn't expect you to all be here. I thought I could talk to you privately." She lifted her eyes to Aibek's.

He frowned. "Are you sure that's a good idea? It hasn't worked out well in the past."

Ahren stood and sighed. She toed the pattern in the plush carpet. "Look, I just wanted to apologize for the way I acted last week. I know it wasn't your fault the council went to Kasanto. I was wrong… again."

She spat the last word, then spun and ran through the door. Aibek blinked in disbelief, glanced at Faruz, who looked equally dumbfounded, then jumped up and ran after her. He caught up with her in the hallway, where she was leaning against the wall, apparently trying to steady herself.

"I have to admit… I'm more than a little confused. What is going on?"

She glanced down the hall, and then looked at the closed sitting room door. "I feel terrible about the way I acted after the council meeting. I shouldn't have been so quick to blame you."

Aibek's expression softened as she spoke. "There's a room down the hall where we can talk if you want a bit more privacy. They're probably listening at the door." He hitched a thumb at the closed door behind him.

"That would be great."

He ushered her into the dark room, then felt his way across the wall to the hearth, where he knew there was a lamp. After several tries with the flint, the new wick finally caught, and he made himself comfortable in a richly upholstered pale green chair near the empty fireplace. It was a cold morning, and the unheated room was chilly. Ahren wrapped her cape tightly around herself and sat in a chair near him. Aibek realized he could see his breath and wished he had brought a blanket or a cloak.

Even as he waited to hear what she had to say, his mind worked to unravel what had triggered that prick of memory when she'd entered his room. He'd tried not to pay much attention to her during the weeks at Valasa's home, but he was certain he'd never seen her wear that cloak before. Still, for some reason, it looked awfully familiar.

"I don't know what else to say…" she began slowly, dragging him back to the moment. "I've acted like a fool since you arrived. I'm not normally like this. I can't even explain why."

"You're worried about your family and friends. I understand that. I know several villagers who said they thought I was an impostor sent by Helak.”

Ahren nodded. “That’s part of it. Truthfully, I don’t even know why I’ve been so awful to you.” She paused and heaved a long sigh. “You’ve never been anything but nice to me in return. I hope you can forgive me.”

“Why don’t we move on from here?” His tone was gentle. “As I said before, I would really like to call you a friend.”

“Thank you; I think I’d like that, too,” she whispered.

“Now, let’s get another cup of famanc. I’m freezing.” Aibek stood and gestured to the door, then followed her through it and back to his sitting room.

He wanted to be happy that she’d finally accepted him, but for some reason, he had trouble trusting her motives. Something felt off about this visit, and he wished he could remember whatever was niggling at the edges of his thoughts.

Faruz and Serik greeted them with curious looks, but both men resisted the urge to ask about their conversation. They were perfectly polite as Aibek seated himself and poured another cup for the visitor, though Aibek knew the questions lurked just beneath the surface. He wasn’t sure what he would say to Faruz later since he hadn’t told his friend about the arguments he’d had with Valasa’s daughter.

Ahren stayed for another hot drink, then excused herself and hurried home. As soon as she was gone, the men dressed and left to spend the day training with their teams. The warriors were making improvements every day, but they still had a lot of work to do.

Within another week, the workers finished the repairs on the rest of the council members’ homes along the square, and their new owners moved in and settled quickly. The four remaining houses along the square were repaired and readied for the visitors expected from the other villages. Valasa exchanged daily messages with those neighbors who had agreed to come and help Nivaka and told the council he hoped visitors would begin arriving soon.

Two of the largest, most comfortable inns in Kainga were prepared to receive the evacuees, and the villagers had made travel arrangements for those who were unable to fight. Aibek thought the townsfolk had accomplished a dizzying amount of work in a very short time and was proud to call himself one of them.

Late one morning while the army was training, a watchman interrupted the council meeting.

"Excuse me, sirs, there's a group of people at the East entrance. They say they came from the southern edge of the Tsari and are here to help us fight."

The mayor, Valasa, and Dalan went with the watchman to meet the newcomers and verify that they were friendly.

When they arrived at the East Entrance, Aibek immediately saw a group of eight men dressed in brown and green zontrec, each wearing a sword and carrying either an axe or a bow and quiver of arrows. They stood at the base of the stairs, murmuring among themselves. When Aibek appeared at the top of the staircase, their leader, a brawny auburn-haired man with an axe slung over his shoulder stepped forward.

"Greetings friends. We've come to answer your call for help. I'm Vayna." He bowed to his hosts.

Aibek looked to Valasa, who nodded once. These visitors were expected. Aibek bowed in return. "Welcome. We're extremely pleased you've come. Come along, and we'll show you where you can stay while you're here."

"We want to hear all about how you managed to rid

yourselves of your governors. We've been very curious about that," the man called Vayna said as he turned to follow his host. Their path took them past several groups of Nivakans training with swords, spears, and staffs.

"Let's get you settled in your rooms and then we can talk more," Aibek suggested. "How did you manage to bring such heavy weaponry with you? I didn't expect your governor to allow you to arm yourselves."

Vayna shrugged. "We told them we couldn't travel through the forest without being able to defend ourselves from the elves, dwarves, bears and such." He looked at the activity around them. "They argued at first, but eventually agreed it would be foolish to travel unarmed."

The guests fell in line behind their leader as he followed Aibek through the village, eyeing the groups of Nivakans training in the parks as they passed.

As the council had planned, they gave the visitors rooms in Valasa's house. When more came, they would fill the Gadonu's home, then the mayor's and the rest of the council's homes. When the hosts' houses were full, they would use the empty houses along the square. Aibek was a bit disappointed that the first group was so small, and wondered if they would have enough people to mount an effective defense.

~*~

Late one morning, about a month after the first visitors arrived, Aibek again walked alone beneath the village. His official duty was checking the fortifications that the villagers had added to the area around the tree-top town, but it had also become his favorite way to clear his mind. The sounds and smells of the forest calmed his spirit like nothing he'd ever known. As the homes above had filled with visitors, he'd found it harder and harder to find time alone. He chuckled to himself as he remembered his concern when the first small group had arrived. Every day after that, more visitors had come. Some groups had been small, with only two or three individuals making the trip; others were substantial. One village sent nearly a hundred and fifty fierce-looking men and women.

Two weeks after the arrival of the first visitors, Valasa had taken the floor in their daily council meeting to announce that everyone who was expected had arrived. All totaled, they had received five hundred, seventy-one individuals from thirty-two villages. Nivaka was nearly overflowing with the unexpectedly large number of guests, a fact that both satisfied and concerned Aibek. The surprisingly large response was straining the village's resources. The fairies, no longer needed to coordinate with travelers, had been tasked with helping the local cooks keep up with the enormously increased demand for food, and the warriors went out in hunting parties to provide enough meat for so many hungry individuals.

Aibek stopped and waved to a hunting party returning with a large deer strung on a staff between them, then smiled to himself once again.

As the remainder of the leaves had fallen, the newly-formed Nivakan Army trained, fortified the town, and got to know one another. Within a couple of weeks, an outsider wouldn't have been able to guess which were the Nivakans and which had come to help. As Aibek watched, the warriors had melded seamlessly into a cohesive force.

As the days had passed, so had his frustration with Tamyr and the situation surrounding Alija's attack. Once the guards had begun keeping records, the secretive visitors had stopped coming to see the woman. Her only visitors now consisted of the council members, Valasa, and a few women who tried to get the woman to talk. Ahren spent a great deal of time there but swore the woman wouldn't talk to her, either. Aibek hadn't found any more clues about the attack. Maybe he'd been wrong, and Tamyr had been the one who'd stabbed Alija. Still, Aibek had tried to find another solution for keeping the woman monitored.

He'd insisted on keeping a constant guard on her, but the men were growing tired of spending their time making sure a small washwoman didn't escape. Aibek had spoken with the woman's family on several occasions. They wouldn't take responsibility for her. He couldn't free her, so he'd had her moved into a slightly larger room with a bed and more space so she could move around. They'd reinforced the window so she couldn't use it as an escape route. Still, Aibek worried.

What'll happen to the girl when the battle starts? Will she take the opportunity to turn on us and fight with the enemy?

He kicked a stone down the path and turned to examine a spiked collar that had been fixed to a large oak tree just beyond the village borders. He tested its strength, pulling downward and away with all his strength. It didn't budge. The cured sap held it firmly to the tree trunk. The blacksmiths had made two types of collars: large, heavily armored devices fitted with wicked spikes like the one he had just tested, and smaller, lighter collars that would break loose, dropping enemy soldiers onto large spikes driven into the ground below. Both types were attached to the shadow trees with varying amounts cured sap, so there was little chance the trees would be damaged.

Aibek looked up, gazing through the barren tree branches at the exposed boardwalk above. Spikes the size of his forearm lined the top rail, with small nails covering the wood beneath the railing. The combination would make climbing over the rail difficult and dangerous. As he watched, a group of archers peered over the side, shouting that they were about to begin practice for the day. His time on the ground was over. Aibek sighed and made his way to the West Entrance, only a short walk to his left.

21.

Visitors

Throughout the preparations, planning, and training, Aibek spent time every day with the spirits of his parents. Some days Faruz came, and those visits were always filled with laughter and boisterous energy, while other days it was just Aibek and one or both of his parents. On one of these nights, Aibek was talking with his father about the challenges of leading a village overrun with visitors and his fears about the upcoming battle.

"I don't know how to do this," he told his father's ghost. "I'm terrified that I'm leading these people into a massacre, like what happened before, only worse."

"You're doing just fine," Eddrick replied, "you've done very well. Keep listening to the will of the people, and lead them in the direction they choose. Fight alongside them, and you can't go wrong."

Aibek shook his head, then lowered it to the table. "There's just so much we still don't know. We don't know how many are coming, or when. What if they show up tomorrow?"

"Then you'll engage them tomorrow. I've been watching your men train; they've come a long way, and I think they're nearly ready for battle."

Aibek looked up at his father. "It won't matter how ready we are if we're outmanned or caught by surprise..." He trailed off as an idea occurred to him. "Can you help? Can you find their camp and tell me how many are coming… and maybe when they'll arrive?"

The ghost answered slowly. "That's a brilliant idea, but I'm not sure if it's allowed. I'll have to ask my father or one of the ancestors."

Aibek raised his eyebrows. "You have rules? What can they possibly do if you break them? You're already dead."

The ghost laughed. "Yes, we have rules. We can't interfere in the lives of the living. We must let them make their own mistakes. We can only answer a direct question. They can't kill me again, but their punishments are worse, in some ways." He shuddered. "I'll ask the ancestors, and if it's allowed, I'll find out everything I can about your enemy."

Following this discussion, they chatted for a few more minutes; then an exhausted Aibek dragged himself to bed.

~*~

Later that night, while their son was dreaming, Eddrick and Kiri met with Agommi in their room to ask about the rules. They both wanted to help Nivaka and seek out the enemy, but neither wanted to risk another lengthy confinement, especially with the battle looming. "I don't know what the rules are on this," the oldest spirit began. "You were asked a direct question, and would only be rendering aid that was requested. That said, it is a critical task and could turn the tide of the battle. I will have to confer with the ancestors."

Before the others could respond, the old man was gone. He didn't bother using the door this time—he just vanished off the sofa.

Eddrick and Kiri looked at each other, shrugged, and went on with their evening as if Agommi had never been there. They weren't willing to proceed without the permission of the ancestors, so they would wait it out.

~*~

The next morning, the council met as usual to discuss the progress of the army and any issues that had arisen. They had almost finished with the business of the day when Faruz entered and asked to be allowed to speak.

At Aibek's nod, he began, "I know you've all seen how hard the villagers have been working. I don't think we should stop training, but I'd say our army is ready for battle."

Kai cocked his head to the side. "I know they've worked hard, and we've seen some amazing improvements, but what makes you say they're 'ready'?"

Faruz stepped farther into the room and stood in the middle of the circle. "While you were meeting, we held a large-scale practice battle. We divided everyone into two equal teams and fought with sticks and blunt arrows. It lasted over an hour, and ended in a draw." He grinned broadly. "I watched each side closely for weaknesses, but I saw none; everyone fought as if their lives depended on it. I would have let them go longer, but they fought so fiercely I was afraid someone could be injured. I am as confident as I can possibly be—they are ready."

Zifa looked up at the captain and smiled. "I trust your judgment. You've spent every waking minute working with this army making sure every move is perfect. If you say they're ready, then they are. We should celebrate."

She turned to smile at each of her friends. Everyone knew she loved a party.

"Does this mean we're done training?" Wayra asked.

Faruz shook his head. "Not at all. As I've said before, no warrior should ever stop learning and improving. It just means we're sure we can face our opponents. Honestly, I do think they're ready, but they still lack confidence." He sat next to Zifa on the couch. "A celebration sounds perfect. It would show them we believe in them."

"Then it's settled. We'll have a feast," Alija replied. "Our warriors should never doubt the council's support."

"Should we vote on it?" Aibek asked the group.

The council members looked around at each other for a minute before Zifa nodded. "Yes, let's have a vote."

It was unanimous. They decided on a day one week away, then concluded their meeting. The council members filed out of their meeting room, talking and laughing down the hall.

~*~

The news spread through the village like wildfire. The excitement was palpable, and all the villagers and visitors began making plans for the event. Some secured dates for the evening, but most planned to simply enjoy the festivities. Most of the visitors hadn't been allowed to host a large celebration since the Helak's troops had invaded the Tsari twenty years earlier.

The week passed in a blur as everyone continued to train and prepare for the upcoming feast. Some of the women sent messengers to Kainga for new ribbon or lace, and the men planned to dress in their finery for the special event. A large group went to the lake the day before the celebration to gather enough fish for everyone, and another group hunted for big game. The cooks worked feverishly through the night to prepare the quantities of food required for such a large number of warriors.

Finally, the day of the feast arrived. Faruz had announced a training holiday, and every citizen of Nivaka primped and preened and got ready for the party.

The mayor's home, like every other house in the village, was in chaos as everyone vied for the attention of the servants. Aibek, Faruz, and Serik helped each other as they had done back in Xona for so many events. Faruz had spent a great deal of time learning the steps to the popular dances and hoped to make a better impression this evening than he had at Wayra's wedding.

"Do you think she'll dance with me again? I really want to show her how much I've learned."

Aibek glanced at his friend as he tightened the knot of the broad neckcloth he'd ordered from Kainga. It was very similar to the neckcloths he'd worn as part of his uniform in Xona, and Aibek thought it looked formal and official. "Which 'she' are you referring to?"

Faruz discarded yet another shirt and put on a deep blue one. "You know I mean Zifa. I can't wait to show her I've learned all the dances. Do you think she'll dance with me?"

His best friend laughed. He had never seen Faruz this besotted with any girl. "I'm sure she will. She was awfully quick to suggest the party."

They laughed and joked as they finished getting ready for the celebration, then left the house along with all their houseguests. They walked down the boardwalk in a loud, boisterous group, and then scattered when they reached the Pavilion.

Within a few seconds, Aibek found himself alone with Faruz at the edge of the party. He took a deep breath, looked at his friend, then stepped into the celebrating crowd. The fairies had strung lamps along the beams as before, but this time they continued for nearly a hundred yards down the boardwalk in every direction. Revelers were walking and dancing along the boardwalks, while others strolled in the lamplight engaged in private conversations.

Inside the Pavilion, people were packed shoulder to shoulder. Some danced, while others strolled around with plates piled high with food, and still more pulled chairs up to small tables to eat. The men had arranged larger tables with chairs around the outer perimeter of the space, and parents sat there with their families, encouraging their young children to eat. Many of the children stared wide-eyed at the activity around them and showed no interest in their meals. Aibek stopped for a minute and smiled encouragement to a mother who was struggling to control four small children who were dancing and giggling instead of eating, then proceeded farther into the heart of the celebration.

~*~

As Faruz expected, buffet tables overflowing with food filled the dais. The fish was featured prominently on the front table and surrounded by roasted elk and other large game meats. Nearby, root vegetables and autumn squash dishes were displayed in a colorful array. Flanking the meats and vegetables were tables filled with luxurious deserts. His stomach grumbled, and he was glad the music was loud enough to drown out the sound.

Faruz made straight for the buffet line, with Aibek trailing close behind. Neither man had eaten anything since breakfast. Aibek had been too busy dealing with a minor dispute during lunchtime, but Faruz had been too nervous to eat. He'd been unable to think of anything but showing Zifa his new dancing skills.

His hands shook as he picked up a wooden plate, and he took a few deep breaths to calm himself before heaping food onto it.

It would be awful to start the night by spilling food on

myself, he thought.

He made his way to an open bench on the boardwalk where could eat without being jostled by dancers. Aibek did an extraordinary job of staying close, even though revelers dogged his steps, congratulating the mayor and the captain on the work they had done to prepare the village for battle. Each time, both smiled and thanked the speakers, then dodged away to avoid getting pulled deeper into a conversation.

They ate in silence, Faruz focused solely on filling his empty belly. He finally looked up when Dalan and Wayra walked over. Their friends joined them on the bench.

"What do we do now?" Dalan said.

Faruz gulped as the last bite of fish caught in his throat.

Is it time to dance already? Where's Zifa?

He craned his neck, searching the crowd for the raven-haired beauty.

Wayra laughed. "I think I saw Zyana with Zifa and Ahren at the dessert table, so we should have a little time before they drag us onto the dance floor."

Faruz laughed along, though it sounded a bit too loud to his own ears. The butterflies in his stomach had transformed into a violent churning, and he took another sip of wine to ward off the impending nausea.

Aibek gave a cheerful nod. "Good! Let them enjoy the sweets. I haven't seen much of you lately, at least not outside of our meetings. How's everything going? I hated to fill your house with travelers so soon after your marriage, but I didn't have anywhere else to put them!"

Wayra smiled. "I appreciate that. I know you held off as long as you could. I'm trying to convince Zyana to evacuate with the others next week." He dropped his eyes to the table and added, "She just told me yesterday she's with child. I'm going to be a father."

The announcement hit Faruz like a club. How would he keep his friend safe during the battle? His new wife shouldn't have to raise their child alone. Though there was no way to make sure every deserving father survived the battle, Faruz felt as if he'd taken a punch to the gut. He felt responsible for this man, as well as all the others. Each one had a family—someone who was counting on him to survive. They were fathers, mothers, sons, and daughters. He had to do everything in his power to make sure they could defeat the enemy army.

Aibek and Dalan slapped Wayra on the back and shouted their congratulations, while Faruz sat stunned by the sudden realization of the scope of his responsibility.

His friends laughed and joked while Faruz looked from face to face, wondering if these men would still be alive next week, or next month... or whenever the assault came.

Before much time had passed, a group of ladies approached, looking for dance partners. Faruz immediately offered to partner with Zifa and quickly spun her onto the dance floor, relieved to escape the prison of his melancholy thoughts.

~*~

Aibek wasn't sure who he should ask to dance, and so was relieved when Ahren grabbed his arm and led him into the throng. He didn't look back to see who his other friends chose for partners, but instead focused on the spritely young woman in his arms. He still didn't quite trust the girl, but he'd set that aside for the night.

He danced the steps as if he had known them all his life, easily keeping up with the fast rhythm of the song. Ahren smiled and led him farther into the heart of the party. They danced and laughed until they were both out of breath, then retreated to the boardwalk for some fresh air and rest.

"That was great!" Ahren smiled up at her companion. "You've been practicing."

"Yes, I had Serik teach me," Aibek replied sheepishly, then pointed to his friend in the Pavilion. "Faruz has been working on his dancing, too."

They both laughed as they watched their friends dancing feverishly along with everyone else on the floor in a fast, complicated routine.

"He's doing great." Ahren clapped along with the beat. "This one is Zifa's favorite."

"Then I'm glad he practiced it." Aibek gave her a slight smile. "He was really hoping to get to dance with her tonight. I think he was a bit embarrassed the night of the wedding." He led her to a bench under a string of lights.

"I noticed that. You were both kind of a mess that night." She laughed.

He chuckled with her. "I guess we were."

He looked out into the darkness beyond the rail behind her and wondered what she thought of him now. How would she react if he reached over and put an arm around her shoulders?

She shivered in the evening air, and he frowned in concern.

"Are you ready to go back into the party? It's a little cold tonight."

She waited for a group of partiers to pass on the boardwalk, then slid a little closer to him and looked up into his face. "It is a bit chilly, but I'd rather stay out here for a while longer if that's all right with you."

Aibek grinned and stretched an arm around her, pulling her close to his chest. She sighed, shifted closer, and snuggled into his warmth. Aibek tried to stay calm, but his heart was pounding in his chest. She felt so warm and soft in his arms. Should he try for a kiss? He wasn't sure how she would take it, and he wasn't sure it would be wise. He didn't need a romantic relationship right now, with the battle looming ever closer. Besides, he couldn't be sure she wouldn't turn on him again tomorrow. She hadn't been predictable or reliable so far.

He'd enjoy her closeness for now, and maybe try to take things further after they had won their freedom. That would be the best option. Besides, he wasn't even really sure she liked him. He enjoyed her warmth for a few short minutes, then took a deep breath, stood, and offered her his hand.

"We should get back to the party before someone misses us."

With a confused expression on her face, Ahren slowly placed her hand in his. "I guess you're right. Do you want to dance some more?"

They walked toward the Pavilion side by side.

Before he had a chance to respond, a group of warriors from a nearby village approached them.

"You've done a fantastic job getting everyone ready to fight together," a tall, dark-haired man said.

"It's been amazing to see people progress so quickly," said another, "Your captain is truly amazing."

"Thank you." Aibek watched Ahren slip silently away to her friends, who were sitting on the other side of the party. "I've enjoyed working with all the warriors and watching you improve."

Soon, another group of villagers joined him, and the conversation he'd just had was repeated nearly word for word. He glanced out into the crowd, hoping this wouldn't be the pattern for the rest of the night.

~*~

Ahren slipped away from Aibek when the visiting warriors approached.

What am I doing? Did I really just cuddle with the interloper on a bench for everyone to see?

She shook her head in disgust and searched through the crowd until she found Ahni on the other end of the Pavilion. Moving with the rhythm of the loud music, she shoved her way through the crush of bodies until she stood beside her friend.

Ahni glanced at Ahren, then returned to watching the dancing couples. It was enough for Ahren to see the tears in her eyes. The two girls had only become close after Tavan's murder, but it had been long enough for Ahren to understand how hard that day was for her friend. Even so, she was beginning to question the validity of Ahni's arguments against the council. None of her predictions had even come close to the truth. All of the council members, including the interloper-mayor, worked hard to make sure they knew the will of the citizens. They encouraged input from the people and often took the suggestions and made them happen.

She cast a sideways look at Ahni just in time to see what the girl was focused so intently upon. Aibek was walking with a group of men toward the front of the Pavilion, his back to them. He was laughing, a sound Ahren hadn't heard much since the visitors had come.

Almost before Ahren could react, Ahni slipped a small dagger out of her sash and moved toward the mayor's group.

"No!" Ahren shouted, struggling to shout over the noise of the boisterous crowd.

She ran toward Ahni, arms outstretched. Before she would have reached the armed young woman, Ahni turned, surprise evident in her dark, tear-filled eyes.

Ahren reached to grab the weapon, but Ahni was faster. She swung the dagger in a clumsy arc, but it connected with the flesh at the top of Ahren's left arm. A bright red stain bloomed across the top of Ahren's pink gown, and pain flashed through her mind.

Ahni screamed at her, "What are you doing? I have a clear shot. Let me take it."

"No! He isn't what you think. He's kind. He'll help you if you'll just talk to him." She grabbed at her friend's wrist with her uninjured arm, desperate to get the dagger away from the girl.

Ahni had the advantage of size—there weren't many people smaller than Ahren—but the latter had considerably more strength from the weeks spent training with Zifa.

She wrestled the dagger away from Ahni, then was caught completely off guard when the girl lunged at her, tackling her to the ground. Ahren dimly heard the screams of partiers around them as her head struck the hard wooden floor. Dizzy from the impact, she tried to roll to her side, then Ahni was on top of her, crushing the breath from her lungs. Ahren gasped once, then Ahni's head crashed into her own. Darkness descended upon her like a curtain, and the screams faded into silence.

~*~

Once again, Aibek found himself running through the crowd of revelers toward the source of the screams. This time, he discovered Ahren unconscious and pinned beneath her friend. An alarming pool of blood grew around them, though he couldn't tell where it was coming from. He rolled the girl off of Ahren and saw a slender dagger protruding from the larger girl's upper abdomen. The blade pointed upwards, toward her lungs and vital organs. It had to come out. Blood gushed from the wound as soon as he pulled the knife free.

Faruz appeared out of the throng and dropped to his knees beside the wounded woman. He pulled off his neckcloth, immediately pressing the fabric into the wound to try to stop the bleeding. It was no use. No matter how hard he pressed, the blood continued to flow. The woman made a gurgling sound in her throat, and Aibek looked up at her face. Blood bubbled on her lips, frothing with each breath.

He groaned, "Oh, no."

There was nothing more he could do for the girl. He left her care to Faruz and turned his attention to Ahren, who lay still and silent on the edge of the dance floor. She had a distressingly large lump on her forehead, and she had a wound just below her left shoulder. More blood oozed from somewhere beneath her, but he wasn't sure if it was Ahren's. She was frightfully pale under the blossoming bruises. Aibek pressed his fingers to the inside of her limp wrist, feeling for a pulse. It was steady and strong.

"Where's Valasa?" He shouted. "Someone bring the Gadonu!"

Beside him, Faruz checked the other girl's pulse, then shook his head. She was gone.

"What happened here?" Aibek shouted at the gathered crowd. "Did anyone see what happened?"

22.

Ready

"I can't believe they approved this," Eddrick whispered to his wife as they crouched in the bushes near the enemy encampment.

Ilodus had risen overhead, and Koviom was climbing the eastern horizon. They provided enough light for Eddrick to see the camp beyond their hiding place. The army's camp sprawled over the grassy hillside, a mobile city filled with energy and aggression. The soldiers were mostly short, heavily muscled, and hairy. They all wore beards down to their waists and had unkempt, long hair. Eddrick shuddered at the sight. He'd been watching the army for most of the day but hadn't grown accustomed to their dirty, ragged appearance.

"Me, either," Kiri whispered in return. "I'm glad they did approve it, though."

A taller man in an immaculate yellow uniform strolled into the clearing. He wore his hair neatly trimmed and his face clean-shaven, and Eddrick assumed he must be an officer. The soldiers gathered around the fire leapt to their feet at the man's approach.

"Listen!" The officer shouted to the men who were still milling around. "We'll be in the forest within the week. Make sure you're training and getting plenty of rest. Remember the plan—the first wave will go in and wear them down, and the second wave will finish them off a few hours later." He gestured to the men standing around him. "You all are in the first group. You have to hold steady until backup arrives. It shouldn't be too hard. These people haven't fought a battle in over a hundred years." He laughed, and the soldiers joined in.

As he spoke, he began pacing the circle that had formed around him. He stopped now, waiting for the laughter to die down.

"Remember, this time we leave no survivors. Our job is to send a message to all the villages in the forest that Helak's army is not to be taken lightly. If we like the place, we might just move in and stay a while."

He chuckled, then straightened and began scolding one of the younger men for some small problem with his appearance.

Horrified, Eddrick and Kiri hurried to tell their son of the enemy's plan.

~*~

Unsure how badly Ahren was injured, Aibek and Faruz carried her to Valasa's house on a makeshift stretcher. The wound on her shoulder had stopped bleeding, but the knot on her head was still growing. Her right eye was blackened and swollen, and the bruising continued to march down her cheek and into her hairline. To make matters worse, Aibek had found another lump on the back of Ahren's head, likely from where she'd hit the floor.

Just as when Alija was stabbed, no one could tell them exactly what had happened. This time, however, one witness came forward. The woman had pulled Aibek aside before they'd decided to move Ahren, and told him Ahren had been holding a dagger when the other girl lunged and knocked her to the ground. The description fit the way he'd found the women and most of the injuries. But he couldn't explain how Ahren's shoulder had been injured. Perhaps, there had been a fight for the weapon.

Aibek paced in Valasa's den, waiting for word on Ahren's condition. Would she be able to pull through this? She was awfully small. He'd been struck by how tiny her frame was when he'd held her against his chest earlier in the night.

What did that embrace mean to her? Was it a distraction? A way to get me to trust her so I'd let my guard down? Had she meant that dagger for me?

Answerless questions vied for his attention, but he pushed them aside. Dalan had stayed behind to notify the other girl's family and help them prepare her for the funeral. Maybe he'd have more information when he returned.

When the large clock chimed midnight, with no more information than he'd already gathered, Aibek bid goodnight to the house-staff at Valasa's home. He trudged down the boardwalk to his own house, Faruz walking silently beside him. Valasa still hadn't emerged with news of Ahren, and Dalan hadn't learned anything from the other woman's family.

Aibek hoped Ahren would wake soon, both so he'd know she would survive and so she could fill in the holes in the story. Part of him didn't want to admit that she was likely the force behind the poisonings and the attack on Alija, but it was hard to ignore the evidence he'd gathered tonight. Still, there were so many unanswered questions. Tomorrow, he'd go and question the prisoner once more. Maybe she'd talk, now that her friend was severely injured and another woman was dead.

As soon as the men entered their home, Faruz said

goodnight and disappeared into his chamber. Aibek followed suit, bone-deep fatigue making his body heavy and sluggish. He needed a good night's sleep if he was going to figure anything out.

~*~

Aibek woke with a pounding headache, rolled to his side, and pulled the blankets over his face. The sunlight streaming through the curtains felt like knives in his head. He knew he needed to be up, checking on Ahren and questioning the prisoner, but he couldn't force himself upright. Every time he tried, the room spun, and the pounding in his head became almost deafening.

Have I been poisoned again?

He stayed in bed for most of the morning, until Valasa brought him a vial of some foul-smelling liquid to drink. Aibek tried to decline the medicine, but the Gadonu was firm. He stayed at Aibek's bedside until the tincture was gone, then walked away mumbling something about childhood diseases. Aibek couldn't bring himself to ask about Ahren. He'd face that situation once he felt a little better.

He didn't know what the old man was grumbling about. He wasn't sick; he just had an awful headache. He forced himself out of bed long enough to build the fire up to a blinding blaze. It must have been an unusually cold night because it was freezing in his room this morning. Before long, Faruz came stumbling into the room. He was shivering, too, and several large, deep red blotches covered his head and neck.

"What happened to your face?" Aibek asked.

"There's nothing wrong with my face. I'd be fine if I could get rid of this headache. I'm so glad you have a good fire going. I can't get warm. Have you heard anything about Ahren?" At that point, Faruz got a good look at his friend. "What's all over your face?"

"Oh, no!" Aibek stumbled to the mirror on the dressing room door. His face had spots just like Faruz's. "We must have caught some weird disease! That must be what Valasa was talking about. And no, I haven't heard anything about Ahren or the other woman yet. I haven't had the energy to ask anyone."

Faruz peered at himself in the mirror over Aibek's shoulder, turning this way and that to get a better look at the angry red splotches. "What do we do now?"

Aibek met Faruz's eyes in the mirror and saw his worries echoed there. Their enemy would arrive any day now, Ahren lay wounded at Valasa's house while another woman was dead. They still didn't know what Tamyr's role in the attacks had been, and now they were both feverish and spotted. They had too much to do to spend time in bed recovering from some bizarre disease. Before he could get too worried, Valasa strolled into the room.

Aibek pounced on him without preamble. "What's going on? How long am I going to be sick?"

"It looks like you've caught a very common illness. Usartma usually only lasts a day or two. But I've never seen it in an adult before. I guess you didn't have it as children?"

Aibek sank into his favorite chair by the fire. "I've never even heard of it. It's common here, then?"

The Gadonu nodded. "Nearly every child here gets it before the tenth birthday. It generally isn't serious. It just wears you out for a few days. The spots only last a day. You need to get plenty of rest if you want to get over this quickly. Now, off to bed. I'll have Serik bring you some broth."

Aibek caught Valasa's sleeve. "Wait! I have to know.

How is Ahren? Has she awakened? Who was the other woman?"

Valasa sighed and dropped his hands to his sides. "Ahren will be fine. She's been awake several times now, but only for short periods. She'll need time and rest to recover from the head injuries. Her arm should heal without any problems." The healer sighed again, and a look of sorrow crossed his normally cheerful countenance. "The other girl was Ahni, the daughter of one of the elders. Her father said she's been acting strangely for months now, since before the boys overthrew Tavan. She was apparently expecting a child. Her father said they had no idea who the father could be."

The room spun around him, and Aibek dropped into the closest chair. What did all this mean? It would be much easier to think it all through if the room would stay put.

"You need rest. Off to bed. We'll figure this out once you're feeling better."

Valasa ushered Faruz back to his room, and Aibek basked in the comfortable silence of his empty chamber. He sank into the mound of blankets on his bed, balled himself in the center of the enormous cushion, and shivered. He wished he could get warm and wondered why he was sweating and freezing at the same time.

While Aibek shivered under the covers, his parents appeared just inside his bedroom door. As soon as they noticed their son huddled in bed, they rushed to his side, and Eddrick laughed.

Kiri swept Aibek's hair off his sweaty, spotted brow "That's right, you never got any of Nivaka's childhood illnesses, did you? It never even occurred to me before now."

Her son shivered harder at the icy touch, so she pulled back and sat on a chair by the fire.

He wrapped the largest blanket around himself and sat on the edge of the bed. "I'll be fine. Valasa said this only lasts a couple of days. What did you find out? Can you help us?"

Eddrick's expression fell slightly, and he drifted to the chair before he spoke. "We… we can help. We've already found Helak's army, and we spent some time watching and listening to their conversations."

They all looked up as Serik entered the room with a tray. The elderly servant placed the tray on the table, then handed Aibek a steaming mug of broth.

"This will help you feel a bit better." He turned to the spirits. "Do you have good news for us?"

"Well… we have news," Kiri answered, "but not all of it is good. We were just saying that we located the army. They're moving slowly because they are bringing a huge number of fighters with them—"

Aibek interrupted, "How many? Do we have a chance?"

"Yes." Eddrick frowned. "But only because of their strategy. They plan to send half their force in, then the other half several hours later once your warriors are already exhausted. It won't be an easy win, and you have to convince your army to save some reserves for the second wave."

"There's more," Kiri interjected when her husband paused for a breath. "We overheard one of their officers saying they plan to kill everyone in the village. He said they want to send a message to the other villages not to try the same thing."

They were all silent for a moment as the warning reverberated in the small space. Finally, Aibek looked up from his broth. "Well, we knew they'd be angry. I guess I'm not surprised they want to make an example of us. Do you know when they'll be here?"

Eddrick replied grimly. "They'll likely be here by the end of the week."

They sat in silence for a long time as everyone considered the implications of this information. Eventually, Serik stood and gathered the dishes onto the tray. "Do you want me to call a council meeting, sir?"

Aibek nodded. "Yes, thank you – immediately. They need to know this."

Once Serik was gone, Kiri drifted over and kissed her son on the forehead. He felt it as a cold whisper of breath on his face. Of course, they couldn't stay for the meeting.

"Are there any rules I should know about? Am I allowed to tell them I talk to you?" He asked his parents before they could vanish.

His mother replied, "You can tell them… if you think they'll believe you. Otherwise, tell them whatever they need to hear to believe the truth of what we said."

Aibek wrapped his blankets tighter around him as another chill came over him, and when he looked up again, he was alone. He wondered if he had time for a nap before the others arrived. The conversation with his parents had left him feeling weak and tired. He lay back on the bed and hoped it would be at least an hour before anyone else disturbed him.

When he woke again, the sun shone through the windows at a different angle, and he realized it must be afternoon. He thought he'd heard someone knock on the outer door, so he pushed himself to a sitting position despite the dizziness and tried to prepare himself for visitors.

As Aibek expected, Serik led the council members into the sitting room, where Aibek joined them.

Kai laughed. "You look terrible. That color red isn't

becoming on you at all."

"Thanks." Aibek chuckled, then grew serious, "I got an update this morning that we should discuss."

They all leaned in to hear what he had to say. Aibek spoke softly because of his headache, and the council members leaned close to hear his words. He relayed all the information he had received from his parents without revealing his source. He wasn't sure how they would accept the thought that the new mayor was talking to the dead.

He kept the meeting short and to the point. The evacuees had left that morning, so only those who would fight were left in the village. They would instruct each division to save arrows and energy for the second wave of Helak's warriors, and make sure to complete all the final preparations by the end of the week. The council members agreed they didn't need to divulge the rest of Helak's plan to the combined army. There was no need to create panic in their fighting force.

Thankfully, no one asked where he had gotten his information. They accepted that as the mayor, he had sources they didn't need to know about.

The discussion finished and the visitors filed out of Aibek's room. He immediately retreated to his bed and was asleep in moments. Before he drifted off, he thought it was probably a good thing he was too sick to worry about the approaching army and the new situation with Ahren. That was a serious mess… He might never figure it out.

~*~

As Valasa promised, the spots were gone when Aibek awoke late the next morning. However, the shivering chills continued to rack his body. He was so thirsty; he gratefully drank the vile broth Serik brought. He didn't ask what it was made from. He suspected he didn't want to know, anyway.

Before long Faruz joined him, wrapped in a fluffy robe to ward off the chills. They sat quietly for a few minutes, choking down more of the rancid brew Valasa kept sending them.

Finally, Aibek broke the silence. "Well, the party was a bit of a disaster, wasn't it?"

Faruz grinned. "It certainly ended badly. I had a great time with Zifa before the commotion, though."

"I saw you dancing together. You looked like you were having fun. Did you get any time alone?"

"No, we were walking to a bench to catch our breath when the screaming started," Faruz lowered his eyes, a disappointed look on his face. He raised an eyebrow. "What about you? I saw you getting close to Ahren. Did she have a change of heart before she tried to kill you?"

"Ha. Ha. Ha. Yes, we spent a little time together on a bench beside the Pavilion, but I don't know what it meant to her. I'm not sure she tried to kill me, either." He sighed, then yawned. "I'm reserving judgment on the whole situation until I have a chance to talk to her."

"That's fair." Faruz grinned again. "Zifa was incredible, though. I have no idea how she keeps going through dance after dance like that. I was out of breath after one, but she wouldn't stop for a break!"

Aibek smiled as his friend chattered on. He wasn't at all surprised to hear that Faruz was falling head over ears in love with Zifa.

"Hey, what do you think?" Faruz blurted after a pause in the conversation. "Is 'captain' a high enough title to earn a home? It wouldn't have to be on the Square. You know I love staying here with you, but it would be great to eventually have my own place."

"Let's get through the next few weeks; then we'll ask the council. You really want to stay here, then?"
"Of course. Who wouldn't want to stay here? It's a perfect place to build a life."

23.

Signals

Aibek spent the rest of the day alternately napping and chatting with Faruz. As the day wore on, some of the fatigue and achiness of the illness started to diminish, leaving him alert and hungry. It became more difficult to suppress the frustration with his weakness, and he yearned to venture into the village once again. At the same time, he worried about the needed preparations for the coming battle and longed to resume his daily checks of the battlements and reinforcements.

By the time the sun set, Aibek was hungry for something besides broth, so he asked Serik to fetch a dinner tray. The simple meal smelled delicious; the steam rising from the roasted meat, root vegetables, and toasted nuts made his stomach rumble painfully. He devoured every morsel, then soon found himself nodding off in his chair. As he prepared for bed, he hoped he would be free of the fever when morning came.

Aibek slept until the dawn lightened his bedroom window. He felt stronger and thought the fever might have passed. He enjoyed a long, soaking bath, and was curled up in his favorite chair, sipping famanc by the fire, when Faruz joined him in his sitting room.

They were halfway through their breakfast of famanc and muffins when Serik said, "You look as if you're feeling better today, sir."

Aibek smiled. "I am. A lot better. I think I'll get outside today. I've missed checking on the army and watching them train."

Faruz had just stuffed a whole muffin into his mouth, but he nodded his agreement.

They sat quietly for a few more minutes, then Aibek cocked his head. "Serik, do you think our enemies have ever been exposed to Usartma?"

Serik frowned. "I'm not sure. I guess it would be reasonable to think not since it doesn't seem to have spread to the city. Why do you ask?"

"I was wondering if we could find a way to spread our illness to the enemy's army… It knocked me down for a full three days. If even a fraction of the army fell ill, it could help us gain an advantage."

Faruz agreed, "Or, it could slow them down if they have to stop and let their men recover. That would give us a few more days to prepare."

Serik nodded. "And how do you plan to spread this disease to the enemy, sir?"

"Well… I was thinking maybe my parents could take some of the rags we've used and plant them in the enemy's tents. Do you think they'd do that?"

Eddrick appeared next to the fireplace. "I think that could be arranged."

Aibek gasped in surprise and turned toward the unexpected voice.

His father stood there, calmly handling a small carving of a deer that had been on the mantle. "Your mother learned how to move things from place to place years ago, so she could knit scarves and hats for the orphans in the city. It kept her busy and made her feel useful while you were growing up. We could easily put some cloths in their tents. I was coming to warn you that they're getting close."

"Thank you, Father." Aibek rose and gathered some of the dirty cloths, including his pillow cover, and placed them in a pile near his chair. He hoped this would work. He wasn't quite sure how Usartma spread, but it seemed reasonable to think the linens would carry it to the enemy.

Eddrick gathered the linens in his arms and vanished just as suddenly as he'd appeared.

With a loud sigh, Faruz stood and stretched, then pointed to the faint light coming through the window. "We should go watch the sun come up. I've spent too much time indoors these past three days

"That sounds perfect." Aibek led the way into the courtyard behind his home.

A few visiting warriors were already outside, lounging on benches and talking softly among themselves. They greeted Aibek and Faruz and emptied a bench for the recuperating men. Aibek sat quietly next to Faruz and enjoyed the bright pinks and oranges that washed across the sky as he watched the sun rise over a frosty morning. Before long, the morning sun warmed the courtyard, and Aibek thought it was late enough to venture out.

He turned to Faruz. "Where should we go first? Should we check on the army? Or try to talk to Ahren or Tamyr?"

"Let's check on the army. They're closest. You can talk to Ahren and Tamyr after the morning's council meeting. And I want to see Zifa. I haven't been able to talk to her since the banquet. I hope she's handling everything all right. Ahren's her best friend."

Aibek sighed. "That's true."

He wanted to believe Ahren was innocent, but the witness from the banquet had called her the attacker. He picked up his pace a little as they walked toward the Pavilion. The sooner he met with the division leaders, the sooner he could see Ahren. He wanted to hear her side, even if the evidence contradicted her.

They found the division leaders at the Pavilion, waiting for the remaining soldiers to join them for the morning's training. Aibek was pleased to learn that the training and preparation had continued full-force in his absence, though he'd expected nothing less. As he'd requested, the archers had put the fairies to work making arrows, so now they had more than twice what they thought they should need.

Everywhere Aibek looked, the village was abuzz with activity as the army prepared for the imminent battle. Men and women trained together with ferocious energy but still managed to laugh and enjoy a warm comradery. At this point, it was difficult to tell who was native to this village and who was visiting from elsewhere in the Tsari, because they had grown so close during their time training.

Aibek walked through all of Nivaka beside Faruz, watching the army train and verifying that their orders had been carried out. They discussed their strategy as they walked, and conversed with division leaders and fighters who approached to express their joy at seeing their leaders well again. Aibek hoped he wasn't leading these good people to their deaths. He examined each face and hoped to see that person uninjured after the battle was over.

Aibek and Faruz declined to join in the training, but Aibek was happy to be out of the house and among the people again. He reveled in the sights and sounds of a training army. The soldiers wore matching leather and steel armor over colorful, reinforced zontrec, and the clanging of metal practice swords filled the wintry air. He shivered a little and wondered how much colder it would get—the winter was just beginning.

~*~

The council meeting was short and to the point; each council member gave an update on the activities of the past three days, then they adjourned to spend their time training. The army would arrive any day now. Aibek didn't feel well enough to train, but he had other matters to attend to. First, he wanted to question Tamyr. Maybe she'd be more willing to talk, now that the other members of her group had shown themselves.

He climbed the stairs to her room, though it took him longer than it should have. He quietly cursed his illness as he stopped to rest halfway. For some reason, there was no guard outside the girl's door. Aibek scowled at the breach, then knocked and entered the room. The guard was sitting on his chair just inside the room, a surprised look on his broad face. The girl sat on a small chair, holding an empty plate and a fork. An empty cup sat on the floor next to her chair. She looked neat and clean, though her dress was worn and faded.

The guard rose awkwardly from his chair. "Good morning, Mister Mayor, I didn't expect to see you today. I mean… it's good to see you up and about."

"Do you normally sit in the room with the prisoner? Wouldn't that make it rather easy for someone to sneak up on you?"

The guard flushed and rushed to answer, "No, sir. I only just came in here to give the girl her breakfast. I have to stay until she's done so I can take her dishes out. We can't leave any potential weapons in the room, sir."

Aibek nodded. "I guess that makes sense. I'll stay in here with her for now. I need to ask her a few questions."

The guard ducked out and pulled the door closed. Aibek lowered himself into the chair the man had vacated and regarded the young woman. She sat with her head down, toying with the fork in her hand.

She began abruptly. "You sure took your time in coming. I was starting to think you'd forgotten about me."

"I've been ill. I wanted to talk to you days ago, but I couldn't leave my room." Aibek explained, then stopped himself. He didn't owe this woman any explanations. "I guess you've heard about what happened at the banquet?"

He struggled to keep his voice gentle but accusing.

"Yes. Valasa came and told me the next morning – after Ahren woke up." She kept her head down, still refusing to meet his eyes.

"What do you know about what happened? I haven't talked to Ahren, yet." He waited for a response, but Tamyr stayed silent. After a moment, he added, "All I know is that the witness at the celebration said she saw Ahren with the knife, then Ahni tackled her. Why did Ahren have a knife at the banquet?"

"Why should I tell you anything?" She spat the question with a venom he hadn't seen since the first time he'd questioned her.

"I've done my best to see you properly cared for, rather than left to rot in that upper room like a common criminal. I've ensured you have clean clothes and proper meals, and I've honestly tried to get to the bottom of the whole situation. I know you hate me and the council, but I still don't think you stabbed Alija." He shifted slightly in the hard chair, leaning back against the wall for more support.

"So, you think because you treated me decently that I'll tell you everything? That's not much of a strategy." She gave a humorless laugh.

"I'm not one for strategy when it comes to people. In my experience, kindness and honesty goes further." He leaned forward again, silently willing her to meet his gaze. "Please, tell me what you know about Ahren. Was she trying to kill me? Or one of the other council members?"

Finally, Tamyr looked up. Her soft brown eyes met Aibek's, stunning him with the depth of her sorrow and pain.

"Ahren is innocent." Tears streamed down her face as her words flowed faster. "She never, ever, wanted anything bad to happen to anyone, and she wasn't sorry to see Tavan overthrown. She just talked to me about how she thought a local should have had your place. No outsider should have a role in running this village."

Stunned by the unexpected proclamation, Aibek sat silently. After a moment, he asked, "Where did the dagger come from? Was it Ahni's?"

"Yes. It was always Ahni. She's the one who stabbed Alija, too. She was Tavan's mistress, though she believed he'd marry her eventually. It was only a few days before his death when she found out she was with child. She'd been trying to hide her condition while plotting to overthrow the council."

She paused, sobbing silently, and Aibek wondered how this woman had stayed captive so long to protect her friend.

"Is she really dead?" Tamyr whispered, another sob escaping as she struggled for control.

Aibek nodded slowly. "I'm sorry."

He couldn't think of anything more to say. He handed her the handkerchief he had brought this time and waited while she regained control of herself, then excused himself and escaped into the open boardwalk below.

He dropped onto an empty bench just outside the prison-house and cradled his head in his hands. He yearned to believe everything Tamyr had told him—that Ahni was behind everything and Ahren was completely innocent. It was a little too convenient.

It was easy to place the blame on someone who couldn't defend herself, and wouldn't face any further consequences. True, Ahni was dead, but this version of events allowed both Tamyr and Ahren to clear their names. He thought again of those few precious moments on the bench outside the party. Ahren had felt so soft and warm and had molded herself against his chest. The moment had felt… what? Right? How would he know if it were right? Even at that moment, he hadn't trusted her.

With a great heaving sigh, Aibek shoved himself to his feet. His head swam a little, so he stood for a moment and waited for the sensation to pass. When he could see clearly, he set off for Valasa's house. He had to hear Ahren's side of the story.

~*~

It felt strange to knock on the heavy wooden door. For several months, this house had been his home, and he'd gone through this door without a moment's hesitation. Now, he waited outside until the housekeeper cracked the door open and peeked through, then swung it wide and welcomed him inside. They exchanged pleasantries while he waited for Valasa. Finally, the healer strolled into the den from his workroom.

When he spotted Aibek, the large man grinned. "I heard you were up and out today. I'm glad you're feeling better."

"Yes, thank you for the broths. I think they helped." Aibek flushed and lowered his eyes, mentally tracing the circular pattern on the plush rug. "Um… would it be all right if I talk to Ahren? I'd like to ask about how she got hurt."

Valasa barked out a short laugh, then grew serious. "Of course. I've already asked those same questions, but I know you have to ask for yourself."

They trailed quietly down the hall toward Ahren's room, and Valasa knocked softly on the door. He didn't wait for an answer before he pressed the door open and gestured for Aibek to enter. They stood just inside, in a small sitting room furnished in green and silver. Hundreds of tiny figurines and carvings crowded every available shelf and table. Some depicted dancing fairies, like the ones in the painting in Aibek's meditation room, while others were forest creatures, trees, and flowers. Aibek snapped his mouth shut and looked questioningly to his host.

Valasa smiled. "Yes, she carved all these. She's very talented."

Aibek blinked and tried to reconcile the patience and skill required to create these beautifully detailed works of art with his image of the impulsive and impetuous young woman he was here to see. Before he could regain his composure, Ahren moved slowly through a door to his right. He had to work to stifle the gasp that rose in him at her appearance. A deep purple bruise covered the entire right side of her face, and her right eye was still swollen shut. She moved gingerly to a soft-looking chair near the window and lowered herself into it without appearing to notice his presence.

Uncomfortable with watching her pained movements, Aibek shifted his weight from one foot to the other and cleared his throat. Finally, slowly, Ahren raised her good eye to his face, and he had to resist the urge to look away.

"I know. It looks awful."

Before Aibek could respond, Valasa cleared his throat. "I'll be in the hall. Maybe she'll tell you more than she's told me." He swept out the door without waiting for a reply. The soft click of the latch echoed in the silence left behind.

"How are you feeling?"

"I heard you've been sick. Are you all right now?"

They both talked at the same time, then they laughed.

"You first." Aibek smiled a little.

"I'm sore, but my father says I'll be fine. What about you? You were ill?"

"Yes, I caught some random forest disease, but I'm better now." He stopped and took a breath, then blurted out, "What happened? Where did the dagger come from?"

Ahren shook her head. "I don't know. I was standing next to her, watching the dancing, and suddenly she had the knife in her hand."

She continued, relaying the tale from the beginning and ending with Ahni tackling her to the ground. She'd woken in her bed the next morning.

When she'd finished, Aibek sat quietly, thinking. Her story didn't contradict the witness, but rather expanded on what the witness had seen. Ahren had the dagger in her hand because she'd wrestled it away from Ahni a moment before.

The seconds ticked by in silence and Ahren looked at him with a stricken expression. "You don't believe me, do you?"

"I want to," he said honestly, "but I'm having a hard time putting it all together." The pounding behind his temples had returned with a vengeance, and he had to concentrate to hear her words. "I don't think I'm quite back to normal, yet," he added. Aibek pushed himself to his feet, then turned to face Ahren again. "I'll come back tomorrow if you want to talk more. I'm not feeling very well right now."

"I think I'd like that. I haven't given you much of a chance before now, and I'm sorry for that."

Silence answered her once again. Aibek couldn't find the right words, so he kept his mouth firmly clamped shut. He wasn't quite sure what he thought yet, and he didn't want to offer false promises to the battered young woman. He bowed slightly in her direction and then pulled open the door. Valasa stood in the hall, apparently listening at the door. Aibek smiled and made his way down the hall and back to his home.

~*~

By the time he'd dragged himself across the Square, Aibek had conceded that maybe he wasn't as recovered as he wanted to believe. He ate a light lunch and crawled back into his bed. He slept through supper and didn't wake until the morning sun shone through the window.

The day dawned bright and cold, and the light streaming through the window had a different gleam to it. Aibek peeked out between the curtains, then exclaimed in wonder at the layer of white fluffy snow covering everything outside. He ventured outside.

Having grown up in the warmer climate of the city, he had never seen snow except in children's stories, so he was shocked when Serik grabbed a handful of it and hurled it at his chest. With a shout, Aibek stepped backward in surprise, then promptly slipped on the icy wood floor and fell onto his backside.

Carefully getting up from his cold landing, Aibek immediately scooped some snow to retaliate, but before he could throw his new weapon, Faruz stepped into the courtyard, and Aibek decided he made a better target. Faruz shouted in surprise when the snowball struck and disintegrated, and then bent to gather a snowball to defend himself.

The three friends gleefully hurled wads of snow at each other until they were soaked through and out of breath. At that point, the housekeeper ushered them inside to change clothes and warm up with some hot famanc. When they looked out the front window, they saw similar scenes being played out around them as their neighbors and guests emerged and discovered the newly fallen snow. The morning was a blur of snowball fights followed by warm blankets and famanc by the fire.

After lunch, the division leaders called their groups to order, and training resumed. They needed to be confident enough to fight efficiently in the icy cold, slippery conditions. No one had any trouble adapting, though. After the shenanigans of the morning, everyone had already grown accustomed to sliding around in the snow.

During a short break, Aibek thought he heard a shout ring out from the north. He peered over the rail and confirmed his fear. The groundfolk had lit the warning lamps. The enemy was in the forest.

He bellowed, "Everyone to your stations! Prepare for battle!"

All scrambled to comply, exclaiming to everyone they passed that the siege was coming. In a deafening cacophony of clanging metal and anxious shouts, the fighters frantically donned their battle armor and took up their weapons. Swords had been filed to a razor edge, and every arrow was deadly sharp. This was the moment they had trained for. The division officers urged their subordinates to keep quiet, so they didn't alert the coming army to their readiness. The invaders expected them to be unprepared, like the last time.

24.

Attack

Breathless and tense, they waited. Faruz shivered as the icy wind howled through the barren trees. He waited along with his division at the northern border. He peered through the dark trees, searching for signs of the enemy's approach. How many would come?

He looked around at the soldiers assembled near him, saw the anxious looks on their faces, and tried to project confidence. Maybe Aibek's plan to infect the enemy with Usartma had been successful, and Helak's ranks would be weak and ill.

He stretched onto his toes and looked in all directions, inspecting the assembled force. Nivaka had brought together an army of twelve hundred warriors: not a large army by city standards, but a huge force for this small town. They stood ready, swords and shields gleaming in the afternoon sun. And still, they waited. After a while, the villagers near him began to mumble and complain. Some brushed the powdery snow away from spots on the boardwalk, making dry patches where they could sit. Some soldiers whispered to each other that the ground folk had deceived them.

Faruz considered the possibility; his eyes narrowed as he continued to stare out into the forest. What if this was a joke? Why would the elves or dwarves light the lamps if no one was coming? What would they gain from such a prank? No, this had to be real.

Though he couldn't explain what was taking the enemy so long, Faruz did his best to reassure the anxious men and women this was real, and that the enemy was coming. He struggled to keep order as small spats broke out among individuals who claimed they had been fooled and those who insisted they should wait it out. The tension was so thick he could smell it on the wintry air.

The warriors waited for an eternity before the definitive sound of boots marching in time through the snowy forest drifted to their fearful ears. The sun overhead was blinding as it reflected off the pristine snow. Twigs snapped and leaves crunched under the wintry cushion beneath the feet of the advancing army. The rhythmic pounding grew until it was almost enough to make some overwrought villagers lose their nerve, but their leaders kept them still.

Faruz crouched low against the rail at the north end of Nivaka, watching and waiting for the perfect moment. Fighters perched in the trees outside the village twitched at the nearness of their enemy. All eyes turned to Faruz, waiting for the signal.

Finally, he raised both hands and waved his soldiers forward, mouthing the word, "Now!"

~*~

At their captain's quiet command, Zifa and her group of agile warriors swung through the trees above the enemy force. With a dagger between her teeth, she signaled to her team without making a sound, and together they dropped to the ground amongst their adversaries. With lightning quick movements, she drew her weapon across the throat of an enemy soldier and leapt back to the branch above. From her perch, she surveyed the scene below and noted with satisfaction that each of her fighters had killed at least one enemy soldier.

As soon as Zifa and her team were out of danger, Faruz waved the archers forward, and each shot three arrows in quick succession onto the advancing army. Immediately after the archers, the spear throwers stepped forward and launched wickedly sharp javelins into the bewildered horde. Many enemy fighters had tilted their heads to follow the retreating villagers and were easy targets for the swift arrows and spears. Screams pierced the air as wounded men fell, and areas of snow turned red.

When enemy soldiers turned to tend their wounded, Zifa and her warriors once again dropped from the trees and attacked the flanks. Again they killed several fighters before returning to their branches. This time, they swung and climbed their way back into the village, carefully avoiding the sharp spikes on the rails. They wouldn't take the chance on a third attack. Their friends were waiting to help them back onto the boardwalk with words of praise and encouragement.

~*~

Faruz watched for Zifa's return to the boardwalk, and personally congratulated her on a well-executed attack.

"Well done! You were perfect." He clapped her on the shoulder, then turned to the man coming over the rail behind her.

"Great job!" he exclaimed as he helped the man to the relative safety of the boardwalk.

Once all the soldiers were within the boundaries of the village, Faruz ducked behind the line of archers and spear throwers. He directed them to shoot at will. He was pleased to see that nearly a quarter of Helak's army lay wounded or dead on the ground, and more were falling every moment from the incessant attack. In the confusion of the surprise assault, some of the less determined soldiers scattered into the trees, further decreasing the size of the invading army.

"Look, they're already running away!" he yelled over his shoulder to Wayra. His tall friend nodded and fired another arrow without stopping to respond, and several others within hearing distance erupted in nervous laughter.

All too soon, the leaders of the enemy force regained their footing and commanded their men to begin trying to gain entrance into the village. Faruz watched with satisfaction as their grappling hooks slid impotently off the spiked rail, unable to find traction on the icy barbs. Without much success, other soldiers tried to find ways to break or climb over the spiked collars protecting the trees near the village.

The archers maintained a steady barrage of arrows while the enemy sought entrance to the village. Before long, Helak's warriors fastened their grappling hooks onto the ends of rope ladders, which they then flung up over the spiked rail. The ladder caught on the barbs, and the soldiers began to climb. They kept their heads down so their heavy iron helmets would repel the arrows, but many were wounded and fell when they looked up to seek their next handhold. Several long minutes later, the first of the soldiers reached the top of the rail. They tried to shield their faces from the arrows but then were quickly dispatched by villagers with swords as they attempted to climb over the rail along the boardwalk.

From his vantage point on a crate behind the archers, Faruz could see the enemy breaching the top of the rail. At first, coming one or two at a time, soon they were like a sea of iron and steel pouring onto the boardwalk.

Faruz swung his father's broadsword off his back. He ripped it from the scabbard and scrambled to help stem the tide. A shield cracked beneath his sword; he felt the satisfying crunch of bone as his blade connected with an enemy's chest. And then he felt a tremor in the board-walk, ice rushing through his veins as he turned to see the most colossal soldier he had ever faced.

Blanketed in iron and bearskin, the soldier stormed for-ward; his snarl baring pointed black teeth. Faruz felt himself bouncing on the boardwalk with every step closer the solder came to him. "Oh, no!" was all he had time to say before the enemy's axe swung for his head.

Faruz shot in, putting all his training to the test. He swept his sword out, but the goliath jumped back and brought his axe down again. Faruz side-stepped, the axe chiming off the railing, sending wood chips flying. Faruz then brought his sword over his head, chopping for the man's arm but only finding the haft of his axe. The enemy kicked, and Faruz felt the wind knocked from his lungs as he tumbled across the boardwalk.

Terror filled Faruz's eyes as he looked up. Not only was this giant coming for him, but more and more spilled over the rail. Archers fired; swords clashed. But for each one his men sent back over the rail, two more took their place.

He filled his lungs with icy air and rolled to the side, then lay perfectly still and waited for the enemy to advance again. When the hulking soldier stamped over to finish him, Faruz rolled and swung his sword with all his might. He felt the blade slice through his opponent's thigh and heard the man scream in pain. He leapt to his feet and swung again, slicing through the giant's neck and sending his head rolling across the slushy board-walk. His stomach churned, and he gagged once at the sight, then turned away and looked to see if any villagers needed help. He noticed with a start that the arrows had ceased flying.

"They're still coming over the rail!" He shouted to the head archer, who nodded, then turned and gave the command for his men to continue firing.

Even though he had been warned, Faruz was astonished by how many there were. Soon the enemy warriors would outnumber the force waiting for them on the icy wooden walkway. His only consolation was that nearly a third of the advancing force had bright red splotches over their faces, and even more looked weak and ill. Aibek's plan to weaken the force with Usartma had worked.

Most of the advancing soldiers carried swords strapped to their backs or around their waists, but some held large battle axes and maces. Faruz was thankful they couldn't use the latter effectively in the limited space on the boardwalk. Some of the larger battleaxes were equally ineffective, and after a couple of tries, the enemy fighters discarded those frightening tools in favor of more practical options such as swords and daggers, as well as smaller axes.

~*~

Meanwhile, a hundred yards to the east of the main battlefront, Aibek waited with his segment of swordsmen. Their assignment was to reinforce the fighters at the front when they began to tire, but Aibek immediately noticed a problem. He watched quietly from a crouched position by the rail as about three hundred men broke away from their formation and circled around toward the east side of the village.

Aibek silently raised his arm and pointed toward the smaller section, then gestured to his archers to nock an arrow. He allowed the battalion to get several hundred yards from the body of the enemy force, then pointed to his archers and shouted, "Shoot!"

Arrows rained down on the unsuspecting enemy, who were stunned for a moment by the sudden attack. They took half a second to regroup, then began a furious rush toward the village.

Aibek looked around and realized where they were, then pointed to several strong men and said, "You! Bring the spiked balls from the blacksmith's shop!"

The army had decided not to use the spiked balls the council had requested because they were too heavy to move around the village. Plus, the captain had no way of knowing beforehand which way the enemy would come. However, since they were this close, the balls would be perfect. Similar to the spiky weapons chained to a mace, they were larger and heavier. He waited while the runners retrieved the weapons, then ordered the men to hand them off to soldiers at the front lines and return for more spike balls.

It only took a few moments before this group copied the main army's strategy of throwing the ladders over the spiked rail. His men hacked at the rope, but their swords clanged against the steel spikes. They managed to cut down some of the ladders, but more came. Aibek watched as they climbed toward the rail, biding his time. When the enemy had almost reached the rail, he shouted, "Throw them, now!" and watched as the first barbed weapon fell. It immediately crashed into an enemy soldier, piercing his helmet. Blood painted his shoulders red before his body fell, knocking three other soldiers down.

"It's working," he shouted. "Keep them coming! Bring more as fast as you can!"

The villagers kept tossing the spiked balls, which bounced from one enemy to another, piercing armor and knocking a number of enemy fighters to the ground below. Most who fell were badly injured or killed, but a few regained their feet and continued their relentless climb toward the village.

The villagers created a working chain, passing the spiked balls from the shop to the battlefront in mere moments.

Aibek thought his plan worked beautifully. Between the spiked balls, large boulders they'd collected, and the efforts of the archers, they cut the enemy faction down to a third of its original size. Aibek knew the rest would breach the rail soon, and warned his swordsmen to be ready. He could hear the clamor of shouts, screams, and clanging of swords coming from the north end, and knew the enemy had reached the village on the main front.

He held his men steady and led the fierce attack when the first of the enemy soldiers climbed the rail. He yelled to the archers to pull back and keep firing from a safe distance; they would be needed again later. All around him, he saw his friends and neighbors engaged in fierce hand-to-hand combat. Before long, the last of the enemy soldiers had entered the village, and Aibek shouted for his men to move back toward the main battlefront. He didn't like being separated from the reinforcements.

~*~

"Let's go!" Aibek roared as he rushed into the wave of enemy soldiers a short time later. He ducked under a sword aimed at his neck and brought his weapon around, planting it between the plates of armor on his foe's chest. He jerked his sword free just in time to block an axe coming toward his head. He dodged to the right and found an opening. The man fell in the snow clutching his abdomen where the sword had ripped it open.

"Attack! Attack!" He screamed to bolster his men.

After a moment, he found himself matched against a short, stocky man who looked very similar to the messenger Siddet, except that this man had red spots all over his face. Aibek couldn't help but smile a little as the man bared pointed black teeth and rushed in to attack. Aibek blocked the assault and moved to his left, looking for an opening in his enemy's defense. They matched each other move by move, and Aibek realized that, for once, his height gave him a disadvantage. He hunched over to bring himself closer to his adversary's size.

They circled slowly until Aibek felt the crunch of snow give way to the crack of ice. He glanced down and saw they were standing on an area of solid ice left from a small leak in a nearby cistern. Drawing on the lessons he'd learned that morning, he used the slippery surface to slide quickly toward his opponent. The sudden move caught the shorter man off guard, and he stumbled, slipped, and fell backward in the snow. Aibek finished him with a swift slash to the throat, then looked up and saw they had rejoined the villagers at the north end. Breathing hard from the exertion of the fight, the mayor glanced around and noticed that the villagers were holding their own, but they were starting to tire. He wiped the sweat from his face with his sleeve and wondered how long they could hold. As he'd hoped, some of Helak's soldiers appeared to have contracted Usartma, but it didn't seem to slow them down much. How would the villagers manage when the second wave of enemy soldiers arrived?

The fighting dragged on as the afternoon shadows grew, and their enemies slowly gained ground. The villagers were being pushed farther down the boardwalk and toward the center of town. He defeated his most recent opponent, then stepped back from the battle for a moment.

~*~

A short while later, Faruz stepped back and glanced around at the chaos. All his friends and neighbors were locked in fierce combat. Even the weaker, obviously ill enemy soldiers were formidable warriors. Would they have had a chance without the advantage of disease? Faruz wasn't sure.

As he watched, Dalan ducked under the swing of his opponent's broadsword and thrust his sword between the plates of the enemy's armor, ending the fight. Faruz caught his friend's eye and nodded his congratulations, then turned to see another enormous soldier moving toward him. He took a few breaths to steady himself then rushed forward to engage the enemy.

He swung his father's sword even before he had stopped running, sending up a shower of golden sparks when it made contact with his adversary's shield. Faruz swayed as his feet slid on the slushy boardwalk. Before he had fully regained his balance, his opponent moved to take advantage, thrusting his sword toward the captain's undefended throat. Faruz ducked under the attack and rushed his attacker. This time he connected with the armor plating on his enemy's chest, and he heard the gargantuan man exhale in a sharp "Oof!"

Before the giant could recover, Faruz swung again. The enormous enemy gathered his wits and blocked the swing with his sword, and Faruz felt the impact vibrate through his arms and chest. With his arms and lungs burning with exertion in the icy air, Faruz thrust lower, toward his adversary's legs. Again, the gargantuan opponent blocked the move.

Faruz stepped back and wiped the sweat from his brow. His chest heaved as he struggled for breath and moved slowly to his right, never taking his eyes from his enemy as they circled. Without warning, Helak's soldier let out a bloodcurdling scream and lunged at Faruz, who relied on all of his training as he quickly dodged the attack and thrust his sword blindly toward his opponent. He felt the weapon connect with flesh and looked up to see that he had managed to wedge his weapon between the plates of armor protecting the giant's upper body. He jerked the sword free and watched, transfixed, as a fountain of red erupted from the man's chest. The enormous man opened his mouth and tried to shout in surprise, but only managed a wet gurgling sound, then flailed wildly as he fell. He released his weapon as he struggled to breathe, and the blade tumbled through the air.

Standing with his hands on his knees as he struggled for his breath, Faruz didn't notice that the weapon was falling dangerously close to him until it was too late. Before he could jump aside, the weapon sliced through the flesh above his knee, then clattered to the icy wooden floor. A river of blood ran down his leg, and he dropped to a sitting position as his head swam from the pain.

~*~

Aibek watched the battle raging around him, considering the plight of his soldiers, then sought out the commander of the archers.

"Shoot into the melèe," he ordered. "Whenever one of your archers has a clear shot at an enemy, let him take it."

"Are you sure?" the commander asked, "What if we hit our own fighters by mistake?"

"I'm sure," Aibek answered, grimly. "We need something to give us an edge. I can't think of anything else, can you?"

"No," the archer said. "I don't have any ideas. We'll do our best. He shook his head and ran back to the group of archers who were trying to stay clear of the combat.

Aibek left the commander and returned to his division, still locked in ferocious battle. He nodded encouragement to Dalan, who stepped forward and ended the fight he had been in with an enemy warrior. Then Aibek spotted a younger man who was tiring and leaving himself vulnerable. Aibek strode over to the fighter and stood next to him with his sword drawn, providing enough distraction that the young man found an opening and thrust his sword between the armor plating the enemy's chest.

At that moment, Aibek spotted Faruz sitting on the ground surrounded by a puddle of red. Aibek was relieved to see his friend sitting up and holding a sword, but he couldn't get to him to find out what had happened. He had to stay with his division and lead them through the battle. He couldn't desert them now, though he wanted to run to his childhood companion and make sure he would survive his injuries.

Within a few minutes, the first arrow flew. It hit an enemy soldier in the neck, and the man stumbled and fell. No one noticed except for the villager he had been fighting. A moment later, several arrows flew into the melèe. Each hit and wounded an enemy fighter. This time, everyone noticed. Several villagers shouted in relief as their adversaries fell at their feet, and others won easy victories due to their foes' distraction.

~*~

From his vantage point on the boardwalk, Faruz couldn't tell what had caused the sudden surge of energy in the villagers. He craned his neck to see around the wall of friends who had been defending him since he fell. A large red puddle surrounded him, and he had grown too weak to hold his sword, but still, he tried to keep track of the battle.

Wayra came to where Faruz was sitting. "I don't like how much blood you're losing, Captain. I'll tie something around your leg to stop the bleeding."

Faruz took a deep breath, nodded and watched as his friend ripped a strip of cloth from his shirt and pressed it over the wound. Wayra bent, removed the captain's belt and tied that an inch above the improvised dressing. He held pressure to the bandage until the bleeding stopped, then loosened the tourniquet slightly.

"That should do." Wayra turned away and resumed his battle position.

The archers continued to fire into the melèe whenever they had a clear shot at an enemy warrior, but the energy of the battle had shifted. The villagers finally outnumbered their opponents and were defeating the enemies that remained.

At the moment when it looked like they'd won the battle, Faruz heard a shout. The villagers around him groaned and lifted their weapons. More enemy soldiers had been spotted advancing through the forest.

~*~

"The second wave is here!" Aibek yelled to the weary defenders. "We knew they were coming, and we're ready!"

He leaned over the rail, slicing the discarded rope ladders loose. They tumbled to the ground in a useless heap, and Aibek turned to the assembled archers and shouted, "Hold nothing back! We only have to defeat this group and its over!"

The archers managed to eliminate nearly half of the advancing brigade, but the others didn't slow their assault. They quickly figured out how to loop their ladders onto the barbed rail, and even though the villagers cut down half the ladders, the enemies climbed into the embattled village on ladders that wouldn't budge and attacked the exhausted defenders.

Frantically, Aibek searched for an angle, any advantage he could use to defeat the newcomers. He considered telling his warriors that these enemies intended to kill them all and move into their homes, but discarded that idea when he saw how tired his men looked.

Upon second look, these new warriors didn't look all that fresh, either. In fact, some of them appeared to be wounded, in addition to the spots marring their faces and necks. He wondered what they had encountered before they arrived here, but then decided it didn't matter. They were here now and must be defeated.

Aibek wasted no time engaging the new enemy alongside his men, even though he was distracted. He blocked and thrust as he mulled over the villagers' situation. Helak's men outnumbered them again. How much longer could they hold out? As he fought, he searched desperately for a winning strategy, even as he shouted encouragement to the villagers fighting for their lives around him.

~*~

Faruz heard the groans of the weary guard as the clanging of armor signaled the approach of the enemy battalion. Some of his defenders moved off to fight the new division, and he wondered if he would live to see the end of this battle. He wanted to see his army succeed against their enemies. He had been weak before Wayra placed the tourniquet, and now he was starting to feel dizzy, too. He'd been sitting in the snow for so long; he could no longer feel his feet. He tried to wiggle his toes but gave up when he realized he couldn't tell if they moved or not. He was so tired. Maybe he would feel better after a little nap.

~*~

"You can do this!" Aibek screamed to the exhausted defenders. "Oof," His breath rushed out as something crashed into his back.

He spun around in time to see an enemy soldier kick at Alija, who fell against the rail. Another adversary sprang toward him with his sword raised, and Aibek moved to save his friend. He attacked the aggressor from the side, knocking the sword out of his hand, then driving his weapon through the man's neck. Before his adversary hit the ground, the other assailant rushed at Aibek with a scream of rage.

Aibek dodged the assault and swung his sword around, sending a shower of sparks when it connected with the armor plating the enemy's back. Helak's warrior stumbled forward with the force of the blow and slid in the slushy snow. Aibek took the advantage while his foe was flailing for balance, and drove his sword through the man's unprotected flank.

Alija stirred slightly against the rail, though he didn't open his eyes. Reassured that his friend was still alive, Aibek planted himself in front of the injured man, determined to protect him.

When he turned his back to Alija, Aibek saw the full scope of the battle. His eyes swung north, then south. Everywhere he looked, exhausted villagers desperately battled enemy soldiers. They were outnumbered nearly two to one. His heart sank to his boots as he saw another adversary rushing toward him. How would they ever win?

"Great job! Keep fighting!" He fought to keep the uncertainty from his face as he shouted encouragement to his men.

~*~

Faruz blinked his eyes open and peered at the gray clouds above. He must have dozed off, he realized with a start. What was happening?

He listened to the clanging of steel and the screams and groans of men and knew the battle raged on. How long could this continue? How much longer could the villagers hold? They'd been fighting since early afternoon, and now the sky was turning orange with the sunset. His head spun as he struggled to a sitting position. He loosened the tourniquet on his leg and felt the painful prickle of blood returning to his toes. The wound on his leg trickled blood, but it was nothing compared to the unabated flow he'd had earlier.

Pulling himself forward, Faruz craned his neck, trying to gauge the progress of the battle. He had to get a better look around. Panting from the effort, he leaned against the splintered rail. He closed his eyes to stop the spinning and waited for the ringing in his ears to cease, then opened his eyes again. He blinked several times and then squinted into a familiar face, wondering if he was seeing things.

With a worried look in his eyes, Eddrick asked, "What are you doing way over here?"

"I didn't expect to see you today." At his sudden outburst, several nearby fighters turned and stared.

Eddrick placed a finger to his lips. "Shh. Remember, they can't see me." The ghost laughed and gestured to the nearby warriors. "Watch this."

Faruz was sure he was hallucinating when he saw hundreds of spirits descend on the village and join the battle. It was hardly fair since the opposing army couldn't see their attackers. The ghosts grabbed the enemy's swords and used them to attack their owners. Helak's warriors exclaimed in fear, and those who weren't killed by unseen opponents wielding their own weapons began to flee.

The confused villagers clustered together and watched to see what would happen next.

"Thank you!" Aibek shouted to the spirits. "I never expected your help today, but we couldn't have won without you." He heaved a sigh of relief as the last of the enemy warriors escaped through the woods.

Looking around, Aibek couldn't believe how many spirits had come to their aid. He searched the nearly transparent crowd for a familiar face and finally found his mother.

"I thought you said you couldn't intervene."

"Normally, we can't. But your father learned that Helak's been breaking the rules for a long time, so the ancestors decided we could come to your aid," She scanned the boardwalk. "I'm sorry we took so long."

Aibek followed her gaze. Dead and dying enemy soldiers, weapons, and injured villagers littered the boardwalk. The snow had been dyed red around the boundary of the village. His gaze swung north, searching for his best friend.

"Faruz!" he shouted when he spotted the man on the walk.

Aibek ran to his comrade and crouched to his eye level. Faruz didn't say anything, but his eyes were open and alert. He was surrounded by an alarmingly large pool of blood, especially since some was dripping through the cracks between the boards.

"Let's get you to the infirmary." Aibek, relieved that his friend was alive, was alarmed by how pale the army's captain had become. Aibek hoped he wasn't too late.

25.

Aftermath

His muscles screaming from the day's exertions, Aibek hefted Faruz into his arms and carried his friend to Valasa's home, where a small hospital had been set up. Other weary warriors helped the rest of the injured soldiers to the infirmary in a slow procession. Serik and Ahren waited with some of the community elders and the fairies to care for the wounded, and others were ready to feed the exhausted warriors and render aid to those with less severe wounds. Aibek deposited an unconscious Faruz on a cot in Valasa's den, then returned to the scene of the fight to help the others.

Back at the battleground, the silence was deafening. All Aibek could hear was a constant ringing in his ears from the noise of the day. He thought all the birds and small animals of the forest must be huddled in their homes, hiding from the terrifying commotion. Everywhere he looked along the boardwalk; he saw signs of the day's violence. The rails were splintered in places, the snow was stained red, and bodies of the deceased lay where they had fallen. The stench of death mingled with the smell of smoke from the fires burning inside the homes. He helped the exhausted villagers tend to their dead. There weren't as many as he had feared.

The sun would soon set, so the villagers brought their slain loved ones into the chapel to be prepared for the funeral, and covered the bodies of their enemies with blankets and sheets. When the work was finished, Aibek walked slowly among the corpses in the chapel, spending a moment with each. Too many lives had ended today. These were husbands, fathers, sons, daughters, and wives. Could he have prevented their loss? Was it his fault they lay on cold tables awaiting a funeral?

He wept for every villager they'd lost, each smile he'd never see again, and every debate he'd never have with some of the outspoken men who had died. These were his friends, his comrades-in-arms, his citizens. He was responsible for their well-being, and he was responsible for their deaths. Had the old man been right in the beginning? Should they have surrendered? No. They were free. They'd lost much today, but more had survived. Now, they could begin to move forward with their lives. Tomorrow, he'd have to figure out how to clean up the mess, but tonight he was looking forward to a hot meal and some well-deserved rest. He couldn't believe everything that had happened that day. From the joy of his first experience with snow to the devastation of the battle and the grief for those they had lost, he felt emotionally drained and wasn't sure how to carry on. Also, with every moment his muscles stiffened, and soreness settled into his arms, legs, and back.

After dinner, while the village was preparing for the night's hard-won rest, Aibek went straight to his meditation room. He couldn't wait to consult with his parents. He had no idea what had really happened today or why they had suddenly stepped in to help. As soon as he entered the darkened room, he knew he wasn't alone. He felt his way to the mantle and fumbled a moment trying to light the lamp. Finally, the wick caught, and he blinked in the sudden light. Slowly, he turned and looked around at the spirits he could sense nearby.

In the dimly illuminated room, he could see his parents and several other spirits who didn't look familiar. They watched in silence as he crossed the room and lit the lamps on the table. Now that the room was fully illuminated, he was amazed by how many spirits filled the space. What had happened to bring so many here today? A few whispered amongst themselves in the far corner, but the rest stared mutely at Aibek as he walked to his favorite chair near the fireplace.

Once he was seated, his father approached and patted him firmly on the back. The cold touch was shocking in its strength—the spirits' touch had always felt like a winter wind before now.

"You learned to lead today. Well done."

Aibek searched his memory for any event that could have warranted this unexpected praise as his exhausted legs gave way and he dropped into the chair.

He heaved a great sigh. "I don't know what you mean. I failed. My plans would have led to the death of every citizen without your help." He dropped his head and stared at the toes of his shoes. The weight of his failure bowed his back and squeezed the air from his lungs. "As it is, far too many good people are dead or badly hurt."

Eddrick laid a hand on Aibek's shoulder. "You made decisions based on what was right, instead of waiting to see what everyone around you wanted, and you saved a lot of lives in the process."

"Um… thank you, I guess. But you—all of you—won the day. We would have lost if you hadn't stepped in." He gestured around the room. "What happened, anyway? What made you decide to help us?"

"While you were recovering this week, I did a little more spying. I found out that Helak hasn't exactly played fair—"

"What?" Aibek jerked his head up and spun in his seat to look at the spirit. "What do you mean?" He was too tired even to try to guess at his father's meaning, so he stared blankly at the spirit and waited for an answer.

"I'm not sure how much I can say..." the older man glanced around at the other spirits in the room.

Aibek followed his father's gaze and answered, "That's all right. I don't have to know all the details."

"Well, I'll just say that he hasn't been following the same rules we have. If Helak's ancestors had followed the Dictates of the Eternal, he never would have known that the Tsari exists, and Nivaka would never have been invaded."

Aibek frowned in confusion. How could that be? Nothing his father was saying made any sense. Were they speaking the same language?

He sat silently for a long while, so Eddrick continued. "The ancestors decided that since he's had extra help, you should have some, too."

The spirit paused for a moment and looked at the crowd of spirits crammed into the small space. Aibek bit his cheek and waited impatiently for his father to continue.

"Everyone here is related to a council member or warrior. We all want to see you succeed. Eddrick took a deep breath. "I'm just sorry it took us so long to show up. That was truly a vicious fight."

Aibek nodded. "Yes, it was. It would have been worse if you hadn't come when you did. Thank you." He glanced around the room at the crowd of spirits. "I thank all of you. We would have lost without you."

Aibek stared at the darkness beyond the window, realizing again how close they'd come to failure and death. How much worse would it have been if so many of the enemy soldiers hadn't been feverish and weak? He silently thanked whatever fates had sent him that disease less than a week before the assault. Finally, Kiri broke the silence and startled Aibek out of his reverie.

"You're falling asleep sitting here. You should get some rest. We'll talk more tomorrow." She crossed the narrow space and kissed his forehead, then ushered the others out of the room.

Aibek stared after her for a moment after the door closed, then forced his aching body upright and extinguished the lamps before he trudged to his room and the welcome oblivion of sleep.

~*~

Early the next morning, Aibek rushed through his breakfast alone, then hobbled on aching legs down the icy boardwalk to Valasa's house to check on his friends. This time, he didn't bother knocking. His knees nearly buckled with relief when he spied Faruz sitting up on the bed and enjoying a cup of famanc.

Aibek pulled up a chair and examined his best friend's pale face. "Are… are you all right?"

Faruz smiled a wan smile. "I'll heal, I suppose. Valasa said the sword cut into the muscles above my knee. It's a good thing it missed all the major blood vessels, or I wouldn't be here, but it'll be tough to walk after this."

His grin widened a little, and he pointed to the empty plate on the table next to his bed. "At least Valasa's letting me have real food and isn't pushing any of his vile concoctions. He says I need meat to heal."

"Well, that's a good thing." Aibek mirrored Faruz's smile. "Those tinctures and potions are awful!"

They laughed together for a moment, then Aibek looked closely at Faruz. He thought his friend looked more pale and tired than he had a few minutes ago. He gently excused himself and promised to return later in the day. Dizzy with relief from knowing Faruz would be all right—provided he didn't catch a fever—he left his friend to rest and went to check on the other injured soldiers.

Aibek was pleased to see that many had only minor injuries and would return to their homes that day. Only about twenty, including Alija, were injured severely enough to require prolonged care. Alija had bandages around his head and chest, and smaller ones tied around both arms. The old man sitting nearby told him Alija hadn't regained consciousness since the battle.

Aibek stayed with his friend for a while, talking softly to the unresponsive man. His aunt had told him once about a man who was injured and slept for several days, but when he awoke, he recalled what his loved ones had said to him. Aibek rambled about the weather and the damage to the boardwalk. He told Alija about Faruz's injury, and couldn't contain his joy that Faruz would recover. He tried to keep his tone light and cheerful. An injured man certainly didn't need to hear bad news. When he ran out of things to say, Aibek stood and went to visit with some of the other soldiers.

He tried to find a moment to talk to Valasa, but the healer was busy tending to some of the more critically wounded men and didn't have time for conversation. Instead, Aibek made his way out into the bright, wintry day. A fresh layer of snow had fallen during the night, making the village look peaceful and lovely. He stretched his sore arms and shoulders and trudged toward the north end of town.

All along the boardwalk, villagers and visitors worked side by side to clean up the mess and begin the repairs. The hoist system, normally used for moving dead trees, had been modified and was now being used to lower the bodies of their enemies to the ground. The warriors had carried their fallen comrades to the chapel the night before so they wouldn't freeze solid on the icy boardwalk. The loss wasn't as bad as Aibek had feared; a hundred and twenty of their soldiers had fallen during the battle. A funeral ceremony was being arranged for the next day.

As he wandered through the village, Aibek frequently stopped to speak with the workers and lend a hand with challenging tasks. While he was helping a group lift a new rail into place, the archery captain approached.

"Good morning, Mayor. I'll take over for you here. They need you at the east entrance—there's something about a visitor."

Aibek stepped away and allowed the other man to take his place at the rail. "Thank you, sir. I hope nothing's terribly wrong; I don't know of anyone who would be visiting today."

They hadn't sent fairies out to inform their neighbors of their victory last night since Valasa had been occupied tending the wounded. It was unlikely to be anyone from the neighboring villages since they probably didn't know the battle had even taken place. Who else could it be? The more he thought about it, the faster he moved toward the appointed entrance.

Messengers had been sent to Kainga that morning to fetch home the villagers who had evacuated ahead of the battle, but they hadn't had time even to reach the river city yet. What if it was another wave of enemy soldiers? No one had accounted for the enemies who scattered into the woods. The walk took an eternity as he ruminated on such thoughts.

Finally, he came close enough to see the entrance. A

large group of villagers had gathered in a close circle next to the entrance. He couldn't see the focus of their attention, but he didn't hear any fighting or shouting, so he relaxed a little. Whoever was visiting must not be much of a threat, but also hadn't been invited further into the town. His curiosity intensified. As he slowed his stride and approached the group, Wayra looked up and nodded in his direction.

"Aibek! There you are. There's someone here to see you."

Out of breath from his run-walk across town, Aibek smiled and moved into the circle. There, standing at the top of the lowered staircase, was a single elf—the same one who had led him repeatedly to the cave-room to meet the king and queen. The villagers had circled him, effectively keeping the visitor from proceeding farther into the town without overtly guarding him.

When Aibek stopped short, the elf stepped forward and raised his hand in a traditional greeting.

Aibek returned the gesture, then greeted his guest. "Hello. It's good to see you this morning. What can I do for you?"

"I'm Aylan. I've been sent to bring you a message from the king."

"Are you alone?" Aibek cocked his head, regarding the visitor with curiosity. "I've never known elves or dwarves to travel unaccompanied." He looked pointedly at the elf's unadorned waist. "Or unarmed."

"My companions are armed, but they prefer to wait below. I shouldn't be long. Is there a place where we can speak privately?"

"Of course. Follow me."

He led Aylan to his home, the group of villagers trailing behind, then invited the elf to join him in the small office near the front door. He ushered the visitor into the most comfortable chair available, then sat next to him in the other visitor's chair.

"You said you have a message for me?"

"Yes." Aylan pulled out a letter and passed it across the small space. Aibek broke the seal and eagerly perused the short memo.

Dear Mayor Aibek,

Congratulations on your victory. We were extremely pleased with the outcome of yesterday's battle. I wanted to make you aware that our warriors eliminated those enemy fighters who fled into the forest. We are pleased to be rid of them, at least in this corner of the Tsari. Good luck to you as you attempt to resume a normal routine in your town. Please remember to keep the terms of the old treaty.

Sincerely,

Turan

King of the Elves

Aibek smiled as he read the missive, then lowered it and considered his guest.

"I'd like to send a gift of thanks, as long as it won't offend your king… Or the queen… I'm still not quite familiar with all the traditions."

Aylan sat up straighter and smiled at the mention of gifts. "A gift would be appropriate and would not offend."

"Hmmm…" Aibek looked around the room. What would be an acceptable gift for the elf king? A sudden breeze ruffled the stack of furs lying on a chest in the corner, and the elf shivered.

Aylan asked, "Is your home always so drafty? Was it damaged in the fighting?"

Aibek cocked his head to the side, trying to suppress

a grin. "Maybe it was damaged. I'll have to inspect it more closely this afternoon."

Of course, there was no damage; the fighting had never moved beyond the edge of the village. Still, he was grateful to his parents for the hint. He stood and crossed the room to the furs and ran his hand over the thick pelt on top.

"We have an abundance of furs from hunting to feed the army this fall. Would these be an appropriate gift of gratitude?"

The elf's eyes widened at the prospect of carrying home the luxurious pelts. "Yes, they would be much appreciated. Winter has come early and may be long."

Aibek tied a length of cord around the gift, making the furs into a soft bundle, then ignored his complaining muscles as he lifted the roll to his shoulder. Maybe it would be wise to haul it to the entrance himself, where the other elves could help carry it home. His guest didn't protest but smiled and followed him from the house.

The growing crowd of villagers moved aside, staring silently as Aibek carried the bundle past them and down the stairs. Once on the ground, he handed the pelts to a small group of elves, again thanked Aylan for the message, and waved the unusually cheerful ground folk on their way.

Once he'd made his way back to work in the village, Aibek sought out the uninjured council members and relayed the information he'd gained from his meeting with Aylan.

Kai frowned. "It was probably a good idea to send a gift, but did you have to give them the furs? We could've used those to get through the winter."

Dalan shook his head. "We'll get through the winter just fine, but our extra hunting didn't leave much for the ground folk."

Wayra's eyebrows rose. "Who cares? Let them freeze. That means fewer of them to attack us when we're not looking."

Aibek held up a hand. "Regardless, they did help us, and they do deserve our thanks. I'd rather hoped this could be the beginning of better relations with our neighbors on the ground."

His last words were drowned out by Kai and Wayra's laughter, but he held on to a sliver of hope that things could be better.

26.

Goodbyes

Later in the morning, Aibek was helping repair the boardwalk when he overheard some of the workers whispering about a celebration feast. Again, he sought out the council members where they were working nearby and asked what they thought of the idea.

Dalan raised his head with a huge grin. "I think that's a fantastic idea. You know Zifa would vote in favor of a party, too."

Wayra hesitated. "Could we wait until the others are back from Kainga? I'd love to dance with Zyana."

Aibek nodded. "Yes, I think we should wait until the evacuees are home. They should be back tomorrow. So, are we doing this?"

Kai pointed at Aibek with a worried expression. "I hope we've defeated all our enemies. All the parties we've had since you got here have ended badly. We really don't need another attack."

Aibek chose not to respond, calling for a vote instead. If they counted Zifa's expected vote, the measure passed. Aibek walked away from the others on aching legs, heading for Valasa's house. He found the Gadonu mixing broth in the kitchen and asked him to set some of the fairies and cooks on the task of preparing the Pavilion for the party.

Smiling, Valasa scooped some of the steaming liquid

into a small bowl. "Of course! That sounds like a wonderful idea. I'll do that just as soon as I get everyone fed properly."

Before Aibek could say anything more, the healer turned and strode down the hall to the sickrooms where the most critically injured warriors were bedded down. As he opened the door, Aibek caught a glimpse of Serik, who had stayed to help nurse the wounded.

Alone in the kitchen, Aibek sampled the aromatic broth, then made a face. It smelled amazing but tasted vile. He dropped the spoon back on the counter and hobbled toward his own home. He'd checked on Faruz and Alija on his way in and found Faruz sleeping. There had been no change in Alija's condition, according to the old man sitting with him.

~*~

Back at the mayoral home, Aibek lingered for a while in the den with some of the visiting warriors, but the small talk soon left him irritated. He wanted to be alone, but his sore legs didn't want to carry him down into the forest. Instead, he made his way to his private sitting room and dropped into his favorite chair. He missed Faruz and Serik. Maybe they'd be able to come home after another day or two. Aibek sighed and laid his head back against the cushioned chair.

A soft, feminine voice roused him. "I wasn't sure I'd be able to catch you alone."

Startled, Aibek sat up and looked around, searching for his visitor. He must have been dozing. Who was in his room? And how had she managed to open and close the door without waking him?

After a quick scan of the space, he frowned. He was alone. Could he have dreamt the voice?

"Sorry, I'm not very good at this."

The voice sounded as if it were near the fireplace, so Aibek stared hard in that direction. A moment later, the apparition of a young woman appeared. She was more transparent than Eddrick and Kiri had ever been, at least as far as he could remember. He looked closely at her face, trying to place where he'd seen it before. Her pale features were familiar, but she kept fading in and out, making it difficult for him to identify her. He blinked the sleep from his eyes and tried to focus.

Finally, his overwrought mind made the connection. This was the girl Ahren had killed—the one Tamyr had claimed was the mastermind behind the poisonings and both attacks at the banquets.

What was her name? Oh, yes, Ahni.

She stood next to the blazing fire, which made it even more difficult for him to see her transparent form. He waited for her to say something, but she remained silent, staring at him with a mixture of sorrow and hatred painted on her delicate features. He felt a stab of fear.

"Is there something I can do for you?"

"No. I just need to tell you what happened, and then I'll be gone. I won't cause you any more trouble."

"All right." Aibek gestured to the empty chair next to him. "Why don't you have a seat?" The way she stared made him uncomfortable, and he shifted in his chair.

"I think I'd rather stand. Look, I'm only here because the elders think it will help me gain 'closure,' not because I actually care what happens to you."

He frowned at the sudden anger. "Um… I… think I understand. What do you need to tell me?"

"Everything Tamyr told you was true. I was Tavan's lover." She dropped her gaze to the floor before her feet. "I truly believed he cared for me—that he'd marry me. I found out I was carrying his child just a few days before your friends killed him. Then you arrived, and every-one acted like it was such a wonderful thing that he was dead. I was angry, scared, and alone. Tamyr listened to my rants without judging me, and eventually agreed to help me get my revenge."

She shook her head and sighed.

"She's such a gentle soul. I should've known better than to drag her into my plans. I felt terrible when she got caught with the knife, but I couldn't come forward. My family wouldn't have understood."

Aibek blinked and tried to make sense of her words. So, she had been behind the attacks.

"And Ahren?"

She heaved another great sigh and kicked at imaginary dust on the highly polished floor. "Ahren is completely innocent. She had no idea about any of this. I… I think she just wanted some friends who opposed the new mayor as much as she did. She used to call you 'the interloper.'" Ahni barked a humorless laugh. "I… she didn't mean to kill me, you know. She was trying to stop me from killing you. Anyway, that's all that I had to say. I need to go now. I have to talk to Tamyr." She turned away, then vanished.

Alone once again, Aibek stood and stretched. He couldn't believe how sore he was; he'd never felt like this after a tournament. Maybe Noral had been right, after all, and he should have taken those bouts more seri-ously. For now, at least, there was nothing he could do with the information Ahni had given him. It was nice to know he could trust Ahren, though. Maybe once every-thing settled down, he'd try courting her.

More tired than he'd like to admit, he slowly lowered himself into the inviting heaps of blankets and pillows on his bed. A short nap wouldn't hurt anything. He rolled onto his back, stretched once more, and slept through until morning.

~*~

The next day, as the workers were finishing their noon meal, the villagers who had evacuated to the city returned home amid cheers and hugs and a few tears. The town came alive with the shouts of children and the loud chatter of reunion. Tired and wet from their journey through knee-deep snow, they all went to their homes for a meal and a nap before the evening's festivities.

Aibek stopped at the infirmary on his way home to talk to Faruz. He had dearly missed his friend and knew Faruz would want to know what was happening in the village. He paused outside the door and took a deep breath. Determined not to stay too long and wear out the patient, he pushed open the door and ducked inside.

Once his eyes adjusted to the sudden dimness, Aibek made his way to Faruz's room. He scooted a chair next to Zifa, who was murmuring as Faruz ate something from a small bowl perched on his lap.

Faruz looked more cheerful now and had a little more color than he had that morning, and Aibek smiled as he eased into a chair. He was still sore. In fact, he was sorer today than he had been yesterday. His smile turned into a grimace as he dropped the last few inches to the seat.

Once he'd shifted to a more comfortable position, he turned to his injured friends. Faruz was watching him with a worried expression.

"You're not hurt, too, are you?"

"No, I'm just sore from the fighting. I'm not used to quite so much activity. I'll be fine in a day or so. You look a little better today."

"Yeah, Valasa said some of the swelling's going down. Hey, watch this. I can move my toes now!" He wiggled the toes on his left foot, then grinned. "Valasa said it was the swelling that kept them from moving yesterday."

Aibek swallowed and forced a smile. The relief that swarmed him almost made it hard to breathe. Faruz would walk again. Valasa had been openly worried about the lack of movement below the injury, so this was a very good sign, indeed. Aibek laughed as Faruz wiggled his toes again, a gleeful expression lighting his pale face.

"That's fantastic!" Aibek cheered. "You'll be dancing again in no time."

"Not tonight, though. We're celebrating here. Right, Zifa?"

Zifa's smile stretched wider, and she nodded. Aibek looked from one to the other, and back again.

What do they have planned for tonight?

Whatever it was, they both seemed pretty excited.

"We won't be doing anything too wild, but Zyana brought some wine back from Kainga, and Valasa said we could each have a glass or two. We'll spend the evening together until we get tired, which probably won't be very late."

Faruz laughed again, but Aibek thought he detected a hint of fatigue in the sound, and some of the color had drained from his face.

"It sounds like you have a great evening planned." Aibek rose with a grimace and smiled. "And I think it's time for me to get ready for the celebration. I'll see you both later."

He strode out of Faruz's room and went to check on Alija.

"Any change?" he asked the elderly man sitting with his friend.

The old man, Eder, shook his head, then sighed. "Not so

much as a blink or a twitch, I'm afraid."

"Well, keep up the good work." Aibek clasped Eder's skinny shoulder for a moment, then slipped quietly out of the room. It was time to get ready for the night's celebration.

While he walked toward his home, Aibek smiled at the picture Faruz and Zifa had presented, leaning close together to plan their evening. He would suggest to the council that perhaps the army captain deserved a home of his own. He had no doubt the rest would agree, and thought it likely his best friend would be married before the end of summer.

He let himself in through the front door, then maneuvered through the throng of visitors socializing in the main rooms of the house. Aibek thought he would be glad to have his home to himself again, though he was extremely grateful for the travelers' help yesterday and today. After he found his housekeeper and requested a hot bath, Aibek spent a long while enjoying the quiet solitude of his rooms. His thoughts were a tangle of elves, parties, and funerals, and he wasn't sure if he wanted to celebrate the victory or mourn those they had lost. He was also very concerned about Alija. The Gadonu wasn't optimistic that the young man would survive his injuries.

Soon, however, the servants peeked in to tell him his bath was ready. He resolved to enjoy the evening and save the melancholy thoughts for tomorrow.

A short while later, as he walked toward the Pavilion in the midst of a large group of revelers, Aibek couldn't stave off an odd stab of loneliness. Faruz and Serik should be walking with him, and Zifa and Alija should be meeting them at the party. The distance felt endless in the gathering darkness, though the walkway had been swept clean of snow. Aibek clasped his gloved hands and watched his breath puff before him, the mundane sensations occupying his rebellious mind.

When they reached the structure at the center of town, he was pleased to find that the fairies had somewhat limited the festive décor. He looked around and knew immediately that he was not the only one feeling the loss of their fallen warriors. Several men and women gathered near the back of the space, talking quietly among themselves. Their hunched postures and reddened faces betrayed their grief. Aibek made his way to them and offered condolences for their loss. He felt responsible for each one. He wondered how the great military generals in Xona dealt with these feelings after a battle. Surely there was some technique he hadn't learned in school.

Within moments, however, he was pulled toward the center of the dance floor and tossed about among the partygoers. He couldn't help but laugh along with them; their joy was infectious, and he gave himself gladly to the celebration. He danced with the warriors for three songs, then Dalan grabbed his arm and pulled him onto the dais at the front of the large space.

Alongside the buffet, a smaller table was set for the council members. Three chairs remained empty after everyone was seated, and Aibek again missed his best friend. Still, he smiled and let the joyous atmosphere seep into his soul like a balm. He listened happily to the cacophony. The music was nearly drowned out by the sounds of laughter and dishes clattering.

The fairies had lit lamps throughout the building, and a warm golden light illuminated the scene. The crush of feverishly dancing bodies helped to warm the space somewhat, though everyone wore winter furs and heavy layers, and puffs of breath were visible toward the outer fringes of the crowd.

The council members ate in silence, and Aibek considered excusing himself to dance among the villagers again. He hated being held separate from the warriors after they had fought side-by-side. When he had finally gathered his courage and was about to speak up, Valasa strode onto the platform and signaled for the music to stop. A sudden hush fell over the crowd as they waited to hear what the Gadonu had to say.

"Welcome!" The great man began in his resonant voice. "I won't stop the celebration for long, but I want to take a moment to thank each one of you for all you have done in the past months, and especially during yesterday's campaign. You all fought bravely, and I am proud to call you my friends."

Aibek dropped his head into his hands and felt a sudden knot of tears in his throat at Valasa's words as he remembered the struggle. The villagers had indeed displayed remarkable valor. Their fallen warriors would be missed, but would always be remembered as heroes.

"There will be a brief service at sunrise to lay our fallen comrades to rest," he continued in a more serious tone. "Their loss has not been forgotten, even in tonight's celebration. We will assemble at the south entrance at dawn to proceed to the lake, so we can conclude the service early enough for some of you to begin your journey home afterward."

Aibek's head snapped up. He hadn't considered that their guests might leave so soon. The village would feel empty without their new friends.

"You will be missed here," Valasa echoed Aibek's thoughts, "but I know you are ready to return to your families. Please know that if you should at any time decide to free yourselves from your governors, Nivaka will gladly help you as you have helped us."

Aibek stared at his plate and swallowed hard against the threatening tears. He had tried to enjoy this evening without dwelling on the ones they had lost.

"On a happier note, I want to give special recognition to our mayor, who bravely made some very difficult decisions in the heat of battle. The call to fire arrows into the fray was risky, but doubtless saved many lives."

Aibek flushed a deep red at the unexpected compliment. He thought he had done what anyone would, given the circumstances.

"And finally, I want to ask each of you to send positive energy to our captain, Faruz, and Councilwoman Zifa who were badly injured yesterday. The captain will survive, though it will take some time for his wounds to heal completely. His bravery was commendable, as he continued to fight even after he could no longer stand. Zifa's wounds are much less severe, and she should heal well as long as no fever sets in. Unfortunately, Councilman Alija's injuries were much graver, and he passed on into the arms of our ancestors and the eternal protection of the Shadow trees just before this celebration."

At this pronouncement, the tears which had been threatening to overwhelm Aibek finally overflowed and ran in rivers down his cheeks. Alija had sacrificed all he could to ensure the freedom of his people. He would be missed. Aibek choked back the tears and tried to bring his emotions under control as Valasa continued his speech.

"Thank you all for everything you have done this autumn. You can each be extremely proud of yourselves, your families, and friends." When he had finished his speech, Valasa waved for Aibek to say something, then walked briskly off the stage and out of the Pavilion.

Aibek fought for composure as he pushed himself to his feet.

"Thank you for your kind words, Valasa." He glanced at the spot where his friend had disappeared into the darkness, then turned his attention to the silent crowd.

"You fought well. I'm proud to have served alongside such a determined and fierce group of friends and neighbors. For those who will leave us soon, please know we are grateful and that you are welcome here at any time. Be assured we will help you in times of need as you have helped us. Nor will we forget those we lost. Their bravery and selflessness will live on in our hearts and minds forever as an undeniable part of our history." He considered the faces of the assembled warriors and villagers, trying to meet every gaze at once.

"You all know I'm new to this, but I'll do my best to be a fair and just mayor. In the coming days, the council members and I will work to establish a new, peaceful norm for this lovely village, and I look forward to returning my friends to their previous prosperity. We will soon resume actively marketing our goods, and you will have the opportunity to sell your wares as Nivakans have for generations. Together, let us look forward to a future of peace and prosperity." He gave a small bow.

The crowd erupted in a roar of applause, and Aibek took his seat once again. He wished Alija could be here to see the result of his revolution, and tears swam in his eyes once more.

Soon, the villagers swarmed around the table where he sat. Only after several minutes was he was able to lift his eyes and look around him. He was relieved to notice the wet cheeks of the other council members, and tears shining in the eyes of many villagers. They clapped him on the shoulders and back, each congratulating him for taking the lead when it looked as if they couldn't possibly win.

He endured this for what felt like hours, then scraped his chair back and stood abruptly. "This is foolish. I didn't win that battle—we all did. Let's dance!" He strode to the center of the dance floor.

Even though his aching body was screaming in pain, he danced with every ounce of energy he possessed. He remained at the center of the space for several songs, then squeezed through the revelers toward the edge of the Pavilion.

Panting for breath, he sat on the same bench he had shared with Ahren just seven days ago. It felt like a year. So much had happened, between Ahren's injuries and Ahni's passing, his illness, and the battle—the past week had been longer than any other he had ever known.

Thinking of that seemingly long-ago party, he looked for the young woman he had held on this bench. He searched the throng of dancing warriors for her bright white hair.

While he watched, she left the Pavilion with Vayna, one of the visiting warriors. They laughed together and huddled against each other in the shadows, then moved into a close embrace. Shocked, Aibek stood and moved quietly away, toward the dancers. The couple might want some privacy.

He danced for a while longer with the other soldiers, but his heart wasn't in it. He had hoped last week had signaled the beginning of a new relationship with Ahren. But seeing her with another man proved otherwise. He laughed bitterly to himself and strode away from the party. He needed to spend some time with Faruz.

~*~

He found Faruz reclined on a sofa in Valasa's cozy den with a mug of hot famanc.

"Where's Zifa? I thought you two were celebrating together tonight."

Faruz grinned. "We did. Zifa and I drank to our brave friends and allies who fought side-by-side with us. But after we talked for a while and finished two glasses of Zyana's fine red wine, I could see Zifa was tired. I kissed her, and she went to get some rest. So here I am."

Aibek pushed a stool over and perched near his friend. "I like Zifa, but I'm glad you're alone. I need to talk to my oldest friend."

They chatted about their friends and the celebration until Ilodus dipped below the horizon and the gray light of dawn seeped through the windows.

When he stood to leave, Faruz blurted out, "You know, you've turned into a really great mayor."

"Um, thanks… I think." Aibek paused. "Where did that come from?"

"Zifa told me the council's been giving you a hard time. I just thought you should know you've done a great job." His friend gave a little laugh. "Not perfect, but pretty great."

Aibek grinned and hugged his friend, then headed home. While he walked, he wondered what would come next for this town, these people, and for his own life. So much had changed in such a short time, he couldn't wait to see what the future would hold.

The End

27.

Preview of The Tsari's Last Hope

Over the next day, the terrain roughened and the close-packed trees grew denser as Aibek and his group picked their way toward the center of the forest. They came to a stop at midday, when the trail they had been following disappeared in the thick underbrush.

Kai stepped around trees and friends to the front of the group and stared at the ground where the path should have been.

"Well, what do we do now?"

Aibek, Serik, and Aylen crowded near him, peering into the dim forest.

Serik cleared his throat. "We'll have to press on. Look, the moss is only on the side of the trees towards us. We'll use that as our guide and just keep moving forward."

With a nod and a grunt, Aylen stepped forward and pushed the thick ferns aside. There, under the heavy leaves, was the faintest hint of the path. "It shouldn't be too difficult. The path is there; it's just harder to see now."

"Wonder–" Aibek cut off as an eerie screech pierced the air. It dragged out into a long, plaintive sound, fading into silence.

"What was that?" Kai's hands trembled, and his hold on his waterskin lessened.

Aibek glanced down at his own hands, they were steadier than Kai's, but not much. He took a deep breath and held it, waiting.

"Emrialk," Serik and Aylen said, concern marring their features.

Aibek frowned. "Oh, well…good then. At least it's nothing dangerous." He barked a nervous laugh.

"Nothing dangerous?" Kai turned to Aibek with an incredulous laugh. "Are you mad? Emrialk are about the most dangerous thing out here!"

"Oh. I thought they were friendly, helpful creatures. I learned that touching their mane gave a man special powers. Aunt Ira used to tell dozens of stories of wanderers that they had helped." Aibek shook his head in confusion and sought Serik.

"Tell me you're not that naive!" Aylen laughed hard enough to stumble.

"Not everything is as it is told in nursery tales." The elderly servant laid a papery hand on Aibek's arm and gazed up into his face. "You must be careful to avoid the creatures in this part of the forest. We're getting close to the Heart of the Forest, and I suspect we'll meet the Bokinna's protectors soon."

"All right, then someone else should take the front for a while. I'll hang back, so I don't accidentally rush into anything. Aylen? Would you lead on?" He waved an arm out in front of him, waiting for the elf to step to the front.

"Me?" Aylen stepped back, eyes wide.

"Yes." Aibek nodded. "You're the one who found the trail when we all thought it was gone. It makes sense for you to lead."

"All right, I guess. Just stay–" He cut off as another long screech reached them. It sounded closer this time. The hairs along Aibek's neck stood as he stared into the dense brush.

Hopefully, the animal making that awful noise wasn't about to attack.

Aylen took a noisy breath and plunged into the dense forest, holding aside ferns and briers to find the diminishing path. They moved, slow and steady, through the forest. The haunting calls of the emrialk continued, but Aibek couldn't see the creature. He craned his neck with every screech, both wishing for and dreading a glimpse of the fabled emrialk.

Surely all the stories weren't wrong; they must be stunning to inspire such fantasies. Aibek's aunt had always said the emrialk were giant wolf-like creatures with a thick mane like a lion's, and a long, narrow face. They were reputed to be as sleek and limber as a summer fox, but with the hunting habits of a lone wolf.

Aylen led the way through the undergrowth, stopping every few paces to examine the trail and look up into the trees.

Aibek peered into the deepening forest, his steps slowing. Was it out there, watching him?

Will I even be able to see it if it decides to attack?

Another screech rent the air, this time closer. Aibek's heart hammered against his ribs, and he resisted the urge to run into the forest toward home. Instead, he closed his eyes and took a deep breath, forcing down the panic and waiting until calm had replaced it. When he opened his eyes, he froze, not even daring to breathe. There, where he had stood only a breath before, sat the largest creature Aibek had ever seen.

It lowered its sleek brown neck and brought its face to Aibek's level, watching him through angry, intelligent eyes. The emrialk cocked its head to the side. Without a sound, the creature lowered itself to the ground in a hunting crouch, folding legs as tall as Aibek under itself. Its red and white striped nose stretched out the length of Aibek's arm, the black end quivering as it sniffed at the travelers. Aibek cringed at the foul breath blowing in his face, but couldn't make himself move.

A curtain of chestnut hair concealed much of the creature's shoulders, but the back and legs revealed powerful muscles under a dappled brown coat. It stretched closer, its head larger than Aibek's entire being, and flattened its pointed ears against its skull. The black fury in its eyes, focused and intent, made his blood run cold, and Aibek tried to scream. Unable to force a sound from his mouth, he flailed his arm, smacking at the air beside him until he connected with flesh.

"Ow! What was that–" Kai fell silent when he glimpsed the creature behind them. "Emrialk!" Kai's scream broke the spell, and Aibek reached for his sword. "You can't fight it! Get in the trees!"

Panic clawed at Aibek's throat, but he yanked his sword free of its scabbard. Behind him, Serik grunted, and Aibek glanced over his shoulder. Serik stood at the base of a thick Shadow Tree.

"Drop your pack!" Aibek backed toward Serik, keeping himself between the creature and his mentor. "It's too heavy!"

Serik did as Aibek said, and Kai reached down from the same tree and gave Serik a hand up into the low branches. Aibek watched as his friends retreated to safety, holding his sword at the ready.

As Serik climbed, the creature screamed again and leapt at Aibek. Lightning fast, it swung a paw edged with claws as long as table knives at his head, but Aibek ducked behind the nearest tree. The skinny trunk cracked under the blow and toppled.

The beast swung again, and Aibek leaned away as the rest of the tree exploded in splinters. With nothing left between them, Aibek found himself face to face with the giant canine again.

"Aibek! Get in the trees. It can't climb," Kai shouted from somewhere above.

The emrialk looked up, distracted by the yell. An opening. Aibek darted forward, poised to strike, and thrust his sword at the creature's exposed neck. Faster than Aibek could react, the beast raised a foreleg and swatted at him. Aibek's sword connected with the pad of its foot and thick, purple blood squirted from the wound. The emrialk screamed, withdrawing the injured paw and swiping again. Aibek dodged, but couldn't move fast enough. The blow threw him backward into a skinny birch tree, which splintered and dug into Aibek's back, knocking the air from his lungs.

No time. He had no time. The beast descended on him in a heartbeat, its hot, foul breath blowing in Aibek's face before he could recover.

Frozen in terror, Aibek held his breath as the emrialk lowered its massive head and looped dagger-like teeth through his belt. Recognizing what was about to happen but powerless to stop it, he grasped his sword tighter. His first fighting teacher's voice rang through his mind, admonishing him to relax his muscles before falling to minimize injury, and he concentrated on following that advice. Wind whipped past his face, robbing him of breath, as the creature lifted him from the remnants of the tree and flung him through the air. Aibek landed in a mossy clearing, though the vegetation did nothing to cushion his landing.

Pain flashed through him as his head collided with a log. Blood stung his eyes. He struggled to open them and see through the red. Somewhere nearby, the emrialk screeched, the sound creating an explosion of pain in Aibek's head.

Above him, Kai leapt across a gap between trees, staying out of the beast's reach.

"Climb!" Serik yelled, joining Kai. "You have to get in the trees!"

Gasping, Aibek dropped his sword and scrambled up the nearest tree, his ribs and shoulder aching with every move.

Another piercing scream, this time closer. Without stopping, he clambered up the tree toward the safety of its topmost branches.

Fire ripped through his leg, and Aibek clawed at the limbs above. Unable to pull himself up, he glanced back at the ground and the creature intent on his death. The emrialk had buried its claws in his calf, pinning him to the side of the tree halfway up. It screamed in fury as he kicked, struggling to free himself from its deadly grasp. With another swing, the emrialk crushed his knee against the tree trunk.

The bark crumbled and dug into his leg, the torn leather failing to protect him. Aibek's head swam from the pain as he desperately grappled with a branch above. He had to get away. His pack caught on a nearby branch, yanking his hand off the limb and leaving him dangling far above the ground. His friends climbed through the branches above, following his movement from the safety of the canopy. He yearned to climb up to them. Instead, he lowered himself until the pack came loose, swung it off his shoulders and tossed it down into the creature's face. The knapsack connected with the creature's twitching snout and it screeched, tossing its head to dislodge the bag. The emrialk moved its paw and

Aibek scrambled up the tree.

Aylen and Kai pulled him further into the branches, and Aibek leaned against the tree trunk. Blood poured from three deep gashes in his right leg and several on his head. Dizzy, Aibek remembered the packet of herbs Tamyr had given him on his last night in Nivaka. The pack had been sacrificed to the emrialk and was now being tossed and crushed as the creature used it as an outlet for its unsated fury.

Head swimming, Aibek tried to focus on stopping the crimson flow. His hands fumbled at his belt, but he couldn't untie the knot.

Someone pushed his hands away. "I'll take care of it. You just sit back and rest." The voice came through a long tunnel, echoing off the sides before Aibek succumbed to the blackness.

Keep reading, get your copy at http://mybook.to/TheTsarisLastHope

About the Author

Leslie E. Heath lives in rural North Carolina with her husband, children, and an unsettlingly large number of rescue pets. She enjoys writing, which is important because she plans to do a lot more of it. When she's not writing, she enjoys spending time at the beach, training for and competing in long-distance running events, and working as a registered nurse.

The Last Mayor's Son is Heath's publishing debut and the first volume of a trilogy. Visit her webpage at: www.LeslieEHeath.com

Sign up and get access to sneak peeks, updates, and backstory not available anywhere else!

Have you wondered what made Serik leave his mountain home? Why does the wise old man spend his years serving Aibek's family? Find out in Journey to Nivaka, an exclusive short story. Sign up and get access to sneak peaks, updates, and backstory not available anywhere else! Go to https://mailchi.mp/4f01668a6ded/journey2nivaka or click the cover below